"Witty and sagacious . . . The persistence of anti-Semitism after the Holocaust has been an enduring theme for American writers, from Bernard Malamud and Philip Roth to more contemporary writers like Michael Chabon, Shalom Auslander, and Steve Stern. Gross earns a spot in that company. . . . People want to know about a place that escaped a slaughter, which frees Gross to write a fine and often funny speculative novel. But he knows people are less eager to confront the roots of that slaughter, which makes 'The Lost Shtetl' a potent cautionary tale as well."

—*USA Today*

"A gorgeous debut."   —*New York Post*

"[A] dose of fabulism may be the best cure yet for a psychologically intolerable contemporary moment. . . . [*The Lost Shtetl* is] a riveting narrative about the costs of living in one's own time as opposed to the benefits and disadvantages of living in a 'lost horizon' that has been overlooked by the contemporary world. It's filled with a slew of intriguing characters. . . . If this novel doesn't take your mind off being holed up in a shuttered-down city or trying to escape the reality of the pandemic by socially distancing somewhere in the country, nothing will."

—*Vogue*

"Lively and imaginative . . . alternately reminiscent of early Isaac Bashevis Singer and a Catskills comedian. Gross's entertaining, sometimes disquieting tale delivers laugh-out-loud moments and deep insight on human foolishness, resilience, and faith."

—*Publishers Weekly* (starred review)

"[G]reat fun, packed with warmth, humor, and delightful Yiddish expressions. . . . Reaching into the storytelling tradition that stretches from Sholem Aleichem to Isaac Bashevis Singer to Michael Chabon, the author spins an ingenious yarn about the struggle between past and present."

—*Kirkus Reviews* (starred review)

"I was blown away. . . . 'The Lost Shtetl' is a Jewish fantasy in the vein of Michael Chabon's 'The Yiddish Policemen's Union' and Steve Stern's Jewish magical realism novels. There are even echoes of Simon Rich's New Yorker story, 'Sell Out,' about a time-travelling Orthodox Jewish immigrant, soon to be the major motion picture 'An American Pickle' starring, yes, Seth Rogen. . . . The novel's narrator, a kind of first-person collective, sounds both contemporary and folkloric, as if one of the great Yiddish writers had somehow survived, like Kreskol, to tell its story. . . . 'The Lost Shtetl' stands on its own."

—*The Jewish Week*

"Gross is hilariously funny as he weaves this story. . . . We laugh, but . . . do we? Yes . . . The miracle of this book is that it provokes theories about its intention and doesn't let you stop trying to figure them out."

—*Literary Hub*

"Novelist Max Gross poses precisely this question in *The Lost Shtetl*. Gross' debut novel unfolds with a transfixing, howlingly funny and achingly sad tale of incompatible cultures colliding with the looping, shaggy dog humor of Jonas Jonasson, and delightful echoes of Washington Irving's *Rip Van Winkle*, Mark Twain's *A Connecticut Yankee in King Arthur's Court*, Michael Chabon's *The Yiddish Policemen's Union*, and Woody Allen's *Sleeper*."

—New York Journal of Books

"Judging by *The Lost Shtetl*, his brilliant debut novel, author Max Gross is the metaphysical love child of Sholem Aleichem and J. K. Rowling."

—*Hadassah Magazine*

"With warmth and charm, Gross spins a resonant and poignant tale of village life complete with gossip and matchmakers."

—The National Book Review

THE LOST SHTETL

A NOVEL

MAX GROSS

HARPERVIA

An Imprint of HarperCollinsPublishers

THE LOST SHTETL. Copyright © 2020 by Max Gross. All rights reserved. No part of this book may be used or reproduced in any manner whatsoever without written permission except in the case of brief quotations embodied
in critical articles and reviews. For information, address HarperCollins Publishers, 195 Broadway, New York, NY 10007.

HarperCollins books may be purchased for educational, business, or sales promotional use. For information, please email the Special Markets Department at SPsales@harpercollins.com.

FIRST HARPERCOLLINS PAPERBACK EDITION PUBLISHED IN 2021

Designed by SBI Book Arts, LLC

Library of Congress Cataloging-in-Publication Data is available upon request.

ISBN 978-0-06-299113-3

21 22 23 24 25 LSC 10 9 8 7 6 5 4 3 2 1

For Jane and Harry

For Jane and Henry

"To a worm in horseradish, the world is horseradish."

—YIDDISH PROVERB

THE METEOR

Even in a happy, peaceful town, such as ours, it is possible to find someone you never want to see again.

Pesha Lindauer found one such person. A man whose visage drove her to rage, and whose voice made her clench her fists and grit her teeth. A man who haunted her dreams, tormenting her with whips and fire, and whose appearance always left her with the faint smell of sulfur upon waking.

It was doubly unfortunate that the personage in question was her husband, Ishmael.

A few months after a marriage contract had been signed and a dowry paid, Pesha asked her husband for a divorce.

This was not exactly a surprise to most of the people in our town. We had all observed the frostiness between husband and wife when they walked through the market square on Friday afternoon to do their Sabbath shopping. We had heard the scintillating gossip that Pesha was a woman of peculiar appetites and that she slapped her husband when they were in bed together. There had been plenty of reports from the neighbors that the two of them roared at each other late into the night like a pair of caged animals. And there was a story making the rounds (who knows if there's any truth in it) that Pesha went to her father the night before the wedding contract was to be signed and begged him to call the whole thing off. The only real surprise was that Pesha had the nerve to end their marriage so soon after it had begun.

"Shouldn't the woman at least give the thing a year before she calls it quits?" Esther Rosen asked the women hovering around her stall in the marketplace. All of whom clucked in agreement.

The Rebbetzin* was sent to pay Pesha a visit and see if there was anything that could be done to rescue the marriage. "Is your objection based on something that happens in the dark?" the Rebbetzin asked, getting straight to business. "Because if that's the case, there are things that can be done. A serious talk can be had with Ishmael behind closed doors where he can be wised up about the facts of life."

"No," said Pesha. "The marriage never should have happened in the first place. We were wrong for each other right from the beginning."

"Why do you say that? Give me reasons."

"It's nothing I can put my finger on," Pesha said a little cryptically. "I just can't stand to look at him anymore."

"You can't just divorce him," the Rebbetzin said. "There must be a reason."

Pesha Lindauer dutifully outlined a smattering of her husband's flaws— from ox-like silence, to bad breath, to fits of temper and crankiness—all of which the Rebbetzin listened to without interruption, and then waved away.

"Nevertheless, you must try to reconcile," said the Rebbetzin firmly. "Divorce should always be the last resort. Besides, nobody wants to marry a divorcee, Pesha. You'll be damaged goods for the rest of your life. Give up on him at your own peril."

Which was a slight exaggeration, of course, but I suppose a rebbetzin has a duty to make a divorce sound dire.

Pesha and Ishmael were told to be on their best behavior for at least a week. "You are to try to find common ground," Rabbi Sokolow instructed them late one winter afternoon in his study. "You are to treat each other with dignity. You are to be humble and courteous. And you must stop

---
*Wife of a rabbi.

your bickering—you must both promise here and now not to raise your voice." ("For goodness sake, Pesha," the Rebbetzin whispered when they were alone, "the Coopermans hear your yelling next door almost every night. Try to control yourselves.")

A week later, Pesha showed up at Rabbi Sokolow's study and told both the Rabbi and Rebbetzin that her and her husband's attempts at treating each other nicely had failed. Instead of yelling, they had retreated into a murky, ominous silence. The tension in the house—that uninvited visitor, who nipped at their heels and whispered into their ears at all hours— refused to leave peacefully.

"And he did this to me," Pesha said, rolling up her sleeve and showing the Rabbi and Rebbetzin a large black-and-blue bruise along her arm, which made Rabbi Sokolow's face redden.

"It's quite possible that things will change once you have children," the Rabbi offered. "A barren house is a lot less happy than one brimming with youth."

Pesha sat up straight in her chair, with her eyebrows arched. And the immediacy of her reaction made Rabbi Sokolow feel like a fool.

"Maybe not," he mumbled.

And over the course of the next few weeks, many people took both Lindauers aside and tried to straighten them out individually. "Let me ask you something," Rabbi Sokolow said to the husband when they were alone together. "Have you ever struck your wife?"

Ishmael Lindauer looked mortified.

"Who told you that?"

"It isn't important. Rumors have a way of getting around. And this one has gotten back to me."

"An utter lie!" Ishmael Lindauer spat, his wedge of a black beard quaking. "That's the foulest piece of slander I've ever heard!"

The Rabbi was a pacifist by nature, and he edged back in his chair, spooked by the violence of the young man's reaction.

Rabbi Sokolow had known Ishmael Lindauer since he was a baby, and always regarded him as a somewhat odd but quiet boy. No one in the Lindauer family had ever come to him with tales of woe or heartache over something Ishmael had done to make their lives miserable. There were no sisters driven to tears by meanness or teasing. (In fact, the boy had no sisters. Only brothers.) Ishmael Lindauer was simply the wigmaker's son, who had taken up in his father's store after he had finished cheder.* The boy had been unfailingly quiet and unexceptional, and had grown into a slender, olive-skinned man—also quiet and unexceptional.

"Look, Ishmael," Rabbi Sokolow said calmly, but with firmness, "we all know that things happen behind closed doors that a husband and wife could not possibly explain to anyone else in the world. But I'm telling you right now that if you're hurting your wife there will be consequences."

Ishmael's face was purple with rage.

"I haven't laid a finger on her," Ishmael said. "Whoever told you that is a liar. A liar!"

Both men sat quietly for a few moments, as the words lingered in the air.

"If she's telling such lies about me, then maybe she should get her divorce," Ishmael finally said. "I have no interest in being married to a liar like her. I've never walloped anybody in my life. Certainly not a woman. *Certainly* not my wife! But I just want to let you know that not only is she a liar, she's a horrible wife."

Rabbi Sokolow said nothing.

"The woman can't sew to save her life," Lindauer thundered after taking a moment to silently compose his complaints. "I gave her a pair of socks to mend two months ago and it still hasn't happened yet. And she's a horrible cook."

These were serious matters, so Rabbi Sokolow fought off the impulse to smile. He simply stared intently at Lindauer, who looked as if his anger were a rabid dog he had completely lost control over.

---

*Elementary school.

"Well, obviously, that can cause problems," Rabbi Sokolow said. "Keeping a good house is nothing to sneeze at. But that can't be the only thing that destroys a marriage. What's been going on between the two of you in your marriage bed?"

For a moment, Lindauer had a look on his face that you would have suspected on a boy who had opened a closet door and discovered his mother in some stage of undress. He couldn't summon the words necessary to answer. His anger was countermanded by embarrassment.

"Nothing."

"Nothing's been going on?" Rabbi Sokolow asked. "Or nothing, and by that you mean nothing's wrong and everything's fine in that area."

"Everything's fine."

The way Lindauer said this—with his eyes turned away from the Rabbi—made Sokolow doubt the young man's sincerity. And as he sat watching Lindauer, it occurred to Rabbi Sokolow that the husband was so angry that he might decide not to grant his wife her divorce, in a fit of spite. It certainly wouldn't be the first time, although nobody could remember when it last happened in Kreskol. Rabbi Sokolow put his hand through the gray wool of his beard and tried to carefully work out what his next words would be. But Lindauer spoke first.

"Is that all?" he asked, suddenly on his feet.

Actually, the Rabbi had plenty more to say. The conversation hadn't even begun to scratch the surface of this peculiar marriage. But sometimes when one party is determined to trespass no farther, it's pointless to engage. Rabbi Sokolow simply nodded.

With that, Ishmael Lindauer bowed his head and stormed loudly out of the Rabbi's study, stomping his shoes as he walked.

"To be honest with you," Rabbi Sokolow later told his wife, "I can't tell who's lying."

"What's there to tell?" asked the Rebbetzin. "I thought you said that he was violent. He's obviously the one who's at fault."

"Oh, certainly," Rabbi Sokolow said. "I thought he might slug me then

and there. But you don't get that worked up over an accusation that's true."
Which was one point of view, I suppose.

And his worry that Ishmael might punish his wife by refusing to grant
her a divorce proved prophetic. A few days later, Shmuel Lindauer (Ishmael's youngest brother) appeared in Rabbi Sokolow's chambers and announced that his brother had no intention—none whatsoever—of granting
his wife a divorce. Under any circumstances.

Of course, the Lindauers would hardly have been the first two people to
have been divorced in our little town.

If you were to consult the Kreskol archives you'd discover at least seven
instances of divorce over the last twenty years. Which makes us, I'm proud
to say, well below average as far as divorces go.

This does not mean that there couldn't have been many more. Men and
women are the same everywhere, and as much as we liked to believe that
we were better than the glumps in Pinczow or the know-it-alls in Bobowa,
Kreskol isn't really any different. Many more people came to Rabbi Anschel Sokolow (and Rabbi Sokolow's father, Hershel, before him) request-
ing bills of divorce than actually received them.

However, we were fortunate in that one of our dayyanim,* Meir Katznelson, and his wife, Temerl, possessed an exceptional talent for smoothing
over problems between husbands and wives and talking both parties out
of rash action.

There was, for example, the famous case of Yasha and Miriam Greenberg. Yasha Greenberg (with his elderly father, Zalman, in tow) came to
Rabbi Sokolow and Rabbi Katznelson asking for a divorce because he believed that his wife was a witch. An amulet had been discovered by Zalman
in his daughter-in-law's wardrobe, among the undergarments, as well as a

---

*A judge in a rabbinical court.

deck of tarot cards. Yasha Greenberg had been too horrified to confront his wife with the discovery—he had gone straight to the beit din.*

"Who can abide having witches in our town?" Yasha asked. "She's apt to cast some kind of spell and turn us all into a bunch of frogs."

A farfetched concern, certainly, but it is the duty of guardians of the law to consider everything.

Miriam Greenberg was summoned to the beit din and confronted with the amulet and cards.

She burst into tears. "I didn't mean any harm," she whimpered. "I traded the amulet for a necklace from one of the gypsy girls who had come through town."

The gypsy caravans had come through a few months earlier as they had every spring, when the band of black-haired, black-eyed peddlers with gold hoops in their ears would hawk pots, and pans, and yards of cloth, and enormous metal contraptions no one in town knew the first thing to do with.

"I figured, a little extra good luck couldn't hurt," Mrs. Greenberg said, dabbing her eye with a handkerchief. "There was no harm."

"What about the cards?" asked Rabbi Katznelson.

"The girl showed me how to use them," Mrs. Greenberg explained. "She told me that they predicted the future. I didn't see the sin in that."

Of course, Mrs. Greenberg was set straight. The cards and amulet were taken to the town gravedigger, who was charged with destroying them. And Mrs. Greenberg swore up and down, the holiest oaths she could think of, that she would never again chant the black spells the gypsy girl had taught her.

"And you!" Rabbi Katznelson said, pointing his finger at Yasha. "You should be more forgiving. The woman didn't know any better. And she who does not know cannot sin. Besides, what kind of a husband asks that

---

*A rabbinical court.

their wife be chased out of town like she was a korva* without even talking to her first?"

Greenberg, with tears running down his cheeks, apologized to the woman that only an hour earlier he claimed he had been wronged by. The request for a divorce was withdrawn.

What's more, the mothers and daughters of Kreskol felt they had a champion in Rabbi Katznelson. Even though Mrs. Greenberg was decisively in the wrong, Rabbi Katznelson seemed to take the position that she was not *fully* wrong.

So in the middle of all the Lindauers' woes, he was called upon to expedite either a divorce or a reconciliation.

"What does she mean she 'just can't stand to look at him'?" asked Katznelson. "I've never heard such nonsense in all my life. Why did she marry the fellow in the first place if she doesn't like him?"

A relevant question, one would suppose.

The marriage between Pesha Rosenthal and Ishmael Lindauer was, in retrospect, too hasty in its arrangement. The day after Pesha turned seventeen, Mira Rut, the matchmaker, appeared on the Rosenthal doorstep with a long list of bachelors to whom Pesha could be married off.

"How about Avigdor Lipsky?" Mira Rut said, referring to the sturdy, straw-haired fishmonger, who was indisputably one of the more handsome specimens in Kreskol.

"Lipsky?" Pesha replied. "He'll come home every night stinking of fish!"

There was no sense pretending that wasn't true. Mira Rut then suggested Yakov Slibowitz, whose family ran one of the dairy farms. "But he's cross-eyed," Pesha protested. Then Reuven Brower. ("Too short.") Or, possibly, Reuven's younger brother, Itzik. ("He laughs like a buffoon.") Or Asa Shanker, who mooned about Pesha in a constant quest for her favor and attention. ("He gives me the creeps.")

---

*Yiddish: whore.

"Very well," Mira Rut said, getting up from the Rosenthals' kitchen table. "This might take some thinking."

Mira Rut—never one to be done out of a broker's fee—came back several weeks later with more ideas; first, there was the sexton, Reb* Zelig Minkin, a widower. ("Too old.") Second, there was Zachary Mandell, whip smart and almost of marrying age. ("He looks like a crow.")

"What about Ishmael Lindauer?" Mira asked.

Pesha didn't know the Lindauers very well. The family consisted exclusively of boys, and Pesha didn't have any female counterparts to compare him with. All she knew of the Lindauers was that they ran the dress and wig shop on the other side of Kreskol, which she hadn't had occasion to visit since her mother died seven years earlier.

"I don't know," Pesha replied, which was the most encouraging thing Mira Rut had heard out of the girl.

A meeting was arranged between prospective husband and wife at the Market Street Tea Shop, halfway between each of their homes, and the conversation was polite enough. Reb Issur Rosenthal sat at the table behind his daughter, and Ishmael's oldest brother, Gershom, sat at a table nearby.

"Why didn't you stay in yeshiva?" asked Pesha when her father appeared to be distracted.

"Because it's just about the most boring way to spend a life that I could ever dream up," Ishmael replied.

Which elicited a smile.

"Nu?"** asked Mira Rut the next morning when she came around to the Rosenthal house. "What do you think?"

Pesha considered the question. "He's funny," she finally pronounced. Which was a misreading, on her part. He was mocking, perhaps. Sarcastic, certainly. But few people would have characterized Lindauer as humorous.

---

*Honorific, like "sir."
**Yiddish: "Well?" or "So?"

Still, that was good enough. Issur Rosenthal was enlisted to tell his daughter that in a town of our size, she couldn't afford to be picky. Pesha's sisters began saying that they found the quiet, dark-complexioned Ishmael to be handsome and admirably modest. ("That's why I think he's so quiet—he clearly doesn't want to boast," said Hadassah Rosenthal. "Maybe he doesn't have much to boast about," Pesha replied.)

After three or four weeks of nagging, Pesha agreed to the marriage; the canopy was raised and the inn was rented for the evening. But Pesha barely smiled when the wedding jester came to entertain her aunts and her sisters. Throughout the signing of the contract, Pesha looked pale and she stumbled slightly as she circled Ishmael for the second time. Only Esther Rosen thought this was a bad omen. Everyone else just assumed Pesha was nervous.

The wedding party had the fanfare one would expect. A procession, led by the four klezmer musicians, paraded the bride and groom back to Pesha's house. They were showered with wheat kernels along the way. When they got to the Rosenthal house they were presented by Pesha's aunt Elka with a large challah* and a clay jug of salt. The subsequent feast was as sumptuous as anyone could remember, and after the bride and groom had retired to a back room in the Rosenthal house, Yetta Cooperman came back to the wedding party a half hour later to triumphantly report that there was blood on the sheets. The occasion was deemed to be a success.

Nobody quite knows what happened between husband and wife in the ensuing months, except that neither of them looked happy. And there had to be some explanation. What could sour the joy of two young people unless there is something terribly wrong?

After their birth, rumors can grow into large, untamed beasts—and the ones about the Lindauers grew particularly oversized and savage.

Some wondered why Pesha had been so hesitant to accept the match in the first place. The thinking went that this must have been because she was doing something illicit, like carrying on an affair with one of the ye-

---

*A braided bread.

shiva students or, god forbid, one of the married men. (Which was not impossible. Pesha stirred sinful thoughts in even the pious men of Kreskol.) The fact that she would sometimes walk through the market with her wig slightly skewed and was once noticed with a button undone on her blouse caused tongues to wag in every direction.

These rumors culminated a few months later when Ishmael came into shul one morning and, just as the amidah* ended, sat down on the sharp end of a ram's horn that some mischievous person slipped onto the bench.

As he jumped into the air, the congregation broke into raucous laughter. Even Rabbi Sokolow smiled. Ishmael could barely contain his pique, and stormed out of shul without a word.

It was a week later that Pesha requested a divorce.

"All this is past," declared Katznelson to the beit din. "Now our only task is to look forward. Be that a divorce or a continuation of the marriage."

"I'll tell you what I'm worried about," said Rabbi Sokolow. "Even if we all agree that divorce is the best thing for everybody, he seems so angry that I don't know if he'll accept anything."

"We'll talk him out of any craziness," Katznelson said. "Those two haven't been married long enough to truly hate each other."

Temerl Katznelson was dispatched to the Rosenthal house, where Pesha had decamped, and after tea was poured and a lemon cookie offered and accepted, the two women unsheathed their blades and inspected the nuts of the matter.

"Honestly, you're going about this all wrong, Pesha," Temerl said. "If you're really hoping to get your husband to agree to a divorce, you're not going to convince him to do anything if you run around town telling everybody that he broke your arm."

Temerl later recalled that Pesha looked disoriented. Her dress was wrinkled, and her face gaunt. Her eyes were sunken into two enormous gray bags falling into her cheeks, as if she hadn't slept in a long time. And she

---

*An important part of a prayer service that involves standing and facing Jerusalem.

had an air of disquiet around her, as if she would drop any dish or cup you placed in her hand.

"I never said he broke my arm," Pesha replied, her voice drained of any emotion. "I said he hurt my arm. Which he did."

"You've got to think strategically," Temerl said, having long since worn through her patience with young brides who hadn't learned the illogical nature of men and the necessary sacrifices in placating them. "If a woman is serious about a divorce, she can't turn the thing into some big battle of the heart. You want him as clearheaded as possible. Don't you think that when he stops and thinks things through he's going to realize that it's pointless being married to a woman he doesn't get along with?"

Pesha didn't say anything, she merely grunted.

But it appeared that Temerl Katznelson's advice was taken seriously. A few days later, Pesha appeared at Ishmael's dress shop with a honey cake. Her dress was free of wrinkles and her wig was combed. Before she entered the shop, she was observed pinching her cheeks to bring out their rose.

The encounter between husband and wife was observed by Ishmael's brother Gershom, who reported that everyone in the store held their breath when she entered.

"Hello, Ishmael."

Ishmael had been hanging a dress on a mannequin and he froze, his fingers tightening around the white fabric.

"I brought this for you," she said, presenting him with the honey cake.

"Is it poisoned?"

Gershom cackled, which caused both Mr. and Mrs. Lindauer to turn in his direction.

"Let's go in the back," Ishmael said.

Husband and wife went into the stockroom as Gershom and their brother, Shmuel, lingered around the front of the shop, occasionally craning their necks toward the back. The store had a haunted silence for the fifteen or so minutes in which the Lindauers vanished into its viscera.

Eventually, Pesha briskly walked out of the back without bothering to say goodbye to either brother. Ishmael emerged with the heavy air of a man who had just discovered an unexplained lump on his body.

"What happened between you two?" Shmuel asked.

Ishmael didn't look at his younger brother. He shuffled over to the yard of fabric by the worktable and lugubriously sat in his chair.

"Nu?" Shmuel said again. "What happened?"

Ishmael didn't say anything. When he finally spoke it was in a whisper. "None of your business."

Gershom and Shmuel exchanged a look of puzzlement.

"Are you two getting divorced?" Gershom asked, taking advantage of his prerogative as an older brother, who could not be answered so curtly.

"No," Ishmael said, not looking up. Then he added, "I don't know."

It was an odd incident, certainly. Later, Gershom and Shmuel went over to Kreskol's tavern and parsed the brief episode as much as within human reason, looking for hidden meanings and possibilities. But they ended up as confused as when they sat down.

To their surprise, Pesha appeared again at the shop the next day. The snow had begun dissolving, and Pesha had gone searching for wildflowers in the forest. She presented a bouquet to her husband, who accepted it with obvious embarrassment.

"Let's go for a walk, Ishmael," Pesha suggested.

Ishmael hesitated for a moment. He stole a fleeting glance at his brother. "I'll be back in a little while, Gersh."

He put on his coat, kissed the mezuzah,* and disappeared with his wife for a half hour.

When he returned, he appeared to be in a better mood than he had been after Pesha's previous visit.

"What happened?" Gershom asked again.

---

*A small case affixed to the doorposts of Jewish houses that has a prayer written on parchment inside.

"We talked," Ishmael said. "Just talked a little. Don't concern yourself with it."

A marriage is a funny business.

For a few weeks, anyway, it looked as if all of the revulsion and abhorrence between Ishmael and Pesha Lindauer had thawed and melted away with the snow on the ground, and perhaps even turned into love.

Pesha would come to the dress shop every afternoon, usually with a gift as if she were the suitor and he were the pursued, and the two of them went for a walk in the forest.

"Could it be?" asked Esther Rosen at her stall. "Could they have put all this nastiness behind them?"

"You never know," answered one of the women.

"Hmm," Esther said. "I'll believe it when she moves back in with him."

Of course, Pesha Lindauer did not move back in with her husband. A month after she had begun courting her husband, Ishmael said that he was ready to agree to a divorce.

"This is ridiculous!" exclaimed Gershom Lindauer. "One minute, the two of you are acting like a couple of honeymooners—now you're agreeing to a divorce?"

"I know what I'm doing."

"I don't think so," Gershom replied. "I think you've been sold a bill of goods, brother. I think she tricked you."

But Ishmael couldn't be dissuaded. As he explained to those who asked, he believed that giving his wife a divorce would pave the way for a reconciliation. His willingness to seem reasonable would make her love him more; it would prove that he trusted her, and it would show the entire world that she would come back to him of her own true volition. Theirs would be one of the few love matches in Kreskol.

"You're crazy," Gershom said. "Completely crazy."

The beit din was summoned, where Rabbi Katznelson, Rabbi Sokolow, and Rabbi Joel Gluck all conferred with the sofer,* and after the divorce agreement was drawn up, Ishmael was given a piece of parchment and a goose-feather quill with which to sign it. He made his mark, and after the document was inspected a final time, it was given back to him.

"Now drop it in her hands," Rabbi Sokolow instructed.

He did so.

Rabbi Sokolow turned to Pesha.

"Turn and walk away from him."

She did as she was told, stepping across the Rabbi's study and stopping at the door.

The three men of the beit din exchanged a look, to make sure that everything had proceeded according to the ancient regulation. Rabbi Sokolow nodded.

"You're hereby divorced."

Ishmael nodded solemnly, but when he looked over to his former wife he was surprised to see that she had tears in her eyes.

They were not outpourings of grief—they were tiny crystals of happiness and relief. She threw a hand over her mouth to stifle whatever joyful exultation was about to leap out. And as Ishmael followed his ex-wife out of Rabbi Sokolow's chambers he felt his brother's words more acutely than he had been expecting.

Walking into the daylight, Pesha skipped ahead of him.

"Why are you walking so fast?"

Pesha didn't answer, but nevertheless she slowed her pace to appease him.

They wordlessly strolled for a minute along Cobbler's Row. Pesha's tears had dried—but she looked as if she was trembling even though the weather was warm and she was bundled up in a wool coat.

"Well, that wasn't so bad," Ishmael finally said. "I thought it would be much worse."

"Mmm."

---

*Scribe who handwrites legal documents and scrolls.

"Why are you being so quiet?"

Pesha kept her eyes on the ground.

"I don't feel like talking."

Ishmael stopped. He stood firmly as she kept walking. "Pesha!"

She turned around.

He didn't quite know what to say, I suppose. Those who witnessed the scene say the flash of temper was the same as Rabbi Sokolow had seen a few months earlier. If you didn't know any better, an unprejudiced observer would have had no trouble believing that he was a violent man. Moreover, the language he used was the kind that would make a Cossack blush. I myself debated whether or not to commit the actual words Ishmael Lindauer used to paper, but I finally decided that it was more important to be truthful than to hew to the most delicate sensibility. So those readers who are sensitive to such matters might wish to skip a few pages ahead.

"You really are a cunt, aren't you?"

Pesha's mouth flung open.

"I beg your pardon!"

"All this time," Ishmael said, his voice now rising, uncontrollably. "All this time that you were being nice to me! It was all a trick, wasn't it?"

"You're disgusting."

"And you're a whore!"

Pesha turned and began walking away.

"Whore!" Ishmael thundered at the top of his lungs. Needless to say, this was not the kind of scene that we witnessed every day in Kreskol. A crowd surrounded Ishmael, to make sure his crazed words wouldn't digress into action.

"I married a disgusting, filthy little whore!" Ishmael shouted loud enough for half the town to hear. Not even the sight of the holy Rabbi, who had come rushing out of his study with the rest of the beit din, did anything to assuage Ishmael's anger.

"Calm down!" Rabbi Sokolow begged. "Please, Ishmael!"

"Whore! Whore!"

"Ishmael—everybody's watching!"

He turned back to Rabbi Sokolow. "I want to take the get* back! I want to take the divorce back!"

"You can't," Rabbi Sokolow said. "It's too late."

"But she tricked me!"

It was useless to tell him that there was nothing to be done. He jumped up and down and howled like a child. Tears came to his eyes and he swore by everything that was holy that he would someday be avenged for this humiliation and disgrace.

"She'll pay!" Ishmael bellowed. "She'll regret this! I swear it! I swear on the Ark of the Covenant and the holy Torah!"**

Pesha took off running. She ran past the synagogue and the mikvah***— past the candlemaker's shop and Garment Lane, past the marketplace and the cemetery—and she did not stop running until she was safely inside her father's house, with the door securely locked behind her.

An unpleasant affair, certainly. And throughout the rest of the day, we all speculated about what would happen next between this loopy pair, because no one could believe that the story was over.

"I have a theory," said Esther Rosen, as she sat on the bench outside the Rosen household, holding court with four other Kreskol wives. "The two of them will wind up married to each other again."

"How do you figure that?"

"Neither of them will emerge from all of this nastiness able to marry anybody else. Who would marry Ishmael Lindauer after what we all just witnessed?"

It would be difficult to challenge that.

---

*A bill of divorce.
**The Ark of the Covenant is where the Ten Commandments were kept; the Torah is the first five books of the Old Testament written on a scroll. In a Jewish service the scroll is kept in an "ark."
***Ritual bath.

"And I think Pesha ruined her reputation a long time ago. No man in his right mind would agree to marry a woman who could drive her husband to such madness. I don't think it will happen tomorrow. I don't think it will happen next year. But when the woman hears the last gasps of motherhood calling, she'll realize she doesn't have anybody else."

"Oh, I don't know," one of the other matrons postured. "Pesha Rosenthal has the face of an angel and the figure of a nymph. Maybe she won't get her hooks into a rabbi, but she'll find somebody willing to take her."

Esther Rosen smirked, and the women continued chattering for the next hour about what fate would bring, before, one by one, the coven stood up to go home.

But what happened instead was something nobody had been expecting: Pesha up and vanished the next morning, leaving nary a trace of herself behind.

Her sister had come to her room to wake her up, and found that her bed was made and her room empty. Hadassah went out into the barn to see if she was milking the cows, or tending to the goats, but the animals were undisturbed. She walked into the woods and began calling Pesha's name. The only answer she got was from the chirping of the birds.

"Wake up! Wake up!" Hadassah rushed through the Rosenthal house shouting. "Our sister is missing!"

Within an hour, the beadle had knocked on the doors of all the town elders with a wooden hammer and they had assembled at the synagogue to discuss this latest development.

"What do you suppose happened to her?" someone asked.

"She probably ran off," another answered.

Foreboding words, among the people of Kreskol. Few townspeople ever roved deep into the forest that lay beyond the town walls; once or twice a decade an unhappy widower or an adventurous youth would make the journey without telling anyone, and, to a man, they were never heard from again. Certainly, they could have made safe passage to the nearest town. Or, for all we knew, they could have died of thirst with the vultures left to pick over their remains. Nobody knew for sure. But the consensus was that leaving Kreskol was a decision not dissimilar to suicide.

"Ran off?" the first elder said. "Into the woods? By herself? But she'll be torn to pieces by wolves!"

"Don't worry. If she's run off, we'll find her."

There was, of course, another sinister fear that didn't dare speak its name for the first thirty minutes of the meeting. "You don't suppose that husband of hers did something to her?" one of the elders finally asked.

"Preposterous," said Rabbi Katznelson.

Rabbi Sokolow, however, refused to dismiss it. He merely ran his hand through his beard. After a few moments, he pronounced: "I wouldn't put it past him." The meeting ground to complete silence.

"God forbid!" Katznelson finally replied.

"It must be considered," said Rabbi Sokolow.

"Yes, it must be," someone else chimed in.

"Just be careful," said Rabbi Gluck. "For those who falsely accuse the righteous lose paradise for themselves."

"Yes, yes—very worrisome," said Sokolow. "But what if we have a murderer in Kreskol?"

It was an astounding thought. A murder had not been committed in Kreskol in a hundred and eleven years.

Back then, according to our town archive, an expedition was sent out to the Polish authorities while the murderer (a man who knifed his brother over a business dispute that was complicated by the fact that the victim had seduced the assailant's wife) was kept locked away in the cellar of the town's shechita,* under constant watch, alongside an ox that was marked for slaughter. It took weeks before the murderer left our fair town in chains with a troop of gentile policemen.

"I suppose we'll have to do something similar," Rabbi Sokolow said. "Provided that Ishmael Lindauer is guilty."

---

*Slaughterhouse.

Reb Dovid Levinson, the ritual slaughterer, and Reb Wolf Shapiro, who operated the kiln and led Kreskol's fire brigade—two of the biggest men in town—appeared at Ishmael's house and took him to the synagogue with an arm around each shoulder.

When Ishmael appeared before the town elders, the furious fire-breather had dissolved into a frightened man. His face was ashen. Sweat poured from his brow and fell into his dark eyes. Every time he wiped the sweat away, Reb Levinson and Shapiro shared a glance.

"Have you heard what this is about?" asked Rabbi Katznelson.

"Yes."

"Your wife is missing," continued Katznelson.

Ishmael said nothing. He merely turned his head and gazed at the assembled elders.

"Do you know anything about it?"

"No—nothing."

A floorboard creaked, as someone in the room shifted from one foot to the other.

"You didn't do anything to her, did you?" asked Rabbi Sokolow.

"Of course not."

"I recall you saying yesterday that you would be avenged against Pesha," Sokolow said, evenly. "I recall you swearing this on the holy Torah."

Ishmael started to protest, but thought better of whatever he had planned to say.

"I didn't touch her."

Of course, none of the men of Kreskol were skilled in the arts of investigation and interrogation. After a few more tense questions were asked and answered ("What were you doing last night?" and "How do we know you're telling us the truth?"), it was decided that Ishmael should be allowed to leave.

"The Torah says at least two witnesses are needed," Katznelson explained to the suspect. "And we're not sure if anything happened to Pesha in the first place."

A dazed Ishmael nodded.

"Just remember," Katznelson said as Ishmael stepped out of the study, "we might need to ask you further questions."

Ishmael was sent home with Levinson and Shapiro at his side, but it was the last time the elders would see him.

Levinson and Shapiro stood watch outside the Lindauer family dress shop into the night, waiting for the candles to get blown out in the residence above. When the house went dark, they quietly stood across the road for a full ten minutes before deciding that its inhabitants must be asleep, and it was safe to go home.

But Ishmael Lindauer managed to slip away before morning. Bread, cheese, and butter from the Lindauers' larder were missing. A few pieces of ripe fruit had been picked off the trees behind their house. And a note was left on Ishmael Lindauer's pillow, written in Ishmael's childlike, blocky script and addressed to his older brother.

Dear Gershom—

I've decided to leave Kreskol. I don't believe I will ever again be at ease here. Every single person in town thinks that I'm a murderer.

The charge is a lie. I never laid a finger on my former wife. She might deserve all sorts of punishment—much of which I'm sure she'll receive in the world to come—but the fact remains that I never touched a single hair on her head.

My only hope is to start anew in a new city.

Forget all about me, Gershom. If it makes it easier, pretend I was struck by a bolt of lightning. Or got crushed by a horse. Or came down with pneumonia. Your brother is dead and gone. Forget that you ever heard the name Ishmael Lindauer.

There was no signature affixed.

"Well, there we have it," said Rabbi Sokolow after the beadle had again assembled the elders of Kreskol and the note was examined. "The man is guilty of something."

Which many of the elders felt was worthy of dispute. "But he says in the note that he's innocent," Katznelson replied. "He knew he was leaving, yes? Why should he lie in his farewell letter?"

"Isn't it obvious?" scoffed Sokolow. "We might catch up with him. The real question is what will we do when we apprehend him."

It was finally decided that Yankel Lewinkopf, the baker's apprentice (who it happens was an orphan whom nobody would miss), should get on a horse and travel in the direction of Smolskie. Upon his arrival, he should find whatever official he could from the district and relate the whole case. As far as the elders of Kreskol were concerned, this might be too important not to get the gentile authorities involved.

Yankel was outfitted with twelve days' worth of food and water, the town archives were rifled through for maps of the forest, and a compass was procured from Dr. Moshe Aptner. But hours before Yankel was about to get on the road out of Kreskol, we were all relieved to see the caravan of gypsies in their horse-drawn wagons coming through for their semiannual visit, which everyone agreed was too great a coincidence to be a mere whim of fate. Our heavenly father clearly wanted to help his children in Kreskol.

In the broken Polish that Rabbi Katznelson spoke, he got the gypsies to agree to lead young Yankel Lewinkopf to Smolskie in one piece.

"Maybe I'm crazy," said Esther Rosen that night, as she sat on the bench outside her house with four others, taking in the May breeze, "but I have the feeling that this is the start of something terrible."

"Like what?" one of them asked.

"Like who knows."

When two weeks had passed, and neither Pesha, Ishmael, nor Yankel returned to our village, most of those who had known and loved the trio began their descent into despair. What hope could these poor souls have of crawling back to our town after weeks alone in the forest? Issur

Rosenthal tore his garments, draped the looking glasses in his house with black cloth, and began reciting the kaddish* every morning. He stopped going into his shop and just sat in the Rosenthals' clay house in unhappy, tortured silence.

Likewise, the Lindauers went about their business under a cloud of grief, as if their brother was never very far from their thoughts (but they refused to appear in synagogue, on the off chance that they'd run into Issur Rosenthal).

Yankel Lewinkopf, however, didn't have much family—only a few aunts, uncles, and cousins who bothered with his welfare—so nobody kicked up much of a fuss that he had gone missing. Besides, he had been the most prepared. Of the three, he had the most chance of returning, even if nobody cared very much whether he did or not.

"Do you think the gypsies knifed him for the twenty zlotys in his pocket?" Reb Shapiro asked.

The question, it would seem, had been answered by being asked in the first place.

We are, of course, a town with many hundreds of inhabitants, so the grief of two particular families is not enough to stop the business of Kreskol in its tracks. The spring labors were conducted as they always were, with an eye on the summer and fall. Naturally, tragedies such as that of the Lindauer and Rosenthal families thankfully do not happen very often, so all through the spring its aftertaste lingered and worried us, and made Rabbi Sokolow say at the end of every sermon: "We all hope for the speedy return of Pesha Rosenthal, Ishmael Lindauer, and Yankel Lewinkopf."

However, I would probably not be telling this story if all three had simply vanished. One August afternoon a boy's voice came whooping through the streets of Kreskol, singing a single word over and over again.

---

*Prayer for the dead.

"Moshiach!"* young Ezra Schneider cried. "Moshiach! Moshiach! Moshiach!"

When somebody asked the boy what he was going on about, he pointed a pink finger up in the air, and we saw something remarkable.

An iron chariot appeared in the sky, thrashing its metal wings in the air like the sound of a thousand scythes busily at work. It came with a great gust of wind which blew a cloud of dust up in the air that sent some of those who had gathered in the town square doubling over in fits of coughing and wheezing.

Indeed, the boy was not touched in the head. He was not seeing ghosts and demons. The Messiah was flying into Kreskol!

Somebody thought to summon Rabbi Sokolow, and the sexton recovered the ram's horn from the synagogue. The horn was blown as if it were Yom Kippur, even though it couldn't be heard under the noise of the chariot. Heads started peeking out of their shop doors and homes to see the spectacle.

Several women fainted dead away. Others crumpled to their knees and broke into tears. The wisest of the wise looked as helpless and humbled as little children, too scared to speak. A draftsman ripped his apron off, hunched over, and was sick all over the earthen ground. Even Rabbi Sokolow's hands were trembling.

The only ones who didn't seem surprised or worried were the yeshiva boys. They looked merely enraptured. Their eyes turned glassy, and they began to form a circle, singing and dancing to herald the glorious destruction of the world as they had known it. They seemed to accept this miracle as having happened in due course, rather than something extremely unusual. (Several little children joined them in their dancing and good cheer.)

After hovering above the ground for a few moments, the chariot found a spot it approved of in the town square and floated to earth. A painted door opened and a white-bearded man set foot on the ground.

"Moshiach!" someone shouted.

---

*Hebrew: "Messiah!"

The rest of the town shouted the word at the tops of their lungs, and bowed to their knees.

The white-bearded fellow looked surprised to be addressed in such a manner. He gazed at the multitudes of devotees. But before he had a chance to speak, a younger man emerged from the chariot—this one without a beard, and dressed like a gentile.

The two exchanged a few words that no one in town understood. And if we had been readying ourselves for an outpouring of emotion, we hesitated. Of course, we had seen gentiles like the gypsies before. But it was puzzling, nonetheless, that the Messiah should be traveling with a non-Jew.

What happened next was even more bizarre: Yankel Lewinkopf hopped out after the gentile.

Yankel's clothes looked spiffy and cared for. And although he was the same rail-thin creature who had left Kreskol three months ago, he looked healthier than he did when he left, like he hadn't been forced to stew roots and grass to keep himself alive in the forest.

The three men who had stepped out of the chariot all conversed with one another, as the roar of the chariot's wings died down.

"Yankel?" Rabbi Sokolow finally ventured.

"Hello, Rabbi," the boy said, before turning back toward the Messiah.

"What is going on here? Is this the messiah?"

"They want to know what's going on," Yankel said, loud enough for us all to hear him. "What should I tell them?"

The messiah turned to the gentile and spoke furtively, as Yankel looked on. The messiah leaned over to Yankel and whispered something in his ear.

"No, Rabbi Sokolow," Yankel said to all those who had gathered in the town square. "This man is not the Messiah. The end of days has come and gone already. We missed it."

Rabbi Sokolow stopped trembling. He was too absorbed in what he was hearing to do anything other than listen raptly. The weeping and the hysterical invocations also died down.

"The Messiah came many years ago," Yankel said, plucking a handkerchief out of a trouser pocket and mopping the heat off his brow. "His name was David Ben-Gurion."

Well, what a shock we all experienced!

Of course, many of us had resigned ourselves to the fact that the Messiah might never appear in our lifetimes—but none of us thought that he could have returned and Kreskol simply could have been left out of this miracle. Where was the sounding of the ram's horn? Where were the disasters of the end of days? When had our loved ones risen from the graves, and when had the era of peace been heralded?

Several of the town elders took a step back from Yankel, as if he had uttered some black witchcraft, and Lazer Frumkin, the town sofer, burst into helpless tears.

"When did this happen?" asked Rabbi Sokolow, who appeared to be the only member of our town who kept his head well enough to ask questions. "How did we miss out on the end of days? Wasn't there supposed to be terrible disasters that would destroy the whole world?"

"There was," Yankel replied. "Many years ago a terrible war was launched by Germany, with the intention of destroying each and every last Jew in Europe. And the war was very nearly successful. Every shtetl in Poland was destroyed—except for one."

The town was silent.

Yankel looked as if he didn't quite know what to say next. The Messiah whispered again in his ear.

"Our beloved Kreskol was the only one to survive the onslaught," Yankel said, this time with a note of triumph in his voice. "The armies somehow overlooked us! We were spared!"

The town was quiet again before someone said loud enough for everyone to hear: "Oh."

Yankel looked as if he had been expecting a greater, more exultant response, and one could see the disappointment on his face.

"A lot has happened in the last few years," Yankel said. "These men will explain everything."

2

YANKEL

Of course, when I described Yankel Lewinkopf as an "orphan," I was speaking euphemistically.

He was, indeed, an orphan in that his mother had contracted typhus and perished before his eighth birthday, and in that he had grown up in several different broods. He lived with an aunt one year. With an uncle another year. And with his grandmother until he was old enough to begin his apprenticeship in his cousin's bakery.

But he was decidedly not an orphan in that his father was surely alive and well among Kreskol's pious men—even if no one could say which man his father was, precisely.

Devorah Lewinkopf, the boy's mother, had married young, and before she had reached her twenty-first birthday her husband had vanished one night from their bedchamber. He had the foresight to pack a bag before this disappearance, but that was the only detail that was known. What had happened to Yehuda Lewinkopf is anyone's guess, but since her husband had never divorced her and his whereabouts remained a mystery, the beit din ruled that Devorah was forbidden to remarry until she got some word of her husband's death or she formally received a get.

But despite this somewhat dire fate for a lively woman still in her childbearing years Devorah seemed at ease with her new status as an agunah.*

---

*A "chained woman": a woman who has not received a divorce from her husband and is therefore forbidden to remarry.

In fact, she seemed happier than she did in the days when her husband was lord and master.

No one could figure out the source of her good cheer at first, but after a few years it was noticed that she had almost entirely withdrawn from the society of other women. She lived alone in a little cottage on the edge of Kreskol, supporting herself without taking up knitting, or washing, or baking so much as a basket of cookies to sell in the marketplace. After a few years, when the other women of Kreskol saw the way the men looked at her, Devorah became widely despised.

They called her a seducer of the young. A spreader of disease. A destroyer of morals. A blasphemous buffoon. A promiscuous whore from whom no good was possible.

To this very day if you asked one of the older women—years after the worms have given up feasting on whatever remained of Devorah Lewinkopf—you will get sour looks and deep frowns upon mention of her name.

She was not a particularly tall creature. Her skin was dark, and her hair was pitch black. She had a wagging tongue that she used to tell jokes, curse, swear oaths, whisper endearments, and sing rhymes that could redden the face of any coachman in Warsaw. (She could do other things with her tongue that were rarely spoken of, and then only in hushed tones.) But there was no denying that there was something alluring in her dark eyes, which gleamed with secret mischief.

And the mischief had its intended effect. It was not uncommon for two yeshiva boys to run smack into each other during moonless nights directly in front of Devorah Lewinkopf's lawn. These boys were often so frightened that they would charge off in different directions, not to be seen again until morning. But this rarely stopped them from returning to Devorah's hovel at some point in the future.

When they were feeling crude, and when they were absolutely certain that the Rabbi and the teacher's assistant were nowhere in sight, the yeshiva boys talked among themselves about "Dirty Devorah." They would speak of Devorah's plump breasts with their brown nipples. Her round rump. The thicket of hair between her legs with its musky odor that left one weak-kneed and light-headed upon examination.

Some of the talk was make-believe, to be sure. You were considered less of a man if you had not called on Devorah at some point, and not every student had the courage to do so. In some cases, midway through his sojourn, a boy would be visited by the spirits of long-departed grandparents, or disappointed mothers, and, with tears running down his cheeks, beg Devorah not to say anything to anybody about what had transpired between them. He would steal away, leaving her the zloty or two in their pockets.

But others were not by any means telling tales. They had spent the extra effort and money necessary to make certain that their stories of Devorah were at least partially accurate.

When she died, she was buried in a plot outside the walls of town where the bastards and whores and thieves of Kreskol were planted, and the general consensus among the wives and mothers of our town was that we were well rid of her, and that it was a fate no other woman in town had so richly earned.

The fact that she left behind a little boy, who was good-natured and intelligent, was not much of a consideration.

However, it should be noted that her bastard, Yankel, was the complete opposite of her in almost every respect—and the females of Kreskol should have been more compassionate with the unfortunate boy. Where the mother had been bawdy and immodest, the son was exceptionally decorous and well mannered. He had his mother's cheerful good nature, but little of her carnality. At least none that anybody could detect. It was believed that he not only didn't know anything about the dubious way his mother kept food on the table, or her shameful nickname, or the older men who would tiptoe in and out of their house in the dead of night, but he probably wouldn't have understood it even if one of the other boys had been indiscreet enough to mention it in his presence.

Indeed, most of the cheder boys subscribed to the theory that the chief difference between Yankel and his mother was the fact that he was an imbecile, who didn't understand much of anything.

This was almost certainly untrue. While never quite at the top of his class, Yankel Lewinkopf was not at the bottom, either. He could memorize Talmud* and Chumash,** and recite it well enough. (His teachers, who more or less assumed the same thing about his intellect, were often taken by surprise that he could answer their questions thoroughly and with obvious quickness.) And even though he had a reputation for being an innocent, this was probably exaggerated as well.

When the conversation turned to the female sex, as it does with boys of a certain age whose imaginations must fill in the details not yet gleaned through experience, he did not cover his ears, or turn away, or brighten with embarrassment as the more prissy children did. He was not stupid—rather, he was reflective. He listened to the ribald half-truths that his fellow boys told one another about women when they were alone, and he kept his opinions on these matters to himself. But he surely thought something.

Fortunately, the misperception that he was both innocent and simple kept the other boys from ridiculing his mother to his face. It was believed he couldn't take any ribbing. The one time that Falk Goreman—the biggest boy in the cheder, and two years older than Yankel—had shouted, "Hey, Lewinkopf! I think I left my tzitzit*** on your mother's bedside!" the incident did not end well.

Yankel looked puzzled by Goreman's words. "What do you mean by that?"

"Figure it out."

Yankel stared at the big, lumbering Goreman, who had turned his attention away from Yankel and back to the other young men. But Yankel

---

*The central text of Rabbinic Judaism, comprising the "mishna" and the "gemarah," originating as the oral teachings in ancient Israel.
**The Bible, or Torah.
***Tassels affixed to the garments of religious Jews.

strode toward his nemesis, tapped him on the shoulder, and said, "Would you repeat what you said?"

"I said I think I left my tzitzit on your mother's bedside when I came around for a visit last night." Goreman smiled, unfazed. "Why don't you be a good boy and run along home and fetch it?"

The other boys stopped what they were doing to observe the scene.

Those who witnessed the incident said that in the ensuing minute or so, every boy felt his heart thumping in his chest. A challenge had been proffered, and all the boys wondered whether Yankel would accept it. Some were waiting for him to break down in tears. Others assumed he was too dumb to realize he had been insulted. A few half-expected him to go running for the Rabbi. And a handful were hoping that Yankel would throw the first punch at Goreman, which would lead to Yankel's subsequent pummeling—something that held a macabre fascination for every boy. One and all studied Yankel's face for some clue as to what would come next.

The pummeling happened—but it was not *of* Yankel. It was *by* Yankel.

He lunged at Goreman so quickly that no one had time to stop him. His hands grasped Goreman's throat with every ounce of his strength.

The other boys fell on them both and tried to tear Yankel away, but to no avail. Falk Goreman's thick, fleshy throat was firmly locked in Yankel's hands, and for a moment it looked as though the boy might in fact be choked to death.

An adult was summoned, and slowly Yankel's fingers were pried off Falk's neck by the young teacher's assistant, who looked more terrified than any of the children that a charge might actually die on his watch.

Falk—the large, immense lummox of a boy, whose size had always made him a purveyor of fear in the schoolyard—now collapsed in the dust. He was beet red, gasping for air, with tears streaming down his cheeks. His blond sidelocks had become matted and hair was strewn every which way over his face. Even after he had caught his breath, he continued to sob and howl and quake in misery.

But Yankel still had a crazed look about him, and no one dared trust him not to lunge again. The teacher's assistant held him down, and the other boys all hovered over him, waiting to pounce, as the minutes ticked by and the lunacy finally left his eyes.

Once Yankel had calmed down and seen the terror he had inflicted on Falk Goreman, he burst into tears, too. Each boy was made to apologize to the other. And despite this pathetic display of cowering misery, after a few weeks Falk returned to his rightful role as the biggest (and therefore the scariest) bully in the cheder.

But Yankel was forever afterward treated as a leper. Not only was he an idiot, it was reasoned, but he was violent. Like one of the goyim. And the son of a whore, anyway. He was thereafter spoken to only when absolutely necessary. Even the other outcasts, who were reviled and picked on, refused to have anything to do with him. As did the pious boys who, knowing they should steer clear of a mamzer,* had avoided him for ages.

When Yankel's mother died a few months later, rather than feeling any sympathy for the orphan a theory emerged among the cheder students that it was an act of divine retribution.

"This," declared Manis Fefferberg on the playground that afternoon, "is what God does to you when you act crazy. This is how he repays you."

The other boys nodded, solemnly.

"Even when you act crazy toward a bully like Falk Goreman."

Another nod.

"I suspect that Yankel Lewinkopf is cursed."

And this was the perception that remained forever after etched in stone whenever his name was mentioned: Yankel was jinxed.

For the aunts and uncles who took him in after his mother perished, they did not think of him as jinxed per se, but as a reminder of the family's

---

*A child born of a forbidden relationship; i.e., conceived in adultery or incest. The designation brings various restrictions and forbids a mamzer from being counted in a quorum or serving as a judge.

abiding shame and as an inescapable slab of dead weight who had to be fed and clothed and washed and educated.

While Devorah Lewinkopf might have been a low, lewd creature, who spent the day of atonement with the other riffraff at the beggars' synagogue on Thieves' Lane, it would be a mistake to assume that she had come from a bad family. In fact, there was a time when the Sandlers (her surname before she became a Lewinkopf) were considered one of the better families in Kreskol.

The Sandlers were once moneylenders. Pincus Sandler, Yankel's great-great-great-great-grandfather, had been a rich man who had built one of the village's more splendid houses, just outside the old medieval walls of the village. Sandler women were given diamonds and pin money and gentile maidservants to clean up after them, and all sorts of other goodies that most women in Kreskol could only dream about.

But, of course, that was a long time ago. The Sandlers' fortunes had fallen several generations earlier when a recession caused numerous families to pick up and leave Kreskol. The Sandlers eventually drifted out of the lending business and into different lines of work. But they remained respectable. While they might not have the riches they once possessed, they hung on to a hoard of silver and diamonds. They never wanted for meat on their Sabbath tables. Their sons studied at yeshiva and became educated men. They had decent dowries to give to their daughters.

Moreover, Devorah Lewinkopf's mother, Zipporah, although not a Sandler by birth, had lent the clan added respectability as the daughter of Rabbi Reuven Nussbaum, one of the most pious and educated men to ever reside in Kreskol. Zipporah had widely been known to feed the poor, scrupulously say her prayers, and share all the important attributes of a saint. It was a shame, the other females lamented, that her faculties deserted her so early in life, because she would have never allowed her daughter to turn into such an abomination.

"Do you think she even knows?" the women would ask at the marketplace.

The answer was, as always, a shrug.

No, Zipporah Sandler did not seem the slightest bit aware of the whispering about her daughter as she trudged through the stalls, examining eggs and cabbages, or on her way to the tailor to have a dress mended or her wig restitched. She held her head high and wasn't hesitant about volunteering some nugget of information or news about her youngest daughter if the subject seemed to fit into the discussion. She could never quite figure out why gazes would suddenly fall and the conversation would grind to a halt.

What went on between mother and daughter when a seed took root in her daughter's supposedly abandoned womb?

Lord only knows if the old lady had wit enough to understand the implications. But, nevertheless, Devorah told her mother that her husband had reappeared one evening to reassert his matrimonial privileges and—just as quickly—vanished again into thin air. At least, this was the public story that Zipporah gave to anyone who asked her. (Not that too many felt compelled to ask.)

When Devorah died, and the rabbis met with the family and discussed what should be done, Devorah's sister and brother each prayed fervently that they would not wind up with their sister's young bastard.

Rabbi Sokolow was firm. Devorah's kin had an obligation to raise Yankel—mamzer, bastard, orphan, or whatever he was—as one of their own, and Zipporah Sandler was too feeble in mind and body to do it herself. The Sandlers hewed to the Rabbi's ruling with the most grudging sense of duty possible.

Indeed, Yankel was given a place in his aunt's house. But he was never made to forget that he was a transient, subsisting on her charity.

"I don't know what other aunts would do for you, Yankel," Shosha Markowitz would tell her nephew. "But aren't you lucky to be here with me?"

The boy nodded.

"Other relatives, they just might leave you to the wolves," Shosha continued.

"I know."

"But not me. You've got a warm house here. You've got three hot meals a day. You have it awfully good."

"Thank you, Aunt Shosha."

She winced, slightly, at hearing the word "aunt" affixed to her name.

"And you shouldn't forget that you have obligations, too, young man."

The boy nodded.

"This house doesn't run itself. Food doesn't magically appear on the dinner table every night. It takes a lot of work to put it there."

"Yes, Aunt Shosha."

"If you want to live here, you're going to have to work for it—just like everybody else."

Yankel helped his aunt wash floors, iron clothes, peel carrots and potatoes, pound out flanken, render the chicken fat, beat out the rugs and carpets, preserve fruits and vegetables for the winter, chop firewood for the stove, and anything else his aunt could think of—even though the "just like everybody else" part of her pronouncement was decidedly false.

Yankel's cousins were rarely asked to contribute the same share of labor. Or any labor at all, for that matter. Even Shosha's daughters, who might be reasonably expected to do more of the household chores than her sons, lifted a finger only if it was to bring a fork up to their mouths.

It should be noted that Shosha Markowitz treated her offspring as if they were a band of wayward royalty who had only accidentally wound up in her care and feeding. She fully believed that her children were talented, intelligent, important people (even if nobody in Kreskol was particularly important), and her responsibility for their happiness was a sacred trust.

Not only did her sons and daughters not have to contribute any labor they didn't want to, Shosha believed that the normal strains of childhood amusement were too much for them, as well.

When they left the house to play with other children, she tearfully begged them to please—*please!*—care for their safety. When they would scrape a knee or bruise an elbow, she would cry along with them and ply them with cookies and potato pancakes and anything else they felt was their due.

But this doting and attention did not extend to Yankel, whom she viewed as if he were part of the hired help. He was never thanked for his efforts; rather, he was led to believe that they were nothing more or less than reasonable compensation for room and board.

Moreover, Yankel's excellence in performing every task put before him did little to endear him to his aunt. In fact, it had the opposite effect. After a few months of living with Yankel, Shosha began viewing his sprightliness and good nature as the sign of something sinister.

"Who is this boy?" she asked her husband one night when they were alone in their bed. "He never speaks his mind, for goodness sake!"

"So?"

"So I can't figure out whether the boy's a simpleton on whom we're wasting all this food, space, and effort, or whether he's truly his mother's son—a little rascal, working up some sort of plot in his head, to cheat us out of house and home."

For the rest of his tenure in the Markowitz house, as he stitched and whittled and canned and ironed and did everything else his aunt desired, Shosha's suspicion remained fixed on him.

Yankel sensed that he had somehow done something to offend his aunt, and he thus put forth greater effort to be as useful as possible. He took on extra chores and duties—things that he was never asked to do—and he did them well, which only exacerbated his aunt's misgivings. Suspicion was calcified into certainty. Shosha would leave Yankel to his chores, and when she was satisfied that her nephew believed that he was alone, she would burst in on him—expecting to catch him, in flagrante delicto, in some violation of the family's trust. Or she would close the door to the kitchen and study him through a keyhole for signs of disobedience.

The relationship between aunt and nephew came to a climax (or reached its nadir) one winter night when all the children had gone to sleep, and the Markowitzes were alone in their bed. Conversation began with the broken stove in the kitchen that desperately needed to be repaired before it got too cold, progressed to mittens and scarves the children needed, and culminated with the question of Chanukah gifts, and what each child deserved.

"I suppose we have to give something to the mamzer," Shosha said, with a little laugh.

Solomon frowned, disapprovingly.

"You shouldn't say that," he said. "It's not nice. The boy can't help who his mother is."

Shosha sighed loudly. "Yeah, not nice," she said. "But, of course, it wasn't nice for my sister to leave us with a mamzer. What did we do to deserve that?"

Shosha's sister was a topic that she never tired of, even after Devorah's ignominious life had been swallowed up by the finality of death. When Shosha was alone with her husband, she still conjured up long-ago memories of her sister to prove what a bad seed she was, right from the start. She told stories of plates of food hurled against the wall when Devorah was a toddler; how she had been shoved by Devorah, knocking out two of her baby teeth; how Devorah had once run stark naked through the house, reached the front door, and galloped outside in the July sun for all the world to witness.

"I still can't get over her," Shosha said. "Still, after all these years. It's not even that she was a whore. But she was such a dimwit. She became a whore because she didn't have the smarts to make a living in an honest way. She couldn't cook. She couldn't sew. She couldn't do anything except spread her legs."

At that, Solomon stood up to close the slightly ajar door to their bedroom, just on the off chance that the children were still awake, and when he reached the door he found Yankel standing in his nightshirt in the hallway.

Both Shosha and Solomon Markowitz's faces reddened. They merely stared at the child in horror.

For his part, Yankel's brown hair was swept over his forehead, making him look, if anything, even younger than he was. His eyes were wide with disbelief. His mouth cracked open, but silent.

"What are you doing out of bed?" Solomon finally thought to ask.

But Yankel didn't say anything. He could only respond in a mousey squeak; as if he were afraid any rumble coming out of his mouth might provoke an avalanche.

"Jacob's awake," he said of his two-year-old cousin, who slept next to him. And before he said anything else, tears began silently falling down his cheeks.

Solomon thanked him for bringing it to his attention and quickly led him back to bed.

"So typical," Shosha said when they were alone again. "Instead of acting maturely, he tries to make me feel guilty. What a number this little stinker is doing on us!"

Shosha's guilt grew strong enough that a few days later Yankel was banished from his aunt's house altogether, and sent to live with his uncle Yitzhak. "It's time for you to live with your uncle now," Shosha said by way of explanation. "You've been here long enough."

Yankel nodded obediently, betraying neither great disappointment nor exhilaration.

"Watch him," Shosha instructed her brother upon delivering their nephew to Yitzhak's doorstep. "He's up to no good."

Yitzhak Sandler was more sympathetic to the young boy than his sister. He believed that Shosha's stories about all of Yankel's evil plotting were just stories—the work of a female with an overstuffed imagination.

Which is not to say that Yitzhak, or his wife, Geneshe, liked the idea of caring for another child. Whereas his sister's objections to Yankel had to do with the shame of bringing a bastard into an otherwise spotless house, Yitzhak and Geneshe Sandler had more practical reasons: They already had thirteen children. Their house was a maelstrom of chaos and noise. Someone in the house was always crying. Someone was always accidentally hurting themselves. Someone was always lodging a complaint or leveling an accusation.

Things had eased up, somewhat, when their eldest son, Avraham, left to be married, followed six months later by their eldest daughter, Gitel. But the house still hiccupped and rustled and creaked late into the night. The idea of caring for another youngster wasn't just daunting, it was depressing.

However, as with his aunt, Yankel was determined to prove himself useful. He did every chore Yitzhak and Geneshe could dream up, even if they never really felt the boy had anything to prove.

They grew to like having Yankel around, and unlike with his aunt Shosha, the boy was never made to feel like too much of a freeloader. Of course, everything changed once their daughter, Gitel, her husband, Favish, and their infant twins, Alte and Itzel, showed up at the Sandler home one night and announced that Favish had not finished his studies adequately and had been asked to leave yeshiva. Favish's parents threw them out of their house and told them not to return until he was reinstated.

Suddenly, a marginally tolerable situation was made unbearable. A house of fourteen (if you considered Yankel and the adults) ballooned to eighteen. Two of whom were wailing, screaming, colicky infants. And in a matter of months that number would become nineteen owing to the fact that Gitel was already expecting yet another child.

"This is ridiculous!" Geneshe said to her husband the next night. "There are going to be nineteen people living in four rooms. Nineteen! Such a thing is not possible!"

"I know . . ."

"Who knows—it might be twenty! After all, that daughter of ours gave birth to twins once. Who's to say it isn't possible for lightning to strike a second time?"

"What can we do?"

"Remind me again why Shosha can't take in your nephew?"

"She doesn't like him."

"That's it?"

"I think so."

"That can't be it. There has to be some other reason. And if that's the reason, it's ridiculous. We're going to have twenty people living in this house. She has eight. She should take Yankel in."

"She thinks that Yankel is a bad seed."

"Why?"

"Lord only knows. Because he was too nice, I think."

"Too nice?" Geneshe repeated.

"I think so."

Geneshe considered this for a minute.

"That's the most ludicrous thing I've ever heard," she finally pronounced. "I mean, is the woman insane?"

"Of course she is."

"Well, sane or insane, we have a serious problem," Geneshe continued. "As dear as Yankel is, he's going to have to find some other place to live. We simply can't have four adults and sixteen children living in this house. We'll go crazy."

"Fifteen is more likely," Yitzhak said. "Gitel won't be giving birth to twins, so far as we know."

A week of strained and moody negotiations took place between brother and sister. Sensing that her husband was getting nowhere, Geneshe Sandler paid a visit to her sister-in-law, and after laying all her cards on the table (and being told in no uncertain terms to drop dead), Geneshe stormed back to her house, slammed the door behind her, and declared her sister-in-law a horror, whom "Yankel shouldn't live with under any circumstances."

Yitzhak assumed this meant that his nephew would remain, and was, for the moment, relieved, as he had grown fond of the boy. But, alas, it was not to be.

"He can't stay here, either," Geneshe declared. "And it's not just because of the issue of space. Now it's a matter of principle. We can't let that cow win. She can't just walk out on her responsibilities and leave us with the bill. There's something at stake here."

And so, setting aside their instructions from the rabbis, Shosha and Yitzhak went to their mother, Zipporah, and told her that they couldn't abide having Yankel in their houses anymore. Zipporah didn't quite understand the objections to her grandson, but she was too docile to argue. Besides, a child is a child. She had borne seven—three of whom reached adulthood. As old as she was, she could raise one more. It was settled. The boy would stay with her, and that was all there was to it.

The boy grew.

He didn't grow particularly tall. Or particularly sturdy. But after his fourteenth birthday—as he spent his days kneading flour and water, and shoveling dough in and out of the baking oven—he turned into something resembling a fully formed man. The whispers of a beard came inching down his chin alongside red zits. He developed calluses and blisters on his hands, working without complaint from the time the cock crowed in the morning until the sun went down at night, and he kept his eye on the fires even during the Sabbath, when the housewives of Kreskol would come in to retrieve pots of cholent* and soup that he kept warm. He greeted every man and woman who entered the bakery with a hearty smile. He jumped like a trained dog to retrieve a challah for the most dour housewife.

Yankel was not liked, exactly. The people of Kreskol were not sophisticated enough to overlook their innate distrust of a mamzer. But he had earned a certain place in our town. He was not fully accepted, but he wasn't scorned, either.

Of course, that didn't mean his illegitimacy wasn't always lurking somewhere nearby. When he was seventeen, he went to Mira Rut, the matchmaker, and asked her to find him a wife. She laughed in his face.

Not that he was ugly. Nor did he have terrible professional prospects.

---

*A long-simmering Sabbath stew.

(There was a reasonable possibility he might, after all, run the bakery in which he was now working.) But—Mira said—an *orphan* is always impossible to marry off. His only hope, she told him, was Hodl Lebowitz, who, in addition to being hunchbacked and missing most of her top teeth, was the daughter of the town ragpicker; or Lila Tanenbaum, who was blind and feebleminded.

Yankel brusquely told Mira Rut he would call on one of her rivals. (It was the only time anyone could remember the boy being choosy about anything.) But the other matchmakers must have told him the same thing, because his eighteenth birthday came and went and he was still a bachelor.

And, yes, some of the good people of Kreskol felt pity for him.

It was difficult to think of any interests the young man had, aside from his work and the time he spent every day in prayer.

He attended services at the beggars' synagogue (the good synagogue, off Market Street, would never count a mamzer in its quorum), where his mother had said her prayers, and led what anybody would agree was an upright life. And we all wondered how he could possibly fill the hours without a wife and children to occupy him. He might be jinxed; he might be a bastard; but it was widely believed that Yankel Lewinkopf was largely blameless in his misfortunes.

And he could have easily spent the rest of his life blameless—a footnote in this book, whose existence was on the edges and not in the center of Kreskol—if he hadn't been visited in his bakery by Rabbi Katznelson the day after Ishmael Lindauer went missing.

"Yankel Lewinkopf!" Katznelson said upon entering the bakery. "I've got good news for you."

Yankel had been tending the fire. He cast an eye in the corner toward his cousin, Avraham, before he shut the oven and turned to the man who had entered.

"Hello, Rabbi Katznelson," Yankel said.

"Yes, yes. Hello Yankel. I hope you're well. I'm here with some big news, my lad. Don't you want to know what it is?"

"Certainly."

"You're about to go on an adventure!"

Yankel was unsure what the Rabbi meant. He looked over to Avraham for some clue, but his cousin was busy kneading a challah into two white braids.

"What do you mean?"

"I mean we're sending you to the big city. You're going to Smolskie."

Avraham evidently heard this, because he stopped kneading and craned his neck around.

"Smolskie?" Yankel repeated. "Why? Who's sending me?"

"Kreskol is. You're going to be our ambassador there, you see. We have a very important mission. You've been following this whole business with Pesha Rosenthal and Ishmael Lindauer?"

"People talk," Yankel acknowledged. "It's only natural to overhear."

"Have you heard the latest?"

"That Pesha is missing? Yes, I heard that."

"Old news," Katznelson scoffed. "Things have changed completely since then, young man. Completely. No, the *latest* is that Ishmael has run off, too."

For a moment Yankel thought the former husband and wife had run off together in an elopement, which sounded unusual, to be sure, but piqued his interest.

"Oh?"

"We don't know what happened, of course, but we've decided that it's time to alert the gentile authorities that a murderer might be on the loose."

"A murderer?" Yankel repeated. "You think the wife was murdered?"

"Anything's possible. We just don't know. But the goyim have much more experience in these kinds of things than we do. We need to alert them. *You* need to alert them."

Yankel considered this for a moment.

"That sounds dangerous."

"Why?" Rabbi Katznelson asked. "No one's asking you to go out and catch a murderer. You're only going to report one. And who knows—it might be nothing at all."

"But I've never been out of Kreskol in my life."

"Who has?"

"But I wouldn't know the first thing about contacting the authorities."

"Nobody does," Katznelson answered. "It's not as though we're going to send you out without maps and a compass. Or without food and water. You'll be provided for."

"But who will look after my bubbe?"*"

It was true that not long after he moved in with his grandmother Zipporah and Yankel switched roles, and he was the one who cared for her. He had prepared the meals for her, and washed the linens for her, and gone shopping for her, and done everything that an old and demented woman could not. "Don't fret about it, my lad," Katznelson said. "If that's the worst of your worries, you'll be fine. Your cousin Gitel can take your place, no? I'm sure that your uncle Yitzhak and aunt Geneshe would like to get her and her family out of their house, wouldn't they?"

"I can't do that," Yankel said. "I would never dream of leaving her."

Rabbi Katznelson didn't have the patience to flatter the citizens of Kreskol into doing his bidding. "Maybe this was a mistake," he said loudly enough for Avraham to hear. "And here I thought we were sending you on an adventure. Here I thought I was giving you what was practically a *gift*! I thought, 'What a lucky man! I wish I was young and off to the big city!' Here I was wishing I could trade places with you. I guess I was wrong."

As I have said before, Yankel was no fool. He had never yearned to see the city—certainly not a gentile city—because it had been drilled into his head from the time he was still a toddler that the world outside Kreskol was a dangerous, treacherous place, and that he should consider himself fortunate that he was born far away from it.

---

*Yiddish: Grandmother.

The other students in cheder told ghost stories of what happened to boys who had strayed too far into Kreskol's woods; how there were demons and warlocks lying in wait, ready to rip the flesh from one's bones and fry one's liver in chicken schmaltz.* He had heard tales that the howling in the trees at night were the moans of disobedient boys who had trespassed and been turned into wolves by whatever witch they had come across. Not all of it was witches, either. There were stories of boys who had been chased, captured, put in cages, and turned into bars of soap at the hands of mad, bloodthirsty gentiles who only did so out of a limitless loathing for Jews.

And he had heard that the cities were temples of iniquity, sin, and antisemitism. These were the places where loose women prostituted their bodies. Where every sin known to man—from theft to adultery, to the eating of filth—existed to be performed and celebrated. Where evil men would slit a little boy's throat simply for the coins jangling in his pocket. (In point of fact, they wouldn't even need pocket change as a pretext; they would kill you if they didn't like the look on your face.)

However, Yankel's cousin's interest was piqued.

"Wait a minute!" Avraham cried out. "Just wait a minute, here!"

Katznelson turned.

"Yankel! You heard the man. This is a great adventure he's proposing."

"But who will take my place here?"

Avraham waved this away with a white-powdered hand. "We'll manage."

"But I don't speak Polish."

"Sure you do," Rabbi Katznelson chimed in. "All the boys learn Polish."

Which was true, so far as it goes. Polish was treated as a kind of secret language among the young. Still, Yankel hadn't spoken it in years.

"I don't remember a word."

"What are you so worried about?" Katznelson asked, pinching his

*Rendered fat.

ruddy nose and sniffling. "You don't think there will be other Jews in Smolskie? You don't think *anybody* there speaks Yiddish? If that's your only objection, I think you'll get by just fine."

And while Yankel couldn't exactly get excited about his mission—or as excited as Avraham and Katznelson appeared—he felt a natural inclination to do what he was asked. It was something that he had been taught since he became orphaned: to be useful. He believed that he should trust in the wise elders of Kreskol, because they knew what was best for everybody.

"Very well," Yankel said. "I'll go, if you want me to."

A pair of new boots were procured. As was a satchel that was filled with nuts and raisins and dried berries, and enough salted beef that he could withstand a couple of weeks out in the wilderness if he got lost. Rabbi Katznelson and his assistant, who still owned a Polish grammar book, sat down together with the town sofer and wrote out two notes, one in Polish and a second one in Yiddish, which Yankel should present to the authorities when he reached Smolskie. (This would, it was reasoned, save Yankel the trouble of summoning the necessary Polish, just in case his linguistic skills deserted him.)

He was taken to the town's archive and he sat patiently as he was instructed on what route he should take through the forest—where the trails would turn into dirt roads, and where the dirt roads would turn into paved ones—and how he would know if he had veered off course. Ancient maps had the dust blown off them and were placed in Yankel's young hands.

Dr. Moshe Aptner, the keeper of all the scientific devices and doodads in our town, produced a dull golden compass.

"What's it used for?" Yankel asked.

Dr. Aptner looked, for a moment, as if he wasn't quite certain of the answer. "Why, it tells the difference between north and south," he finally declared.

"How?"

"I'm not sure."

If Yankel felt nervous, he took pains not to reveal it. A mule was taken to the blacksmith and fitted with new shoes, and then loaded with supplies.

However, I'm not going to say that we didn't all breathe a great sigh of relief when, only hours before Yankel was to depart, the caravan of gypsies came through Kreskol's market for their spring visit. "Thank god," Katznelson whispered when he thought no one was listening. "Oh, thank god!"

The gypsies had taken the primitive, unpaved path through the forest that their ancestors had beaten several centuries earlier. Why they remained faithful to this route was something of a mystery. Some in Kreskol believed that it was more out of a respect for custom than anything else—they certainly weren't coming back for any money we could offer. As poor and unsophisticated as the gypsies were, they let us know that we were much worse. Our cash offers were too insulting to even be countered; they would only accept trade.

Still, every spring and every fall they hitched their horse-drawn wagons to a fence that stood just outside the walls of town, and dragged the elaborate birdcages and grandfather clocks and baskets of puppies to the market square along with more practical items like sewing needles and boxes of nails and castor oil and Epsom salts that were unquestionably in demand.

As much as nails and sewing needles were needed, we were never exactly welcoming. We treated trespassers suspiciously and didn't mind if it came off as rudeness—but the gypsies weren't exactly polite or effusive, either.

They would spend hours thoughtfully examining Szeina Rifkin's embroidered aprons and summer frocks, or Shalom Shmotkin's sheepskin slippers, before making an offer for the entire inventory.

"A box of five hundred matches for each dress," a gypsy would say in Polish, and then hold up the box in her left hand and the dress in her right, indicating a one-for-one trade. Seeing that she could turn around and swap these matches for shoes or gloves or even a goose, it didn't seem like a bad bargain to Szeina, and for a few weeks thereafter she was in the match distribution business. A hand was offered and accepted. The gypsies spent the afternoon sifting through our market and making their offers before turning around and heading on their way.

This time, however, when Rabbi Katznelson was summoned out of the study house and he saw who was riding into town, he waved hello, gave them his best smile, and said in broken Polish, "Too long, too long!"

The main plenipotentiary of these wanderers, a man in his fifties who wore a gold ring in his left ear, was named Washo Zurka, and he looked as surprised as we had ever seen him to be greeted so warmly.

"Well, hello," Zurka said.

"Good!" Katznelson said. "Good to come!"

Zurka didn't know what he meant, exactly. "Yes," Zurka replied with a nod, scratching nervously along his plump cheek. "It's good to be here."

The rest of the conversation was hammered out in a broken, piecemeal way, but led to Yankel being plucked from the blacksmith's and Rabbi Katznelson telling Zurka, "This boy needs to go to Smolskie. You will take him?" And Zurka shrugged before agreeing, "Why not?"

A price was offered of twenty zlotys, but it was laughed off.

"But twenty zlotys?" Katznelson said, looking alarmed. "That's a fortune!"

Zurka smiled with sympathy. He was not an unfriendly person. While he hadn't yet quite figured out what this crisis was all about, he could sense that something was wrong among these Jews and he was willing to help them if it didn't cost him anything. Nevertheless, even a charitable man couldn't help but be taken aback by these Hebrews' sense of money. "You have not been to Smolskie recently, have you?" Zurka asked.

"Never. I never been."

"Well, then you would know that twenty zlotys is not very much of anything."

For a moment, Rabbi Katznelson looked dumbstruck. He would have to take the twenty zlotys from the synagogue's treasury, and it would take some time to replenish it. Months and months. But if Yankel Lewinkopf's safety was at issue, he was willing to spend it. However, how was it possible that twenty zlotys was "not very much of anything"?

If they had been speaking Yiddish, Katznelson might have been able to ask better questions, but the surprise had thrown him. He shook his head before saying: "Forty."

Zurka laughed again. He watched his partner in this negotiation with fascination more than anything else.

"You laugh?" Katznelson said. "*Forty* zlotys and you laugh?"

"It's not much more than twenty."

"Two times twenty! Two for one. Double!"

"I know the math."

"That's a lot."

"For you, maybe. But it's just not very much money today in Poland."

Katznelson wondered if this gypsy was tricking him. He had no way of knowing what went on in other places, but in Kreskol two groschen bought you a loaf of bread, therefore forty zlotys would buy two thousand loaves of bread. It was a staggering figure. Could it really be that worthless in the rest of Poland? Besides, all he was asking was that the man take Yankel through the woods and to safety. What could the man want for that?

"Forty-five," Rabbi Katznelson said. "That's final."

Zurka said nothing. He merely looked at the Jews of Kreskol who had come to watch the negotiation. Zurka imagined that they rarely saw anything this exciting play out in their daily life, and he decided to give the villagers their money's worth. He looked as if he was weighing the decision carefully and was unsure of how he would decide.

"All right," Katznelson said, unprompted. "I will make one more offer. Take it or leave it. I cannot spend another penny . . ."

Zurka waited for Katznelson to say something, but he didn't. Katznelson's eyes were cast on the dirt ground, as if he were stealing himself for his next concession.

"Yes?" Zurka said.

"Fifty. Fifty is it. If you want more, we'll let the boy find Smolskie on his own."

Zurka smiled. "Fifty?"

"Yes, fifty. And he'll bring along his own food and water."

"Very well. I accept. In fact, you can keep your fifty zlotys. What I want is for you to give me the mule he was planning on taking. And two dozen of Shmotkin's gold slippers."

Rabbi Katznelson looked not just relieved but ecstatic. They shook hands and—after the yearly negotiations commenced and more swag was exchanged—Yankel was led with the little mule back to the four covered wagons on the outskirts of Kreskol.

The gypsies stared at Yankel as if they were encountering a never-before-seen animal, whose passivity or malevolence they were unable to fully gauge.

The horses were untied, and one of the gypsy teenagers mounted the mule and started on the forested path ahead of the other animals.

"You'll ride in that one," Zurka said to Yankel, pointing to the last wagon in the caravan, where he had put the cache of slippers, as well as shawls, boots, summer vests, and pottery the gypsies had successfully traded for.

Yankel had a hard time understanding the gypsy. The conversation between the gypsy and Rabbi Katznelson had been agony to follow, and things weren't any easier now that Zurka was speaking directly to him. He recognized terms here and there, but the words had shot out of Zurka's mouth far too quickly for him to fully grasp. Yankel simply stood, dumbly.

Zurka repeated the instruction and pointed to the wagon.

An old mother with a black kerchief wrapped around her head was standing guard, and Yankel turned back to Zurka, who was watching him at a distance. Yankel pointed to the wagon. "Go in?"

Zurka nodded.

The old woman opened the curtain to the back of the wagon, pointed out a seat in the middle of a sea of metal and wooden junk, and began talking to him in a language he was fairly sure wasn't Polish.

At first, Yankel didn't know what the gypsy mother—whose fingers were long and bony, like the fingers of a witch—meant as she pointed to the empty space in the back of the wagon next to a large wooden wardrobe lying on its back, and a faded gold candelabra that could have been replicated from the Arch of Titus.

He turned in the finger's direction and stared mutely at the great mounds of clutter, stacked from the wagon's floor to its canvas top.

The gypsy repeated her command.

Hunched over, like an old man who had to make every move with the deliberateness of age, he navigated around the silk scarves, cardboard boxes of plastic-wrapped shirts (transparent wrapping was something Yankel had never seen before), crates of lightbulbs and electric irons.

The old woman followed, and took a seat across from Yankel. After a minute the horse was whipped, and the caravan began the next leg of its journey.

For some reason, even though she knew not a word of Polish or Yiddish, the old woman took a liking to Yankel.

It might have been the fact that there was something childlike in the esteem with which Yankel held the mess surrounding him. It occurred to her that the poor boy, all the way out there in the boondocks, probably had never been exposed to these things before. Every digital clock or stereo brought a glint to his eye, and the old woman could not help but admire his wonder.

She held up a blender and began to explain the instrument's purpose in the Romani language. Yankel gave her his full attention and nodded vigorously as she spun her fingers around to illustrate the thrashing manner in which the device smashed and pureed vegetables.

She held up a cardboard box containing a hot plate, which had on its box a Chinese family poised with chopsticks over a wok full of sautéed vegetables, and Yankel marveled at the image, having never actually seen a photograph before or features as distinct as those from the Orient.

The old gypsy mother was a talker, and she liked having an audience. She produced a white stick from her jacket, which she put in her mouth and lit on fire. The fire did not consume the stick, however; after its tip was lit, blue rings of smoke drifted out of the old woman's nose. And she proceeded to ply her audience with great, long-winded monologues.

Yankel was the ideal audience because he was unable to interrupt. When she wasn't explaining the technical marvels in the back of the wagon, or smoking cigarettes, she passed the hours recounting gypsy folk stories and bits of worldly wisdom. She accepted his smiles and nods as the only affirmation necessary.

She occasionally pulled back the wagon's canvas curtain and pointed to some oddity of nature, or the dirt road they were traveling on, or a deer studying their caravan, and Yankel looked eagerly on, as any explorer setting foot in the unknown.

When the wagons stopped for the night, and all the gypsies spread out blankets and mattresses on the ground, built a bonfire, and took out their mandolins, the old woman kept Yankel away from the youths who were smoking pot and drinking beer. "He's too pious to sit with you," she told her teenaged grandson. She gave Yankel a blanket, lay down next to him, and continued talking to him until Yankel was snoring soundly.

The next day, the forest path gave way to a dirt road that, in turn, gave way to a paved highway that the horses walked slowly along. When, on the third day of their journey, a loud buzzing and vroom could be heard, much to her young guest's bemusement, the old woman pulled back the curtain and pointed to the cars and trucks burping and zipping ahead of the wagon.

Yankel's reserve vanished almost instantly.

"What's that?" he asked in Yiddish, and then repeated the question in Polish.

"Automobile."

Yankel barely knew what to say about the enormous, gleaming, red, silver, and blue metal cans that flew past them.

"But how does it work?"

It was a useless question. The old mother didn't understand him.

Yankel was almost tempted to find a way up to the front of the wagon to ask Zurka what these contraptions were, exactly, and what they were doing. He stuck his head out of the back and stared at the men and women who were sitting quietly behind the steering wheels. He waved at them with barely containable excitement as they whizzed by.

"What's it called again?" he asked the old woman, but this time she didn't understand his question. She just shrugged. He turned back to the machines and watched them as they glided over the highway and honked horns at one another and gave bewildered looks at the young bearded Jew in the back of a horse-drawn gypsy caravan, flapping his arms wildly.

The old lady was somewhat surprised by the man that Yankel had suddenly become. Once the levee of words had been breached, the flood that followed was almost too much for her.

"How do you like that!" he kept saying. "How do you like that!"

The old woman nodded politely, just as Yankel had done an hour or two earlier.

"Maybe when we get to Smolskie, we could stop one of these *buggies*"— which he decided was the best fitting word for the contraptions—"and ask the owner how the thing works."

The old woman nodded, again.

"It's like it's being pushed along by magic! I still cannot believe it. They keep running and running."

The old woman said nothing.

"At first, I thought they must have rabbits inside, pushing the wheels along. But those things are far too big and heavy for rabbits. There are no rabbits inside, are there?"

No answer.

"And besides, look at those things. They look as if they're made out of metal. How could they move as fast as they do being moved along by rabbits? It doesn't make any sense."

Not that she disliked Yankel's newfound enthusiasm, but she was an old woman and no longer possessed of the energy or willpower to match it, so she kept quiet. (And, in truth, the fact that her stories and explanations had failed to capture the young Jew's interest as strongly as these modern marvels was a small blow to her vanity.)

As the day wore on, and the speeding contraptions grew into a harder and more unalterable reality, Yankel continued to dominate the creaky back of the wagon with stories and speculation.

"There's a horse in Kreskol who was the fastest thing I had ever seen. I once saw him get spooked by something—maybe a mouse, I don't remember, exactly—and gallop from the market square to the cemetery in what must've been ten seconds. It was something to see. But I don't think he could run half as fast as those buggies."

Yankel loved the roar of the highway. "Listen. I've never heard anything like it." And he was fascinated by the calm of the drivers. "How could they all look so bored? Are they really so normal, these machines?"

The gypsy had no explanation.

The road to Smolskie was adorned with traffic lights, and once the caravan hit the town limits, the wagon slowed to a stop at a small shoe seller.

Without a word, Zurka opened the back curtain and grabbed the golden slippers he had traded for Yankel's safe passage to town. He disappeared into the shop and returned a quarter of an hour later, counting a thick stack of zlotys, which he put in his front pocket.

Yankel watched this side of the transaction with quiet fascination. Not that it shouldn't have occurred to him—and everyone else in Kreskol—that the gypsies kept returning to our backwater, year after year, for some practical purpose.

Yet, for a moment, Yankel felt wiser and more sophisticated than his fellow townsmen; like he had just uncovered for himself one of the mysteries of adulthood that children are never privy to.

"All right, young man," Zurka said upon his return. "This is as far as we're taking you."

Yankel grabbed his satchel of food, clothes, and maps, and said farewell to the old crone.

"How do I get back?" Yankel asked once he was on the paved sidewalk.

Zurka shrugged.

"Will you take me?" Yankel asked.

"We're not going to be near Kreskol for quite some time. If you want, I can give you my cell, but I doubt you're going to want to wait four months."

Yankel looked puzzled.

"Here," Zurka said, and he reached into his pocket for a slip of paper on which he wrote his mobile phone number. He handed it to Yankel, who stared at the Arabic numerals blankly. "Goodbye, and good luck."

I'm sure the sophisticated reader will think very little of the sights that Yankel observed in the city. They were ordinary things, and Smolskie is not by any means a large or memorable town.

But those scattered members of the human race whose homes are still far from the reaches of civilization will no doubt understand how humbled Yankel felt as he stepped out onto a mostly abandoned sidewalk.

He had never seen a building more than two stories high, and he stood staring at a five-story apartment in quiet revelry. He looked at the windows that studded the side—which were blinking in the afternoon sun—and quietly tried to figure out where all this glass had come from; how it had been fitted so seamlessly into the bones of the building; how the building's draftsmen could make a structure so symmetrical and unblemished, unlike the coarse, homespun-looking ones in Kreskol.

Yankel looked across the street and saw another, grander structure.

And as he gazed down the block, the line of buildings stretched off into the distance—some of which were shorter, some taller and stouter—and made him hold his breath. He felt like a pilgrim stepping foot in Jerusalem for the first time, or among the porticos of Ancient Greece.

The cars on the street slowed down and stopped at a traffic signal, which lit up in red, and then switched to amber and green—something that also drove Yankel to contemplation. The lights had a will of their own. No candles were poised behind the colored glass. No sentry was switching the light from amber to red. It worked automatically, as if by witchcraft.

Raised above his head was an enormous fresco of a blond gentile woman—with a beautiful white-toothed smile, wearing a low-cut blue top that revealed the cleavage between her breasts—holding a plastic tube of dishwashing liquid in her hands.

Yankel took a step backwards when he saw it.

He had never seen such immodesty in public before, and this first glimpse reddened his cheeks and made him recoil. He looked around to make sure no one else was watching him before he looked up at the billboard again and studied it carefully.

And as he took his first few steps along the sidewalk, like a newborn infant encountering the fully formed world for the first time, Yankel had the sensation he got late in the night on Purim,* when he had forgotten how many glasses of vodka he'd drunk, and the room suddenly spun free from its earthly moorings.

The people he started to see as he walked closer to the center of town were all gentiles—there wasn't a single Jew in the mix. They were a race of beautiful, hearty men and women, whose clothes were short and revealing, in deference to the warm weather.

At first, Yankel stepped forward to approach the men, but they all walked with far too much determination to stop.

---

*A spring holiday that celebrates the defeat of Haman and openly encourages inebriation.

As for the gentile women, Yankel's courage faltered there, as well. He was too shy and embarrassed to ask for help. But as he stared at them— ripe women whose shoulders were uncovered in the sunshine, and whose breasts clung to white cotton halter tops—he thought for the first time since he had left Kreskol that perhaps Rabbi Katznelson was more right than he imagined. Maybe he was lucky to go on this mission, after all.

So Yankel wandered out into this strange city, his eyes gleaming at every bus that roared past him, at every mother who pushed him aside to make way for her perambulator, at every supermarket with their crates of lemons and oranges out front, at every bakery, at every hardware store, at every electronics outlet.

It was hours before he would say to anyone, "Police . . . ? Police . . . ? Would you help me to find the police?"

"Do . . . you . . . speak . . . Yiddish?"

Yankel knew those words reasonably well. He had practiced them with Rabbi Katznelson as he had been fitted for his boots. If the answer had been in the affirmative, the rest of his memorized questions would become unnecessary, Rabbi Katznelson said. So they were the best ones to learn, backwards and forwards. However, Yankel spoke these words haltingly, considering each syllable before they left his mouth, just to make sure that no one could fail to understand.

Nevertheless, the policeman he directed the question to managed to miss it.

"What's that?" the officer said. "Do I speak what? Speak up, son."

The policeman had strawberry blond hair, which had been sculpted into a crew cut. And despite the fact that this officer—whose bulk filled out every spare inch of his uniform—spoke diminutively toward Yankel, he was not quite old enough to make the word "son" sound convincing.

"Do. You. Speak. Yiddish?"

"Yiddish? No."

Yankel took this as a matter of course, and jumped to his next question. "Does *somebody* . . . speak . . . Yiddish?"

The policeman stared at the young buck before him for a few moments before answering. The buck, when he had entered the station a few minutes earlier, had caused a considerable stir. Not everyone in Smolskie had ever seen a Jew in the flesh—much less a Jew fully outfitted in the black-and-white trimmings—and as Yankel had wandered into the precinct, the station came to a standstill, with officers staring at him openly. Telephones rang, and angry prisoners growled from their holding cells, but the police ignored these unseen disturbances. It was a good minute before Yankel was directed toward the strawberry blond officer.

"No. Nobody here does."

Yankel nodded, sagely.

"Can . . . *you* . . . help me?"

For a second, the officer wondered if this were a put-on; if the whiskers on Yankel's face were fake, and if the black trousers and black hat weren't a costume. Some teenager's idea of a weird joke. "That depends. What do you want?"

"I wish . . . to be reporting . . . lady." Yankel looked pleased with himself that he had managed to get as much out. Then he added, "Missing lady."

"You want to file a missing persons report," the officer said, suddenly taking the decorum of his profession seriously. He selected a form from his desk, took the cap off his pen, and went to business. "What is the name of the person in question?"

Yankel looked baffled.

"The missing lady," the officer said. "What's her name?"

"Name" triggered something. "Ah . . . Pesha Rosenthal."

"When did she go missing?"

It was not a question Yankel had been prepared for—and he was not entirely sure he understood what he was being asked. "When?" he repeated, and pondered the answer. He had been on the road for three days. And he had been preparing for his trip for two days while still in Kreskol.

And she must have taken off at least a day or two before her husband had gone missing as well. "A week."

"Are you a relative?"

Yankel didn't understand the query.

"Are you a relative?" the officer repeated. "Are you her brother? Or her husband?"

"No."

"Are you colleagues?"

Yankel certainly didn't understand that one.

"Do you work together? Have the same job?"

"No," Yankel replied. "I'm a baker."

"What's your name?"

"Pesha Rosenthal," Yankel said, understanding only the word "name."

"No," the officer said. "What's *your* name?"

"Ah!" Yankel said, and told him.

"How do you know her?"

"I don't."

A peculiar response, certainly.

"How do you know she's missing?"

Yankel figured this was the opportune time to produce the two parchments and hand them over to the official.

To the most honorable court of Szyszki—

We, the humble people of Kreskol, founded under the auspices of the great and honorable reign of Casimir III, wish to report a most dastardly and treacherous circumstance in our village.

Pesha Rosenthal, daughter of one of our tailors, Reb Issur Rosenthal, has gone missing from our town.

The young lady left neither a note, an explanation, or the smallest evidence of why she abandoned a loving home and family. If the decision to abandon Kreskol was hers in fact. We have reason to suspect something more sinister. She was recently divorced from her husband, Ishmael Lindauer, who in a fit of anger cursed his former wife with violence in his voice, and swore great and bounteous oaths to do all manner of harm to her.

Since Pesha's disappearance, Ishmael Lindauer has also disappeared and, as a small town whose resources are modest and police is nonexistent, we thought it best to present the court with these facts and leave it to your discretion as to how we should proceed.

The messenger of this epistle, one Yankel Lewinkopf, is at your disposal.

Your humble servants,
Rabbi Anschel Sokolow, Rabbi Meir Katznelson, Rabbi Joel Gluck

The officer read the note twice. When he finished it a second time, he looked back at the emissary even more puzzled than before. "Where is Kreskol?" he finally asked.

Yankel looked as if he didn't understand.

"Kreskol?" the young officer repeated.

"Yes?"

"Where is it?"

Yankel thought about the question for a moment before he pointed in an eastern direction.

The officer looked around for some confidant to share in the strangeness of the moment, but the rest of the station resumed its normal business with its accompanying clatter and roar. He read the letter a third time—even more perplexed this time by the flowery language; its ecclesiastic authorship; the operatic circumstances it described—and decided that this could not possibly be a serious complaint.

He had to give this young buck credit: This hoax was elaborate. It had incredible backstory. And the Jew (if he really was a Jew) never broke character. He sat with a good-natured grin frozen on his face, completely unbothered by the skepticism with which this goodwill was returned.

There was almost something the officer found insulting about his haplessness. He must believe we're awfully stupid—awfully stupid, indeed—to think we would swallow such a story. And for that reason, the officer was not inclined to deal Yankel any kindness.

"Get the hell out of here," he said, returning the note to Yankel.

Yankel nodded pleasantly. Then he said: "What?"

The officer rose to his feet and pointed a finger toward the door. "Go!" he bellowed. "Get the hell out of here and don't come back!"

The sudden shift in tone frightened Yankel.

"Excuse me!" Yankel said as meekly as one can when turning to run from a tormentor. "Excuse me!"

"Go!" the screaming continued. "Leave! Go!"

And with that Yankel ran out of the police station.

3

WOLF BOY

Yankel Lewinkopf was probably better suited for this mission to Smolskie than the elders realized.

While others might have been driven to the panic or despair that can overwhelm a young man when he first recognizes that the world is a friendless, pitiless place and he is alone in trying to tame it, Yankel accepted what happened in the police station calmly—the way he accepted all the misfortunes life had planned for him.

After he dashed through the darkened streets for a few blocks, not daring to look behind him (and nearly being run over by a Fiat), he slowed to a walk as the office buildings, storefronts, and Soviet-era apartment complexes gave way to freestanding houses in the older part of town. All along the streets, jutting out of the concrete were great iron poles whose tops glowed with light that he stopped to admire.

He ambled along until he reached Powazki Park, and after deciding it would be a quiet enough place to spend the night with only minimal chance of being bothered by hoodlums or vagabonds, he laid out the blanket in his pack and drifted to sleep thinking of the women who had brushed past him in the streets with their mystifying curves.

The next morning he began stopping people in the street. He looked for clean-cut and well-groomed men in their middle years. The more officious-seeming, the better. Yankel decided these were the ones who were least likely to be superstitious about Jews. (Or, at the very least, done enough business with Jews to know that we weren't all monsters and bloodsuckers.) And this time, he was more determined to get their attention.

"Excuse me," Yankel would say, "can you help me?"

But most of these men couldn't be bothered to break their stride. They would murmur, "Sorry," and be on their way if they decided to answer at all.

Some reached into their pockets and came out with fistfuls of coins that they dropped into Yankel's hands. But when Yankel said to these men, "I don't want money," it barely registered. Most of them were in much too great a hurry to hear anything else.

Yankel avoided men his own age. The tall, vigorous-looking youths, clothed in dungarees and ragged summer T-shirts, looked to him like thieves and ruffians. They would no doubt be the ones most eager to taunt him, rob him, and beat him senseless. (Rabbi Katznelson explicitly warned him against associating with the young. "They have the most zeal," Katznelson advised. "And their zeal is reserved for pummeling Jews.")

And despite his immense fascination, he was terrified of the young women. When he tried to summon the words to ask them for help, they lost their way up his throat and came out of his lips in nothing louder than a whisper.

He asked one middle-aged woman, "Where's the nearest synagogue?" on the supposition that he would most likely get help from his own kind, but the woman looked baffled by the question.

"I have no idea," she said.

"Where's the Jewish quarter here, then?"

"There is no Jewish quarter," she replied, and before Yankel had time to ask another question, she darted away from him in what was more or less a sprint.

That was odd, certainly. Rabbi Katznelson had told him before he left that if he had problems finding the local authorities, he should go to the Jewish quarter. Everyone in Kreskol knew that there were Jews in Smolskie—even though we didn't care for these particular Jews very much. (The Smolskie Jews had long ago turned their noses up at us, and no one in Kreskol was inclined to forget an insult. Even if virtually no one remembered the story behind the insult.)

However, Katznelson had assured Yankel they would surely help another Jew in need. "If worse comes to worst, they'll at least be able to help you get around the city. They'll speak enough Polish to translate for you. They'll be able to tell you who to talk to." It had been the primary reason the letter on the parchment had been copied into Yiddish as well as Polish. "And if nobody asks, there's no need to tell them you're originally from Kreskol, my lad."

But Yankel was slightly taken aback by the words *there is no Jewish quarter.* How was that possible? The Jewish community of Smolskie was older and larger than that of Kreskol. Their yeshiva was more respected. Their rabbis were more prolific writers. Their shtreimels* were taller and gaudier. (Supposedly. That could have been an old wives' tale.)

The possibility that the Jews of Smolskie could have just picked up and left didn't dawn on Yankel until later—and even in the warm weather, it sent a chill down his back.

When the church bells struck three o'clock and he hadn't managed to get a single person to look at the parchment in his hands, he decided he would start going into the shops, where the proprietors couldn't escape so easily.

He first chose a bakery. No doubt, it was a welcoming, familiar sight, but he chose poorly. A great wooden cross hung over the oven, and he was met by a stout, middle-aged woman whose glare no doubt unnerved the women and children whom she disliked the looks of. And probably a few grown men.

"We don't have anything for you in here," the baker declared, arms folded across her colossal bosom the moment Yankel passed through the doorway.

Yankel smiled. "I'm not hungry," he said. "I need help."

---

*A large fur hat.

"No help in here."

Nevertheless, Yankel reached into his pocket and handed the baker the parchment. She refused to take it.

"You going to buy something?" she asked.

Yankel nodded. "Yes. I buy."

Not that there was anything he could eat in such a place. Or so he assumed. (Another warning he had been given was to be careful what he ate—the gentiles, as everybody knows, consume filth.) But if it would take a small bribe to get help, he was willing to do so. And he was flush from all the change that the dapper gentlemen of Smolskie had tossed in his direction (he had more than fifty zlotys, if you counted what Katznel-son had given him). He pointed at a small brown roll studded with raisins wearing a thin cap of flour on top.

"I'll take that."

"Five hundred zlotys."

Yankel was taken aback. For a fleeting instant he wondered if that was really the price of bread; if so, he was doomed to severe poverty once he finished the food in his pack.

But when he looked at the various cakes and breads stacked up behind the counter which had price tags affixed for three or four zlotys (or ten for something elaborate) he understood the message the baker was send-ing. With an overly polite bow of the head he thanked her and left. As he opened the bakery's glass door, he looked back. The baker, whose red, corpulent face had remained hardened from the moment Yankel had set foot in the bakery, like a bust sculpted in clay, did not take her eyes off him—but in that moment, she turned her head to the floor and spat.

However, in fairness to the citizenry of Smolskie, the baker was the most overtly hostile person he would encounter.

An elderly, steel-haired gentleman manning the counter of the hard-ware store looked at the note, rubbed his chin, and said, "I don't think there's anything I can do for you—I'm sorry."

A florist laughed cheerfully when she read the note and offered him a long-stemmed rose.

"But can't you help me?" Yankel asked.

The florist smiled again. "You're funny," she replied. "Very, very funny."

It didn't make any sense to Yankel, but he obediently went on his way.

He went to a slender, acne-scarred teenager who was the cashier at a supermarket and gave him the parchment. The boy grew more and more agitated and nervous as he read it. "I don't know," he said. "I don't know what to tell you. You'll have to speak to the manager. And he's not in."

And that was the general reaction of the population of Smolskie. Some treated the parchment like a joke. Others held the view that Yankel was a freak—and thus somebody to be wary of. But most threw up their hands. They all told him to go to the police, and when he said that he had already been, they shrugged.

The greatest sense of menace came not from the young, but the old. He appeared to them like some apparition they thought they were long rid of. Women's eyes would narrow into slits and their noses would turn up. Yankel didn't need to be told he was being given the evil eye.

One elderly man, whose spine was crooked and whose hands shook as he gripped the gray rubber handle of a cane, turned to Yankel as they waited for the light to change on a street corner and barked, "I thought the krauts took care of all of you."

Yankel didn't know what he meant, so he smiled, even though he sensed no measure of kindness in the old man's voice.

As the light changed and the old man inched across the street he threw his chin back over his shoulder and said, "It was the only thing the Germans ever did right."

He ate very little the next day. He had looked in his pack that morning, and his food supplies were dwindling. He resolved to be more conservative. When he began wandering the streets the next morning he no longer looked as cheerful and pleasant as he had the day before—he looked famished. The people to whom he handed his parchment no longer thought he was a nut; they assumed he was a charlatan and the pathetic story on the parchment was the best one he could come up with. Patience grew thinner. Responses were more rushed. The chimera of politeness he had enjoyed the day before evaporated.

And if he had been amazed by the whirl of progress he had seen in his first full day in Smolskie, he had grown disturbed by it in his second. Toward four o'clock, with the sun beating down and his head light, Yankel went into an appliance outlet to catch his breath and was so stunned by what he saw he could barely stay on his feet.

He saw a couple of dozen glowing black boxes mounted on the wall. Some were fat and some were thin. Each had a glass window along its side, with images of enormous trucks, tropical islands, soaring airplanes, madcap explosions, and a dozen other things continually, effortlessly, moving and shifting shape.

The boxes chortled and hummed, as if they had a life of their own, and Yankel's face turned white, as if he had seen a ghost.

"Have you seen those . . . paintings?" he said to a bored-looking girl behind the counter of a café, trying to grasp the proper word for what he had witnessed. It was the wrong word, of course. The surfaces were too flat and seamless to be called a painting. But it was the only word that seemed to match what he had seen.

"What paintings?"

"The paintings that are on those boxes," Yankel said. "They're this big." He parted his arms at roughly the length he had seen. "It's a store a few blocks down . . ."

"So?"

"They're alive."

He spoke those words with a kind of unsettling intensity. Even though the teenage girl hadn't the slightest idea what he was talking about, she was unnerved by the conviction in Yankel's voice.

"Oh," the girl said with a nod, but also with a look on her face that seemed to indicate she was uneasy. "Would you like some coffee?"

Yankel said nothing. He handed the girl the note he had been carrying with him without a word. She studied it for a few moments and then looked over the exhausted, vagrant man standing in front of her.

"Please leave," she ordered. "Now."

A policeman was sitting in the café, and had observed the bizarre exchange.

As Yankel turned to leave, the girl looked over at the officer, desperate to share her alarm with someone. She only spoke with her eyes, but the policeman stood up and began to follow Yankel into the street.

Yankel did not know he was being tailed at first. But after a few moments he felt the presence of the officer, and when he turned, he saw the officer vigorously charging in his direction.

Before he knew what he was doing, Yankel had taken off at a sprint and the officer gave chase.

Yankel was fortunate that his pursuer was a good fifteen years older than him, and soft around the middle. As tired and run down as he was, Yankel felt the jolt in the legs that one feels when nearing trouble, and raced around a corner, and then around another, ducking and weaving, as various pedestrians stepped out of his path.

When he turned a third corner and didn't see the policeman behind him, he decided that he should take refuge somewhere until he was certain that his adversary had given up.

He stumbled into a candy shop with frosted windows, where he was greeted by a tiny middle-aged woman dressed in brown and tweed who stood behind the counter. "Hello," she chirped. "What can I do for you?"

But Yankel couldn't get the words out of his mouth. He started to breathe heavily, winded from his sprint, and thought for a moment that he would collapse.

"Someone was chasing me," he whispered.

"Calm down, young man."

But Yankel simply could not stop himself. If anything, he was growing more excited. And as the sweat poured out of him, he felt his knees begin to buckle. He backed into a chair upholstered in red velvet and flopped down.

"Oh my!" the confectioner said.

She disappeared into the back of the store for a moment and returned with a glass of water. "What's the matter with you?" she asked, edging closer to him. "What's wrong?"

"I don't know."

With a familiarity between the sexes that surprised Yankel so much that he sat up straight in his chair, the confectioner put a hand on his clammy forehead and swept it over his cheeks.

"Well, you don't feel like you have any temperature, even if you're awfully sweaty," she said calmly and with matriarchal expertise. "Do you feel weak?"

Yankel nodded.

"Drink this," she said, handing him the glass.

He obeyed.

"When was the last time you ate something?"

"This morning."

"Hang on," she said, and went behind the counter to select a piece of candy. She returned with a flat and light brown chocolate disk. "Here," she said, extending her hand. "Eat this."

Yankel shook his head. "Not kosher."

The confectioner considered this for a moment, and disappeared again, this time returning with a red aluminum can of cola.

"You guys drink Coke, right?" she said. "They sell Coke in Israel, don't they? Here. Have some."

Yankel shook his head again. "Not kosher."

"Of course it's kosher," the confectioner said, examining the can. "I'm certain Jews drink Coca-Cola. Now, don't be a child. Drink it."

Yankel was too weak to argue. She put the small cylinder—which was as freezing to the touch as if she had given him a dry icicle—in his hands. He stared at it for a moment, unsure of what he was supposed to do next.

"Go ahead and drink it."

But Yankel couldn't quite figure out how this woman expected him to drink what she had given him. He turned it around and around, looking for a way to open it, and saw none. He tried to twist the lid off the top, and when that didn't work he tried to pry it off by digging his fingernails under the metal lip.

"You've never had a soda before?" the confectioner asked with a raised eyebrow.

"No."

She plucked the can out of his hands and snapped open the top. "Drink," she ordered for a third and final time.

Yankel put the can to his lips, but the moment the caramel-colored liquid touched his tongue he stood up, as if a surge of electrical current had run through his body, and spat the soda out on the floor.

"That's alive, too!" Yankel cried. "There are things jumping up and down on my tongue!"

"Are you crazy?"

But Yankel didn't hear her. He was on his feet, and after an instant he ran out of the shop, nearly crashing through the glass door. The pedestrians on the sidewalk all jumped away, but Yankel was too far gone to take note of any of them. He ran straight ahead for about fifteen feet when a BMW, going full speed, crashed into him.

The confectioner wasn't sure whom she should call. She called for an ambulance first. And after she had stepped outside the store and heard someone say, "Yeah, he's alive," she reconsidered the general strangeness of what had taken place, and came to believe she was within her rights to lodge a complaint. So she called the police, too.

The police came first, and she described all that had happened with a growing sense of outrage.

"There's something wrong with this young man," she said, pointing to the crowd that had formed outside her shop. "He spat on me, for goodness sake! He says he never saw a Coke before. When he started drinking it, he said that it had living things in it. I've never heard such nonsense in all my life. He's got a screw loose."

The cop scribbling notes for the official report didn't seem to share her alarm. "The ambulance will be here in a minute."

Once Yankel had been strapped onto a gurney and wheeled into the back of the ambulance and had his vital signs checked, the ambulance workers were less impressed with the incident. "He's fine," one of them said to the other after listening to Yankel's heart beating normally. "Maybe a broken leg." The siren was turned off, and the driver began staying in the traffic lanes.

They went through his pockets when he was admitted to the emergency room, and found only thirty zlotys in cash and a few collectors' coins. The young man had no driver's license, no passport, no ATM card. Not even a wallet. There were three pieces of paper in his pocket—one a piece of scrap paper with a phone number scribbled on it, and the other two were weathered yellow parchment. One of the documents was written in Hebrew, and the other one was a letter, which nobody thought to read. The nameless patient, after all, had bruises, a concussion, possible internal bleeding, breaks and fractures, and was dehydrated, so there were more immediate concerns than figuring out the young man's identity. Or in remarking on how bizarre his custom-made clothes were. Or how rank the young man's odor was.

It was only after he had been moved into a private bed and the doctor on call asked for the young man's chart and found him listed as a John Doe that anyone thought to actually read the parchment.

"Admit him to the psych ward," the doctor instructed a nurse after examining the document.

That was where Yankel would stay for the next few months (long after he recovered from his most serious injury, a fractured leg), and that was where he tried to tell anyone who passed his bed—be it a doctor, or a nurse, or another patient—the story of poor Pesha Rosenthal and murderous Ishmael Lindauer. But the doctors at Our Lady of Mercy Hospital had much more interest in the messenger than his message.

"Tell us about your village," they all said when they sat down to examine him.

Most addressed him in Polish, which Yankel spoke as well as he could. (And which improved as the weeks went on.) But after the first month—as the questions directed at Yankel got more specific and detailed—an elderly professor of Germanic languages named Johann Fishbein, whose father was Jewish and wore the white whiskers of a rabbi, was summoned from Uniwersytet Fryderyka Cybulskiego* to act as translator.

Yankel, ever obliging and eager to do what was expected of him, answered all queries without complaint.

Some of the doctors were content to simply sit and listen. A few were willing to engage him on the subject of Pesha and Ishmael. But most of them were curious about Kreskol's history, and economy, and system of local government—which Yankel tried to answer as best he could. The doctors nodded solemnly. Smiled frequently. Some took notes. A few asked skeptical questions. And more than one was outspokenly dubious of every word that left Yankel's mouth.

"We should start with the truth, Mr. Lewinkopf," one middle-aged psychologist said. "We know there is no such place as Kreskol."

"But of course there is. Where do you think I'm from?"

"I don't know—but you're speaking of an imaginary place. Let's start with the truth, shall we?"

"Maybe you don't know about it," Yankel insisted, "but Kreskol is there."

_____

*Frederick Cybulski University.

"No, it isn't," the doctor stated, firmly. "There are three realistic pos-sibilities for your story about Kreskol. One, you have been lying to us this whole time. Two, you are mistaken about the name of your hometown. Or, three, you are completely crazy. Those are the realistic possibilities. Now which is it?"

Even if Yankel hadn't been a polite person, he had been very concerned about how to comport himself among the gentiles. He certainly didn't have the courage to contradict one directly. He felt like a child whose honesty has been called into question by a capricious adult.

"It's been called Kreskol as long as I've known it," Yankel said, turning his head away from the doctor. "I've never heard it called anything else."

The doctor stared at Yankel for a few lingering moments before he said, "All right—now we're getting somewhere. Why don't you tell me where you're *really* from."

But none of Yankel's subsequent answers satisfied this psychologist. After spending another hour trying to wheedle the name of a different town out of Yankel, the doctor stormed out of Yankel's room with the parting words: "The man's impossible!"

In addition to the many hundreds of questions asked about our home-town of Kreskol, Yankel was asked hundreds more about himself and his views on life—the majority of which he hadn't the slightest idea how to answer.

He was asked about his departed mother and his phantom father.

"How old were you when you realized your father had abandoned your mother?" asked a female psychiatrist in her early fifties named Dr. Maria Babiak.

"I don't exactly know."

"And how did it make you feel?"

Yankel shrugged. "I never gave it much thought."

"Do you think your father was a bad person for leaving your mother and you like that?"

It was a question no one had ever thought to ask him before, and

Yankel was more surprised by the novel realization that his father might have been a wicked man than he felt a duty to defend him.

"That never occurred to me."

Some of the questions were of an impropriety that nearly brought Yankel to tears. He was asked whether he had ever made love to a woman. He was asked how frequently he masturbated. He was asked to describe erotic dreams and nocturnal emissions. He was asked whether he had homosexual yearnings. "That's immodest" was his constant reply—which he always delivered in Polish.

And even though the doctors assured him that they wouldn't tell anyone his answers—that everyone had prurient thoughts from time to time; that they were only there to help him; that what he said would be held in the strictest confidence—sex was the one topic which he refused to indulge the doctors on. Which had the ironic effect of making the psychiatrists at Our Lady of Mercy more convinced that Yankel's sex life was essential to understanding this improbable fiction about Kreskol.

He was quizzed on his knowledge of the modern world and its history over the last century.

He was asked if he had ever heard of Pol Pot or Joseph Stalin or Winston Churchill. (He had not.) He was asked if he knew of Vladimir Putin or Barack Obama or Donald Trump. (He also had not.)

But, then, Yankel didn't know much history from any epoch, except for that of Ancient Israel.

He vaguely knew a few names such as Columbus and Napoleon—and even knew that Columbus had made his mark in history when he discovered the New World and that Napoleon made his when he conquered the Old—but those were exceptions. Most of the other great, earth-shaping figures from centuries ago were unknown to Yankel, especially if they came from the gentile world. He was equally unaware of Martin Luther, Johannes Gutenberg, and Genghis Khan. Likewise, he had never heard of Marilyn Monroe or Michael Jackson or Greta Garbo or Charlie Chaplin. One psychiatrist simply could not accept the fact that Yankel seemed familiar with the writings of the rabbis Moses ben Maimon and Joseph Karo,* but had never heard of William Shakespeare. "You never heard of *Hamlet*?" the psychiatrist nearly bellowed. "'To be or not to be'—you never heard those words before?"

Yankel simply frowned. "Hamlet who?"

And the longer he stayed in the ward, and the more calmness he showed in the wake of his doctors' incredulity, the more confounded the psychiatrists at Our Lady of Mercy grew. There had to be some explanation for this strange fellow and his story.

True, the doctors had encountered their share of delusionals floating through the hospital who claimed to be the mighty and accomplished of history, from St. Augustine of Hippo to Alexandrina Victoria of the House of Hanover, reborn in modern times. And, like Yankel, these cranks had detailed explanations for how they wound up in this lonely corner of Poland.

Some knew the particulars of their former incarnations fairly well; from the silverware and china patterns at the Golden Jubilee to the six months spent in Cassago Brianza with Saint Monica. But none of these yarns sounded as convincing or straightforward as the story Yankel told.

"He's very intelligent," Dr. Babiak declared during one of the biweekly meetings the staff convened to discuss their most puzzling patient. "But he's like a feral child—those boys raised by wolves or bears. He's never been civilized. I'm not saying that he couldn't learn the rules of modernity and civilization, but I don't believe he was putting on an act when he said he had never seen a TV or an airplane before."

Just to be safe, the doctors punched "Kreskol" into Google when Yankel first told them where he was from, and found nothing. They tried misspelling it in more than a dozen different ways without luck. And the doctors all told themselves that it was impossible for a Jewish village

---

*Moses Ben Maimon, better known as Maimonides, was a twelfth-century Jewish philosopher considered one of the greatest sages of the medieval era; Joseph Karo was a sixteenth-century rabbi who authored the Shulchan Arush, one of the largest compilations of Jewish law in history.

to have survived the onslaught of World War II in one piece. It was a preposterous story. The Germans were simply too efficient; too attentive to detail; too committed to whatever otherworldly voices induced them to conquer and exterminate to allow an entire town to escape their notice and remain untouched through the ensuing decades. "Nonsense," they all told themselves. "Complete nonsense."

Eventually, they started the patient on a drug regimen.

Yankel was given an antipsychotic drug called risperidone, which dried his skin out, made him constipated, and caused him to gain seven pounds—but his story about Kreskol remained unaltered.

They then tried quetiapine, which put him to sleep for most of the day and turned his waking hours into a dreamy, narcotic haze—but changed nothing about his life story.

One of the doctors suggested fluphenazine, which made Yankel roam around the psychotic ward all night and kept him from sitting still for more than thirty seconds. He grew moody and bored and his customary politeness waned. He offered only one- or two-word answers to the doctors' questions. And one night he was discovered in the bathroom digging under his fingernails with a beard scissor, which had left his hands drenched in blood. (Scissors were henceforth taken away from him.) But the next morning, with his fingers bandaged and rapping on the table in impatience, when he was asked where he was born he responded with the same simple answer he had for weeks:

"Kreskol."

When drugs failed, a hypnotherapist was summoned from Krakow who took over an examination room one afternoon with Johann Fishbein, turned on a recording of soft, Oriental music, and spun a white spiral on a black background in front of Yankel until he was in a trance.

When the hypnotherapist emerged two hours later, he could scarcely contain his ebullience.

"Extraordinary!" the hypnotist said. "Just extraordinary!"

Dr. Antoni Polus, the head of psychiatry, and the rest of the staff looked surprised—as if they had not really expected this hypnotherapist to be of any use. The psychiatrists, psychologists, and neurologists monitoring the case all filed into the conference room and eagerly awaited the hypnotist's diagnosis.

"Well?" Dr. Polus said. "What's Mr. Lewinkopf's story?"

"This is incredible," the hypnotist said. "Strangest case I've ever seen. But Mr. Lewinkopf is not delusional—not at all."

The doctors all sat up straighter in their chairs.

"He's from a little town in Poland that it appears was overlooked by the Nazis in the war! He's never even heard of Hitler or World War II."

The room was silent for a moment, the doctors unsure of whether this hypnotist was trying out some kind of joke. Only Dr. Ignacy Meslowski laughed softly, more out of politeness than amusement.

"He told me all about it," the hypnotist continued, not appearing to have noticed the discomfort that had settled over the doctors. "It's in a small corner of Szyszki called Kreskol. And it would appear that they've had almost no contact with the rest of Poland for the past century."

At that moment, Dr. Polus looked angry enough that several of the doctors present were worried he might take a swing at the hypnotist.

"Sir!" Dr. Polus nearly shouted. "That's the delusion he's suffering from!"

"No, no. It's no delusion."

"Why do you think we hired you? There is no such place!"

"Perhaps we don't know about it," nodded the hypnotist. "Obviously, if it's as primitive as Mr. Lewinkopf describes, there's no reason it should have a significant paper trail. But you should begin investigating."

"I thought we made it very clear to you before you went in there," Dr. Polus said, taking a breath before he spoke, lest his anger break loose and overwhelm him. "There is no such place as Kreskol. There never was such a place. We've already looked into it. He's invented his whole background! You were supposed to go in there and find out where he *really* grew up!"

The hypnotist looked puzzled.

"Why is it so difficult to believe that there would be a town that would have been missed by the Nazis?" the hypnotist asked. "In the 1930s there were many isolated rural villages in Poland. There still are today. You don't think there are settlements in, say, the White Wilderness or the Carpathian Mountains that were untouched by World War II? Why is it so odd that a Jewish shtetl should be equally solitary?"

"You're an idiot!" Dr. Polus screamed, finally throwing the last vestiges of decorum to the wind.

The hypnotist, who was Dr. Polus's age, looked insulted. He was an elegantly dressed man who carried himself with a patrician air, and was not accustomed to being spoken to in such a manner.

"You told me you had a psychotic in there," the hypnotist said quietly, trying to preserve his dignity.

"What a waste of time!" Dr. Polus said, now on his feet and heading to the door. "What a waste of money! All you hypnotists are frauds. Just a bunch of gypsy fortune-tellers! I'm sorry I let myself get talked into hiring a phony like you."

He slammed the door behind him.

If it sounds like the doctors at Our Lady of Mercy were cruel or callous toward Yankel, I should correct that impression.

In fact, with one or two exceptions, the doctors at Our Lady were extremely fond of their bizarre, cheerful patient—and eager to cure whatever malady had overrun his mind.

Moreover, while Yankel was certainly bored with the questions the doctors asked—and reasked, then reasked again—he was generally not bored with the doctors themselves. In fact, he found their explanations of the world fascinating.

During the middle of one therapy session, a sweet, high-pitched melody began humming out of thin air, and Siwinski, the young doctor who was interviewing him, reached into his lab coat and removed a black iPhone.

"What is that?" Yankel asked when the doctor had finished his phone call.

"The phone?"

"Yes. What is it?"

The basic principles of the telephone were explained, and the explanation was concluded with a demonstration: Dr. Siwinski called his wife back—which left Yankel astounded. He asked if he could phone his grandmother back in Kreskol.

"Certainly," Dr. Siwinski said. "What's her number?"

Yankel had no idea.

The patient could be found staring at the toilet in the middle of the night (long after evacuating his bowels) with the same reverence.

He stared at a digital clock on the wall as intently as if he were watching a child taking his first steps; waiting for its minute to change from 8:58 to 8:59. And then he would watch all three numbers change when it became 9:00. He would count for sixty seconds, hoping (it would seem) to trip the device up—and always looking slightly disappointed when the clock obeyed all its functions faithfully.

When Dr. Polus declared that he had played enough games with the young man, and that he intended to get to the bottom of his candor or madness, ordering a polygraph examination at once, the doctors were too embarrassed to hand down their boss's decree—as if they were questioning the honesty of a friend rather than a patient.

Yankel didn't seem to mind. "What is it?" he said when they asked him if he would submit to an examination. He wasn't offended when told that it would determine his honesty.

When the examination indicated that Yankel had been responding truthfully, the doctors looked more relieved than Yankel.

As if to make up for the bizarre ritual, the next Sunday afternoon, Drs. Babiak and Meslowski took Yankel on his first outing since he had been admitted to the hospital and drove him to the fairgrounds just outside town.

"Have you ever been to the circus before?" Dr. Babiak asked.

Yankel shook his head. He took a seat among masses of shrill, laughing Polish children and quietly observed the wild animals that had never appeared in any forest near Kreskol before: elephants, hippopotamuses, giraffes, and a striped horse. "It's a zebra," Dr. Babiak explained.

As they watched the show, a pink cloud floated past Yankel on a white stick. "Would you like some?" Dr. Meslowski asked.

Yankel shook his head, but was intrigued as Dr. Meslowski took a stick for himself and began breaking off pieces of the cloud and popping them into his mouth.

"What does it taste like?"

"Sweet," Dr. Meslowski answered. "You sure you don't want? You can't go to the circus without getting cotton candy."

When the doctors realized that he had never heard classical music before, Dr. Meslowski began playing Mozart for the patient.

"Do you like it?" asked Dr. Meslowski.

Yankel considered the question.

"I'm not sure," he finally said. "It just sounds so . . ." Yankel's eyes flittered around the room as he searched for the proper word. "Gentile."

"Is that bad?"

Yankel nodded. It was the first suggestion of impoliteness Dr. Meslowski could recall from the patient.

After Mozart, the doctors played Bach and Beethoven. Then Vivaldi and Rossini. Then Schumann and Schubert.

"Why are you only playing classical music for him?" Dr. Polus asked. "Have you tried any pop music?"

"Not yet," replied Dr. Meslowski.

"What's stopping you?"

"Nothing."

So the next morning they played him *Beggars Banquet* by the Rolling Stones.

"What do you think?" Dr. Meslowski asked.

Yankel stroked the soft stubble on his chin and considered the question. "Not as good as Mozart," he finally pronounced.

Yankel's musical tastes were old-fashioned. The doctors played Elvis Presley and Louis Armstrong for Yankel; he preferred Armstrong. He couldn't have understood it, still he liked the quick and clever ditties of Gilbert and Sullivan but had little to say about Grandmaster Flash.

When Yankel heard the Ray Charles number "The Mess Around," he laughed and clapped, and even got up to dance. Which might have come across as comic, because the only dancing Yankel knew was the horah,* but he looked so sincere as he circled Dr. Meslowski's office with his arm raised in the air that the doctor didn't have the heart to laugh at him.

"This is wonderful!" Yankel declared.

"Duly noted," Dr. Meslowski said, and smiled.

"It sounds like a klezmer** tune!" Yankel exclaimed, which Dr. Meslowski had to admit was a good description.

And in a moment of bliss, Yankel erupted, "Everything here is wonderful! I feel bad for everybody back in Kreskol. They have no idea of how interesting the world became."

The next morning, Dr. Meslowski came into the staff meeting with a list of other things that they could show Yankel for the first time: Paintings. Sculptures. Movies. Television shows. "He's got the whole world at his feet!" Dr. Meslowski cried. "To think what it must be like to see Michelangelo and Renoir for the first time!"

And as they spoke of modernity, in all its variety and splendor, a sinister thought appeared in Dr. Babiak's mind: "Do you think he knows about the Holocaust?"

The question dangled in the air for a few moments, ominously, everyone too frightened to furnish the obvious answer.

"Who knows," Dr. Meslowski finally said.

---

*Jewish circle dance.
**Traditional Ashkenazic Jewish music.

"Shouldn't we tell him?"

No one quite knew the proper response.

"Why is it up to us to tell him these things?" asked one doctor. "We aren't here to educate him in European history."

"Well, of course not," said Dr. Babiak, "but don't you think an observant Jewish person would want to know that kind of thing?"

"Not everybody cares about history," Dr. Meslowski offered.

But no one believed that the Holocaust would be an issue of no importance to a man who had devoted every waking second of his life to being a devout Jew.

"And what about Israel?" Dr. Babiak asked. "Wouldn't he like to know about that, too?"

Dr. Polus nodded. "Probably."

"But how do we explain it all to him?" Dr. Babiak asked. "All these events happened so long ago. How do you let him know how important they were?"

"Maybe we should just show him *Schindler's List*," one doctor suggested.

The idea was deemed acceptable (after all, it wasn't as if Yankel *knew* anyone who was killed in the Holocaust) until someone asked the unarguably practical question: How would he understand it?

The dubbed version in Polish would no doubt go too fast for Yankel. And weeks earlier the doctors had discovered (to their surprise) that Yankel spoke no modern Hebrew—so a Hebrew-dubbed version wouldn't make any sense, either.

"This is just silly," Dr. Babiak said. "Forget *Schindler's List*. I'll try to explain the Holocaust to him."

And so when Yankel's next session was winding down, Dr. Babiak began to try to explain the complicated history of World War II, in simple terms that her patient could understand.

She decided that the tortured saga would be impossible to tell without going back to the establishment of the Second Polish Republic, after World War I. "Actually," Dr. Babiak tried to explain, "there were *two* wars. There was a war against the Germans, which was World War I, and after that one, there was another war right after against the Soviets." She hadn't even mentioned Marshal Józef Piłsudski taking Kiev from the Soviets in 1920, before she realized that her patient was asleep.

The next day Dr. Babiak started at the beginning of the hour—when he wouldn't be groggy—and failed again. She lost her nerve as she looked into the simple, trusting eyes of her patient. "I have delivered bad news before," she later told her husband. "But it felt like I was telling him that overnight his species had gone extinct."

The next day she told her colleagues that someone would have to figure out a different solution, because she didn't have the heart for this.

"It should really be explained to him in Yiddish," declared Dr. Meslowski. "There should be no mistaking what he is being told. Frankly, I think Dr. Fishbein should be the one to tell him."

Dr. Meslowski's use of Johann Fishbein's academic title made the rest of the staff feel less troubled assigning a man who had no experience in such matters the grim job none of them preferred to do themselves. And Fishbein, while hesitant, had to respect the importance of telling a man a tragedy in words that he didn't have to puzzle over.

"Yankel, do you remember how you told me that when you first got to Smolskie you asked for the Jewish quarter and that woman had no idea where it was?" Fishbein said late one Friday, after most of the staff had gone home for the weekend.

"Yes."

"Why do you suppose that was?"

"I suppose she didn't want to talk to me."

Fishbein nodded. "Yes, that's always possible. But did you know that there was no Jewish ghetto in Smolskie?"

"Oh—I heard there was."

"Certainly, there was. But no more. Do you know what happened to the ghetto?"

"No."

"It was destroyed."

Yankel did not respond.

"More than three-quarters of a century ago. The Germans came through Smolskie, rounded up all the Jews, and massacred them."

Yankel nodded his head, glumly. "Terrible," Yankel pronounced, but with an element in his voice that implied these sorts of tragedies happen now and then.

"It was not just in Smolskie either," Fishbein continued. "All over Poland, Jews were rounded up and destroyed. The German army went from town to town, hunted down Jews wherever they could find them, and they slaughtered them."

Yankel shook his head. "Terrible," he repeated. "Very sad."

"Almost all the Jews in Poland were killed."

Yankel's eyes, which were cast on the floor, suddenly shot up with surprise.

"All the Jews of Poland?" he said. "How could that be?"

"The Nazis . . ." Fishbein stopped. He was unsure of whether he had used the word "Nazi" as opposed to "German" when he had first begun the conversation. "The *Germans* were very efficient. They kidnapped the Jews, took them out into camps, and gassed them to death. The old and the young. Women and children."

"But how could they have killed all the Jews of Poland?" Yankel asked. "You're still here, aren't you?"

Fishbein smiled. The professor's father was Jewish, it was true. But the professor's mother had spent his childhood rigorously instructing him that he was not to consider himself Jewish—no matter who told him otherwise.

Sonia Fishbein had good reasons to be concerned: her son's Semitism had been written on the curve of his nose, the olive tinge of his skin, and the richness of his dark eyes. No one needed to hear the Jewish sound of his last name to guess his ancestry. And the children he grew up with never let him forget it, calling him every dirty name they could think of for a Jew, and even coming up with a few original ones.

"I am not Jewish, Yankel."

Yankel looked surprised. "You could have fooled me."

"My father was Jewish. But my family became Catholic a long time ago."

"Oh," Yankel said. He meditated on this for a moment before he said, "So did all the Jews convert? Like during the Inquisition?"

Now it was Fishbein's turn to be surprised. It was the first time Yankel had alluded to a commonly known historical event. And had alluded to it so casually; as if the Spanish Inquisition was something every adult should be familiar with. Fishbein thought he should probably make a note of this and tell the other doctors. (He promptly forgot.)

"No," Fishbein said. "All the Jews were killed. Most of them anyway."

"But how could all the Jews have been killed?" Yankel replied. "There must have been hundreds of thousands."

"There were millions," Fishbein said. "No longer."

"What about the Jews of Krakow?"

"They were killed."

"Warsaw?"

"Killed."

"Bialystok?"

Fishbein nodded grimly. "They were killed too. There are no more Jews in any of those places. Only a few hundred."

"Come, come," Yankel said with a wave of his hand. "You're kidding me."

"I wish I was."

Yankel stared into Fishbein's eyes, expecting the man would burst into laughter. And he wondered if he shouldn't just play along, like some straight man waiting for the inevitable punch line.

"It wasn't just Poland where the Germans went on their rampage,"

Fishbein continued. "They killed Jews all over Europe. Greece, France, Russia, Ukraine. Everywhere the Germans set foot, they killed Jews."

"You're saying there are no more Jews in Europe?"

"Yes. Six million were killed, all told."

Of course, a mind like Yankel's didn't traffic in millions. As Fishbein later told the other doctors, he no doubt was struggling to wrap his arms around the sheer volume. "I didn't know there were that many Jews in the whole world," Yankel finally said.

Fishbein's lip curled into what he hoped was a smile that could be interpreted as understanding. "There were."

Fishbein began recounting (in less detail than Dr. Babiak) a truncated history of the Jews in the twentieth century. He started with World War I, and the dissatisfying peace that had left the Germans feeling rudderless and betrayed. He explained how in the chaos of the Weimar years a charismatic Austrian corporal whipped the masses into hysteria by laying Germany's problems at the feet of the Jews. And then he described what happened after the Germans swallowed the Sudetenland and then bounded east, and their satanic methods of killing Jews along the way.

The night before, Dr. Fishbein had rehearsed what he was going to say; he would end this gloomy history with the triumphant birth of the state of Israel. A land where "the cop and the criminal and his lawyer and his bondsman are all Jews," as Fishbein would exclaim. It was now as mighty a nation as any other on the face of the earth. But he never got that far.

Midway through his explanation of the tragic prologue to Israel's founding, he saw that his audience looked bored.

"What do you think of all this?" Fishbein asked.

Yankel looked as if he were going to say something else, but he stopped himself and it was several minutes before he spoke again.

"Not to be disrespectful, Dr. Fishbein, but just how dumb do you guys think I am?"

4

THE MYRMIDON

After almost three months, the perception took shape among the administrators at Our Lady of Mercy Hospital that too much time, too much thought, too many specialists, and far too much money were being spent on the mysterious patient kept in luxurious seclusion (or so it was believed) in the hospital's eastern ward.

This view took several months to solidify, mostly because the details of the convalescent were known only as gossip. The departmental heads at Our Lady of Mercy abided by an unspoken agreement not to meddle in the fiefdoms of their fellow administrators, and, for several months, this protocol was honored.

While the rumor had circulated that a nut—a *real* nut; a costumed, delusional wacko, with a backstory like something out of a movie—had pitched a tent in the mental ward, and that the entire staff of psychiatrists and psychologists had been utterly flummoxed in trying to treat him, that was the extent of what was known. The nature of what afflicted "Patient X," as he was commonly referred to, was left vague. The doctors and nurses who had seen the patient firsthand, when he showed up in the emergency room with a broken leg months earlier, observed only that he had been dressed in an "old-fashioned costume"—but nobody knew what this was supposed to mean. Some thought this meant he showed up in a Roman toga. Others assumed he had been wearing a suit of armor.

But, nevertheless, Patient X remained safely confined in a high citadel of gossip and nobody had any cruel or petty thoughts about him or his caretakers, until the quarterly budget meeting.

As the department heads sat in the main conference room going through the budget, line by line, several of the doctors in the other departments asked Dr. Antoni Polus what "Lewinkopf Expenses" were.

"They're to study our delusional patient, Yankel Lewinkopf," Dr. Polus answered simply.

This explanation might have sufficed had the expenses been small. (This, despite the fact that most of those in attendance immediately guessed the connection with Patient X, and could practically taste a morsel of scuttlebutt.) But, alas, a simple explanation would never do. The breakdown of the Lewinkopf Expenses was too bizarre—and the figures too oversized—not to demand further annotation.

Of course, tens of thousands of zlotys had been spent on tests, X-rays, physical therapy, CT scans, and drug regimens few doctors would question the use of. But bringing in Dr. Johann Fishbein as a semi-regular consultant had cost well more than a hundred thousand zlotys, and that was the first item that the committee wanted to know about.

"What kind of doctor is he, exactly?" asked Dr. Bartek Krol, the head of radiology.

"He's a professor at Cybulski University."

The answer lingered in the air for a few moments. Dr. Polus turned his head back to the budget, not meeting the eye of any of his colleagues.

"Professor of what?"

"Germanic languages," Dr. Polus answered. He then added with what he hoped was finality in his voice: "Dr. Fishbein's help on the case has been indispensable."

Johann Fishbein at least had some sort of expertise attached to his name. A far stranger expense had been the thousands of zlotys spent every month on food.

"And what's this?" asked Dr. Krol again, who assumed the role of inquisitor in this matter, which suited the other doctors and administrators in the room just fine.

"The patient has an irregular diet," Dr. Polus answered.

The air conditioner had broken in the conference room that morning, and after briefly trying to find another room—and discovering that all the remaining ones had already been reserved—the assembled departmental heads removed their jackets, rolled up their shirtsleeves, and resolved to "just get it over with." But the mood in the room was perceptibly more hostile than it had been when they sat down. Sweat had soaked nearly every shirt and blouse in attendance. And when questions were asked, there was subtext in each that even the most sensitive observer might have missed an hour earlier.

"What kind of irregular diet?" Dr. Krol asked. "We're a hospital. We can't feed him?"

When Yankel was admitted to the psych ward all those weeks earlier, he was deemed undernourished by the examining doctor. He was ordered to go on a diet of high-fat dairy and animal fats to boost weight, iron, and calcium levels. But the patient had stubbornly refused to go along with these recommendations. "Not kosher," he insisted when he was handed his first tray of beef stew, butter noodles, and eggnog, agreeing to consume only the banana and the bottle of water. The nutritionist had told Dr. Polus that the patient couldn't go on eating just bananas and apples if he expected his bones to heal, or reach a healthy weight. Somehow he would need to be fed. "What are you suggesting?" Dr. Polus asked.

"Let's call a kosher supplier. Get some meat and some dairy into his diet," was the answer.

A kosher butcher was found in Berlin who supplied frozen beef and poultry to the Chabad House* in Krakow. The meat cost a fortune, but Dr. Polus shrugged it off at the time. Two new frying pans were procured.

---

*Chabad is the largest Hasidic movement in the world and the only one that offers outreach to less observant Jews; Chabad Houses are the study and outreach centers worldwide.

On one of them was written the words "Yankel Lewinkopf, meat," and on the other, "Yankel Lewinkopf, dairy." The pans were given to the patient to examine along with a special cupboard where they would be kept, away from the other pots and pans, and it was solemnly promised this cookware would be reserved exclusively for him. An orderly went to the supermarket to look for orange juice and pints of ice cream bearing an Orthodox Union stamp, which the doctors took great pains to assure Yankel was a universally accepted insignia for kosher food.

Yankel's weight rose—and everyone was more or less happy. Except the hospital administrators.

"No," Dr. Polus explained. "He's on a kosher diet. He refused to eat until we brought him kosher food."

"Kosher diet?" Dr. Krol repeated.

"Yes."

Despite the fact that Judaism and its accompanying orthodoxy were the first things that had been noticeable to everyone who laid eyes on the patient, this fact had somehow failed to make it into the hospital's tattle about Patient X. Most of the doctors just knew that the patient was "strange" and "mysterious." Some took the word "strange" to mean a physical deformity; a case of elephantiasis, perhaps, or dwarfism. But this was the first true explanation of Yankel's oddity. Several brows rose around the conference table, filling in the first murky details of the patient in their mind's eye.

"So we've become a restaurant now?" Dr. Krol asked. "We're here to suit everybody's palate?"

No one responded.

Dr. Krol stared at the budget for another second. "And what is this four-thousand-zloty expense for . . . Aldar Kosa?"

"Who?"

Dr. Krol looked at the budget line again. "Aldar Kosa," he repeated. "The note says 'Hypnotherapy.'"

Dr. Polus blushed.

"Oh, yes. Yes . . ."

Dr. Polus's voice trailed off, as if he expected the matter to end, but the assembled doctors and administrators would wait for an explanation.

"We tried hypnotizing the patient. We thought he might be able to talk more freely under hypnosis." After a few moments, Dr. Polus felt compelled to add: "In retrospect, that might have been a mistake."

The room was quiet, as the doctors now stared at psychiatry's budget with a second, vivified eye. The last few minutes of the meeting had been an almost unprecedented exchange as far as these sorts of meetings went. Not that there hadn't been expenses that were challenged—that happened all the time. But they were never quite this colorful. Each doctor and administrator present hoped for yet another explosion.

They would not have long to wait. The administration of a polygraph exam was next.

"Very necessary," Dr. Polus said.

"Why is that?"

"We had to be certain that the man was mentally ill and not a con artist."

There were three tickets to the circus.

Dr. Polus reflected on that for a few moments. "I concede, that shouldn't be in the budget," he said. "I'll pick up that expense, personally."

"What's this fellow's problem, anyway?" Dr. Krol asked.

For the first time since the conversation had begun, Dr. Polus stared directly at his adversary. Radiology, like every department, had to weather cuts. And Dr. Polus wondered if his colleague wasn't just projecting some of his personal frustration and rage on Yankel Lewinkopf. Or, perhaps, his colleague was simply hot and sticky. Was he eager (as the rest of the hospital staff undoubtedly was) to plunge into the intriguing details of another man's madness? Maybe he had just never outgrown the voyeurism of youth, and it was not an unreasonable assumption that Dr. Krol was simply a more aggressive hoarder of detail than his fellow hens.

And Dr. Polus was sorely tempted to say to Dr. Krol—as he might say to a fresh child—"None of your damned business," and defend himself later against Dr. Wojciech Kowalski, the head of the hospital, in a less public setting. (Dr. Kowalski was not in attendance that day.) But just as quickly as this thought sprouted, he abandoned it and assumed the most diplomatic tone he could muster.

"He's suffering from a mixed type of delusional disorder," Dr. Polus said. "We have yet to isolate the root of the disorder."

The other doctors in the conference room all moved their eyes back to Dr. Krol, as if they were watching a game of Ping-Pong. Dr. Krol scratched the chin of his beard for a few moments before he spoke.

"What's the delusion?"

Dr. Polus sighed almost imperceptibly. "He thinks he's an eighteenth-century Orthodox Jew from an imaginary shtetl in the forest."

A peal of laughter erupted from a female department head in a cocoa blazer, and the rest of the staff followed suit, albeit with more tempered, polite chortling. Dr. Polus's face reddened in embarrassment.

"Who's managing his case?"

"Doctors Babiak and Meslowski are managing the case on a day-by-day basis. But the whole staff has taken part in attempts at a prognosis."

"Babiak and Meslowski aren't working on this full-time, are they?"

"Yes."

It was difficult getting into a scrum with Dr. Bartek Krol. Dr. Krol was the youngest department head, and had risen in the hospital bureaucracy because he was an efficient doctor who had a reputation for not suffering fools lightly. Moreover, Dr. Krol was slender and dark, and favored almost universally by the female staff.

Another strain of gossip that had worked its way into the hospital's bloodstream was that Dr. Krol had carried on romances with at least four of the more comely nurses on staff, and two of the female doctors—one of whom was married. Nobody could say when these romances had begun, or if they had ever been called off. (It was strongly suspected that at least two of them were still ongoing.) And while Dr. Krol remained discreet, the same could not be said for his partners in these frolics.

One nurse, who had been carrying on an affair with the doctor, overheard a rival talking to one of her friends about the man whom she had assumed was her property. She marched over to Dr. Krol's office and scrawled "Cocksucker!" on his door seventeen times in red lipstick, triumphantly put the cap back on the lipstick and returned to her rounds. The nurse was dismissed, but, as if honor-bound to treat someone who had shared his bed with some minimum courtliness, Dr. Krol talked the administration into letting her keep her job provided she paid for the damage and promised to keep private affairs out of hospital business.

These stories did little to scare away future lovers. If anything they heightened Dr. Krol's value in the eyes of the women at Our Lady of Mercy. Every single nurse believed that she would be the one to tame his oversized libido. It was rumored that his seduction method both in administrative and private matters was the same: his extreme confidence. It was an unfeeling, arrogant beam of entitlement that unnerved any man or woman he chose to shine it on. Including Dr. Polus.

As he sat in the swivel chair with each doctor and administrator waiting for his reply, Dr. Polus wondered—briefly, for only a few seconds, really—if the Lewinkopf case didn't sound silly in the cold light of day; if his odd patient wasn't any more or less of a mystery than the other derelicts and schizophrenics encased in a padded cell. Perhaps too much money had indeed been spent on Yankel Lewinkopf.

"Dr. Polus," Dr. Krol said with undue formality. "I submit to you that this patient is a waste of resources. In looking to make this year's budget projections, I suggest that you alter his treatment."

The conversation did not go much further. When he next spoke, Dr. Polus could feel the air sucked out of his corner of the room. "I'll manage my own budget, thank you," he replied, meekly. "And I have cuts that I'll have to deal with the same as you, Dr. Krol. Mr. Lewinkopf's treatment will not be altered." But the witnesses that afternoon came away with the distinct impression that it had ended with a decisive winner (Krol) and loser (Polus).

Dr. Krol merely shrugged, and as the committee began examining

Gastroenterology and Hepatology's budget Dr. Polus experienced the dreary sensation one gets not when ending an ordeal, but beginning one. Word of this embarrassing exchange would no doubt escape the meeting. Dr. Kowalski (who was at a fundraiser in Krakow, and was expecting budget recommendations on his desk next week) would probably ask him to take even more money out of his budget. Overnight, he would become a laughingstock. It was all very depressing.

And, indeed, Dr. Polus was correct; the hundreds of thousands of zlotys that had been designated as "Lewinkopf Expenses" became a source of effrontery and amusement to the hospital staff at large. It became a font of speculation and gossip. It became the punch line to several dozen private jokes. And, finally, it evolved into such outlandish and bewildering falsehoods that it resembled nothing approximating the truth about the patient or the department.

The patient's kosher prohibitions were translated into a diet of champagne and caviar. And it was assumed that this food was not just for a patient but for the pampered departmental head and one or two of his choice deputies.

The fact that Dr. Polus had put a professor of romance languages in his budget meant that the shrinks were taking German and English lessons, at the hospital's expense. In the weeks that followed, Dr. Polus had to turn two doctors and three nurses away who came knocking on his office saying they heard that the department was offering free English lessons, and could they sign up, too? When he told them that there were no such lessons, they assumed he was just hoarding them for his staff and his friends.

And the hypnotist—the same meddlesome quack whom Dr. Polus had instantly regretted hiring—was painted by the same malevolent brush of gossip as nothing more than a pricey astrologer hired for kicks. Hospital funds, it was said, were being used by the psychiatrists to have their fortunes told. The department was taking field trips to the circus. They were testing out polygraphs on one another—for lord-only-knows-what!

The patient barely came up in all this. But when Yankel's name was mentioned he, too, was viewed with cynicism and exaggeration.

Some made the claim that he was a missionary, out to convert (or, as one doctor put it, "Zionize") the staff. Others told a wild story that Yankel had come to the hospital seeking Holocaust reparations; in this fetid account, the hospital had been built on land that Yankel's family had once owned, and he had come to the hospital demanding an ownership stake. "Why do you think they're spending so much money on him?" asked one anesthesiologist. "They're doing it to shut him up."

And as he sat in Dr. Kowalski's office two weeks after the budget meeting, and listened to the litany of distortions being spread through the hospital like Spanish flu, he could scarcely find his voice. "Wojciech," he finally croaked, "that's the damnedest list of lies I've ever heard."

And as he tried to go through the list and defend each expense and correct the misrepresentations, he was defeated by their sheer volume. (It should be noted that Dr. Kowalski didn't bother mentioning the stories that were obviously untrue, such as the whopper about Holocaust reparations.)

"Antoni, I don't doubt that every item has some solid purpose behind it," Dr. Kowalski finally said. "Each could be defended just fine in its own individual day in court. What bothers me is the totality of it. I'm seeing a larger picture of excess and waste."

When Dr. Polus limped back to the mental ward he reconciled himself to the inevitable—he would no longer have money to lavish on Yankel. Perhaps he would no longer have money for anything.

Certainly, it was a depressing blow to science. And to his patient. But mostly Dr. Polus felt the rage of impotence; the humiliation of suddenly losing control of a budget he had managed for almost twenty years. He spent the night in the throes of violent self-pity.

The next afternoon, Dr. Polus summoned Drs. Babiak, Meslowski, and four other psychiatrists who had been attending the case part-time, and told them that there would be a decision in the coming days about Yankel Lewinkopf's status, and whether he could remain at Our Lady of Mercy.

"Yes, yes," Dr. Polus said from behind his desk, not looking directly at the startled expressions of the doctors in front of him. "We've all found

Mr. Lewinkopf fascinating. No question. And I would like someone here to get the chance to publish. But at this point there have been no plausible theories about the genesis of his condition. So we are going to have to come to a decision; should we keep him in the ward with only one of you looking in on him in your roster of patients, or should we release him."

"We should keep him," Dr. Meslowski said quickly.

Several others nodded and murmured in agreement.

"Pardon me, Dr. Meslowski," Dr. Polus said. "But when I said 'we' what I really meant was 'I.' I have to decide. And I should add that I'm not terribly inclined to keep a healthy, grown man in a hospital against his will, if he's not a danger to himself or others. If, in the next few days, someone here could offer me something useful about him, maybe I'd change my mind. Otherwise, I believe we'll be releasing Yankel Lewinkopf."

And with those final words, Dr. Polus put on his reading glasses, picked up one of the folders on his desk, and bid the staff a good afternoon.

Several of the doctors retreated to the tavern two blocks from the hospital to toast shots of vodka to the memory of the Lewinkopf case, but Dr. Meslowski went straight to his office.

Dr. Meslowski was alone in taking seriously the idea that their work could continue if there was a breakthrough in the next couple of days. Not that Dr. Meslowski didn't appreciate the unlikelihood of a reversal, but Ignacy Meslowski was thorough. He opened his file cabinet and examined every note he had made, every scrip he had written, and every X-ray taken, for something the collected doctors missed the first time around.

In recent weeks, after Johann Fishbein had sat him down for the grave report on the fortunes of the Polish Jewish population, the patient had grown distrustful of the medical staff, refusing to believe anything they told him.

This had not been anticipated.

A few of those on staff predicted that Patient Lewinkopf would have been more or less undisturbed by the misfortunes of World War II. After all, he was of an age where such large-scale global tragedies do not carry the same weight that they do with men of more sober years.

Plus, the doctors at Our Lady of Mercy had tiptoed around the most grue-some truths. They spoke of the vast numbers of dead (millions and millions), and the fact that the war altered forever the trajectory of world events—but declined to show Yankel the photos of emaciated survivors; the industrial ovens; the ghoulish lampshades fashioned out of Jewish and Gypsy skin which any other student of the Holocaust could find in an internet search. Hopefully, the lack of visual aids would make the whole thing less traumatic.

But much to everyone's surprise, Yankel was utterly dubious of everything.

When he was asked in the next therapy session what he thought about all that Dr. Fishbein had recounted for him, he told Drs. Babiak and Meslowski that he didn't believe a word of it. "I'm still trying to figure out the punch line," he said.

When all the doctors swore up and down that no, honestly, this horri-ble event occurred and the Jews were really and truly driven out of Poland and the rest of Europe, Yankel seemed to think that the staff had con-spired together to play a prank on him. "Keep on telling me this till I'm ninety years old," Yankel said. "I still don't get it."

"Why would we lie to you?" asked Dr. Babiak. "Why do you think we're so interested in you and your story? We didn't think there were any Jews left in Poland."

Yankel merely nodded his head, glibly.

"You think we're completely making this up?" asked Dr. Meslowski.

"Well," Yankel said, sounding a little like a rabbi in all his preening and sagaciousness, "might there have been *some* sort of big massacre of Jews? Perhaps. That sort of thing is not unheard of. But all of them driven out of Europe or killed? Every last Jew? Millions of them? I don't think so. The Jews have been in Poland for a thousand years—they'll be here for another thousand."

When Drs. Babiak and Meslowski said that no, not *every single* Jew had

been killed or driven into exile—a few remained here and there in Warsaw or Krakow—Yankel nodded his head, knowingly, as if he were right
to treat what they told him warily.

"Dr. Babiak," Yankel said, careful as always to be respectful of the gentiles, "maybe I am a chump who doesn't understand big-city ways. But I'm
not dumb enough to fall for this nonsense."

And over the next few weeks, Yankel grew doubtful not just about the
Holocaust, but about everything that the doctors had described during
his three months at Our Lady of Mercy. He became distant during his
therapy sessions. He stopped eating the meat that they cooked for him,
and consumed only fish and roughage.

Indeed, when one has heard a lie—a grand, operatic lie that no one in
their right mind could take seriously—one has to take stock of the source
of this falsehood. With a suddenness that startled Yankel as much as any
of his doctors, he began to wonder what else these seemingly kind, seemingly knowledgeable, seemingly competent gentiles had been lying about.

Of course, the world of Smolskie was a surreal one, and there were too
many technological advances to figure out at once, but every explanation
they had proffered now seemed suspicious. When he first moved into the
ward, he had asked a doctor how the light switch worked, and had heard
convoluted ravings about "electric current" and "heated filaments."

"What's electric current?" Yankel had asked.

"The movement of electrons," said Dr. Babiak.

"What's an electron?"

"You don't know what an electron is?"

Yankel shook his head.

"Well, the whole world is made up of atoms," Dr. Babiak explained.
"These are the smallest particles known to man. And each atom is divided
into three parts . . ."

Yankel stopped paying attention after the first ten minutes or so of
Dr. Babiak's exegesis. But even the cursory introduction to the periodic
table struck him as far-fetched. "You see, Yankel, gold and oxygen are re-

ally made out of the same basic matter—atoms—just a different number of protons, neutrons, and electrons."

At the time, this hadn't made sense. How could everything be basically the same, and yet completely different? But the doctor had answered with such authority that Yankel assumed she knew what she was talking about. As he sat in his room weeks later, he wondered how he could have possibly been so trusting.

"May I ask you something, Dr. Meslowski?" Yankel said. "What if I wanted to go back to Kreskol—could I go?"

Dr. Meslowski was surprised by the question.

"Now?" Dr. Meslowski asked. "You want to leave right now?"

"Yes."

Dr. Meslowski reddened slightly. "If you really want to go, I'm sure you can," he said. "I'd have to ask the doctor in charge. But how will you get home?"

Yankel ignored the question. "Will you ask the doctor in charge, please?"

Dr. Meslowski was nearly speechless. He put his pen in his pocket, put his pad away, and called an emergency meeting of the other doctors. They all agreed that they should stall for time with Yankel and try to talk him out of wanting to leave.

This was shortly before Dr. Polus's fateful meeting with Dr. Kowalski, and the doctors told Yankel that they hadn't yet been able to secure a meeting with the head of psychiatry, who made those decisions.

Now Dr. Meslowski grew more resigned that the patient would walk out on his own into the streets. It broke his heart. He pulled out Yankel's file searching the notes for ideas—crazy or otherwise. Dr. Meslowski's eyes stopped on the register of Yankel's property. It read simply:

(1) Hat, black, custom-made

(1) Overcoat, black, custom-made

(1) Pair of trousers, black, custom-made

(1) Shirt, white, custom-made

(1) Pair of leg stockings, black, custom-made

(2) Pairs of undergarments, white, custom-made

(1) Brown sack (material unknown)

(1) Pair of boots, black, custom-made

(1) Cloth garment with strings, long, rectangular, white, custom-made

(2) Boxes, black, leather, 31 millimeters x 30 millimeters, containing
    compartment with small scroll and two black leather straps

(1) Velvet "yarmulke," black, custom-made

(2) Loaves, black bread

(3) Onion rolls

(1) Quantity of nuts and berries (weight 1½ kg)

(6) Strips of dried beef

(4) Apples

(1) Pocket-sized hardcover book, title unknown, language unknown
    (probably Yiddish or Hebrew), antique

(1) Map, antique

(2) Sheets, antique paper

(1) Slip of notepaper, current

(20) Zlotys, coins, collector

(30) Zlotys, coins, current

He read the list twice over. It had the veneer of authenticity—the index of possessions for a poor, country hermit who had been sheltered from the machinations of the industrial age. His clothes had been made by hand. His food had come from the forest and the farm. Even the prayer book— which the patient carried with him at all times, as firmly as an infant clutching a rattle—had been bought many generations ago. When he had asked Yankel if he might be permitted to examine it, the pages looked as if they might flake off and crumble if they were handled too roughly. (The book was so old that no publisher's information was affixed in the first or final pages.)

The two letters Yankel had been carrying—one in Yiddish, one in

Polish—were also in keeping with the Charles Bertram–like forgery of a fictional shtetl in the wilderness. The parchment had been fashioned out of calfskin (or goatskin, the doctors weren't able to determine which) and, while clearly newer than the prayer book, also gave the unmistakable impression of being the product of a simpler, bygone age.

These letters had been photocopied a dozen times and widely circulated among the staff. Like the other doctors, Meslowski had examined them, puzzled over them, and reread them. The fact that the letters had been written in a different hand from Yankel's (more majestic and with greater flourishes) made the staff speculate that he might have co-conspirators. Another bearded Jew might just pop up with the same harebrained story—even though none ever did.

The only things that looked out of place were the final item (thirty zlotys in coins), the box with the leather straps (which caused a great deal of commotion at first, as a possible explanation of Yankel's carnal proclivities), and the third item from the bottom.

Dr. Meslowski couldn't remember ever looking at any slip of *notepaper*, or hearing any of his colleagues discuss it, and he wondered whether this was a clerical error. (As for the thirty zlotys, Yankel had recounted how the people of Smolskie had treated him like a street urchin on his first day in town. Likewise, the doctors learned that the leather straps were a common Jewish talisman, making them far less interesting.)

Dr. Meslowski went to the patient's room and asked him if he still had the papers he'd been admitted to the hospital with.

"Yes."

Yankel closed his book and removed the three sheets of paper he owned from under his bed and gave them to Dr. Meslowski, who stared intently at the notepaper for several long beats.

"What is this?" Dr. Meslowski asked.

"Paper."

"I know that," Dr. Meslowski said. "But what's the number on it?"

Yankel shrugged.

"This is a phone number," Dr. Meslowski replied, irritated at the patient's obtuseness. "Where did you get it? I thought you said you didn't know about phones."

"The gypsy gave it to me."

Ah, yes. The gypsies. Yankel had told the doctors all about the band of gypsies who had come through Kreskol every six months, and how they had agreed to take him into Smolskie for a mule and two dozen slippers. It had been yet another improbable fiction dismissed out of hand by the doctors (and deemed much less interesting than his stories about the village). They googled the name Yankel gave them—Washko Something-or-other—and when the search turned up nothing, were content to forget this unimportant detail.

"Is this the gypsy's number—his phone number?"

Yankel shrugged.

As Dr. Meslowski left the room—the slip of notepaper still in his hands—he found (almost to his surprise) that his fingers were trembling.

Dr. Meslowski sat down in his office and stared at the number for several minutes before he went back into his files and looked up the gypsy's name. Washo Zurka. He stared at the phone number for a few moments before he dialed.

The phone rang.

A mechanical voice—an automated voice from the service provider—answered, repeating the numbers Dr. Meslowski had just dialed. No name was attached. There was just a beep at the end. Dr. Meslowski hung up without leaving a message, and stared for several long minutes out the window.

And yet in those minutes some assumptions about Yankel and Kreskol began to change.

A phone number—with a real-life person at the other end—seemed like the most critical piece of evidence as to whether Yankel was mentally ill, a fraud, or, in fact, telling some unlikely truth. For the first time, there was a second party that could confirm or deny all Yankel had been saying.

And, also for the first time, Dr. Meslowski came to believe that Yankel's story might be more credible than he, or anyone else, originally thought. (Not that he hadn't wondered—even out loud—if his patient had been telling the truth. But every other doctor seemed to find it impossible.)

He couldn't help but marvel at Yankel's unflappable consistency. Even the minor details had not changed over the months, and in Dr. Meslowski's experience most liars had short memories. He never met one who didn't get tripped up on a trivial point edited somewhere along the way to make the story more credible or succinct that soon sent the whole edifice of fictions collapsing to earth. But that wasn't the case with Yankel.

Moreover, Dr. Meslowski didn't think that a man with serious mental illness would be able to recruit a confederate into his madness. He couldn't imagine Yankel telling a friend: "If someone calls you on this number, just say you're a gypsy." A normal person wouldn't play along months after not hearing from Yankel at all.

But the biggest unanswerable in Dr. Meslowski's mind was that Yankel had seemed so calm and untroubled as he had handed over the gypsy's phone number. He had held on to that number patiently for months, without volunteering it to anyone. No man involved in a hoax could have that kind of restraint—at least not in Dr. Meslowski's view.

The happenstance that seemed most logical, the more Dr. Meslowski thought about it, was that the number had been given to Yankel—just as he said—and that Yankel didn't know what to do with it.

Dr. Meslowski dialed the number again. Again, the call went into the disembodied voicemail.

"Hello," Dr. Meslowski said tentatively, thinking over each word as they left his lips. "My name is Ignacy Meslowski. I'm a doctor at Our Lady of Mercy Hospital in Smolskie. I'm looking for Washo Zurka concerning a very important matter."

Dr. Meslowski paused as he considered what to say next.

"If Mr. Zurka could call me back, I would appreciate it." He left his number twice, and before hanging up he felt compelled to add, "It's about Yankel Lewinkopf."

Dr. Meslowski sat in his office for an hour, not doing much of anything except staring out the window. Another hour passed. He nearly fell out of his chair when his phone rang and a nurse asked him if the nurses' rotation could be switched next week. "Yes, of course," he said—and hung up.

Before he got up to leave for the evening, well after eight, he called the number again and left another message, and this time he left his mobile number at the end.

"Any time, night or day, is fine to call."

Dr. Meslowski went back to his house—which had been empty for more than two summers, since his wife had agreed to let him have it in the terms of their separation agreement—with a pack of Marlboros. With no one around to scold him, he smoked one cigarette after another, all the while staring at his mobile phone until the pack was empty. And when his first indulgence didn't feel comforting enough, he poured himself a glass of vodka, and he fell asleep on the leather chair in his living room, still in his suit and tie. That night, he dreamed he was a shoemaker living in Kreskol.

Dr. Meslowski called again the next day. Twice. But he did not leave a message the second time. He had no intention of frightening these gypsies away before he had a chance to talk to them. So he told himself that he should just be patient and that somebody would get back to him sooner or later.

But Dr. Meslowski thought of little else over the course of the next week. When two days had passed and he hadn't heard anything, he began asking some of his intimates: "What would you say to someone—a stranger—on their voice mail if you desperately wanted them to call you back?"

"What do you mean?" asked his friend, Aleksander.

"Let's say you needed someone to call you back," Dr. Meslowski said, mindful to not reveal any details about Yankel. "Let's say that this person didn't know you. And let's also say that this fellow was a loner. Or, not a loner, but an introvert. He wasn't eager to chat it up. What would you say on his voice mail to make sure he called you back?"

Aleksander considered the question for a few moments.

"I'd say that I found something that belonged to the person," Aleksander finally replied.

An excellent idea. One that Dr. Meslowski should have been able to figure out himself, if he hadn't been so tangled up with nerves.

After a full week had gone by with no word from the gypsies he asked one of the female orderlies, Brygida, to call the number and say that she had found something of Washo Zurka's and would he please call back. (He also threw in a hundred zlotys, for the effort.)

"Just try to sound concerned," Dr. Meslowski told Brygida. "Like whatever you found is important and needs to get back to its owner as soon as possible."

"What did I find?"

"It doesn't matter," Dr. Meslowski replied. "Don't say what. Just say you know that it's his. That's all. There's no need to say anything else. They're not going to pick up the line, anyway. Call from your house, though. I've already called him from the hospital. He might have the hospital number blocked."

Brygida didn't show much interest in the drama or peculiarity of what was going on. "Fine," she said and plucked the hundred-zloty note out of the doctor's hand.

Number 17 Przewoz Row, in the old part of Smolskie, was a much more lordly house than Ferka Gorjer was accustomed to.

As he stood outside in the late summer evening silently smoking cigarettes, Ferka checked the address a second time, just to make sure he hadn't gone to the wrong street. And as he stared at the oversized windows with their baroque casements, he began wondering if he would have to figure out some tricky alarm system.

There were some thieves for whom spotting and disabling an alarm was second nature. They knew exactly where the wires were buried. They knew which cords to cut and which ones to leave alone. It was as if they had gotten the scent in their noses as infants and could sniff them out forever after. Ferka wasn't quite in that league, but he wasn't bad at it. One of his cousins had taught him the fundamentals of the closed-circuit magnet—how to remove the insulation and put a wire across the circuit, thus disabling the alarm—when he was a teenager. Ferka had been caught only three times by a missed wire. Two of these times, he had been younger than sixteen. And it wasn't Ferka who had tripped the alarm those two times—it was his older cousin Chal.

No, in his mature years, he rarely made amateur mistakes—provided he was sensible in choosing his targets. The only time he had been nabbed by an alarm as an adult was at a jewelry store. The alarm was so well hidden that when Ferka came up from behind the counter with a fistful of ruby rings and saw a gang of policemen across from him with their guns drawn, he assumed there must have been a squad car patrolling nearby. It was only at the pretrial hearing a month later he learned that he had accidentally tripped a silent alarm.

However, his uncle had been insistent that this particular job carried little risk. Security would almost certainly be nonexistent. Ferka had asked whether he should bring Boiko and Marko—his brothers—along with him. "Not necessary," his uncle had said. "You'll be in and out of there in an hour."

When the bedroom light had been turned out, and Ferka decided that the only other visible light (the kitchen) had simply been forgotten about, he threw away his cigarette, made sure that the street was empty, and took a long look at the door before deciding that he wouldn't have much to worry about, alarm-wise. He wouldn't even need the more complicated instruments he carried in his jacket. A paper clip and a nail file would do.

The interior of the house was not as nice as its exterior. The furniture looked cheap. There was a brown leather chair and a flat-screen television, but that was the extent of this house's luxuries. There were no pieces of art or soft sofas or glass tables. Only books and papers. And several hundred videocassettes. ("Who still watches videos?" Ferka wondered as he examined the titles.) The house had a certain staleness about it—as if it were the dwelling of a lonely man. On the walls were framed photos of a family, but that was the only evidence of something more than solitude. The spare surfaces were littered with empty coffee mugs, and half-empty glasses of vodka. If Ferka had been hoping for chests of emeralds, he was to be disappointed.

Ferka locked the door behind him, sat on a brown metal folding chair next to a dining room table, and waited for his eyes to adjust to the darkness.

It did not take long. He put his hands into his windbreaker and ran his fingers over the knife and the duct tape in his left pocket and the pistol in his right pocket—just to make sure they were still there.

And as he sat waiting to make sure his prey upstairs was helpless, he quietly went into the kitchen, turned off the lights, and in the darkness selected a butcher knife. (It was the only one in the knife block that was sharp enough to break skin, if it came to that.)

When he was satisfied that whoever was upstairs was now asleep, Ferka removed his tennis shoes and tiptoed up the stairs and toward the open door of the bedroom, from which came loud snoring.

The sleeping man was middle-aged. His eyebrows were two gray tufts of hair, and his face was lined. While not heavy, exactly, this sleeping man filled out his pajamas—as if a healthy metabolism had slowed. The sleeper was tall, too. When all was said and done, he might be as much as double Ferka's weight. But that was never something that Ferka worried about.

He went to the dresser and removed a pair of white socks. The fellow's mouth was wide open as he snored. Ferka stood still as he waited for his nerves to steady, and when he realized that the fellow wasn't going to wake up without some help, he stuffed the socks in the man's mouth.

The fellow woke up.

He gasped and coughed as if he had swallowed a mouthful of water, and his arms flapped and writhed. But Ferka was ready; as swiftly as he had stuffed the socks into the fellow's mouth, he flung his elbow cruelly into the center of the man's exposed stomach like a wrestler, oblivious to the whimpers of misery he fomented.

With his victim stunned and immobilized, Ferka grasped the gray roll of duct tape out of his windbreaker pocket and got to work taping the man down to his bed.

When the muffled gasps of terror and fear began spilling out of the stuffed sock, Ferka merely whispered, "Shhhhh . . ."

To accentuate the point he raised the knife he'd taken from the kitchen, which glinted in the darkness, and the squirming man suddenly stopped flailing his arms.

Ferka did his work quickly. A strip of tape went over the man's chest. Another one went over his legs. "Put your hands together," he instructed his captive. The man's hands were fastened together. Gracefully, more strips of tape were applied to keep the man firmly fixed to his bed.

After half the roll of tape was gone, and Ferka reasonably certain that his victim wouldn't be able to escape without serious struggle, he put the rest of the roll in his jacket pocket, sat down on the chair across from the bed, and lit a cigarette—not bothering to look his victim in the eye until he was good and ready.

"I have a gun right here," Ferka finally said, taking the pistol out of his windbreaker and flashing it before his captive. "And I got this knife. So you just be very careful around me, you understand?"

Like a young child, his victim nodded obediently.

"Now look here," Ferka continued, "I'm going to take those socks out of your mouth. If you scream, I'm going to cut your throat. If you come at me, I'm going to shoot you in the face. Do you get me?"

The victim nodded again, looking as if he might break into tears at any moment.

"I'm going to ask you a question," Ferka continued, "and you're going to give me the god's honest answer—right?"

Another nod.

Ferka still had the gun in hands. He slid back the barrel, which made the frightening locking sound that it was ready to fire, and he crept slowly toward his victim. After looking the man in the eyes, just to make sure he was good and scared, he plucked the socks out of the man's mouth.

The man didn't say anything. He looked far too frightened. He just tried furtively to catch his breath.

"Now," Ferka said, "why are you trying to track down Washo Zurka?"

The victim looked perplexed for a moment, but his face began changing as it slowly dawned on him why this ruffian had visited him.

"Washo Zurka?" the victim said, his head suddenly a little straighter. "That's why you're here?"

Ferka sucked on his cigarette without removing it from his mouth. "You heard me."

"I didn't mean to bother him," the victim said. "Really. Honestly. I had no idea he would send you here."

"Yeah? Then what do you want from him?"

"Nothing," the victim said. "Honestly! I swear, I'll never bother him again."

"Why'd you call him half a dozen times last week and get that girl to call him, too?"

"I just wanted to talk. But it's not important now. Truly."

The smoke from Ferka's cigarette slowly rose to the ceiling and silhouetted his small, childlike body, making him look ghostly. Indeed, Ferka was the sort who knew the tricks to menacing a bigger man. While some of his cousins would never break into a stranger's house without wearing a ski mask or some other disguise, Ferka believed that if one truly intended to throw a fright into someone, it was critical to prove to them that you were fearless. A mask suggested that someday your captor might have the upper hand on you—but Ferka believed it scarier to show that you couldn't be intimidated by threats from the future.

"Listen to me," Ferka said, without moving. "You just said to me that you were going to give me the god's honest truth, did you not? And that's exactly what I came here for. None of this bullshit, you hear me? Now, why are you trying to get a hold of Washo Zurka?"

The victim nodded vigorously. "I just wanted to know if he'd heard of Yankel Lewinkopf."

Ferka continued to stare at his victim. "Who's that?" he asked after a moment.

"He's a mental patient," the victim said with an uneasy laugh. "I was a fool for taking anything he said seriously. But he's a young man in the mental ward at Our Lady of Mercy. And he told me that Mr. Zurka helped him get to Smolskie."

Ferka didn't say anything.

"It's a weird story," the victim continued. "He's a Jew who says he's from a town in the middle of the forest. It sounds stupid now, but he says that a band of gypsies came through his town a couple of months ago and he hitched a ride with them. The only name he remembered was Washo Zurka. I was just trying to find out if there was any truth in the boy's story. That's all."

The ominous mien that Ferka had perfected suddenly seemed to vanish. This burglar now just looked confused.

"You mean the kid from Kreskol?" the gypsy asked. "Slender kid. Not too tall. Couldn't quite grow in a beard. Yeah, we gave him a ride to Smolskie a couple of months back. So what?"

5

JUBILEE

It's peculiar, I suppose, that after our many decades proving to the world exactly how disinterested we were in its comings and goings, we should all have collectively changed our minds at once. But that's more or less what happened.

Yankel's role in our rediscovery came to a relatively speedy conclusion after Dr. Meslowski's brief capture.

The kidnapping was never reported to the Smolskie authorities as an "abduction" or a "seizure" as such. It was, however, recounted in all its frightening particulars to Dr. Meslowski's colleagues, seated around him in Our Lady of Mercy's conference room, listening as intently as if he were the lone survivor of a shipwreck.

Dr. Meslowski spoke about how he had trembled violently as he answered his abductor's questions. He tried to be as disarming as possible. He openly wept and made oaths and used every trick he could think of to convey just how innocent his inquiry into the gypsy uncle had been. He begged for his life. He pleaded for mercy.

But for his abductor's part, Dr. Meslowski's anguish proved more of an amusement than a threat. He sat smoking cigarettes, allowing the ash to collect in a small gray heap on the carpet, before he spoke. Yes, he said, the young Jew had been pawned off on one of the widows, who was grateful for the company. What of it?

"So there really is a Kreskol?" Dr. Meslowski had asked.

"Of course."

When his abductor finally agreed to cut Dr. Meslowski loose, it was on condition that he not breathe a word about what had transpired to anyone.

"I'm positive I can tell *you*," Dr. Meslowski assured his audience and then, almost involuntarily, glanced over his shoulder to make sure the young gypsy hadn't somehow slipped into the room. "But I don't think it would be wise to go running to the police."

It was agreed, calling the police would be an unnecessary complication. Nevertheless, phone calls to the voivodeship's office* should be made the same day. Now that it was established that Kreskol was a real place, with real inhabitants, these matters needed to be attended to urgently.

Dr. Babiak took it upon herself to make the first call to the governor, and felt silly explaining it to the administrator who answered the phone.

"There's a secret shtetl filled with Jews which survived the war," Dr. Babiak said when she was asked what the call was about. "There's no danger, so far as we know. They're all living just as they always did. But we thought we should tell somebody about it."

The other end of the line was silent for several moments before the secretary spoke.

"What's a shtetl?"

And while the hospital spent months dithering to and fro, the wheels of government moved surprisingly rapidly. Several deputies called back, and the governor himself got on the phone a few hours later. He apparently believed that this little village had the potential to become a big media story—a modern-day Brigadoon, if you will—and everyone should be prepared. An elderly Yiddish translator was summoned from Warsaw, and several government officials descended on Our Lady of Mercy to interview the various parties involved. When they were satisfied that no hoaxes were being pulled, it was agreed that the government had a duty to visit Kreskol and welcome it to its rightful place in contemporary Polish society.

---

*A voivodeship is a Polish province and area of local government.

"The only thing left to do is to actually locate Kreskol," said Rajmund Sikorski, the slight, middle-aged official the voivodeship sent to Our Lady of Mercy Hospital. "We will take a helicopter over the forest tomorrow."

The helicopter took off from the outskirts of town and landed in the center of Kreskol the next day, and Yankel—who had left town as an expendable, acceptable loss in the course of finding the truly important people—was suddenly thrust into a heretofore unimaginable position of authority and wisdom.

The people of Kreskol had gathered in a crowd, the size of which Yankel had never seen before. They stared in stupefaction. They wept. And for the moment, Yankel was as puzzled as the gentiles. Then he heard one of the townspeople look at the translator and cry: "Moshiach!"

The throngs followed suit, shouting "Moshiach, Moshiach, Moshiach!" over and over.

For not the first time since he had left home months earlier, he realized just how simple and artless the people he left behind were. The poor souls. (Of course, three months ago Yankel would have no doubt had the same reaction.)

"What is going on here?" the Rabbi asked. "Is this the Messiah?" And Yankel began to explain what I recounted a few chapters earlier.

After the initial shock had worn off somewhat, it was decided that the succeeding business should be conducted in a less public setting.

"Who are these people?" Rabbi Sokolow asked Yankel, after the trio had been trotted into his study and examined by the old and esteemed of Kreskol. (The younger and less educated were crammed into Rabbi Sokolow's hallway, each with their ears pointed to the Rabbi's oak door eager to hear the miraculous news for themselves.)

"This man is Rajmund Sikorski," Yankel said, introducing the short, bespectacled gentile with the receding hairline who carried with him the aura of leadership. "He is with the voivodeship."

"And who is he?" Rabbi Sokolow asked, pointing to the aged, shrunken Jew who had jumped out of the chariot with the gentile.

"His name is Gerard . . . something," Yankel replied. "He's here to translate."

Rabbi Sokolow looked as if he tried to weigh his words before he spoke—anxious not to offend anyone's sensibilities, particularly one who might have the imprimatur of holiness.

"So he's not the Messiah?" Rabbi Sokolow asked.

The translator chuckled softly to himself. "No, I'm not anybody important," he ventured in Yiddish. (A more worldly observer would place his accent in Riga.) He then gestured to the gentile chieftain. "He's the important one." Which were largely the last words he would speak for himself.

"Good people of Kreskol," the translator said a few moments later for the chieftain. "I am here to fill you in on everything you might have missed."

Yes, we missed a lot.

I have sometimes lost track of what Sikorski told us that afternoon and what we later learned over the next few months, but the fundamentals of the last century were recounted: World War II; the Cold War; the creation of the state of Israel; the collapse of the Soviet empire; a man on the moon; the eradication of polio; the instant coffee powder (even if normal coffee was an unfamiliar commodity in these parts).

When Sikorski spoke about World War II, he was determined that we would not be left with the same doubts as Yankel Lewinkopf: He produced eleven photographs, which he placed on the Rabbi's wooden desk, for each man to examine for himself. "Millions died," the gentile explained, pointing to the glossy black-and-white images of Babi Yar, Auschwitz, and Treblinka. "Poland was almost completely cleansed of Jews."

As he said the word "cleansed," the gentile's face changed color, as if he had accidentally said something impolite.

We all nodded, respectfully, but I still don't think anybody truly understood the magnitude of what he told us—except, perhaps, Rabbi Sokolow and Rabbi Katznelson, who lingered over the photos longer than the rest.

"This was, of course, only the beginning of Poland's troubles," the gentile said through the voice of his translator. "For the next fifty years, we would live under the yoke of the Bolsheviks."

And with that he proceeded to tell us a condensed version of how Poland, from the late 1940s until the late 1980s, abided according to the whims and dictates of their neighbors to the east, and how cruel and unfair life was in those years.

The gentile was somewhat more animated talking about the Bolshevik calamity than the German one. He told us how the Bolsheviks had taken over the chess clubs and local sports clubs, how they printed phony propaganda sheets dressed up as newspapers and how even after neutering their political rivals they still had to steal elections rather than win them honestly. And I supposed that if anyone had a clue as to what a Bolshevik looked like—or what the term meant—we would have run screaming at their very mention.

Naturally, the names that the gentile sprinkled his talk with—Wladyslaw Gomulka and Witold Pilecki*—were forgotten almost as soon as they were spoken. But a visitor should be allowed to say his piece. Rabbi Sokolow didn't even interrupt him to ask if his wife couldn't, perhaps, offer the man a glass of tea.

We had questions—hundreds of them. And I am a little embarrassed to admit now that they were mostly limited to the contraption sitting in the center of our town. Nevertheless, the gentile patiently explained what he knew about air travel.

"I don't know very much about the mechanics of how a helicopter works," he declared after he had given us an abbreviated history of two Americans named Wilbur and Orville Wright, a discontinued airline called Pan Am, and a fearless pilot named Lindbergh (who was *not* Jewish, despite the fact that Reb Dovid Levinson said it sounded like a Jewish

---

*Wladyslaw Gomulka (1905–1982) was the first secretary of the Polish United Workers' Party; Witold Pilecki (1901–1948), a co-founder of the Secret Polish Army during World War II, was arrested and executed after the war by the Communist government.

name). "But I can tell you that it is *not* magical in any way. I can assure you of that. Not magical."

Nobody believed him.

"Now," said Rabbi Sokolow almost as if it were an afterthought, "what's this business Yankel said about the Messiah coming back to earth and the Jews returning to Israel?"

As he said this, we all turned to the boy in question, whose face reddened.

Shortly after the Polish government became interested in Kreskol, the doctors informed Yankel (with more formality than he was accustomed to) that now they had discovered evidence of Kreskol's existence they took it on good faith that his story must be more or less true and he would be returning to his hometown shortly.

"When will I go back?" he asked Dr. Babiak.

She shrugged. "Tomorrow—maybe the day after."

Yankel was frightened by the immediacy of this. He said nothing at first, but after several hours of meditation, he wondered if it wasn't too late to withdraw his request to leave the hospital.

Not that he didn't still think that the stories of mass slaughter sounded outlandish. But the doctors who had been looking after him (most of them, anyway) were honest people, who looked genuinely hurt when he said that he didn't believe their tales about World War II.

He liked things in the ward, where the climate was cool, even in the middle of August; where the bed was both firmer and softer than any he had ever slept on; where unpolluted water came gushing out of the faucet with a simple turn of a knob; and where everyone cared for his well-being. Maybe they are all crazy, Yankel said to himself, but does it really matter?

It was shortly after he had come to these realizations that he was led—almost by accident—to the topic of Israel and David Ben-Gurion.

None of the psychiatrists at Our Lady of Mercy had ever reached the propitious postscript in their retelling of the Holocaust. Perhaps they were too beguiled by Yankel's skepticism. Maybe the expanse and sweep of history exhausted them. It's possible they thought that if the young man was dubious of the wholesale slaughter of Jews, how could he possibly be expected to believe that a scrounging, scraggly group of refugees fought off a half dozen Arab armies to achieve the historical realization of their race?

Either way, when Sikorski arrived at the hospital for his interview with Yankel, he casually mentioned that the American and Israeli ambassadors would no doubt want to meet him, and Yankel didn't have a clue what he was talking about.

"What do you mean—Israeli ambassador?" Yankel asked.

"The Israeli ambassador. Jerusalem's man in Poland."

"I don't understand."

And after Sikorski realized that nobody had bothered to tell Yankel that the Jews had returned to their ancestral homeland, he took on the duty himself.

"The exile is over?" Yankel asked, incredulous.

Sikorski pondered this question for a moment.

"Yes," he said finally. "Some Jews prefer exile. But they can return anytime they like."

"When did this happen?"

Very briefly Sikorski explained the bare bones story of David Ben-Gurion, the Irgun, the 1948 War of Independence, and the subsequent wars and skirmishes Israel had been involved in ever since.

"It sounds as if this man, Ben-Gurion, was the Messiah," Yankel declared.

Sikorski sat unmoved for a few moments.

"I suppose."

Yankel felt dizzy and needed to spend the rest of the afternoon in bed.

Sikorski recounted the same story in more muted, sober tones a day later in Rabbi Sokolow's study, refusing to enliven the tale with anything that could be considered grandiose—he merely told us that the Jewish Agency (something he never really defined) bought up empty plots of land in the 1920s and '30s; he recounted the can-do spirit of the Russian and

Ukrainian Jews who had settled together in kibbutzes on barren swamps and marshes that they spent their lives draining and turning into farms; how the Jews had terrorized the British administrators of the land and made a successful appeal to the UN before fighting off invading Arab armies. (No one knew what "UN" meant, either, but nobody wanted to interrupt.)

"So Jerusalem is in the hands of the Jews?" asked one of the elders.

"Certainly."

"What about the Wailing Wall?"

"Yes."

"Has—"

The elder almost looked embarrassed by his next question, as if he were trespassing a little too deep into fantasy. He fell silent for a few moments before he decided that he could no longer resist.

"Has the Temple been rebuilt?"

For the first time, Sikorski looked as if he didn't know the answer.

"I'm not sure," he said. He asked the translator if the Temple had been rebuilt.

"No."

A short-lived sense of disappointment draped over the room.

It didn't last, however. Even if nobody uttered the word "Messiah" throughout the rest of the afternoon, we could see how Yankel made the connection. Few in attendance could feel doleful about much of anything. We didn't even feel the loneliness that Kreskol, out of all of the villages in Poland, had survived the German atrocity. Rather, the mood was celebratory.

Although the Rebbetzin and the rest of the women of Kreskol had been excluded from this meeting, they sensed the good news in the air. The wives and mothers all spent the day around dining room tables and asked one another, "What do you think is going *on*?" And they all arrived at the same conclusion: that whatever it was, it was a miracle.

The only disquieting moment came toward the end of the afternoon.

"I'll be back in two days," Sikorski said as the daylight began to wane. "Then we will discuss your future here."

These words sounded vaguely unsettling.

"What do you mean?" asked Rabbi Katznelson. "What is there to discuss?"

"There is much to figure out," the gentile said simply. "This town is important. It will be an important part of Poland, going forward."

"Why can't we discuss it now?" asked Katznelson.

"It will take a long time to go through everything," Sikorski replied. "I'd come back tomorrow and tell you all about it, but the weather is supposed to be crummy. And I'd like to update my colleagues back in Warsaw about our encounter today. It would just be better to wait until Thursday."

And with that, Sikorski and his translator thanked those who had assembled in the Rabbi's study, shook hands with Rabbi Sokolow, and walked briskly through the town, past the throngs of onlookers, and flew back to wherever he hailed from. The only thing he left us with was Yankel Lewinkopf.

Of course, nobody had known what Sikorski meant when he said that the weather was supposed to be crummy. The word he used—*brundy*—had been translated into *shmutzy*. More than one person assembled in Rabbi Sokolow's study wondered how this stranger could be so certain that the weather would be bad when there wasn't a cloud in the sky. However, the gentile had tossed off this pronouncement so casually—as if it was unworthy of additional commentary—that most assumed they had misheard him.

But when we woke the next morning, the sky was black and the rain was pounding down, turning the dirt roads into mud, springing leaks through the roof of the bathhouse, and compelling mothers of our town to keep their children home lest they catch cold, and the men who had been in Rabbi Sokolow's study that afternoon felt a shiver run down their spines.

One by one, they showed up at Rabbi Sokolow's study and asked the Rabbi what explanation there could be of this gentile's predictive powers.

"He's a wizard," declared Dr. Moshe Aptner—adding the flourish of noisily plopping onto a chair in the Rabbi's study. "He can fly. He can change the weather. He's clearly some master of the occult."

"He was too cosmopolitan to be a wizard," Rabbi Sokolow replied.

Dr. Aptner reluctantly conceded that Sikorski did not resemble your typical magician. But that was what made him potentially dangerous.

"I thought you were a man of science," Rabbi Sokolow countered. "Since when do you put stock in wizards and magic?"

And as the day wore on, others came knocking on Rabbi Sokolow's door, eager to offer their own explanation of the gentile's correct prediction. Most agreed that he must be a sorcerer who had conjured up the storm to rattle our nerves. "You don't think the flying coach was impressive enough?" asked the Rabbi.

After Rabbi Sokolow listened to the last of these convoluted theories, he went to his bookcase and examined the literature of Tsevi Hirsh Koidanover and Naphtali ha-Kohen Katz* for something concerning the human capacity for flight or for changing the weather. He couldn't find anything.

When the downpour had not let up by that evening, Rabbi Sokolow decided that he would need a better theory than the ones proffered, so he summoned Yankel into his study.

From the day he got back, it was quite obvious to us that Yankel Lewinkopf had lost his mind.

Not that he exhibited any of the outward signs. There was no muttering to himself. No furious scratching. No bubbles of spittle settling

---

*Tsevi Hirsh Koidanover and Naphtali ha-Kohen Katz were seventeenth-century Eastern European rabbis and Kabbalists.

in the corner of his mouth. No tics. He didn't scowl and harangue and rain curses down on us. He appeared more or less the same man who had left Kreskol three and a half months earlier, except that all the attention melted some of his natural reserve.

Still, he spoke like a nut.

An hour after the gentiles left, the luminaries of Kreskol led Yankel into the yeshiva and asked him to tell us all he had seen and done, lo these many months. (Rabbi Sokolow was not among them.) He told us of the great cities of Poland with their glass-and-steel towers, and their marvels such as moving paintings and horseless buggies and indoor plumbing. After an hour or so, everyone in the study house felt the discomfort of being in the presence of a diseased mind. The assembled men gradually began falling away until only Rabbi Katznelson remained—and even he came up with excuses around eleven o'clock to send Yankel on his way.

Not that Yankel knew exactly where he would go for the night. He thought of making a spot for himself in a corner of the study house, like one of the beggars, but Katznelson told him that he should go back to his grandmother's house.

"I wouldn't want to wake her."

"I'm sure your cousins are still awake. They'll let you in and find some place for you to sleep."

Katznelson began blowing out the candles and putting away books while Yankel quietly watched. When Katznelson was finished he led Yankel out of the study house and locked its doors, bidding him a perfunctory adieu. Even in the warm crepuscular night, the thought of returning to his grandmother's house chilled him.

He had forgotten how dark it got in Kreskol as he slowly made his way over the dirt and cobblestoned streets. The majority of the houses had gone to bed for the evening and were unlit. It forced Yankel to follow the light of the moon, and when he finally reached his grandmother's house, he had an unpleasant sense of déjà vu.

His cousin Gitel, her husband, Favish, and their seven children had moved in the day he had left. (Their brood had grown exponentially since Yankel had lived with his aunt and uncle.) And as he looked at the house, which still had a light burning, he wondered what it would look like now that so many months had passed. He thought of Zipporah, his grandmother. She had never been well, and his cousins certainly wouldn't have been able to give her the attention that he had. He wondered whether his grandmother—who was forgetful in the best of times, living in a different era populated by long-deceased relatives he had never known—would recognize him.

It was many minutes alone in the dark before he knocked on the door and was greeted by an astounded Gitel.

"Oh my!" his cousin nearly shouted. "Oh my! Look who's here!"

Gitel's face had grown fuller than Yankel remembered. She had always been a pretty, slender girl. In her early motherhood she had managed to maintain her figure despite the fact that she kept having more and more children, which she left with her husband when she went to the stalls in Market Street to hawk flowers in the summer and yarn in the winter. But for the first time, she looked less attractive than Yankel had remembered.

"Favish!" Gitel bellowed. "Look who's here!"

As the words left her mouth, an infant inside the house began crying.

Gitel's husband appeared in the doorway, also looking fatter.

"Yankel, my boy," Favish said, warmly. "Welcome home!"

The house didn't look very different, except in the mess that had accumulated. Cloth diapers were draped over a soapy washboard, which sat next to a small embankment of soiled stockings, trousers, shirts, and undergarments. Crumbs, dirt, and raspberry jam were spackled on the floor, the walls, the doorknobs, and the tabletops. Off in the corner Yankel observed a meek, undergrown chicken staring back at him.

The crying infant was brought out of its room to be comforted by its mother. With its hands blindly grasping around, and tiny legs kicking, the baby only added to the general sense of disorder that had taken hold of the otherwise familiar house.

"Please sit," Gitel commanded, cradling her daughter under her breast, and gesturing towards the wooden chair behind the dining room table.

"We've been hearing about you all day," said Favish, taking a seat across from his cousin-in-law. "All rumor, of course. Nobody knows what's true and what's false. But don't let anybody tell you, Yankel, that you're not an important man!"

Yankel nodded, politely.

"Well," Gitel said, "what was it like to fly in the air, anyway?"

Nobody had thought to ask him that question. He had almost forgotten how jarring the helicopter ride had been. Early that morning, he had been driven out to a small field on the outskirts of Smolskie and buckled into the back seat of the aircraft.

But as soon as the propeller began thrashing the air above, Yankel had misgivings. His head began to swim and his hands began trembling.

"Listen, bro," the pilot shouted, observing the greenish tint of Yankel's skin, "if you're going to puke, puke out the window. Don't get any in the cockpit."

A window was opened, and the unfortunate boy regurgitated over the forest the oatmeal, toast, berries, and banana he had eaten an hour earlier.

"It was fine," Yankel told his cousins about the helicopter ride. "You don't feel as good as you do on solid ground. In fact, you feel terrible. But it is, I suppose, something everyone should try once."

His cousins roared at that. Favish laughed so hard that the older children stirred out of their sleep and were led into the living room, where, one by one, they were reintroduced to their famous cousin.

"Tell us about what you saw in Smolskie," said Favish once the children had been sent back to bed.

And while Yankel might have been trusting and good-natured, he was no fool. He sensed the skepticism his story inspired among the wise of Kreskol. "There are no longer any Jews in Smolskie," he said—beginning with the most believable and relevant facts first. "And there isn't a marketplace there, either. At least none that I saw. There's nobody in the town that speaks Yiddish—not a single solitary soul."

"No Jews in Smolskie?" Favish repeated in wonder.

"No *marketplace* in Smolskie?" chimed in Gitel. "How is *that* possible? I can understand a town without Jews. They do it in China, don't they? But how does a town survive without a marketplace? That makes no sense."

"They make do," Yankel answered. "Everything is sold in a store."

Gitel rolled the thought around in her mind for a few moments.

"That's a bad way to run things," she opined. "If a fruitier wants to go into business he has to open up a store? That's such a commitment. What if, after a few months, he decides he's no good at selling fruit? What if he decides to sell fur hats instead? He's got to sell off a whole store's worth of inventory and then switch over? It sounds . . ." Gitel's eyes flitted around the room hoping, perhaps, to find the proper word hiding under a mound of dirty laundry. "Inefficient."

"I hadn't thought about that," Yankel replied.

Gitel laughed, heartily. "Well," she said, "if they hadn't gotten rid of all their Jews, these goyim wouldn't make such mistakes!"

Favish joined his wife in her laughter, which became so loud that for a moment Yankel was worried that the children would again come back out of bed, but this time they stayed put. And these tidbits were enough to satiate Gitel until morning—she announced that she and her husband were retiring.

"The children sleep in your old room, Yankel," Gitel announced. "And we sleep in the spare room."

As if Yankel were suddenly a minor among adults again, he became passive.

"Oh."

"You can sleep on the sofa tonight," Gitel continued, comfortable letting her cousin know that she considered herself to be mistress of the house with the accompanying privilege of doling out permission whether he could stay or go.

Yankel turned his head to the worn red upholstered sofa, which had several stacks of white linen on top and whose wooden leg the chicken appeared to be pecking at.

"Favish," Gitel commanded, "get the linens off the sofa."

Her husband obediently snapped to his feet and indelicately swept the flax sheets and tablecloths onto the floor. On his own accord, Favish disappeared into the bedroom and returned a minute later with a blanket.

"This should do for you," Favish said with a good-natured smile.

The husband and wife were almost out of the room when Yankel said, "Wait a minute—you never told me anything about Bubbe."

"Bubbe?" Gitel repeated. "What about her?"

"How is she?"

Gitel considered the question for a moment.

"Fine," Gitel finally said. "She's asleep now. But no problems to speak of. You'll see her in the morning."

Before waiting for Yankel to follow up, Gitel and Favish disappeared into their chamber.

Yankel sat in the living room for a long time and pondered the way his cousin had said, "You can sleep on the sofa tonight"—and his reluctance to challenge her. Not that he couldn't register an objection tomorrow. But Yankel knew enough about himself to recognize that he rarely asserted his rights when it came to his family, and felt a familiar, crushing sense of disappointment in himself.

His eyes surveyed the disordered living room. How, he asked, could his cousins have possibly kept his grandmother together in body and soul if they kept the rest of the house in such shambles? He had spent years feeding the old woman, wiping her mouth, cleaning up after her, and doing the thousand minor tasks that a feeble grandmother requires. They simply let her wallow in filth.

He silently got to his feet and opened the door to his grandmother's bedroom. The room was dark, but he could hear the heavy, labored breathing of the old woman, deep under the spell of sleep. He took a whiff of the air, to discern whether the squalor of the rest of the house had penetrated her room. But he smelled nothing peculiar. He stood for a few minutes, silently listening to each snore—just to make certain that it, too, was regular and normal-sounding.

As he closed the door to his grandmother's room—may God forgive him—Yankel was disappointed. The realization that his beloved grandmother had gotten along without him brought with it a certain measure of despair.

He blew out the candles, sprawled out on the sofa, wrapped himself in a blanket, and closed his eyes. As he lay there, he pondered how rapidly his life had changed, and then changed back.

His thoughts eventually returned to his time at Our Lady, but he didn't dwell on the comforts he abandoned, or the attention he received from the doctors—rather, he thought of one nighttime incident about which he had never told anybody, and which he sometimes believed to be an extremely authentic dream.

It was a reasonable precept. The incident had taken place during the weeks in which his moods rocked back and forth between extremes of fatigue and restlessness; when the doctors were trying new medications on him every day, prompting a new pattern of behavior. When he slept, his dreams were more vivid than they had ever been. He was mauled by wolves, chased by bears. He was trapped at the bottom of the ocean, or lost deep in the wilderness.

He also saw his long-departed mother in these dreams, at her healthiest and most vibrant, and upon waking he found his cheeks glistening with tears.

On the nights when Yankel didn't sleep, the unending hours exhausted him. Sitting alone in his empty room, he sometimes thought he saw little creeping insects out of the corner of his eye, startling him to attention. But after examining the entire room, from top to bottom, he slowly drifted back into a foggy stupor.

One such night, when he was too bored to sit still, he got up from his bed and wandered the halls. Tomas, the orderly on duty, knew Yankel and didn't bother scolding him for being out of his room after lights-out.

As he drifted near the padded cells of the truly insane where there were no knobs on the doors, Tomas said to him: "Take a walk by number five."

Yankel saw a single light coming from the cell. He looked through a square of Plexiglas at the door's eye level and saw a naked woman pacing the cell, gnawing on her wrist like an animal.

She was young, but not as young as Yankel—probably no more than twenty-four or -five. And although her eyes were wide, and her blond hair matted and unkempt, this mental patient was unquestionably beautiful. Her breasts were small, but her torso was toned, like that of a woman who didn't care for food or any other corrupting pleasure. She might have been mistaken for a child, if not for the thick, untrimmed thatch of hair on her pubis.

Yankel had never seen a naked woman before. He had formed his own vague ideas about what the female form must look like unclothed, but he was unprepared to be confronted with so stark a reality, and for a moment he held his breath, as if this vision would vanish once he exhaled.

The mental patient didn't notice Yankel at first. She had been pacing the room when Yankel passed by and continued her pacing and the frenzied but bloodless gnawing of her wrists. The strides that she took around her cell became wider and more furious—then shorter and slower. Her lips trembled, as if she were muttering to herself and alternating between kissing her wrists and biting them, but it was impossible to tell if she was actually speaking, as her cell had been soundproofed.

However, it wasn't too long before she sensed that she was being watched, and looked up to see Yankel.

At that moment, Yankel jumped away from the Plexiglas, horrified that he had lingered so long over a woman in so vulnerable a pose. Tomas, who was all the way down the hall, turned and grinned.

Still, a moment after he hid himself away, Yankel felt the urge to look again. He wanted to see if the woman was outraged (as he would rightfully expect) or if she was so insane she had simply resumed her crazed behavior. He peered through the window again.

The woman merely stared back at him, arms at her side. She stood proudly, as unashamed of her nudity as Eve before succumbing to temptation.

They gazed at each other for several minutes, neither party daring to utter a word, and Yankel felt a stirring in his loins. After a while, he simply backed away from the heavy door that kept this woman imprisoned and returned quietly to his room.

For the next week, he looked for this blond, brown-eyed siren around the ward and in the cafeteria, but could never find her. (Although, it should be noted, the dangerous inmates were separated from the harmless ones.) And when he couldn't take it anymore, he walked past her room one night to take another look, but the lights were out and the room was empty.

He meditated on all of this, back in Kreskol. After a sleepless hour passed he sat up, put his shoes back on, grabbed his tefillin bag and siddur,* kissed the mezuzah on the doorpost, and left his grandmother's house.

By the time he was out again in the streets of Kreskol, the remaining houses had gone to bed. The light from the moon had vanished under a quilt of cottony fog, and it was now so dark that you couldn't see a hand in front of your face. Yankel inched slowly over the cobblestones, trying to feel his way through the alleys and streets, and had trouble believing how much he had forgotten in less than four months.

And he realized this was the first time since that afternoon alone in Smolskie all those months earlier that he was the sole author of his fate. No one was checking in on him. No nurse would come by to tell him that it was lights-out. No one would wake him in a few hours. There would be no metal tray of watery scrambled eggs and potatoes for breakfast. He hadn't realized how dearly he valued his solitude.

---

*Prayer book.

At the same time, what was the point of freedom in a town like Kreskol, where everyone knows one another's business and his future was more or less written already?

Somehow, in this swirl of thoughts, his legs had taken him to the bakery where he had spent the bulk of his youth. Just then, the clouds opened and rain started crashing down.

He was not about to blindly wander the streets in a downpour until it was time to wake up. So he opened the door to the bakery, found a spot in the corner, propped his head up on a sack of flour, and waited to fall asleep.

Yankel was groggy the next day, walking around the bakery like a man who has weights fastened to his limbs.

Not that he was obliged to perform any physical labor—on the contrary, once his cousin Avraham entered the bakery, shaking the morning rain off his shoulders, and spotted Yankel gently snoring in a corner, he wouldn't let his famous relative lift a finger.

"Welcome back, cousin!" Avraham nearly shrieked.

From the moment the first woman came through the door, each one was giddy that they were in the presence of a celebrity.

"You look good," one of the housewives opined. "Big-city life agrees with you."

"So tell me, Yankel," said Rukhl Weingott, who had two daughters about Yankel's age. "Did you find some pretty wife while you were away all those months?"

For a moment Yankel thought Mrs. Weingott, who had always treated him superciliously, was proposing a match. And he instantly lost the words in his throat, because the eminently marriageable Weingott daughters were universally acknowledged to be beautiful and well mannered, with very decent dowries.

"No," Yankel finally said. "I didn't."

"Too bad," Mrs. Weingott said. "You should have looked. That was your big chance, no?"

Yankel hid his disappointment as well as could be expected. (Yes, even celebrity had its limits.) But throughout the day, more housewives came into the bakery, eager to talk to the boy whom they had always liked—or so they claimed—and pinch his cheeks and tell him how proud they were of him.

Only one woman cast a shadow over the good mood; Bluma Gutthof, whose husband had been among those who had crowded around him in the study house the night before. "Hey, Yankel! Are you really off your rocker?"

Yankel was, at first, too shocked to reply.

"I'm not off my rocker," he said quietly, feeling his cheeks go hot with embarrassment.

"What kind of question is that?" growled Avraham, who had been standing two feet away. "What's wrong with you, you old bat!"

Bluma shirked Avraham off. "Throw salt in your eyes, you big lummox," she told him. "I didn't say he was crazy. Others said it. Don't blame me."

"Get out of this store this instant!" Avraham bellowed.

Bluma left muttering, "Everyone's so touchy," and Yankel's mood quickly shifted from exhaustion to self-pity. Certainly, he had sensed that he wasn't entirely believed last night, but did his fellow Kreskolites think so badly of him that these things he was reporting could only be attributable to madness? (And while it was true, that was also what the gentiles of Smolskie thought of him, Yankel excused it away because they didn't really know him.)

Still, there were more pressing matters to worry about—like where he would be living, for instance. No doubt his relatives would come into the bakery at some point during the day to discuss it. They couldn't leave him in the lurch after he had so selflessly served as ambassador for our town. It was only right that the family make some effort at restoring his past, and they were no doubt negotiating among themselves a proposed arrangement. Besides, Gitel and Favish were probably frantic when they woke up and discovered that he was missing.

Good, Yankel told himself. Let them worry a little.

But as the hours ticked by, none of his relatives stopped by the bakery. The rain continued lustily slapping the roof until Avraham told Yankel that he didn't think there were any more customers coming today, and he would be going home in a few minutes.

"Wait," Yankel said.

"Yes?"

"Am I going home with you?"

Avraham looked surprised by the question.

"Why would you do that?"

Yankel considered this for a moment. He finally said, "Has the family been discussing me?"

"Of course. We're all very proud."

"No. I mean, have there been any conversations about where I would live, now that I'm back?"

Avraham looked taken unawares.

"Nobody's said anything to me."

The conversation might have stumbled along from there, and who knows whether Yankel would have sputtered with rage, or tears, but Avraham was saved when Beynish Salzman came through the bakery's front door and informed Yankel that Rabbi Sokolow wanted to speak to him immediately.

Yankel dashed through the rain (losing his footing at one point, and narrowly avoiding a puddle of mud) and to the Rabbi's court, where he was seated on the bench outside the study for a good twenty minutes and left to shiver. The Rebbetzin didn't feel compelled to offer Yankel a glass of tea or a towel.

"You can go in now," the Rebbetzin eventually told him.

Alone in his study, Rabbi Sokolow looked more imposing than he did the day before when he was surrounded by faces. Tracts and commentaries

Yankel had never heard of lay open on tables throughout the room. Yankel was almost afraid to sit on one of Rabbi Sokolow's chairs, on the off chance it might be too sacred to park one's backside on.

"Tell me everything you did and saw while you were away," Rabbi Sokolow said, dispensing with any unnecessary introductions, and not bothering to address Yankel by name. "Don't leave anything out."

Yankel proceeded to tell the Rabbi all I have related here, more or less. When he finished, Rabbi Sokolow sat quietly for a long time pondering these fantastic developments with a look of bemusement. Unlike the other wise men of Kreskol, Rabbi Sokolow didn't look dubious or skeptical about anything he had been told. Merely fascinated, forcing his great mind to probe deeper into these mysteries.

"Still," Rabbi Sokolow finally pronounced. "None of this explains how this fellow Sikorski can make it rain."

6

AUGURIES

The gentiles arrived in three helicopters the next morning, instead of one. Rajmund Sikorski was in the first, along with the interpreter (dressed in a blue suit and red tie so there would be no mistaking him for a messiah). But there were other strangers who arrived, too. A heavyset middle-aged gentile with a manicured gray beard who wore a homburg hat emerged from another. He was introduced to us as the governor. He immediately went to shake hands with Rabbi Sokolow.

An energetic, orange-haired Jew leaped out of one of the helicopters wearing a blue-and-white knit skullcap and the same sort of contemporary suit that the gentiles wore.

"Shalom!" he cried, extending a hand to Rabbi Sokolow. "The state of Israel sends its warmest greetings to its long-lost brethren!"

This Jew traveled with an aide-de-camp; a dark, muscular fellow, who looked younger and more serious, and didn't bother shaking anyone's hand.

In the third helicopter that had landed on the outskirts of town, there was a battery of reporters, photographers, and cameramen who sprung off the landing skids and hurtled toward us like they were bulls charging the matador. Questions weren't asked so much as growled, the only criterion for being qualified to answer such a question was that your eyes had fleetingly met those of one of the reporters.

"Tell us how you fed yourselves for a hundred years if you had no contact with the outside world?" one reporter shouted.

"Did the Nazis ever come through here even if they never rounded you up?" another asked.

"Who's the mayor of this town?" asked one of two female reporters, with as little delicacy as her male cohorts.

But those were the only questions that the translator would render back into Yiddish before the rest got drowned in the soup of voices and the blare of the local klezmer musicians, who it seemed had taken it upon themselves to spontaneously form in the town square with their clarinets and fiddles to give the occasion musical accompaniment.

"Now, now, boys," the governor said. "There'll be plenty of time for questions later. First things first."

There would be an official ceremony to reintroduce us into contemporary Poland, the governor said. Next, there would be a friendship ritual between Kreskol and the governments of Israel and the United States. He had a proclamation that came from the prime minister's office, as well as ones from the American secretary of state and the office of the secretary-general of the United Nations. Then Dr. Avi Fleishman, the orange-haired Israeli, would make a statement. "After that, you can ask all the questions you like—until two o'clock."

The reporters obediently silenced themselves as the photographers danced around the town square, flashing lights in our faces, while we stared back in mystification. (Esther Rosen's only comment when shown one of the photos was: "Is *that* how I look?")

The day went by in a whirl.

Nearly every mother brought her litter along to watch the spectacle, and the air convulsed with the shrieks and laughter of the young. The old were there, too, propped up on wooden canes and mopping their brows in the heat of the waning summer; their heads leaning forward to better see what they had never dreamed would unfold before them.

Some families came dressed in mildewy gowns and formal wear that they last wore on their wedding day. Many of the older women had spent the previous evening polishing brooches or stone earrings or whatever other family heirlooms they kept hidden away, which they proudly pinned to their breasts. Hawkers were selling fruit juice and small fig hamentashen.*

"Our hearts soar to learn that you have survived the onslaught of history," said the governor, who was the first to speak. "It is a miracle that you and your people continue your proud tradition within Polish history."

We all rocked with laughter when we heard that.

Even a people as ignorant as the Kreskolites knew the falseness of this. This isn't to say that nobody was acquainted with history's multiple instances where a particular fiefdom or county would issue a decree welcoming Jews to settle their land—so long as we didn't forget to bring our moneylenders. But other Poles felt very differently.

The governor was astonished that these sentiments should have been received so raucously.

"Why are they laughing?" he asked to no one in particular.

The translator shrugged.

However, the governor was seasoned in ingratiating himself with a less-than-friendly audience and continued praising the miracle of our survival until the novelty wore off, and the speech grew a little dull.

The American ambassador sent regards from the secretary of state and the White House and presented the rabbis with a certificate of friendship encased in glass and framed with gold leaf.

The representative from the Israeli government told us that we were welcome to visit the Holy Land, and that a delegation from our town was invited for an all-expenses-paid trip in the coming weeks. "You will be treated no less than a visiting head of state," the Israeli pronounced. "Have you ever heard of the King David Hotel?"

No, no one ever had.

"It's the finest hotel in the Middle East," he declared—before adding, "west of Abu Dhabi."

---

*Triangular cookie filled with preserved fruit, typically served on Purim.

No one had heard of Abu Dhabi, either.

All the while, the reporters who had accompanied them kept looking around and scribbling away on their notepads until it was their turn to ask questions and they barked at us as fervently as an unmuzzled bitch whose eye had been poked.

As it happened, in the middle of the press conference Rabbi Sokolow turned away from the questioners and found Rajmund Sikorski staring directly at him.

When they first met two days earlier, Rabbi Sokolow had been impressed by Sikorski. Maybe it was the glasses perched on his nose, which suggested a scholar (or, at least, someone educated), or his title—deputy head of dzielnica* affairs of the Szyszki voivodeship—which sounded important. But whatever the reason, Sokolow innately trusted him.

After their eyes met, Sikorski made a subtle gesture pointing behind him, as if to signal that the two of them should step away from the crowd.

Slowly, so that no one would notice as the questions continued, Rabbi Sokolow ducked away and started to move toward Sikorski. The aide-de-camp of the Israeli ambassador was standing next to Sikorski.

"We'd like to talk to you," the aide-de-camp whispered in Rabbi Sokolow's ear, in an accent the Rabbi could not place. "Privately."

Rabbi Sokolow nodded, and he led the two men away from the crowd and toward the yeshiva, which he suspected would be empty.

"Rabbi Sokolow," the dark Jew said, translating for Mr. Sikorski when the entire party had been seated behind three hard wooden chairs, "the Polish government is eager to improve things for Kreskol, and we wanted to let you know what you should expect."

Rajmund Sikorski enunciated slowly and waited for each sentence he spoke to be translated before he moved on. He was a careful sort of man; one could see it in the punctilious way he was dressed. His jacket and trousers were tweed; his white shirt was ironed and free from the wrinkles

---

*Polish: administrative.

that even the most dutiful laundress can miss; his bow tie—a ribbon of navy blue with small white polka dots—was knotted around his collar with the care of a person who paid attention to neatness.

"You have rights," the translator said for Sikorski. "And you have entitlements. For instance, every town in this district is entitled to be connected to the electrical grid. Do you know what that is?"

Rabbi Sokolow did not.

By way of demonstration, Sikorski took out of his pocket his mobile phone, dragged his fingers along its slippery glass-like screen, and shone a beam of light in the Rabbi's eye. (Not that a flashlight on an iPhone was exactly the same thing, but the details were unimportant.)

"We will run some cables through the town, and when you just flick a switch you will have light in your houses."

Perhaps Sikorski had been waiting for Sokolow to speak, but the Rabbi kept his thoughts to himself.

"You are also entitled to a clean water supply," Sikorski continued. "I saw some of the wells out there when we were walking through town, but it's a very outmoded way of collecting water. And I'm positive it's not as sanitary as it should be. There is a technology that will allow you to turn a knob and have water coming out of a faucet in your sink. You can have as much water as you like."

Rabbi Sokolow said nothing.

"The whole system of plumbing has gone through many, many advances. Nobody uses an outhouse anymore. We all have latrines built into our houses that flush away waste without you ever having to leave your home in the middle of winter."

Rabbi Sokolow's nose wrinkled in disapproval.

"Doesn't anybody complain about the smell?"

The translator grinned before he rendered the question back to Sikorski, who smiled faintly.

"Good question," Sikorski said. "I can promise you that the odor isn't the problem you assume it is."

The Rabbi looked skeptical.

"You are entitled to new roads, coming in and out of town," Sikorski continued. "Obviously, the roads in their current condition are useless for traveling to and from the rest of Szyszki. We will send a crew to clear out a path through the forest and create a service road which will be linked up to the highway."

The Rabbi said nothing.

"This will be a very large change for Kreskol. Maybe the biggest of anything else to come. Once you have working roads you'll be able to go back and forth to the rest of the province in a matter of hours—or less. You will be able to trade much easier with the rest of the province. You'll be able to get shipments of fruit and vegetables in the winter; all the things you want or need can be delivered here."

Rabbi Sokolow was unsure of how he should respond to this, but the two strangers had their eyes focused on him, and he felt he should say something.

"That sounds fine," Rabbi Sokolow said, with a nod.

"Kreskol will be included in the Poczta postal system," Sikorski continued. "When was the last time the town had a working postal system?"

At around the time that Kreskol's reputation began to fade, our forefathers found that messengers refused to come to Kreskol unless there was an exorbitant fee attached. Some messengers left for Warsaw with a parcel or a letter and simply never looked back.

"I don't know," the Rabbi said.

"Well, you'll have one soon," Sikorski said. "Poland has a system of socialized medicine. Do you know what that means?"

Rabbi Sokolow shook his head.

"It means that you're all entitled to medical care. If there is an emergency, the state is obliged to take you to the hospital. Now, we'll need to carefully weigh the pros and cons of how to address this entitlement. The hospitals in Smolskie and Szyszki are a long way off. Are we going to send a helicopter out here every time somebody breaks his leg? Or, would we build a medical clinic here? I have not looked at the numbers yet but this is one of the many questions we are going to have to discuss in the coming months."

"We have a doctor in our town," Rabbi Sokolow said quickly. "Dr. Aptner."

"Naturally," Sikorski said after hearing the translation. "But what training did he have?"

"Why, Dr. Bauer was the town doctor before Aptner," Sokolow answered. "He apprenticed Dr. Aptner. And Dr. Aptner's son is apprenticing with his father now."

"But Rabbi Sokolow," Sikorski said with a grin that might have been mistaken for glibness, "don't you see how much has changed in medicine in the last hundred years? The training your doctor has wouldn't take him through his first month of medical school at one of today's universities."

If Rabbi Sokolow had been inclined to like Mr. Sikorski when they were introduced, he did not any longer. In this lordly manner, Sikorski had just insulted centuries of Jewish medical expertise.

"That's ridiculous," Rabbi Sokolow hissed. "Was Maimonides a fool? Was Moses Tibbon* a fool? Jewish medicine is the best in the world."

"Naturally," said Sikorski. "I'm no doctor, but I assume that Jewish doctors formed the bedrock of much of modern medicine. Still, things have changed very significantly. There are machines now that can see clear through your skin and your tissue and look at your bones. A scientist today could take a little drop of blood from a pinprick on your wife's finger and tell you whether she's going to develop breast cancer in twenty years."

Rabbi Sokolow didn't answer.

"What if I told you that if we found this out in time, we could give her a procedure to make sure she would never succumb to that cancer? All those things are true, and much more. We are living in the greatest era of medical science in human history." For a moment, Sikorski seemed taken

---

*Thirteenth-century French Jewish doctor and author.

aback by the sweeping nature of his own declaration. But rather than re-
treat, Sikorski only seemed to grow more comfortable with the grandeur
of the idea. "A little cold could have killed a person a hundred years ago.
It's a minor annoyance now. Technology has saved us all."

The man no longer looked wise to Rabbi Sokolow. He looked like a
Cossack who was trying to explain how things proceeded in the afterlife.
It was slightly unnerving. Rabbi Sokolow suddenly felt the sweat in his
mustache and beard.

"I'm assuming that no one in this town has collected taxes in quite
some time, correct?"

Rabbi Sokolow shook his head.

"It's not something you should worry very much about," Sikorski continued. "I'm sure your holdings, assets, and revenues are such that you
wouldn't have much to tax right now. And no one in the governor's office
has expressed anything except sympathy for your plight. Tax holidays can
be granted. But you will have to pay taxes in the future. All this land will
have to be assessed.

"But I think you have many more potential revenue streams than you
know about. The reporters who are here right now are all convinced that
your story will be a popular one. It's a little early to start counting your
millions, but there's no reason to think that Kreskol can't become a tourist
destination. Poles, Israeli and American Jews, Germans, and maybe even
Russians will want to visit. You have a yeshiva system here, correct?"

Rabbi Sokolow nodded.

"Modern education is very different. The government in Szyszki is obligated to build a public, secular school in Kreskol for those families who
choose to send their children there. Not that the yeshivas will go away, but
there are standards that the yeshiva will need to uphold."

"Like what?"

"Polish, for one," Sikorski said. "Every child ought to learn the language of the state."

It was a reasonable enough demand, so far as it goes. While the Jews in town knew Polish a long time ago—back when we had gentile neighbors—it faded as Kreskol became isolated and hermetic. But like a vestigial tail that has outlived its original purpose, the language remained spoken as a slang around the marketplace. Every child learned it as a way of speaking blasphemes among themselves. The Aramaic teacher who died a few years ago offered to teach it to anyone who asked.

"The children learn Polish."

"Not well enough, I'm afraid."

Which was true. And, if Rabbi Sokolow's defenses weren't up, he might have even conceded as much.

"Nobody's blaming you for this," Sikorski added. "You haven't had contact with other Poles for a very long time. Learning it today is a lot like seeing a copy of a copy. But today, every student who sits for a matura exam must be proficient in Polish. And have a secondary modern language—English, French, German, Spanish, or Russian."

"What's a matura?"

"They're the standardized exams for higher education," the aide-de-camp offered, without translating the question for Sikorski.

"We don't need it," Sokolow said quickly. "Our yeshiva is education enough."

"Certainly, you may not *need* it, but the young should be acquainted with the basics, Rabbi Sokolow," Sikorski continued. "Judaism isn't everything. Every child should know their multiplication table, algebra, geometry, and trigonometry."

Rabbi Sokolow said nothing as the man prattled on about unemployment insurance and garbage disposal until Rabbi Sokolow felt compelled to interrupt him.

"Excuse me?"

The translator stopped mid-sentence.

"Yes?"

Rabbi Sokolow sat straight in his chair, perhaps remembering the days when he was a schoolboy in the same room and made to feel the same sense of dread when posing a question to a figure of authority.

"Can we say no to everything you're offering?"

A few minutes later, Sikorski could be seen sauntering through the town ahead of Sokolow, and not seeming to care if the aged rabbi kept up. Even the Israeli translator struggled to navigate through the bobbing eddies of humanity, all of whom had their attention fixed on the presentations in the center of town.

Sikorski caught the attention of the governor, raised his palm in the air, and spun his finger around in a few circles, mimicking the rotor of the helicopter.

The governor nodded and proceeded to step into the middle of this press conference. "All very good questions. We shall let Rabbi Katznelson answer this last one, and then that will be all for today."

The press groaned, as if they were a pack of children being put to bed.

"Now, now," the governor said. "There will be other visits. But we've already been here for hours. The people of *Krushkool* need to get on with their lives. I'm likewise certain that you have enough copy to file a story."

And in a matter of minutes, these strangers were back on their chariots and flying away. One of the reporters (a female one) waved at us as her helicopter slowly lifted off the ground. A few of the little boys waved back.

The afternoon was peculiar, certainly, but a few minutes after the chariots took off, everybody went back to work.

Only Rabbi Sokolow wore an expression different from all the others. He looked simultaneously worried and enraged.

"Are you all right?" asked Meir Katznelson.

Rabbi Sokolow merely nodded.

But Sokolow didn't acknowledge his colleague in any other way. He merely walked through the hot summer sun, until he was back in his study, and sat wordlessly down on the sofa.

The Rebbetzin also felt compelled to ask him how he was feeling.

"Fine," the Rabbi said. "Now please leave me alone."

It was a curter answer than the Rebbetzin was accustomed to, and for a passing moment she wondered whether it wasn't worth fighting about. But she was able to discern that her husband was troubled by something serious. She closed the door to his study, leaving the Rabbi's assistant, Beynish Salzman, out on the bench in the hallway.

After six, the door to Rabbi Sokolow's study finally opened.

"Beynish," the old man said in a voice just short of a growl. "Go find Yankel Lewinkopf at once."

Beynish hurried over to the bakery. Avraham Sandler was tending to the fires when he entered.

"I'm looking for your cousin," Beynish said.

"Haven't seen him all day."

"Do you know where he is?" Beynish asked. "Is he with your cousin Gitel?"

Avraham didn't take his eyes off the fires in the oven.

"He didn't sound like he had any interest in staying with Gitel," Avraham finally said. "And he's not at my house. So I have no idea where my cousin is keeping himself. He's not my concern. Maybe the beggars' synagogue, but your guess is as good as mine."

The prospect of a journey to the beggars' synagogue was not one that Beynish relished. It was a little clay house at the far end of Thieves' Lane, and Beynish—like others of his education and pedigree—had been warned against spending too much time in that section of town. It was where Lamkin Fogel sold cheap wine, beer, and vodka. Where the rag-pickers and beggars passed their days. Where the handful of drunks and thieves in our otherwise respectable village lurked when they didn't even have six pennies for a half-beaker of wine. And it was where two unwedded maids—Rifka Steinberg and Binke Singer—shared a hovel.

The only Jews who prayed in the synagogue there were too poor to afford a pew in Kreskol's Market Street Synagogue on Yom Kippur—or bastards, like Yankel, who had no place else to go.

As Beynish walked down the alley toward the synagogue he saw the heavyset figure of Lamkin Fogel step out of his tavern to take in the late afternoon air.

Even though Beynish had never spoken a word to Lamkin, this wicked man's reputation had traveled well beyond his footprints. Beynish kept his eyes on the ground and quickened his pace.

"Yeshiva bachur,'*" Beynish heard a low voice say softly.

Beynish kept his eyes down.

"I said," came the low voice, this time a little louder, "*yeshiva bachur.*"

Beynish might have kept walking if Thieves' Lane hadn't been a small, confined block. And he might have clung to the fiction that this ruffian had addressed someone else if the two of them hadn't been entirely alone.

"Are you addressing me?" Beynish asked.

Lamkin didn't answer.

"What do you want?" Beynish asked after a few moments.

Lamkin rubbed a lightly bearded cheek.

"Don't be shy," Lamkin finally said. "One zloty for half an hour, whether you're finished or not."

Beynish froze, as if the words couldn't be coaxed out of his mouth. All that came were burps of noise that the wisest of the wise could never discern.

"Help!" Beynish finally cried at the top of his lungs.

He took off running as fast as his legs would carry him, down the empty lane and into the beggars' synagogue, slamming the door behind him.

As Beynish caught his breath, he heard shrieks of laughter coming from the alley. The drunks of Kreskol emerged from the tavern to see what the commotion was about and they laughed, too, when Lamkin recounted

*Yiddish: "yeshiva boy!"

the story of the wayward yeshiva student who had lost his nerve the moment he was closest to his prize.

Rifka and Binke emerged from their hovel and listened to Lamkin's story, laughing even as they felt sorry for the poor boy. "Everyone has to have a first time," Rifka commented sympathetically. "It's never easy."

When he stopped listening to the gossip about himself, Beynish realized that the beggars' synagogue was empty. Humiliated as he was, Beynish would have to turn around and go back the way he came at some point. After a few minutes he decided to weather Lamkin Fogel's cruel laughter and try somewhere else that Yankel Lewinkopf might have hidden himself.

"It's no big deal, Yeshiva," cried Lamkin. "God himself commanded you to be fruitful and multiply. You'd just be doing the work of the Lord."

"I wasn't here for that," Beynish shouted over his shoulder as he continued walking. "You ought to be ashamed!"

This provoked another roar of laughter.

"What were you here for?" Lamkin asked. "To wrap tefillin* with the thieves?"

"If you must know," Beynish said, "I was looking for someone."

"Who?"

"Yankel Lewinkopf."

Lamkin, still rustling with joy as the rings of fat around his chest rippled and quaked, tried to calm himself.

"I haven't seen Lewinkopf," Lamkin finally said.

Beynish sharply turned and stomped out of Thieves' Lane, his anger multiplied by the fact that he had been humbled enough to ask these rogues for their help.

When Beynish had nearly gotten to the edge of the lane and out of earshot he heard a barely audible murmur, "I saw Lewinkopf." Just as abruptly as he had turned around to head back to town, he spun around.

---

*Phylacteries; a set of black leather boxes that are wrapped around the arms and forehead during morning prayers.

"Who saw him?"

An elderly drunk with a red nose, whose grayish blond beard had never quite filled in, stepped forward.

"Where did you see him?"

The drunk rubbed his nose. He reeked of vodka, and even in the summer heat he wore a long black coat that was caked with dirt. If Beynish Salzman had ever met the man before, he certainly didn't remember him.

"He's gone," the drunk finally said. "Got on one of those flying machines. Left Kreskol for good."

The drunkard belched loudly, which had the distinct aroma of onions.

7

SCHEMA

It was only by happenstance that Yankel fled.

After his late interview with Rabbi Sokolow the previous evening, he had been grudgingly invited to sleep on the bench outside the Rabbi's study. "For tonight only," Rabbi Sokolow warned. "I understand that you don't know where you'll go, but you shall figure out a permanent solution tomorrow. This is only for tonight and only because you stayed so late." When Yankel woke up the next morning, he was weary and stiff, and wondered why the Rabbi hadn't at least offered him the sofa.

It was the Rebbetzin who had roused him out of his slumber.

"Young man," she said, declining to address him by name. "It's time for you to go. The Rabbi already left for the marketplace."

He spent the rest of the morning wandering the empty streets of Kreskol like a drifter, frothing with rage.

He fumed about his cousin Gitel and her useless, moronic husband. And the aunts and uncles who had despised him all these years with no good reason. And the haughty, fool-headed rabbis who had no real idea of how the world had changed. And Rukhl Weingott, who thought her daughters were too good for the likes of him. And Bluma Gutthof, whose manners were something less than those of a billy goat. In his anger he didn't realize that these complaints were being softly mumbled under his breath, audible to any passerby.

"Are you talking to me?" asked one such passerby in Polish.

Yankel looked up and saw two of the journalists—one with a microphone, the other with a bulky video camera—who had slipped away from their colleagues and were lurking behind the bathhouse.

"No," Yankel replied.

One of the journalists—the one who had spoken—was not much older than Yankel. He wore a barbered, barely grown beard, and longish dark hair. The cameraman with him was a blond, stocky fellow a few years older, who wore a blue cap with a red "C" outlined in white that was stitched to the front.

"Do you speak Polish?" the dark-haired journalist asked, expectantly. His partner wordlessly swung the camera toward Yankel.

"A little."

"Aren't I a lucky man!" the reporter exclaimed. "Where did you learn to speak Polish?"

Yankel was, for the moment, almost afraid to speak—as if these men were delicate, fawn-like creatures and an imprudent noise would scare them away. He had told himself an hour earlier that there was nothing he could learn from the visiting caravan of gentiles. Besides, he had met enough gentiles to last a lifetime. But one doesn't need to be especially learned in matters of human emotion to realize that there was a self-protective impulse at work. He hadn't wanted to go to the town square to see the gentiles because he was afraid once the tears started they would never stop. Or that bile would come spewing from his mouth. Now that he was face-to-face with these two reporters he wasn't entirely sure what he would do.

"We all learn it," Yankel replied. "When we're young."

"I see," the reporter replied. "I don't suppose you were the fellow that they picked up in Smolskie, were you?"

Yankel reddened. The reporter reached into his trouser pocket and pulled out a folded sheet of paper.

"Is your name Yankel—Yankel L.?"

Yankel nodded.

The reporter laughed and looked at his partner.

"I suppose we're even luckier than we thought, right, Karol?"

The cameraman grunted something indecipherable.

"Well," the reporter said, extending a hand to Yankel. "My name is Mariusz Burak. This is Karol. We're with TVP Kultura. Do you mind if we ask you a few questions?"

Before Yankel had a chance to answer, a thought—a dazzling, glittering thought—came to him. The subsequent plot hatched in Yankel's mind in only a matter of seconds; as if he were a painter visited by the elusive ghost of inspiration. Yankel opened his mouth to speak, then closed it quickly, sucking air through his teeth, his mind reeling as these strangers stared at him.

Not every detail in the plot was filled in, mind you. He wasn't sure where to begin, for one thing, and was half afraid that he might destroy this delicate seed of an idea by getting off on the wrong foot. But he could see the larger canvas plainly. More than anything else, he had to temper the impulse not to smile too broadly or sing with joy.

"No," Yankel said finally. "I don't want to answer any questions."

When he was in captivity Yankel had learned the value of selective disobedience. Most of the time he did as he was told and took pains to be helpful and sunny. But he had also found that when a man with good manners raised an objection, it was treated seriously. He learned that when he asked to be returned home, the doctors around him made greater efforts to make him happy. (He also had to wonder if things might have unfolded much faster if he hadn't been so congenial.)

Now this glimmer of willfulness proved a shrewd opening move. From the moment Yankel said no, the reporters were so determined to keep hold of such a precious find—a Kreskolite who actually spoke Polish—that higher costs were paid than might have been under different circumstances.

Not only did the fellow, Burak, plead with Yankel, but the cameraman joined in. It would just be a few questions, they promised. They wouldn't include any personal details that he didn't want them to. It would make their story about Kreskol so much better . . .

The younger reporter, dressed in a white-and-blue checkered shirt and a pair of summer khaki slacks, would have been considered handsome if he wasn't quite so thin. The slightly older cameraman looked a bit more worn; and he didn't make nearly the effort that his colleague made to persuade. But Yankel was determined to make them wait before he said anything. He let them talk.

"I've got something better for you than answering some questions," Yankel finally said after several minutes had passed. "How would you like to know how a boy from Kreskol adjusts to the big city?"

Both reporters looked puzzled.

"Yes," Burak smiled. "That's exactly what we mean. We would love to get your story from your days searching out the authorities."

"You're not understanding me," Yankel said. "How about you take me with you when you go back to Smolskie."

Burak looked over to his partner, and then back at Yankel.

"We're not from Smolskie," replied Karol. "We're from Warsaw."

"It makes little difference to me," Yankel replied. "Warsaw is bigger than Smolskie, yes?"

"Certainly."

"Then Warsaw is even better. I just want to leave Kreskol, right away."

The two reporters again exchanged a glance—much longer than the previous one.

"You want to come with us to Warsaw," Burak said to himself more than to Yankel. "Why would you want to do that?"

"That's my affair," Yankel answered in a tone that surprised even Yankel. "If you just get me there, I'll answer any questions you like."

"Do you know anybody there?" the reporter asked.

Yankel shook his head.

"How will you survive? What will you do for money?"

It was a good question. And, admittedly, it wasn't one that Yankel posed to himself in the fleeting moments he had pieced together this on-the-spot proposal. Surely, they would never permit him back in the hospital, but he also assumed it wouldn't be too hard for a good baker to find a situation. No one had ever complained about his ability to knead a challah. He wouldn't mind working for low wages until something better came along.

"I'll make my way," Yankel replied. "But you can check in on me in a few weeks and I'll tell you all about my adventures."

The fact that Yankel used an old-fashioned word like "adventures"—implying that Yankel viewed himself as the hero of his own story—made Burak smile for a moment. If he had been disinclined to accept the scheme, this moved him slightly—ever so slightly—closer to Yankel's position.

"I'm not sure we're allowed to do that," Karol piped in.

"Why not?"

"Well, are you allowed to leave?" asked Burak.

"Who would block me?"

"Isn't that rabbi in charge?" asked Karol.

Yankel shrugged. "Maybe he's in charge of the synagogue, but he's not in charge of me."

The two reporters turned away from Yankel for a final time and stared at each other.

"All we'd be doing is giving him a ride, right?" asked Karol.

"That's ridiculous," Burak said. "The moment he gets on the helicopter, the other reporters will be all over him. And Sikorski isn't going to let us take one of these guys home with us like he was a lost dog."

For a moment, Karol looked resigned to the fact that his partner was probably right, and began nodding.

"Maybe," Yankel chimed in. He then pointed to the camera that Karol held on his shoulder. "But maybe they wouldn't notice me if I was carrying that."

Burak and Karol looked at the camera.

"And if I was wearing that," Yankel said, pointing to Karol's cap.

Neither of the gentiles spoke. They merely let the notion percolate. And a strong idea takes on a logic all its own. Before any better arguments had been proposed, Burak took note of Yankel's build, and concluded that he could probably switch shirts with him without it being too obvious. He had a pair of scissors on his penknife, if it proved necessary to trim this Jew's beard or sidelocks. And, yes, when he thought about it, there was room in the helicopter. None of the reporters who had flown in that day knew one another very well. At any rate, there were enough of them so that they could conceivably get away with it, as long as their secret passenger kept his head down and his mouth shut.

And there was no question it would make a fascinating story. Everybody in the press corps would be caught flat-footed. Besides, as Karol took pains to remind Burak, was this boy a prisoner? What law was he violating by giving the kid a lift?

So, yes, within a few minutes—and without much more coaxing from Yankel—the unlikely trio found a quiet spot in an empty alley and they cut off Yankel's beard. (Or, rather, did as good a job as one could expect when the whiskers are as uneven as they are on a nineteen-year-old.) With two big snaps they discarded the sidelocks that Yankel had been growing since birth on the ground without ceremony. After they had glanced over each shoulder to make sure nobody was watching, Burak and Yankel switched shirts.

When the press had all found their seats in the helicopter, Yankel was grateful to have the camera to cling to when the aircraft lifted off the ground and began sailing into the sky. The dizzying, sweaty feeling returned, and Yankel closed his eyes tightly and kept his head down, which proved helpful in keeping himself unnoticed by the other reporters—and which made Burak think the kid was sly.

The helicopter landed on a large square just on the outskirts of Warsaw, a few meters from a rail yard. The other reporters hopped out of the helicopter and went straight for the officials who had been flying in the other aircraft. But Yankel seemed much less troubled than Burak or Karol (whose last name he still did not know) as he ambled toward the trains without a care in the world. His two companions had to jog to keep up, looking as if they were the ones at risk of being discovered.

"So these are trains," Yankel said as he walked toward the enormous brown and red cargo cars, taking greater pleasure with every step he took. "Do you know something? I *had* heard of them. Even before I left Kreskol that first time. But I've never seen one."

Burak and Karol shared a confused glance, wondering if this weren't some pearl of wisdom that should be taken note of, or a non sequitur to be ignored.

"Yup, that's a train," Karol said. "Do you think I can get my camera back?"

Yankel handed him the camera and the cap without being asked.

"What happens now?" Burak ventured.

"I suppose we get away from the others as quickly as possible before anybody notices who I am," Yankel offered, as if he were the only calm and rational one in the bunch. His co-conspirators nodded vigorously, and in a few moments they were in the TVP Kultura van, on their way to downtown Warsaw.

Burak spent much of the drive into town wondering if he shouldn't offer to give this Jew some money, and maybe a bed to sleep in for the night. However, it occurred to him that by helping the guy out he would be changing the story.

"You got a place to stay?" Karol finally asked.

"No."

"Well, what are you going to do?"

"I'll get by."

Karol, who had been behind the wheel, turned to his partner and tried to catch his eye. "That sounds like a shitty plan," Karol finally said. "Are you going to sleep out on the streets?"

Yankel said nothing.

"That's ridiculous," Karol said. "You can stay with me for tonight. I've got a sofa that folds out."

Burak shot his partner a reproachful look, suddenly self-righteous and protective of the mores of his business.

"Thank you," Yankel replied politely. "Very kind."

8

TERRA INCOGNITA

Back in Kreskol, Yankel's disappearance was a low-ranked item on the long list of things we had to contend with, and after a few days nobody remembered much about him.

Shortly after Rabbi Sokolow's less-than-satisfactory meeting with Sikorski, the Polish government sent a team of officials to Kreskol to determine how, precisely, we "escaped history," as they put it.

These officials (two of whom spoke Yiddish) spent a week in the town archives, examining birth and death certificates, as well as the minutes of the beit din meetings, legal rulings, and various other archived materials.

Some of the documents were so old that they crumbled and dissolved into thin air the moment they were handled. "Uh-oh," said one of the Poles. The other two nodded, conspiratorially, but they were evidently prepared for such a contingency. Baby-blue rubber gloves were removed from their pockets, and small black boxes unsheathed. They pointed the boxes at these various documents and snapped a button before they proceeded with any further examination.

"What's that?" Kreskol's archivist asked.

"We're taking photographs," one of the Poles answered.

It was not a particularly illuminating answer, but the archivist simply continued painstakingly going through each page of our town chronicles as these strangers snapped many thousands of photographs.

When they exhausted all the material, the officials bid us farewell and visited Szyszki and Smolskie to examine the records there, before prowling through the yearbooks of the Central Statistical Office in Warsaw and tax receipts going back two centuries.

Three months later they issued a report, which I have taken the liberty of summing up here.

I should start by saying that we weren't always called Kreskol—back in the old days we were called Kyrshkow. Nobody, to my knowledge, has ever been able to say how long Kyrshkow stood, but at the very minimum it was four centuries old. According to the town archives, our founding dated to sometime during the reign of Casimir the Great*—but you have to take that claim with a grain of salt, as many laudable deeds were attributed to Casimir that he didn't really have a hand in. (Even the account in our archive was hesitant to commit to this as uncontested fact. "It was widely known that Kyrshkow was *probably* established under an order from the great Casimir," its author wrote, "even though the order itself was lost to history.") Nevertheless, Kyrshkow was solidly established two centuries later when Sigismund II Augustus** took his throne. By then, some government official had sent Kyrshkow a town seal and charter and begun collecting taxes.

We were a happy village, as far as it goes. One-third of the town was Christian, and the other two-thirds were Jewish, and all available sources indicate the residents of Kyrshkow treated one another with relative civility despite a mutual sense of distrust. Naturally, there was the occasional peasant who would lose his wits in a jug of vodka and go rollicking through the fields, hurling dung against barnyard doors, and unmaidening whatever unfortunate Jewess stepped in his path, but this was a relatively rare occurrence.

The Rabbinic Council*** sent a delegate to Kyrshkow every year to cer-

---

*Casimir the Great (1310–1370) was a Polish sovereign who introduced a legal code to the kingdom, founded the University of Krakow, and offered protections to Jews.
**Sigismund II Augustus (1520–1572) was the last male of the Jagellonian dynasty of rulers of the Grand Duchy of Lithuania.
***Eastern European Jewish organization that collected taxes and served as a go-between with local communities and government.

tify that we were milking our cows properly and butchering our chickens in accordance with the laws set down in the Talmud, and our record was unblemished.

Runners went back and forth from Smolskie every week, and peasants came out of the forest to swap silver goblets or pearl necklaces with our pawnbrokers. We sold grain in the market in Lublin, and if a relative set out to make their fortune in Warsaw, we received regular letters updating everyone on their progress. (These dispatches usually included a zloty or two for a widowed aunt or crippled brother.)

No, we were not isolated, exactly. (Or, not *extremely* isolated.) We were simple—and proudly so.

"And what's so bad with simplicity?" Rabbi Yeshkel Slibowitz—the Rebbe of Kyrshkow—asked in one of his surviving writings from a century and a half ago. "It is complication that is evil. Adam and Eve were perfectly happy with their humble, unadorned garden. It was only when they reached for knowledge, for understanding, for an ability to be godlike, that everything started going wrong. We here in Kyrshkow shouldn't want for more."

Reasonable enough, one would suppose.

In those days, however, it wasn't just gypsies, hard-up gentiles, tax collectors, and Rabbinic councilmen who would ferry through our town, but all sorts of other Jews who would stay at one of Kyrshkow's inns and tell us about the wonders of the world. "There's a machine that can take you from Warsaw to Paris in under a week," one such visitor told us. "It is called a railroad."

All the villagers knew that this was nonsense. "That'll be the day" was our reply. The man was obviously touched in the head.

That is, until another visitor came through who said the same thing.

"You people are behind the times," a rabbi from Krakow said. "These sorts of huts will be replaced by the end of the year. Any of you people ever heard of cement?" None of us had. "It's the way of the future."

There were other, greater inventions of the industrial age that seeped into our awareness in dribs and drabs. There was a contraption that eliminated the need for walking from location to location, called a velocipede. There was a miniaturized printing press that you could keep on your desk called a writing ball. And someone told us of a machine that could send a message from Paris to Lyon through the thin air called the pantograph.

When a peddler brought a sewing machine to town and demonstrated it before an incredulous crowd, our thriftiest mothers and grandmothers flew to the floorboards in their bedrooms or dug up the flower beds in their backyards, counted out their savings, and demanded a machine of their own.

And while we didn't exactly have a great stream of current events to worry about, the outside world's comings and goings made similarly dim appearances.

We learned of the brilliant French general who marched a gleaming, fully outfitted army through Europe—to military victory after military victory—only to have it destroyed in the Russian winter. We knew vaguely of the cadet uprising in Warsaw and that almost a quarter of a million men had taken part in the fighting. Several of our young men who had been sent to yeshiva in Warsaw came back telling everybody that a new prophet had been born in Trier. His name was Karl Marx and his evangel was entitled *The Communist Manifesto*—which the students handed out in Yiddish translation and Rabbi Slibowitz attempted to read.

"I don't understand a word," Rabbi Slibowitz said to one of the yeshiva boys who had brought it back.

"This is what will make us all equal, Rabbi," said the student. "This will result in the dictatorship of the proletariat."

"What's the proletariat?" the Rabbi asked.

"We are."

The Rabbi considered this.

"Who's this other fellow besides Marx?" the Rabbi asked. "Friedrich Engels?"

"A goy."

An answer that required no further explanation.

Still, there were other, more painful disturbances from the outside world, including the one that would end our relative normalcy and cast us into isolation and infamy. This happened shortly after two bombs were thrown at the Tsar—the second of which killed him.

The news came in the form of a telegram to the Tartikoff family. The telegram was the first of its kind in these parts (the telegraph office was all the way in Smolskie and needed to be delivered to the recipient by hand), and after giving Yochanan Tartikoff the message, the courier—a pinched, poorly shaven young fellow with brown curls—helpfully informed him: "It's customary to give a gratuity for carrying a telegram such a long journey."

Tartikoff handed him twenty groschen. The courier looked ready to spit in his face, but said nothing. He turned around and left.

The telegram contained within it a minor apocalypse: Tartikoff's brother, who had gone east to marry several years earlier, had been killed along with his wife and three daughters by marauding Cossacks.

Few supplemental details were in the telegram, but a stricken Yochanan Tartikoff came staggering out of his hovel and tried to catch up with the courier before he got too far away.

Tartikoff found him at the tavern, blowing the foam off a mug of ale before heading back to Smolskie.

"What's the meaning of this?" Tartikoff demanded, his voice cracking and his face white, waving the telegram in his face.

The Polish peasants and fur traders seated around tables stopped what they were doing to listen, but the messenger was less impressed with Tartikoff's distress than the rest of the tavern.

"How would I know?" the messenger said with a shrug. "I deliver them. I don't write them."

Tartikoff was in no condition to accept glibness for an answer; he grabbed the young courier by the lapels, spilling his beer, and demanded that he look at the dispatch.

"Take your hands off me," the messenger said, and he grudgingly lowered his eyes to the slip of yellow paper in Tartikoff's hand.

"Sounds pretty standard for what's going on in the east," the messenger pronounced. "Ever since that bitch Gelfman killed the Tsar, the rest of the Jews are taking their lumps."

The tavern continued to stare at the messenger, who, now that he had an audience, felt compelled to explain things.

Among the nine conspirators in the assassination of His Imperial Majesty, Alexander Nikolaevich Romanov, King of Poland, Grand Duke of Finland, Emperor of Russia and Sovereign of the Order of St. Andrew, was a woman by the name of Gesya Gelfman. Gelfman's status as a daughter of Israel was highlighted in the press accounts of the crime, as well as stories about her subsequent conviction and the scandal that she was four months pregnant when the sentence of death by hanging was read. But Gelfman's lineage freed the great Russian masses to commit every dark fantasy that had ever entered their minds upon their Jewish neighbors.

"It's the end of things for the Jews of Russia," the courier explained. "They're doing it in every town. Swarming the Jewish homes. Clubbing the men to death. Raping the women. Cutting the throats of the children. And burning the houses to the ground after, so they don't have to ever think about it again. It's everywhere. And it's spreading like yellow fever."

For the Jews in Kyrshkow, this episode presented a serious crisis.

After all, what was to prevent our neighbors on the other side of town from getting it into their heads to do something similar to the Jews of Kyrshkow? Some of the Poles listening to the courier's account looked as if they were already angry and indignant.

Father Klement Nowak, the priest at the massive, blue-and-white-domed rectory on the other side of Kyrshkow, made no secret of the fact that he despised Jews from the very depths of his soul and believed that each and every one of us was personally responsible for the murder of Jesus Christ.

He was not the first to spread such slander, nor would he be the last, but he did so with unequaled zeal. According to Father Nowak, the Jews were akin to a vampire cult and we each had a consuming desire to kidnap whatever Christian child we could lay our hands on and drain them of their blood. "The devil walks among you," he was known to say in mass. "And the devil—whose cunning knows no bounds, whose treachery is always at work, whose evil is never satisfied—has figured out the best way to disguise himself: He has split himself into hundreds of different people. He is in the soul of every single Jew in Kyrshkow. He spends every night sitting in his synagogue, plotting ways to murder you. Every last Jew—man, woman, and child—is guilty! Take heed, good people, for safety's sake! Do not let these monsters destroy you!" (Father Nowak's sermons were so inflated in their disgust for Jews that even the peasants—never known for their great subtlety—sometimes laughed at the depravity supposedly under way on our side of town.)

Some suggested that a visit be paid to Duke Boleslaw Szyszki and that we get assurances that he would send his royal guard to protect us if things turned violent—but the idea was eventually dismissed. The collective wisdom was that Duke Boleslaw was not nearly as well disposed toward the Jews as his father, Slawomir, had been.

There had long been a story that after discovering one of his prized hunting dogs poisoned, the Duke cast his eye on his Jewish estate manager as the most probable culprit. He ordered his Jew slowly tortured to death over the course of the next several weeks in the hopes of extracting a confession. The estate manager's fingernails were pried out; his kneecaps were smashed with a big wooden mallet; he was lashed with leather whips and his left ear was cut off. However, even in his agony he refused to confess. It was later discovered that the dog had broken into one of the silos and gnawed through a block of poison that had been meant for the rats. No apology or restitution was made to the estate manager's widow.

But in the absence of a strategy, Kyrshkow's Jews collectively held their breath, waiting for the firestorm that was expected.

The gentile burghers of Kyrshkow, sensible enough to know that there were no horns hiding under our skullcaps, warned us that Father Nowak was acting giddy; like a twisted child presented with a kennel of helpless kittens. On the Friday night before his sermon, he had retreated into the rectory with pen and paper, a lusty expression on his face. He gave instructions that he was not to be disturbed for thirty-six hours.

It got around town that "no one should miss Father Nowak's mass" that week—and that there would be at least one surprise from the pulpit.

When he heard this, Rabbi Naphtali Slibowitz (son of the late Yeshkel Slibowitz) heaved a great sigh of nervousness.

On the Sunday in question, Father Nowak was said to have had a glint in his blue eyes. He carefully observed the peasants file into the pews, and when he was satisfied that the church was full and that nobody of importance would miss his exhortation, he picked up a silver pitcher of holy water and began the mass.

But the Lord works in mysterious ways. Before Father Nowak finished the asperges the priest suddenly stiffened. His head jerked up straight, and the wisp of rust-colored hair that was normally brushed neatly over his otherwise bald head fell in a mess over his forehead.

The parishioners fell silent, sensing something was wrong. The priest wavered from his left foot to his right foot. He opened his mouth to give the next invocation but the silver pitcher tumbled out of his hands.

Before anybody had a chance to see if Father Nowak was all right, he keeled over, landing on the carpet with a great thud. It's written that man is born so that he might die, and Father Nowak succumbed to the universal fate.

Some might have expected us to be overjoyed, but when we heard of this on the Jewish side of Kyrshkow, our jitters only intensified. There would surely be some hotheaded peasant who would take it into his head that the Jews had somehow hardened Father Nowak's arteries. And when one hothead goes on a spree, he almost always lures confederates to follow. Calls for revenge were inevitable.

"If there is a way to blame us for this," one of the Jewish housewives opined, "believe me, those mamzers will find a way."

A meeting of town elders was convened in the synagogue and our pending doom was put up for discussion.

"We should move to America!" someone shouted.

"All of us?" replied Rabbi Naphtali Slibowitz.

"Why not?"

"Well, for one thing, none of us know English."

A minor quibble.

"We can learn," said Reb Lev Sanders, who had made the suggestion.

"How are we all going to afford to go?"

Which was a relevant concern, certainly. Steam tickets for more than a thousand men, women, and children would be expensive—and we were not exactly a wealthy village. (That's not even taking account of the inevitable exit visa problems and paperwork we would encounter. Or the fact that plenty of the grandmothers and grandfathers couldn't dream of taking a weeks-long land-and-ocean voyage at their advanced age.)

"We should start a new town," someone else suggested. "In the middle of the forest. Away from all these gentiles. Let's begin again from scratch."

Rabbi Slibowitz's eyebrows rose up into his forehead and he stared quietly at the assembled elders for a few moments before he spoke again.

"Does anybody have a more realistic suggestion?"

The synagogue fell silent.

When the meeting ended, it was agreed that the elders should go home, rack their brains, and reconvene in a week, hopefully with better ideas of how to proceed.

You could probably guess how quickly word spread among the Christians that we were Father Nowak's slayers. By Sunday evening the town was atwitter with rumor and innuendo. The more affluent families didn't wait to hire wagons and coaches to take them to Hamburg, where passage could be secured to America. Others began selling off farm equipment and furniture and family heirlooms, with the expectation that they would have to also flee in the near term.

But then something peculiar happened. Rather than careening onto our side of town with knives and clubs and letting themselves run amok, the Christians of Kyrshkow were utterly discomposed.

When a Jewish butcher or a cobbler or a blacksmith crossed Market Street and went into the Christian part of town, the old women would turn white and cross themselves furiously. The chandler's hands would tremble when a Jew would come into his shop and ask for candles. When the Jewish children would play along the cobblestone streets mothers would come running out of their hovels to scoop up their little boys and girls and bring them back home, lest one of these young monsters lay a curse on them, too. Almost overnight the goyim of Kyrshkow had become frightened of us.

Of course, the gentiles were always afraid of us in some sense. Long before Father Nowak had taken the pulpit they had heard the outlandish stories from his predecessors about all the evil that Jews hatched away from Christian eyes. For generations the priests had said that we poisoned drinking wells. That we were vampires who sucked the lifeblood out of gentiles. (Or, alternatively, that we used the blood of Christian children in our matzahs, depending on which priest you consulted.) They warned their daughters about the lasciviousness of Jewish men and told them they would be kidnapped and sold into white slavery if they responded to our courtesy. They said that we kept millions squirreled away in secret hiding places, and that when the town was asleep and the moon was out, we would commune with the devil.

Still, a legend—an outrageous legend, one filled with the improbable and the occult—takes on a different dimension when it starts unfolding before your very eyes.

While the Jewish evildoers might be only a few hundred feet away, it was also acknowledged our mischief was many hundreds of years in the past. No Christian in Kyrshkow could point to any specific child who had been abducted and found murdered in the forest. No poison had ever been found in the water supply. No devils or dybbuks* had been spotted stalking the graveyard during the witching hour.

In the instance of Father Nowak's death, however, the gentiles of Kyrshkow believed they had witnessed an unambiguous use of black magic, and when faced with this stark reality many of the Polish braggarts and bullies became fearful. If they did decide to run riot on the Jewish side of Kyrshkow and smash up Jewish businesses, beat Jewish men to death and rape Jewish women . . . well, what would the Jews do to them in return? It was a question they apparently never considered before and it tied their stomachs in knots.

So not only did the attack that we had been awaiting never come, but the exodus that was expected unspooled in reverse. One year after Father Nowak's death, no clergyman had been sent to take his place. Suddenly, the gentiles of Kyrshkow were less sentimental about their hometown— they began talking of the village like it was a backwater.

A year later, a factory opened up outside Smolskie that was in need of hearty young men, and hundreds picked up and left.

The next year, two more factories broke ground and the young men who originally beat a path to Smolskie sent for their younger brothers and cousins. Soon, Smolskie was like one of the boomtowns of the old west, and those looking to bid farewell to the demonic Jews of Kreskol now had the ideal excuse. Young women followed the eligible men, and elderly parents followed their adult children.

Then slowly, over time, those who hadn't found a spot in a city vanished into the forest where the swamps could provide anonymity and where game and vegetation was plentiful enough to live on. There were, after all, hermits and mountain people who had lived in the woods for centuries. Better in the wilds, these gentiles reasoned, than sharing their town with demons. Within a decade, there were only a few dozen gentiles still living within the medieval walls of our town. Some of these goyim had begun

---

*Yiddish: an evil spirit.

growing beards and stopped butchering their hogs. They began speaking in Yiddish, rather than Polish, and would disappear completely a decade later—either into the woods, or into our synagogues.

God be praised, the Jews of Kyrshkow were spared!

While I'm sure that this ironic twist of fate may strike some readers as the moment when the Jews of Kyrshkow should have felt most triumphant and smiled upon by good fortune, in truth we never really felt that way.

In the ensuing years, we felt our abandonment was much more a curse than a blessing.

For one thing, with the gentiles of Kyrshkow no longer tilling the land and producing the kind of abundance we had grown accustomed to, the price of food shot up almost immediately.

The vendors who were still able to secure vegetables gouged their customers—they charged three times the normal price and refused to give any goods on credit.

Odder still, the next summer the price of everything else went way down.

Because the price of food had risen so dramatically, nobody had any money to spend on anything else. The Jews assumed it was wiser to save than spend, and everybody from shoemakers to ironsmiths was forced to offer their work for a song.

Rabbi Slibowitz insisted that the solution to this was to take over the abandoned plots and produce as much food (the one commodity that remained expensive) as possible. Several families began planting peas and onions and carrots and cauliflower and beets and dozens of other crops on the unused land—which meant that food was suddenly plentiful again. But this only dropped prices on everything, including food.

The price of a challah was cut in half. And the baker offered house-wives the use of his oven to heat up Sabbath pots—just on the off chance that they would feel charitable toward him and perhaps buy an extra loaf. The shoemakers offered three pairs for the price of one. Yussel Schactman, the coachman, shot and killed his horse, Blueberry, because nobody was using coaches anymore and Schactman could no longer afford to feed the poor creature. He sold Blueberry's remains to the gypsies, who apparently didn't observe any taboos about the consumption of horsemeat.

We probably could have endured all this and more, but in a parting gesture of contempt, the gentiles of Kyrshkow proceeded to ruin our reputation in the cities with which we did the most trading.

It is always impressive how quickly gossip can take root and bloom; it has the wherewithal and adaptability that no crop can match. Even plagues of pestilence can be wiped out over time, but not gossip. Almost immediately after Father Nowak's death, the whispering began in the Smolskie marketplace that Kyrshkow was an evil town—filled with wizards and witches—and thereafter nobody would buy grain, which might very well have been contaminated by whatever voodoo the people of Kyrshkow bestowed on it.

This mumbo jumbo was not confined to the gentiles, mind you. Other Jews seemed to think there was something awry, too. Even the sensible and educated believed that we conspired to head off a pogrom by poisoning our chief antagonist. The legend arose that the night before his sermon, a Jewish boy had been sent into the rectory and instructed to spike the holy wine with cyanide.

Rabbi Naphtali Slibowitz became a character of mythical villainy among the Jews of eastern Poland. He was called a charlatan. A ruffian. A disgrace to his sainted father. An atheist. A thief. A murderer. And a dozen other vile things I won't bother to mention.

Aside from the accusations that he had murdered Father Nowak, others arose that Rabbi Slibowitz was practicing some sort of heretical brand of Judaism—one part based on the apostasy of Shabbetai Zevi, one part on the debauchery of Jacob Frank, one part Karaite, and one part Zoroastrian.*

We supposedly engaged in wild orgies in which not only did men sleep with a dozen or more women at once, but men slept with other men, and women slept with other women. Children as young as eight years old were encouraged to join the depravity. Mothers were married off to their sons. Fathers to their daughters. Brothers to sisters. Marriages between first cousins were permitted, so long as Rabbi Slibowitz gave his blessing, but marriages between non-relatives were forbidden.

We were said to throw dinner parties with free-flowing wine and vodka in which the candles would be blown out in the middle of the main course, and men would blindly swap wives with each other.

And if our degeneracy would have sickened any gentile man or woman, they were doubly revolting to Jews.

Just to prove our defiance, we made Shabbat the one day of the week in which we'd work, and the rest of the week we treated like Purim. We lit enormous bonfires after dark on Friday night and broke every law and commandment we could think of (from gathering sticks, to handling money, to writing out long legal documents). Then, from Saturday night until the following Shabbat, we idled away in our drunken sexual romps.

Finally, we had erected in the center of Kyrshkow a statue to a pagan goddess Demeter, which stopped the flow of Jews willing to go through our depraved town, lest their pious eyes be defiled by our excesses.

When the rumors came back to us, we were stunned. "How could anybody believe such nonsense?" Rabbi Slibowitz would say. But when our merchants would go into Bialystok to sell our goods they were turned away without even uttering a word. Any Kyrshkow face was instantly shunned.

---

*Shabbetai Zevi was a seventeenth-century Turkish rabbi believed by many Jews to be the Messiah, until he converted to Islam; Jacob Frank was an eighteenth-century Polish Jewish figure (ultimately excommunicated) who preached a mixture of Christianity and Judaism advocating "purification through transgression," i.e., sexual swinging; the Karaites are a sect of Judaism that rejects the Talmud; Zoroastrianism is one of the oldest Middle Eastern religions.

"Get out of here!" the Bialystokers would growl, and chuck rocks, or to-matoes, or eggs at the merchant's head. "You people are animals!"

The Rabbinic Council sent an expedition out to Kyrshkow to get to the bottom of these rumors, and the head of the delegation supposedly was taken aback at how unchanged everything had been in our town. "What's been going on here?" he demanded.

"Nothing!"

The delegate looked downright perplexed that a town with such a bad reputation could look so normal and upstanding.

"What's this business with Father Klement Nowak?" the delegate asked after he had poked his nose through the slaughterhouse and the synagogue and the mikvah and the inns and the tavern and every other place he could think to look for signs of transgression. "How did he die?"

"Nobody knows, exactly," said Rabbi Slibowitz. "None of us were there at the time. But it sounds like he had a stroke in the middle of his sermon."

"And what did you do to him before the sermon?"

"Nothing at all!"

"How do you know? Have you spoken to everybody in town?"

"Of course not, but sometimes people just have heart attacks or strokes, don't they?"

The delegate frowned, not seeming particularly satisfied with the re-sponse, but that was the toughest questioning he would venture. When he left town a few hours later, he told Rabbi Slibowitz his report would be favorable, which it was. The Rabbinic Council ruled that we had been the victim of lashon hara* and that nobody should have any reason not to do business with us or stay the night in a Kyrshkow inn. We were given an official pronouncement, signed by five rabbis, and written on sheepskin parchment, with all the necessary legalese to make it sound important. A fat lot of good it did.

---

*Hebrew: literally "evil tongue"; malevolent gossip.

Just as a young girl who gives in to the pleading of a frisky boy will never again be thought of in quite the same manner—no matter how many paupers she feeds—a bad reputation will stick to a town until the day its last hovel burns to the ground.

When our merchants would drive their wagons through the Bialystok market the Bialystokers remained determined to have nothing to do with us. "Didn't you hear?" our merchants would plead. "We did nothing wrong. The Rabbinic Council said so."

The grain merchants would shrug, if they deigned to do that much.

After another year in which Kyrshkow failed to interest anyone in our grain or our furs or our produce or anything else, the town fathers sat down and tried to figure out how we could save our town from economic oblivion.

"What if we change the name of our town?" asked Reb Simon Gluck.

The town fathers hadn't considered this, and there was a moment of silence as the various elders stroked their beards, furrowed their eyebrows, and drank in the suggestion. An hour later everyone agreed that this was Kyrshkow's only hope—even if its chance of success was slender.

A petition was sent to Duke Boleslaw Szyszki's court for the change to be made official, along with a request for a new town seal and charter, and the people of our village were instructed to start throwing the word "Kreskol" into conversation whenever they could—just so we could become accustomed to the name. The record is spotty in terms of who came up with the word "Kreskol," or what it meant, but it was agreed that the name sounded good, was easy to remember, and was close enough to the original that the transition wouldn't be too tough.

Perhaps because he thought he was setting a good example (or maybe because his name had become so speckled with mud in all the swirling gossip), Rabbi Slibowitz announced that in the spirit of change, he, too would alter his surname from Slibowitz to Sokolow. Furthermore, like our great ancestor Jacob, he would adopt Israel as his given name.

A festival was planned that summer to inaugurate the new name. The town square was prepared for dancing, and little Elkana Sanders composed a ditty for his fellow yeshiva students to sing:

> *Kreskol, Kreskol—*
> *My heart belongs to thee!*
> *Kreskol, Kreskol—*
> *Wait until the Warsaw lasses see!*
> *Kreskol, Kreskol—*
> *No town under the sun is finer.*
> *Let them sing it atop the mountaintops*
> *With voices ablaze with fire!*

A great display of honey cake and rugelach and babka* and bagels was planned, along with a table full of lox and pickled herring and sable and pike. It was all, of course, free for the taking.

Tevye Berkowitz practiced juggling knives and forks, and the wedding jester prepared jokes and magic tricks. The young girls of Kreskol took out their holiday clothes, ironed out their wrinkles, and stitched up whatever the moths had eaten.

Several days before the festival, a handful of the more boisterous yeshiva students were dispatched to the marketplaces in Smolskie, Bialystok, Krakow, and Duke Boleslaw's court to tell their fellow Jews of the festival in Kreskol. "Come one, come all!" they chanted, like a pack of carnival barkers. "The first annual Kreskol summer festival! Help us inaugurate the new village of Kreskol in the great Duchy of Szyszki! Entertainment, food, and cider will be provided for all, absolutely free of charge!"

Most of the Jews in other villages who heard this announcement were unsure of what to make of it, exactly.

"Where's Kreskol?" they would say. "Never heard of it."

Some thought that this announcement sounded like a ruse; an effort

---

*Rugelach are small, rolled-up pastries; babka is a yeast cake.

to lure a group of helpless saps into the forest where they could be robbed outside the eye of the law.

"How will we get there?" several asked.

I'd like to think that if coaches and wagons had been provided, it wouldn't have made much difference, but who can say? The yeshiva boys who were asked this question turned red and stammered some evasive response.

"It'll be up to every man to find his own way there," one of the yeshiva boys answered confidently. "It's not like we can take care of everything." But he was the only one who had enough chutzpah to respond with conviction.

When the festival arrived, few outsiders visited our little village. Those who did were mostly schnorrers,* who didn't mind a long journey because they had no place better to go, and didn't mind running the risk of being robbed, as they had nothing worth stealing.

A few of the hermits and mountain people also came out of the forest and helped themselves to glasses of cider. When they were tipsy and sated they staggered back into the woods and we never heard from them again.

The festival was deemed a disappointment if the idea had been to lure visitors back to our town.

However, the Jews of Kreskol felt a great deal of pride in their "new" town. And when the summer moon appeared and we were in the throes of the cider and dancing, everything seemed right with Kreskol—even if the baker, the fisherman, the winemakers, and everyone else lost money on the festival.

It would be the last time our little village would make an effort to reach the wider world.

Loneliness can be an affliction, like typhus or pneumonia—and it wasn't long before Kreskol came down with a serious case of the disease.

---

*Yiddish: moochers.

The longer our village stayed undisturbed by the outside world, the more we grew to resent it and all its emissaries.

No longer did the people of Kreskol think with envy back on their brothers and cousins who had had the money to abandon the town for America. Instead, we began remembering them with sadness; as if they were poor besotted creatures who had never made it all the way across the ocean, but whose ships had sunk halfway and now lay in a watery grave.

In the ensuing years, we grew extremely proud of Kreskol's natural beauty in a way that we had never been before. While we still exhibited all the natural prejudices of our race in favor of the life of the mind over nature and physical exercise, we encouraged Kreskol's young to roll up their sleeves and hike the nearby mountains, or swim our streams. "Go out and get some fresh air," mothers commanded. (So long as they left the forest alone.) Their children obeyed.

Tilling the soil, we realized just how fortunate we were: Whoever it was who founded Kreskol all those centuries ago had picked an excellent plot of land if cultivation and agriculture had been his chief concern.

Even as the economic wind seeped out of our sails, the earth beneath Kreskol kept producing its abundance year after year. Fruits and vegetables appeared every summer, along with corn and grain. A stream flowed a few hundred yards from our town square that was stocked with fish, and helped us irrigate our crops during the droughts. Our cattle and goats and chickens took the invocations of Genesis seriously and multiplied.

In short, if loneliness was to be our lot, we could survive it well enough, thank you very much.

However, long after the infamy of Kyrshkow died down in the marketplaces of Bransk and Bielsk—long after the names of Rabbi Israel Sokolow and Father Nowak and Duke Szyszki had been forgotten by all except the town chronicler—we did not let ourselves forget just how cruelly the rest of the world had treated us.

Rabbi Menachem Sokolow (Naphtali's son) proved to have a knack for figures, and dealt with our economic turmoil by deflating prices. He put a strict ceiling on the price of every commodity, from eggs to female wigs to belt buckles. There was some grumbling at first, but over time the value of money changed in our minds. And those children who grew up when the price controls had been fixed were accustomed to it, hardly thinking twice about the fact that they sold a loaf of bread for a penny—even if their fathers had sold it for three times as much. (Money had always been used in sui generis ways in Kreskol; in decades past when visitors came through town bearing rubles and saying that this was now the currency of the land, Kreskolites hung on to their zlotys. This almost always proved sensible in the end.)

We treated scornfully the few merchants from the outside who still made the trip through Kreskol every few months. When they offered to sell us a teakettle, they were too stunned by our counteroffers to be insulted. After a while, the merchants stopped trying, as did everybody else—save the gypsies, who still saw the value in Kreskol's wares and were willing to put in the time and effort to reach Kreskol in one piece, and were shrewd enough to maximize their profits reselling it.

All the while, we had very little idea just how dramatically things were changing outside Kreskol.

One summer, a member of the Austrian nobility was shot dead in Sarajevo, and the whole of Europe embraced its most violent, most barbarous persona. They clawed and chopped and shelled and sank white hot slugs of lead into one another's flesh. War broke out on a scale never imagined by humanity—but we heard very little about it in Kreskol.

One afternoon, a Polish cavalry officer whose uniform was blackened with soot and grime galloped into our town square and broke into tears when he saw the butter and the bread and the golden pyramids of apples on display in the marketplace.

"What's wrong with the fellow?" Hoda Levy asked another housewife.

"He must be a deserter," came the reply. "Worried that we're going to turn him in."

When the Pole recovered his wits, he began reaching his arms into the barrels of vegetables, frantically filling his pack with our goods. He didn't give so much as a penny in return.

"I'm requisitioning this," he told Rabbi Menachem Sokolow. "By order of the Polish cavalry."

No one could remember a gentile ever attempting something so brazen in the past but the man had a savage, wild look about him—as if he'd lunge at the throat of anybody who tried to stop him. And after all these years free from violence and harassment, nobody felt the need to make trouble now.

"I'll be back," he declared, with a tremor in his voice. "The army will be back, too. You people ought to be ashamed of yourselves, holding on to contraband in a time of war!"

That was peculiar, certainly. One doesn't usually feel shame from a man who is robbing you. The villagers all shared a look of puzzlement after the young officer mounted his horse and galloped away, never to be seen again. No one knew what to make of those goyim. Their morals shifted with a strong wind.

But to truly understand why Kreskol was spared the hangman's fate that awaited so many other towns in the remote regions of the White Wilderness or the Tuchola Forest, it is necessary to relate the story of Jacek Krzywicki, the man whom we later learned would figure most significantly in our rescue.

Not that Mr. Krzywicki ever appreciated his outsized role in our fate. According to all available sources, he had no opinions about Jews, one way or the other, and spent his life as a drunkard and a spendthrift whose gargantuan appetites led to his execrable discovery in an alley in Warsaw one November morning shortly after his forty-first birthday, dead of cirrhosis of the liver. At the time of his expiration—with only two zlotys in his pocket—he owed an obscene amount of money to a range of pimps, gamblers, and innkeepers in Warsaw, Krakow, and Lublin. The division of his meager estate was the subject of not less than seven different court actions.

After our rediscovery, we made an earnest attempt to find out more about unfortunate Mr. Krzywicki, to whom we owed such a great debt—but very little was known about him other than that his cousin was Ludwik Krzywicki, who founded the Central Statistical Office in Warsaw, and that he collected data for the office's yearbook. With a prostitute in Lodz, he had fathered a bastard daughter named Wanda whom he never acknowledged as his own—but it is not clear whether Mr. Krzywicki was even aware of his daughter's existence.

Our own encounter with Krzywicki was extremely limited. We met him on precisely one occasion not too many years after the cavalry officer came and went from our village.

Krzywicki rode into town on a white mare, and several of those who saw him say that they were surprised that a horse—even a strong, sturdy one—could support a man of his considerable girth.

"Where am I?" he asked in Polish when he was in our town square. He reached a swollen hand into the inner pocket of his uniform, pulled out a white slice of paper, and said, "Am I in Kreskol?"

Many of those who now manned the stalls in the market square no longer spoke any Polish, so Rabbi Sokolow was summoned to speak to this elephantine, ruddy-faced official.

"Yes," Rabbi Sokolow answered, "you are in Kreskol."

Krzywicki reached into his inner pocket for a second time and pulled out another slip of paper along with a yellow map, both of which he studied for a minute before he said anything else.

"Now, have you people ever heard of a place called Kyrshkow?"

Rabbi Sokolow nodded.

"Where is *that* place? According to this map, it should be here as well."

"We're one and the same," the Rabbi answered. "We don't go by Kyrshkow anymore. We only go by Kreskol."

It took Krzywicki a few minutes to understand this. He sat on his horse and studied the paper in front of him intensely before he asked Rabbi Sokolow to explain the change, which Rabbi Sokolow did with outright embellishment. "We had discovered that there was a village also called Kyrshkow in Russia where there was a scandal," Rabbi Sokolow said, his voice moving up a few octaves. "We didn't want to be associated with scandal and thought it was easier just to change our name."

Krzywicki listened to this explanation before rubbing his temples and saying, "You don't happen to have any vodka, do you?"

Under normal circumstances, the Rabbi might have noted that nine o'clock in the morning was considered early for indulging in spirits in these parts, but he simply sent Dudel Aaronson to fetch a jug from the distillery.

"You don't get many visitors out here, do you?" the man said after he had gotten off his horse, taken a few significant gulps of vodka, and was suddenly a little more at ease.

"No."

"Well, I'm with the census for the Second Polish Republic's Central Statistical Office."

Rabbi Sokolow had never heard of a census. Or the Central Statistical Office. And he had no idea that there was a first Polish republic, much less a second one.

"What's that?"

Krzywicki didn't look particularly surprised by the question—as if he had heard it before. This was, after all, a time when Kreskol was not the most primitive village in Poland. With greater care than one would have expected from a stranger, Krzywicki took pains to explain all that had happened since the end of the Great War.

The war ended—he explained—only to be followed by a smaller war with the Ukrainians and a third war, with the Russians. With the final peace treaties the kingdom around us was transformed into a republic, and the Duchy of Szyszki was turned into the District of Szyszki. This was part of the Second Polish Republic's effort to organize itself in a more sensible, modern way. For that reason, he would need to make a report on Kreskol, along with every other village in the district.

This was largely irrelevant to us. Rabbi Sokolow was as polite as could be expected, believing our town's best path to peace and prosperity was to smile, nod, and not ask too many questions.

"So see here," Krzywicki said. "What I have to do is evaluate this town. And by that, I mean I have to find out how many people are here."

Rabbi Sokolow said nothing.

"Do you know?"

"No . . ."

Krzywicki looked disappointed.

"Don't you people keep records?"

It was true, there was the archive in the yeshiva's library. There would be records of all Kreskol's births and deaths. But nobody kept a running tally of the various souls of our town.

"Can you estimate?" Krzywicki asked. "It doesn't have to be perfect."

The Rabbi looked perplexed. He cast his eye about the town square, to the crowd of Jews watching the exchange. "Maybe two thousand?" he answered.

Krzywicki's eyebrows leaped up. I suppose he expected a smaller figure. He reached into his uniform yet again and this time pulled out a small, red leather booklet and a pencil. He began scratching out notes.

Krzywicki spent the rest of the day with Rabbi Sokolow and the town archivist, going through our synagogue's records. As the morning wore on, he asked for more vodka. He was sweating furiously even though it was a cool, balmy day, and began wiping his brow and patting down his cheeks with a red handkerchief. Just before noon he asked somewhat sheepishly if he could use the outhouse, and the archivist and Rabbi Sokolow later reported hearing the sounds of heaving and gagging.

He emerged with his handkerchief at his lips, not baring even a hint of the sickness and misery he knew a minute or two earlier.

"This town might have tax problems," the official said. "When was the last time you paid an assessment to the Rabbinic Council?"

It had been more than two decades, and Rabbi Menachem Sokolow had little idea what the man was talking about.

"You haven't paid your taxes in more than twenty years?" Krzywicki said in disbelief. "How did the Rabbinic Council permit you to get away with that?"

"We don't have a good relationship with them."

Krzywicki was silent when he was told this.

"This is serious," he finally said. "You'd all better start saving up, because I'll be back with a tax assessment in a few months."

Rabbi Sokolow nodded, grimly.

Toward the end of the day, Mr. Krzywicki lumbered back to his horse and began the painful process of mounting.

"Easy, Daisy, easy," he said, trying to calm the animal as he kept trying to swing his leg over the saddle. Finally, the ironsmith and the woodchopper appeared, and hoisted him over the top.

"Thank you," Krzywicki mumbled, and as he was about to ride out of town he said to Rabbi Sokolow, "Do you think I can have one more? For the road?"

Another jug of vodka was produced, and as he watched the official gulp the last of it, his brown eyes shining brightly in his doughy face, from the depths of his soul, Rabbi Sokolow felt sorry for Krzywicki even if the man would no doubt be making life difficult in the coming months.

"Thank you," Krzywicki said again—this time with more fervor than when he had been helped onto his horse.

He rode out of town.

However, it turned out that we could not have been more blessed with a census taker than we were with Krzywicki. He didn't return with a tax bill—nor did anyone else. It was the last we would hear on the matter of taxes.

It can only be surmised what went on in Krzywicki's mind after he

had been told that Kreskol had been untaxed for years. The best guess is
that some scheme unfolded between the time he left Kreskol and when he
returned to Warsaw.

He was, as I've said, a man of incredible financial burdens. There was
no doubt he could use a large influx of cash. And he had the privilege of
being one of the few outsiders who had seen Kreskol with his own eyes.
Could he have come back to our town with an official decree, saying that
we had to pay such-and-such a tax bill, and then simply pocketed the
money?

That is the current belief of the Polish government. And it is the one
that makes the most sense, in light of his subsequent behavior.

Krzywicki filed an official report with the Central Statistical Office
saying that he could find neither hide nor hair of Kreskol—or of Kyrshkow, for that matter.

He did, however, say in his report that he had spoken to several of
the local hermits and mountain people who said that the tiny village (of
no more than two hundred souls, anyway) had been destroyed during
the war.

To quote his report directly: "One forest dweller—who would only
give her name as Catarina, who looked about 35 and had two warts on her
chin—said that there had been a scuffle between Russian and German
troops in the town. This led to a massive fire when artillery hit one of the
barns. The Kreskolites, now homeless, all went their separate ways."

Krzywicki then went on to describe the few ragtag remains of the village, as if he were describing a lost civilization. "There is the half-burned
skeleton of a building with a Jewish star," the report states. "This, no
doubt, was the local synagogue."

It appears that Krzywicki had done something similar with several
other villages. Not that he erased any other population centers wholesale, but a decade later—long after Krzywicki had been thrown in a pauper's grave—during the second census, it was discovered that many of
the towns and villages that had been in Krzywicki's region were under-

counted. Suddenly there were great influxes of extra persons. (Moreover, plenty of these extra people had dutifully paid whatever tax bill they had been presented with before Krzywicki's death.)

It was deduced, therefore, that Krzywicki was in all probability a thief and an embezzler on top of his many other foibles, and that he had eaten and drunk and gambled away the treasure he collected. If he hadn't succumbed to an early death, Krzywicki would no doubt have made an appearance in our town to collect our taxes the next year.

The people of Kreskol, however, could find no fault with the man. If not for Jacek Krzywicki we almost certainly would have perished in the monstrous German push to the east twenty years later.

Shortly after our rediscovery, there was talk about putting a statue of him in the town square.

9

GEHEIMNISTRÄGER

Providence might have conspired to save Kreskol from the greatest catastrophe, but there was another conscious hand that kept it preserved after the seething war hardened into cold peace. This never made it into the official report about Kreskol but I would be remiss if I didn't mention it here.

The hand was that of one of Kreskol's residents who died a few years before our rediscovery, unmarried and childless. And he was unique among our citizens in that he wasn't born in our town and had no ancestral connection, rather, he had the distinction of being the sole transplant to move here before the big rediscovery.

Leonid Spektor arrived more than twenty years after Jacek Krzywicki's brief ingress in Kreskol's fortunes. And unlike the typical Kreskolite, he was educated and worldly. He built a small cottage on the edge of the woods and took up in the yeshiva, where he taught Aramaic. Physically, he was short and lithe and his most distinctive feature was a patch he wore over his left eye.

To anyone who asked, Spektor would give private lessons in Polish and Russian and French—telling those who questioned the purpose of this that everyone should know a second language and his fluency in languages had saved his life more than once. (This "saved my life" business was somewhat cryptic, but he never expounded on it.)

While he was willing to teach German on request, he would preface every lesson with the advisory that the only reason to do so was because it was important to know more about your enemy than he knew about you. "Make no mistake," he would say. "The Germans are our enemy. They always will be. Forever and ever."

Why the Germans, his students asked, and not the Poles? Or the Russians? Or the Ukrainians? They hated Jews, too.

"Everybody else is a mix," Leonid pronounced. "I've known good, courageous Poles. I've known others who were perfect swine. But the Germans are consistently bad. They hate Jews with every fiber of their being. They're all irredeemable." He said it with such conviction it seemed fruitless to further contest the point.

Spektor was intimate with the wonders of the modern world that others had merely heard about. Certainly, he had been on a train before—who hadn't? And, naturally, he had been to the picture shows. (A pastime that the inhabitants of Kreskol didn't quite understand, despite the pains he took to explain it.) He had once set off fireworks at a fairground and seen gorillas at the Warsaw Zoo when he was a boy. "They're very manlike," was his main takeaway.

And Leonid Spektor was immensely popular with his students. Not only did he offer to teach the children languages, he told wild, frightening, dramatic stories to the young boys about what awaited them outside the walls of Kreskol.

"Never did a crueler, more bloodthirsty man stalk the earth than Dieter the Demented," he would begin, and he would tell the tale of a sadistic German who would tear the limbs off little children, and flay mothers alive, using their skin to make coats and blankets and birdcage covers, and stomp old men to death with his jackboots.

"When old Dieter would find a pretty Jewish girl, he would throw her on the ground with his friends watching, to make sure she didn't get away. He would tear off her clothes and whip her flesh. And while she was writhing in pain, he would inject her neck with strychnine."

The boys were almost too afraid to ask what strychnine was, but Spektor forecasted the question.

"Strychnine is a poison. Dieter would just watch as she would contort and turn blue before dying. He and his friends would laugh."

He told tales of a blond, rotund witch with a chipped front tooth who hunted innocent little boys for sport, locking them up in cages. She would feed them just enough to develop a little tummy and she would cut them up and dump their bodies into a giant cauldron with horseflesh that would bubble into soap. He spun yarns of mad Germans and Ukrainians who drank vodka until they didn't mind slaughtering anyone who crossed their path, and did so with abandon and joy.

These gruesome, lurid stories tantalized the youth of Kreskol as much as they frightened them. Unlike the folklore that began violently but ended with peace and justice, Spektor declined to sweeten the endings. They reinforced the general perception that the world outside Kreskol was an evil place—but they also aroused a certain morbid curiosity. And whatever lack of realism was inherent in these tales, the youth had the good sense to realize that there was, indeed, something authentic as well.

Their parents, on the other hand, loathed Leonid Spektor and couldn't understand what was wrong with the fellow. Individually, they made complaints to Rabbi Herschel Sokolow (son of Menachem, father of Anschel) about Spektor, but when they could see that they weren't getting anywhere, several mothers banded together and visited the Rabbi's court en masse.

"Yes?" Rabbi Sokolow said upon receiving the redemption coin. "What can I do for you ladies today?"

"Leonid Spektor is filling our sons' heads with a lot of craziness," replied Masha Landau, who was designated spokeswoman by the other mothers, thanks to a deficit of embarrassment about what she said and a surplus in the volume of her voice. "All day long all I hear about is 'Sebastian the

Scavenger' and 'Rolf the Enraged,' and how they torture Jews incessantly.
My boy repeated this dreck to his sister, and she's been waking up in tears
in the middle of the night for three weeks."

"I see," the Rabbi said. "Well, that's a fairly easy thing to fix. I'll have a
word with Mr. Spektor."

However, this promise had been anticipated; Rabbi Sokolow had made
similar assurances to Baila Franken more than a year ago when she first
presented him with the problem.

"I'm not so sure," Masha replied. "I know a few people in this room
have already complained." (Baila, who was standing right next to Masha,
looked sheepishly at the floor.) "Are you really going to talk to him?"

Nobody likes having their word challenged—not even someone as
temperate and wise as a great rabbi.

"I hadn't gotten around to it," Herschel Sokolow admitted. "As you
know, I have many matters to attend to."

Masha nodded, but as far as she was concerned this argument (also
anticipated) was bunk. What matters did the Rabbi have that were so
important that he couldn't have a five-minute conversation where he told
Spektor to knock it off? However, Masha knew enough about men to
recognize that when they were faced with a task that they had no appetite
for, you needed to push them along every inch of the way. "When are you
going to talk to him?" she asked.

"Tomorrow," he answered. "Maybe the day after."

Nobody knew how or why Leonid Spektor had bewitched Rabbi Sokolow,
but it was useless to contemplate whys. It was obvious Spektor could do no
wrong in his eyes, even if nobody could understand it. After all, there was
something practically misanthropic about Spektor. Shortly after he settled in
Kreskol a matchmaker came to see him and said he had a couple of enticing
prospects. "Not interested," Spektor replied, bluntly.

"But you haven't even met them. I'm talking about real beauties here."

Spektor frowned.

"I'm not interested in anybody."

The matchmaker was taken aback. The only thing he could think to say was: "Don't you want children?"

Spektor shook his head.

"There are enough children in the world. I don't intend to bring in any more."

This sounded chilling, especially in the mouth of a teacher who was supposed to be sculpting young minds. The remark made its way back to Rabbi Sokolow. "I'm not his father," the Rabbi pronounced. "Nobody can tell him what to do or what to think." And that seemed to be the end of the episode.

But there were plenty of other reasons Spektor was distrusted. He never showed up to shul. Never. Not on Shabbat, not on Tisha B'Av, and not on Yom Kippur. It didn't seem to trouble the Rabbi in the slightest.

While he was popular with the boys, they, too, recognized something slightly uncanny about the man. Sometimes, in the middle of a lesson, he would stare into the eyes of his pupils and excuse himself. His students would then hear him sobbing and heaving in the next room. When he returned, Spektor wouldn't breathe a word of the emotions that had whipped and flayed him a few moments earlier.

He spent most of his spare time by himself, but when he did seek the company of others it was largely the scum on Thieves' Lane, where Spektor could be seen drinking in the tavern. Everyone disapproved, except for Rabbi Sokolow, who again said that he didn't believe it his place to interfere with the affairs of a grown man.

"Fine," Masha Landau said. "You speak to him the day after tomorrow. But we want to know what he has to say and if he agrees to keep his yap shut. We'll be back on Wednesday."

He was unshaven, bony, ghostly.

Rabbi Herschel Sokolow first laid eyes on Spektor as he was locking up the synagogue for the evening. The stranger was young then, but weathered. He was seated on the last bench near the door, wearing a sooty gray shirt, brown vest, and brown trousers that were held up by twine in lieu of a belt. He looked as if he hadn't eaten a meal in some time. He wore a patch over his eye, which gave even a grown man like the Rabbi apprehensions that this figure was in some way otherworldly.

"Are you looking for something, friend?" Sokolow asked.

The stranger didn't speak for a long time.

"I grew up in a place like this," he said, craning his neck around the synagogue. "Perhaps not quite as rural. But rural. I haven't even seen a streetcar here."

The stranger took his cap off to scratch his head and as he did so the Rabbi noticed a sequence of numbers tattooed on his left arm.

An introduction was made. Spektor said he had been wandering along a path in the forest most of the afternoon and he came here just to rest his legs.

"This is the first place I've seen that looks like it came away unscratched," Spektor said.

"Unscratched from what?"

Spektor laughed, until he saw Sokolow wasn't joking.

"The war, naturally."

The Rabbi nodded, not wanting to be taken for a fool—but after a moment decided there was no real harm admitting he didn't know exactly what the fellow was talking about.

"Yes," Rabbi Sokolow said. "Untouched by the war. Completely untouched. Didn't even really know about it." The word "really" was his single scrap of face-saving guile. "Who was it between this time? The Tsar up to his old tricks?"

Spektor's mouth popped open, slightly, before politely closing. He considered what he would say for a long time before he spoke.

"There is no Tsar," Spektor finally said. "The Russians got rid of the Tsar thirty years ago."

Well, it might have been late but that was certainly a development worth hearing about. And given the fact that the man didn't look as if he was in a hurry to go anywhere, the Rabbi figured he'd do a good deed.

"No Tsar?" the Rabbi laughed. "Well, hallelujah to that. I imagine there's a good story to go with it. You look famished, young fellow. How about you come with me and the Rebbetzin will rustle us up something to eat."

"Very kind."

So the two of them walked through the darkened streets to Rabbi Sokolow's court. And when the Rebbetzin set down roast chicken, kasha with noodles, pickled beets, and gefilte fish for the table, the stranger lost control of his emotions—to the great discomfort of his hosts.

"Are you all right?" Sokolow asked.

Spektor could only nod, tears raining down his cheeks.

Rabbi Sokolow looked to his wife, who led their young son (and his son's friend, who had come over for supper) out of the room.

"Forgive me," Spektor said. "I haven't had food like this—good food—in a very long time."

The Rabbi didn't say anything. He just sipped the glass of wine in front of him and nibbled on several pickled beets as his guest, delicately but ravenously, devoured the entire chicken.

And as his hunger receded, the stranger's garrulousness expanded. "The Tsar," Spektor nearly spat. He had been executed in the middle of the night with Tsarina Alexandra, their five children, and several courtiers in Yekaterinburg years before Spektor had even been born, on orders from the revolutionary government. "But I should tell you, as bad as the Tsar was he was a rank amateur in comparison to what came after."

"Was that what the war was about, then?"

"No," Spektor said. "Not really." And he proceeded to relate the story of an Austrian corporal and his war of extermination.

Adolf Hitler had started life as a painter—Spektor explained—a
profession he practiced ineptly. He spent much of his young
adulthood swept up in the conviction that he was a great man with a
historic destiny. And with Germany's defeat in the Great War (which
Rabbi Sokolow didn't interrupt to ask about) Hitler discovered the
deeper purpose of his life: He preached the gospel of Germany, its
right to conquest, and the unredeeming evil of the Jews, who, in his
convoluted thinking, kept Germany from its unrealized inheritance.

And unlike his fellow novices who fulminated from street corners
in Munich, Hitler's fire and sulfur resonated with an enormous
chunk of the public. Grown men and women leaped to their feet with
outstretched arms, saluting the man whose wisdom they viewed as
godlike.

"Even his looks are something the Germans revere," Spektor added,
"and his looks are objectively weird. Or were. He's dead now, too."

Although Spektor's little town of Bruskevo wasn't in Germany,
the gentiles would crowd around their radios together, and listen
approvingly to the corporal as he worked himself into a froth over
international affairs and world Jewry. They would leave their windows
open and the volume raised so that the unsaved could hear the good
word.

When war was finally declared and the Germans goose-stepped
through his town, the gentiles came out to greet their conquerors
with bouquets of flowers and black crosses raised above their heads.
The town square was festooned with leaflets from the invading army,
promising freedom from international Jewry, Joseph Stalin, and
Franklin Roosevelt.

Leonid's uncle, one of the elders of Bruskevo, was tasked with
selecting a Judenrat.* When he respectfully offered his objections,
he was marched to the town square, where a German in uniform

---

*A council that served as a liaison between the Nazis and the Jewish community.

removed a Luger from his holster, placed it next to the sainted man's head, and calmly pulled the trigger.

Spektor's account had been interesting enough, but at that moment Sokolow sat up straight, as if he had received an electric jolt.

"You saw that?" Sokolow asked. "With your own eyes?"

Spektor didn't answer, but a shadow fell on his hardened, scraggy face. He continued.

The perpetrator was a sallow, dark-haired Nazi captain, who wore gold-rimmed spectacles and a gray SS uniform with the skull-and-crossbones badge. He was not a low-ranking soldier, whom the government could claim had exceeded his authority should the incident ever be examined in a court of law.

The Nazi captain placed his gun back in its holster, took a handkerchief out of his pocket to wipe away a few spots of blood that had spattered on his hand, and walked unhurriedly back to Gestapo headquarters in the Bruskevo town hall.

When the assailant was out of sight, three young men stepped forward to retrieve the body, whose eyes were still open and lifelike.

"Halt," commanded one of the Germans, who had mutely observed the scene. "Don't touch him."

So he lay for three days in the town square, until the stench became too much for even the Nazis and they ordered him tossed in the nearby river.

And this was only the beginning. Leonid witnessed dozens of other summary executions for infractions such as being without papers, being in possession of a contraband hard-boiled egg, being out after curfew, and so on.

The Spektor family sensed that the end was nigh, and the teenaged Leonid and his cousin Gavril were sent to separate gentile families in the countryside. Soon thereafter, the Jewry of Bruskevo were liquidated.

"The Nazis kept it secret," Spektor said. "But not too secret. They did the same thing again and again in towns all over Poland and Lithuania. Word got out. The gentiles I was staying with heard the story a few months later."

Under normal circumstances, the family who saved him—the Rymuts—would have turned Leonid away, but the Spektors had offered such an extravagant sum to house their son that the Rymuts felt they couldn't say no.

Of course, there were plenty of gentiles who accepted a bounty from a Jew and then turned around and accepted a second one from the Germans, but the Rymuts declined to traffic in that kind of treachery. "Once you do that," Adam Rymut remarked to his wife, Maja, "life becomes chaos." She agreed, without second thoughts.

During his first year at the farm Leonid had been given a room in the house and he helped with the chores. However, when rumors came back that Jews were being hidden in a nearby village, and that the penalty for harboring them was death, Leonid was moved to the barn, where he lived in the hayloft above the cows. Six months later, a pit was dug for Leonid with a trapdoor, and he lived among the lice.

But doom was always lurking nearby. One of the Rymut daughters bought Leonid a newspaper in town, which nearly destroyed him.

"What are the Rymuts doing with a newspaper?" Olga Wojcicka asked her sister after observing the purchase. "I didn't think they knew how to read." Wojcicka felt duty-bound to report this suspicious activity to the Germans.

A search of the Rymut farm was conducted two days later, but Olga Wojcicka (whose chipped central incisor, straw hair, and squat stature bore a notable physical resemblance to the witch who boiled children into soap in the stories Leonid later told) had made reports of eight different families in the area whom she believed were harboring Jews, and the Germans had come up empty all but once. When they came for an inspection of the Rymut farm, the soldiers were wary enough of the source to leave without bothering to examine the surrounding property.

A second report, however, was made by a more restrained peasant named Piotr Mazurek, who said that he had come by the farm to trade some vegetables and had seen a pair of trousers on the clothesline. They were too small for Adam Rymut. And Rymut's surviving children were all girls. Mazurek casually asked if anybody was staying with them. No, Rymut had said. Nobody.

This time, the Germans didn't just go through the entire house and remove a floorboard to see if there were any hollowed-out rooms under the kitchen, but they went out to the barn and examined every stall of every animal.

Maja Rymut watched the scene unfold in dread, which she tried to pass off as indignation. "We are a good family here," she barked. "We don't break any laws and we don't hide Jews. You have no right to treat us like criminals."

The Germans asked to speak to her husband alone.

"There was a pair of pants hanging on your clothesline on Thursday," the interrogator said to Adam.

"Yes . . ."

"They were men's pants. And they could not have fitted you, sir— they were too small."

Adam stared at his interrogator, who was shorter and huskier than he, for a few moments before speaking.

"You think that a girl on a farm doesn't have occasion to wear men's pants?" Adam asked.

It was a believable precept, as far as it goes, even though each of the Rymut daughters at that very moment was wearing a dress—all soiled from the morning's labor.

When the German asked to see the garment in question, Adam

produced a pair of trousers that fit the eldest Rymut daughter. (The Germans hadn't noticed that Adam had taken the trousers not from his daughters' room but his departed son's.)

Even though the Germans came away empty-handed, the Rymuts were shaken. "They'll be back," Adam Rymut said to his wife. "He must leave immediately."

And so Leonid was sent away with a pillow, blanket, and sack of food, where hopefully the Poles leading the resistance would help him.

That proved a mistaken assumption. When Leonid ran across two armed figures in the forest they initially appeared to take him into their confidence. He was taken back to their hideout, given a cup of warm milk, and turned over to the Germans the next day.

He was stuffed into a boxcar, cheek to jowl with a hundred others. (More than a thousand, maybe, if you counted every single human being on the entire train.) The train convulsed through the countryside for two days at an unbearably slow speed—starting and stopping in fits—before coming to a halt at a cold, isolated spot where the prisoners were made to sit and suffer for another two days without food or water.

He watched several elderly passengers near him collapse and slip into the throes of unwept, infinite death.

But the Germans refused to tend to them. Refused to listen to their final, pathetic whimpers. Refused to even remove them from the boxcars until their bodies had stiffened and the stink of ordure had settled over the survivors. It was an effluvium that would follow Leonid for the remainder of his captivity.

Upon arriving at the camp, he was looked over by a German doctor, and told to go to the right; he never again saw the people who were sent to the doctor's left.

Some of these unfortunates must have sensed the fate that awaited them. When the fathers of these damned women and children objected and asked not to be separated, the Germans lied mechanically. "You'll see them later," answered the examining doctor.

Leonid was ordered to disrobe with the other men. The room was frigid, which caused him to shiver and his flesh to turn goose-like.

In the stark coldness, the dimness and the nakedness of the scene unfolding around him, Leonid began to sob, silently, certain that all hope was lost.

A few of the other prisoners glared at him. Youth and softness were liabilities, and in the first—but certainly not last—breach of camaraderie, he was told to shut up or someone would shut him up. When he didn't conceal his emotions quickly enough, a tall, square-jawed Russian punched Leonid in the stomach, hard. (He felt it for days after.)

"That would set the tone for the rest of my time at Auschwitz," he told Sokolow. "It was a state of nature, where the only law was that of immediate, unquestioning obedience. Allegiances and friendships could be rescinded for a better relationship with the Kapo,* or a more favorable work detail."

Leonid was led into a freezing shower. He was then given two oversized wooden shoes, a striped uniform that was a size too large (a "zebra suit," as it was called by the inmates), and a yellow star to punctuate his low status as a Yid. His hair was shorn and he was brought before a toothless Polish Jew who told him to stretch out his left arm, and with neither permission nor explanation, six bluish-black numbers were etched onto his forearm.

He asked his brander what would happen to him.

"Don't ask questions," the toothless prisoner replied. Questions were another sign of weakness.

But Leonid Spektor's punishment and unhappiness were destined to be greater than those of his peers in this desolate place. In those

---

*An internal concentration camp police force, populated by prisoners.

first few days, he uncomplainingly went through the rigmarole of finding a bowl and spoon, of learning his work detail, of appearing at the predawn roll call promptly; and his strength was noted.

A week later, three SS officers and a dog attached to a metal chain arrived at his hut and pointed at him and two others. "You three—come with us."

They were escorted out of the barracks and through the camp to a truck, in which they and a dozen other prisoners drove less than two miles from Auschwitz to Birkenau. Leonid was then led into a barracks where he met a Jew who was not dressed in stripes but in normal trousers, vest, and shoes.

"Pick something out," said the Jewish Kapo—a man named Stitz who wore curly black hair—after he led Leonid and two of his companions into a room overflowing with garments.

Spektor came to a sudden halt in his story. He didn't say a word as the tears began welling up in his one good eye. When he finally spoke again, his voice was so soft that Rabbi Sokolow could barely hear him.

"When I was dressed, Stitz unveiled another indulgence: a flask of vodka and four shot glasses."

For a moment, Leonid and his two confederates were not sure what to say, but Stitz just handed each of them the glass and raised it high.

"You are hereby geheimnisträger"—keepers of secrets.

Leonid didn't have the faintest idea what the man was talking about, but nonetheless all four sanctified the declaration by knocking back their glasses. He was led out of the barracks to a large, rambling farmhouse surrounded by birch trees where two Germans stood guard. Leonid and his compatriots descended a short flight of stairs where Stitz stopped in front of an enormous door that was bolted shut.

"Don't lose your wits," Stitz warned. "You won't like what you see. But you won't be able to unsee it. And, just so you know, if you kick up a fuss that will be the end of you."

Gas masks were handed to Leonid and the three others, which they strapped on without questions, and the door was flung open to reveal the full extent of the annihilation.

Words failed Leonid. Imagination failed him. His legs might have failed him, too, if one of the SS officers behind him hadn't barked for him to hurry up and get on with it, poking him with the barrel of his rifle.

It was akin to opening the door to the lair of a lunatic who murdered for pleasure and kept demented trophies of his kills; he had stumbled into an obscenity that was no longer the work of human beings. The dead numbered in the hundreds, maybe more. They were naked, and most of their faces had turned purple from suffocation. But they were also lifelike, indicating the abomination had been committed only a few minutes earlier. (Which was indeed the case.) They were frozen in poses that ranged from wailing grief to hysteria. In the panic after the poison gas was dropped into the chamber, several victims had broken nails and chipped teeth, clawing at the locked door. Included in their number were countless children, many of whom had been trampled as their elders flailed about in hopeless agony. But it wasn't just children who had been crushed; the strong had tried to climb their way to the vents at the top of the chamber, in the wild chance of reaching uncontaminated air, and they had done it at the expense of the weak. Pools of blood had collected on the floor and been smeared on the walls. Also on the floor and walls were feces from those who had befouled themselves in their final moments of torment.

"Cut off the hair of the dead," Stitz ordered. Leonid and one of the other newbies were presented instruments closer to hedge-clippers than scissors.

"You," Stitz said, pointing to a third. "After they finish taking the hair, you look in their mouths for gold." The prisoner was handed a pair of pliers. "Another crew will be here in a few minutes to start moving the bodies to the crematorium."

Back in Kreskol, neither Spektor nor the Rabbi spoke.

In the next room, Rabbi Sokolow's young son, Anschel, and his best friend, Meir Katznelson, had situated themselves in the dark, under the sofa, and quietly listened to everything with rapt attention. But after these last words were spoken, Meir cried out.

As soon as he heard young Katznelson, Spektor turned red. The Rabbi apologized to his guest and sent the boys immediately to bed. But even as they were on their way out, the boys could see that the stranger looked chagrined; as if he had second thoughts about revealing so much of himself.

They sat in Anschel's room for a long time before either boy said anything.

"Why do you suppose they cut off everybody's hair?" Anschel finally asked.

"I don't know. Maybe they sold it."

Which sounded like a strange explanation.

"Who would buy human hair?"

Meir shrugged.

And the boys spent the week raising questions to each other about the stranger's grisly yarn. (They were circumspect enough not to mention it to the other boys.) How did Spektor free himself from such a hellish place? What was the story behind the tattoo? How did he lose the eye? But even as they raised these questions, they did so with utter faith in everything they had heard.

Anschel's father had greater doubts—at least at first. Neither the Persians, nor the Greeks, nor the Romans, nor the Spanish, nor the Cossacks had ever conjured up such insanity. It seemed impossible that it could happen in modern times, a few miles away. The Rabbi wondered if the man was out of his mind and should be sent packing, post haste.

But like his son, Rabbi Sokolow sensed the anguish and sincerity in Spektor's voice. It made him feel protective.

After the two boys had been chased out of earshot, Sokolow listened to the brief afterword: a liberation by the Soviets; a Displaced Persons camp; an endless walk back in the direction of his hometown of Bruskevo, which was how he found himself in Kreskol.

"But you can't go back to Bruskevo," Rabbi Sokolow said. "If what you're saying is true, there are no Jews left in your village."

It was a somber pronouncement. All the more poignant because Spektor—who was so detached and matter-of-fact in his retelling—looked shocked; as if this transparent truth had never been considered.

"Rabbi," he eventually said in a soft, pleading voice that he didn't raise lest it crack, "for more than five years I fell asleep dreaming about Bruskevo. That was all I ever wished for. That I could return home."

Neither man said anything for a long time.

"I suppose I can go to America," Spektor finally said.

"That's not a bad idea," Sokolow replied. "Who wouldn't want to see America? I've always believed it's a second chance; an opportunity to begin again."

However, there was something unstated in Sokolow's pronouncement—as if he understood that the chance to start anew was not what Spektor was after. Rather, he was aiming to pick up in the middle.

"Or you could stay here," Rabbi Sokolow suggested. "Nobody would kick you out. And there are no enemies of the Jews here. No Germans. Not even any Poles—not for years and years."

Spektor smiled.

"It's a very nice town, of course," Spektor said. "But it's not home."

The Rabbi nodded.

"Well," Sokolow quickly added, "you should stay tonight at least."

"Naturally."

"There's plenty of space in the prayer house."

Spektor nodded.

"And, just to be clear, you shouldn't feel the need to run off right away. There's no real hurry, is there? You can stay a few days. Rest. And then figure out the next leg of your journey."

In the succeeding weeks, it was never stated explicitly that Leonid Spektor would relocate permanently. He just did.

A space was made for him in the prayer house that he could use indefinitely. Funds were drawn from the synagogue treasury to buy the poor man some decent clothes. When Sokolow learned how well schooled he was in Aramaic, he let him teach the eleven-year-olds.

And while a general lack of piety prevented the more respectable citizens of Kreskol from getting too close to Spektor, the same could not be said of Herschel Sokolow, who not only felt protective of him, but also grew to love and admire him. He had, in the Rebbe's eyes, the wisdom that comes from torment.

Rabbi Sokolow wasn't such a fool as to believe that there was something ennobling about pain and suffering. (That was a theory for the goyim.) But nobody could deny that he had confronted and survived things that no one else in Kreskol ever had. This humbled the Rabbi in Spektor's presence. The last thing he felt entitled to do was lecture or scold this ghost who had taken up residence in Kreskol.

After his meeting with the disgruntled mothers, Sokolow found himself much busier than he had been in weeks. There had been a long simmering dispute before the Beit Din between Steinmitz (the dairy farmer) and Lowenstein (the grain farmer) about where Steinmitz's cows could permissibly graze. The Rabbi decided that the matter deserved his immediate attention.

The next day he oiled a rusty hinge on the door to the linen closet that the Rebbetzin had been complaining about for six months, and treated a recent stain on the carpet (which was usually his wife's work), and went through his son's cheder assignments to make sure that Anschel had really and fully memorized the Ark of the Covenant's cubit dimensions as they were stated in the book of Exodus. ("Two and a half long by one and a half wide," the boy answered. "I understand." But when Anschel asked his father the length of a cubit, Herschel Sokolow couldn't remember.)

Toward the end of the day the Rebbetzin entered his study and told him that he had a visitor: Leonid Spektor. When he heard this, the Rabbi's face turned crimson.

"Masha Landau said you wanted to see me," Leonid said.

For a moment, Rabbi Sokolow grinned in grudging respect for Masha's tenacity, but the grin quickly vanished.

"Leonid," Sokolow began. "We must talk about the stories you tell the boys."

Spektor didn't say anything.

"You're telling them about your experiences in the concentration camp . . ."

Spektor shook his head. "No, not exactly." After his initial indiscretion with the Rebbe, Spektor only ever referred to the death camps obliquely. "They're just stories. Nobody in them is real."

"Maybe you should lay off," Rabbi Sokolow said. "I'm getting complaints. Apparently, they're giving the children nightmares."

Spektor smiled to himself. "*They*'re the ones with nightmares . . ."

Rabbi Sokolow couldn't even meet Spektor's eye. "Yes," he said. "Obviously it's nothing like what you went through, these nightmares. Or, I'm sure, what your nightmares are like now. Obviously not. But these are children, Leonid. They don't need to think about such things, do they?"

Of course, the boys of Kreskol loved hearing Spektor's stories. They begged for them. (And Spektor told them well.) Plus, if he were going to truly mount a defense he might point out that it wasn't as if he forced anybody to listen.

Still, he could understand a mother wanting to protect her cubs from the world's unpleasantness—even unpleasant thoughts.

"Very well," Spektor said. In his reckoning, he owed it to his adopted town to live by its customs and precepts. After all, he had been designated a keeper of secrets once—it appeared he would remain so.

A few years before Spektor turned up in Kreskol, the gypsies who staked their claim to our modest corner of eastern Poland gave up on us. Evidently, they finally accepted that we were too cheap (or too poor) to conduct business with. Or, so it would seem, because they vanished.

They missed their regular spring visit. Then their fall visit. Then we stopped seeing them altogether.

The gypsy sojourns were irregular enough that it took more than a year before this was noticed and remarked upon. What happened, some of the merchants of Kreskol wondered? What had we done? The salts and soaps and medicines and other knickknacks that we traded were suddenly no longer available in Kreskol's marketplace at any price. It proved to be a significant annoyance. But it was also perplexing.

Then, suddenly, the gypsies returned at roughly the same time as Spektor arrived, without explanation.

Although Spektor couldn't have felt their absence, he was among the happier members of our town to see them. He would be the first to trade with them for aspirin and marzipan. "Do you have any books?" he asked a young gypsy girl the second time he saw the caravan coming through town.

"No," the girl answered. "But I can get you something. What do you want—which books?"

"Could you get me something by Knut Hamsun?"

"You'll pay in advance."

The next time she came through the town she brought an edition of *Hunger*—but Spektor should have been more specific. The copy she presented him with was in the original Norwegian. ("You didn't say what language you wanted," the girl declared. "All sales are final.")

When trading was finished for the day, Spektor would stop by the gypsy encampment for a few hours, just to chat. "What do you talk about with them?" the Rabbi asked.

"Mostly the war."

Rabbi Sokolow looked surprised.

"I thought you didn't like to talk about that."

Spektor nodded. "I can with them."

"Why?"

Spektor shrugged, slightly. "They know what it was like. The Germans treated them as roughly as the Jews."

This particular tribe of Romani was relatively lucky; they had escaped into the forest along the unmarked routes and the Germans never caught up with them. In the aftermath of the war, the tribe took in extended family whose fortunes hadn't been nearly so charmed. The curly haired girl who brought Leonid his books—whose name was Lavinia—was one such wretch. She had seen her mother, father, and teenaged husband all massacred before her eyes, eventually finding herself in the Jasenovac concentration camp.

"I will never complain again about living in a backwater," Lavinia laughed to Leonid. "You Kreskolites know what I mean. It was the fact that we were in a backwater that made the Germans not pay as much attention here as they should have."

"I suppose."

Leonid was eager to hear what was happening in the wider world and plied the gypsies for news, even as each new development portended some fresh harbinger of doom. He asked the gypsies about the Russians; Lavinia told him anyone expecting they would go back to Moscow now that the war was over was looking pretty dumb. If the Russians themselves weren't running things, they found flunkies to hold their place in Warsaw, Kiev, Budapest, Prague, Minsk, Bucharest, Sofia, Vilnius, Berlin—you name it. And they were terrible, she added. Almost as bad as the Nazis. Almost.

"It'll only be a matter of time," Lavinia said. "They'll pay Kreskol a visit. And I'm sure they won't be happy you evaded scrutiny for so long."

The words were all the more ominous because they spoke to a fear that long ago attached itself to Leonid. He spent his first few years in Kreskol waiting for the dark day when the Bolsheviks would rope the village into a local workers council—or whatever it was they did in Russia.

When he thought too much about these unhappy topics Leonid would escape to the forest; he at least took comfort in the fact that these woods were the great barrier protecting Kreskol from encroachment. He would spend hours walking her trails; collecting her berries and mushrooms; listening to her birds sing in the hot sun, trying not to think of the wicked world.

One afternoon, as Spektor hiked along the path out of town, he came across a dirt road. He followed the road for a few miles until he saw another conjoined road that he had never seen before. This one was paved.

As he stared down the gray strip of asphalt, a red Warszawa[*] flew past him, leaving a trail of summer dust.

Spektor was too stunned to speak, but after a moment he turned around and ran straight home.

The episode—ephemeral and seemingly benign as it was—was a grave crisis for Leonid Spektor.

He failed to show up at school the next day, and when a boy, Zindel Schumacher, was sent to check on him, the boy believed at first he had left town.

"Reb Spektor?" the boy called, banging on his door to no response.

---

[*] A post–World War II Polish-manufactured automobile.

Just as Zindel was about to return to the yeshiva, a wan, feeble Spektor opened the door still dressed in his nightshirt.

"What do you want?"

The question was posed rudely; there was no attempt to mask his irritation. And Zindel was taken aback. He might have turned around and fled if he hadn't been instructed to find out what Spektor was up to by the schoolmaster himself.

"Are you feeling all right?" Zindel asked.

Spektor looked more annoyed than before.

"Goodbye, Schumacher."

Spektor began to close the door.

"Wait, wait!" Zindel shrieked, a little louder than he intended, and his voice echoed in the nearby woods. Spektor stopped.

"What?"

"Well," the boy started, "everybody wants to know how you are." Realizing that the word "everybody" was vague enough that it might enflame Spektor more, he corrected himself. "The schoolmaster sent me."

Spektor considered this for a moment, wondering just how short he could afford to be with a proxy of his employer.

"You can tell him I don't feel well," Spektor finally said, and moved to close the door again.

Spektor didn't show up at school the next day. Or the day after. On the third day, the schoolmaster decided to take matters into his own hands. He arrived at Spektor's hovel near sunset, but when he knocked all he heard was stillness and silence. He went around back to see if Spektor was, perhaps, in the outhouse. But the premises appeared to be deserted.

The schoolmaster wondered if the man was too sick to answer (or, god forbid, worse) and if he shouldn't break down the door. But just as he was sizing up the slab of oak in front of him and his chances of knocking it down without injury, the man in question appeared out of the forest.

"Nu?"

While Spektor was never the embodiment of good health, the ashen, sickly figure that Zindel Schumacher reported seeing two days earlier had undergone a miraculous transformation. His face was pink and his hair was damp with sweat. His trousers were muddy and his hands caked with dirt. Most peculiar, he carried a pickaxe and shovel in his hands.

"Reb Spektor?"

Leonid turned hangdog.

"Reb Bernstein," Leonid replied with embarrassment. "It was very good of you to check up on me."

The schoolmaster didn't speak.

"Why don't you come inside?" Spektor moved to open the door.

"No," the schoolmaster said. "I just came to see if you were ill. But it appears that you are very much all right. I presume I'll see you tomorrow."

Spektor looked surprised—as if he had expected the lashing to be much, much worse.

"Yes, of course." And then, as if he wanted to make the man feel better about treating him forgivingly, Spektor added: "I wasn't feeling so good this morning."

However, this was such an obvious falsehood that it only served to infuriate the schoolmaster.

"Good day," the schoolmaster grunted, and seethed with rage on his way home. He remained in such a state the next morning that he decided to tell Rabbi Sokolow everything.

Other reports trickled back to the Rabbi about Spektor over the course of the next week. While Spektor missed no more lessons at the yeshiva, he exhibited increasingly strange behavior. He was observed walking through the town late at night, carrying the same tools the schoolmaster had seen him with. He purchased a number of lanterns and a pair of gloves at Slotnick's shop. He was groggy in the mornings and once drifted off to sleep in the middle of a lesson. But oddest of all, he was never home at night; he seemed to vanish into goodness-knows-where.

"What have you been up to?" Sokolow asked Spektor when he summoned him for one of their semi-regular chats.

Leonid just shrugged.

"I'm hearing peculiar things," the Rebbe said. "That you've been not behaving like yourself lately."

Leonid assumed a puzzled expression. "I don't know why anyone would think that." And that was as far as either party would push things.

After a few weeks, Spektor's behavior returned to normal. His energy was restored in the classroom. There were no more bizarre journeys through town in the middle of the night carrying heavy tools. And whatever anxiety had overtaken him a month or so earlier appeared to have dissipated.

It wasn't until the next visit from the gypsies that anyone else in town received any suggestion as to the source of this new heartiness and good cheer.

"What happened to the road?" one of the gypsies asked Frayda Siegel, as they were trading scarves for tubes of glue.

"What?"

"The road," the gypsy said. "It's ruined. What happened to it?"

The few words of Polish that Frayda spoke were largely devoted to trade. Anything more complicated was almost certainly a lost cause. Besides, she had been taught that when a gypsy asked a question it was in the service of some kind of trickery. "I don't know what you're talking about," Frayda said.

But there was no duplicity or cunning in what the gypsy woman asked. It was as if the modest dirt passage connecting the paths out of Kreskol with the asphalt-and-concrete highway had been deliberately sabotaged. Someone had planted a row of pine and birch saplings along the entrance to the highway. While the gypsies could still discern where to enter, in another year or two nobody else would. Behind the young trees, another attempt was made at camouflage, with transplanted bushes and logs scattered about, causing the path to blend with the surrounding forest—at least for those first critical meters.

Farther into the woods, trees had been felled, landing smack in the middle of the dirt road, making it impossible to drive a normal automobile through. (Luckily, the gypsies traveled by horse and could maneuver themselves and their carts more dexterously.)

In one notably difficult stretch to navigate, pits and trenches had been dug in the once smooth ground that hardened with the spring rains. It was more modest, perhaps, than the work of General Sherman or Lord Kitchener, but it was nonetheless effective. Only a very determined visitor would bother to traverse this path. Someone had formed a moat around Kreskol. And so it remained for the rest of Leonid Spektor's life.

10

SAINT TERESA

"If you're still a virgin," Karol said, "you need to take care of that, pronto."

In the eight weeks that they lived together, Karol Bugaj wasn't shy about offering his advice about the world, and what his new pal, Yankel Lewinkopf, needed to do to fit in and conquer it.

On their first morning together, he had started with fundamentals: "You ever use deodorant?" Karol asked. "'Cause I've gotta tell you, brother, nobody is going to look twice at you if you don't smell good." He then cocked his head and arched an eyebrow in a way to suggest that he wasn't making the point idly, and he handed Yankel a stick of Rexona. "Just rub it under your arm after you take a shower."

Yankel's shower routine got plenty of advice from Karol, too. "You take showers in Kreskol, don't you?" Karol asked. (We do not, but Yankel didn't feel pressed to clarify the point.) He gave Yankel a bottle of shampoo and another bottle of conditioner. "You rub the shampoo in your hair, right? You wash it out, then you put in the conditioner but you let it sit there for a minute or so before you wash it out. You get me?"

Yankel nodded, and Karol never stopped giving him advice thereafter.

Karol took Yankel to the Zlote Tarasy,* telling him, "Nobody wears black pants and a button-down shirt. You look ridiculous." Karol went straight to the Levi's counter and found Yankel a pair of blue dungarees. "The first thing you need to get is a pair of jeans. You can wear them any

---

*An office-and-retail complex in Warsaw.

day, any time of year. And they go with everything." When they found
a pair that fit, Karol handed the clerk his credit card and turned back to
Yankel. "We'll call this a loan, right?"

Yankel nodded.

"Next stop, we'll get you some T-shirts. Those'll come cheap. You might
need some more stuff down the line, but this will get you started." A pair
of gray sneakers, a dozen sweat socks, several pairs of boxer shorts, and a
toothbrush were added to Yankel's tab. "Today, I'll show you around my
neighborhood. Tomorrow we'll start trying to find you a job."

It would be difficult to say why Karol Bugaj felt generous and protective toward his new charge, but he did. It might have had something to
do with the fact that Mariusz Burak had dressed him down when they got
back to the TVP offices that first day. "We're here to report on the news,
Karol," Burak had said when they were alone, and Yankel was waiting in
the break room. "We're not here to make the news. If this guy stays with
you then you'll be part of the story." And Burak continued—on and on—
until an annoyed Karol snapped, "Fine, I'll turn him out tomorrow."

Karol then felt compelled to tell the younger man: "You know, Burak,
you can't talk to me that way. You're not my boss."

The next morning the thought of leaving Yankel on the streets to fend
for himself was put to rest when Karol told Yankel, "When Mariusz in-
terviews you in a few months about what you've been doing, you won't
mention my name, right?"

"Right."

Karol had a son, a few years younger than Yankel, who lived with his
ex-wife in Poznan and whom he was rarely afforded the chance to spend
time with and money on, and doing a good deed for a friendly and helpless
fellow made him feel fatherly. Yankel showed requisite gratitude and good
manners. And he let Karol do as much talking as he liked without filling
the silence with his own opinions. These were qualities Karol admired.

After he bought Yankel clothes, Karol drove him to his barbershop.
"I'm afraid our friend Mariusz didn't do much of a job on your hair,"

Karol laughed. "And there's no point in getting you dressed normally if you've got that shoddy beard and haircut."

"What's wrong with my beard?"

"You ain't old enough to grow one, kid," Karol said. "At least not properly. Look at how patchy it is. All peach fuzz. You shave for a year or two and it'll grow in right."

When the barber finished the shave, he put down the razor and traded it for a pair of scissors.

"How do you want it?" the barber asked.

"Want what?"

"Your hair."

Yankel was dumbfounded. "I don't know," he finally answered.

"Just make it nice and neat," Karol said for him.

Ten minutes later, Yankel looked unrecognizable to himself.

"You clean up good," Karol remarked.

And in the days and weeks that followed, the advice continued. Yankel was advised on how to search for a classified ad, how he should comport himself during a job interview, what the best brand of beer was, why he should always add fabric softener to a wash, why Pepsi was a superior cola to Coke, the reason to keep his wallet in his back pocket (the wallet, a little Velcro item, being another thing Karol added to Yankel's running bill), and a hundred other things.

Yankel followed Karol's advice scrupulously.

Karol told him that finding a job would not be easy, but that he would do what he could. "You got any skills?" Karol asked. "Anything you do better than the average shmoe on the street?"

"I'm a baker."

Karol grinned. "There you go—you're off on the right foot! I thought we'd have to make you a rent-a-cop or something."

The next day Karol took Yankel to the bakery two blocks from his apartment, and presented him to the owner.

"This is my cousin," Karol told the proprietor, after he spent a few moments searching for how he should introduce the young man. "His Polish is okay, but it ain't great. He's from . . . Azerbaijan."

The owner of the bakery smiled. "Is he Catholic, or a member of one of those Russian churches?"

"He's like us."

"Pleased to meet you," said the owner, a middle-aged gentleman with a distinguished gray mustache, extending Yankel a hand. "What's your name, sonny?"

"Yankee," Karol answered for Yankel. "That's what everybody calls him. His nickname is Yankee. Like the baseball team."

So within his first week in Warsaw, Yankel had found gainful employment. The pay was terrible, and he had to rise every morning at 3:00 if he intended to get the bread ready by the time the bakery opened its doors at 7:00, but it was a start. "Besides," Karol said, "you're not in a rush to leave, are you? You can stay with me until you save up a little to get your own apartment."

And Yankel proved to be an excellent roommate. Eager to make himself useful, he would fold up the bed and replace the couch cushions every morning before going off to work. The sink and the tub would always be clean and free from any stray hairs. And he would start making dinner when he got home from the bakery in the afternoon. Karol would come home to find that his apartment smelled of sweating onions and rendered chicken fat.

Yankel enthusiastically washed the dishes when the meal was over and scrubbed the kitchen down. When Karol discovered that Yankel was washing the dishes by hand he had more advice: "Use the dishwasher, for god's sake!" And he proceeded to demonstrate the miracle of this device, which Yankel at first refused to believe could do all that labor automatically.

Women and sex were the only things they didn't talk about in those first few weeks. This was not for lack of trying on Karol's part—but Yankel never responded when Karol whistled quietly at the derriere of a woman they would pass on the street or loudly at the gams of one they saw on TV.

And after observing Yankel turn tomato red and as shy as a church mouse upon mention of the fairer sex, Karol decided not to broach the topic.

But after the two of them had been living together for nearly two months, Karol didn't come home one night and when Yankel found the apartment empty the next morning, he was worried.

When Karol stepped through the door the next evening Yankel was the closest he had ever been to scolding his new friend.

"*Mój Boże,** Karol," Yankel said, copying one of his cohabitant's favorite phrases. "Where were you yesterday? I was worried sick."

Under different circumstances, Karol might have taken the position that this kid had a lot of nerve asking him his comings and goings when he was a guest, living rent-free. But there was little doubting that the concern and relief in Yankel's face was genuine. (He also thought it might be time to get his friend a phone.)

"Sorry I worried you, kid."

"Where were you?"

"Tanya," Karol said with a wink.

For a moment, Yankel thought that his roommate was referring to the great text of Hasidic mysticism, the Tanya, and Yankel had to wonder where this gentile—likable and kindhearted as he might have been— could have heard of this given that Karol's education and knowledge of the Jews had been limited, to put it politely. (After the haircut, Karol had fixated on Yankel's scalp for several minutes. When asked later what he had been staring at, Karol admitted that he had been trying to locate his friend's horns. "You can't blame a guy for *looking*, can you?")

The fact that Karol had said "Tanya" with a wink was even more confusing.

Alas, he was not referring to *the* Tanya, he was referring to *a* Tanya, namely a blond, slightly heavy woman who lived on the other side of Warsaw, whom Karol had known for several years and would occasionally

---

*Polish: "My goodness!"

spend the night with when they were both feeling lonely. "I guess I hadn't seen her since you've been here," Karol said. "But she called me at work yesterday. You know how it goes."

It was clear from the expression on Yankel's face that he didn't know how it went. Not in the least. And for the first time it occurred to Karol that his roommate might not just be shy but completely innocent in matters of sex.

It was slightly difficult to believe, given that Yankel cut a surprisingly handsome figure once he stopped wearing his yarmulke and sidelocks, and dressed a bit more normally. Karol had observed women checking him out as he strode past them in the streets.

"You never had a girlfriend—not once?" Karol asked.

Yankel shook his head.

"And you've never kissed a girl?"

Yankel blushed before he shook his head.

It was then that Karol advised Yankel to lose his virginity at once. "It's not like it's all that difficult," Karol assured Yankel. "We can take care of it tonight, if you want. I know a place."

Half an hour later, they were in Karol's car on their way to the place in question.

The cathouse was in a crummy, run-down part of town, and Yankel grew steadily more anxious as they got closer. Drifters and criminals seemed to be loafing on the street corners, lazily smoking cigarettes, waiting to commit some act of mischief on an unsuspecting, inexperienced party like himself. The sidewalks were salted with broken glass.

Karol pulled up across the street from a molding, scabby building where all the shades on the top three floors were pulled down. The ground floor had a fluorescent-lit commercial space with a red-and-white sign advertising "30 Minute Massage" out front.

"A couple of things to remember," Karol said to Yankel when he had turned off the engine. "First off, don't let them charge you more than two hundred zlotys. If the girl says you owe more, she's trying to hustle you. Second, this is for you." Karol reached into his pocket and handed Yankel a tiny square of golden foil. "This is a condom. You open it up and roll it onto your dick once you're hard. Do not take the condom off until you finish. I'm serious about this, brother. God only knows what these girls have. Do *not* take it off until you finish."

Yankel nodded, solemnly.

"Don't look so worried." Karol laughed, raffishly. "Just remember one thing. You're the one paying her. If you're finished in thirty seconds? Trust me, she's not going to care."

Yankel nodded again, and tried to smile, but once they were out of the car and headed across the street, he found himself trembling. The words "God only knows what these girls have" didn't make much sense to Yankel, but they sounded dire, particularly since Karol rarely issued *those* kinds of advisories.

It all happened very fast; they walked through the massage parlor, with Karol giving a little nod to the Chinese girl at the front desk, and up the stairs to an apartment on the second floor. Within a few seconds, Karol was talking to the short, elfin, middle-aged woman named Kasia with bleached blond hair and a pair of thick glasses that made her eyes seem immense, who ran the cathouse.

"He's shy," Karol said. "This is his first time. And he doesn't talk much. Who can you set him up with who'll treat him real nice?"

Yankel winced slightly.

"Don't worry about it," Kasia said, trying to catch Yankel's eye, and grinning at him. "We'll find somebody right for you. Do you have a particular type, teddy bear?"

Yankel had never been called an endearment by anybody except his grandmother, and it caught him off guard. "No," he said in a voice that came out garbled, as if he hadn't spoken all day.

She looked him up and down, as a horse trader might examine a prospective stallion, and after a moment grinned to herself. "Teresa," she finally said. "Oh, I think you'll like her. She's my most beautiful girl. And a bit shy herself. Come with me."

Kasia then waddled like a little duck down a darkened hallway, and found an empty bedroom that she led Yankel into.

"You can leave two hundred fifty zlotys on the dresser," Kasia said. "Right?"

Yankel nodded, and was left alone in a dimly lit bedroom, perfumed to smell like an indeterminate flower. The room was not much more than a bed, a nightstand, a lamp, and a vanity with an aged chair with faded roses and blue-green vines on the upholstery. The only decoration was a vintage poster of Tahiti hung across from the bed, but the room was dark enough that you could barely make out the beach and palm trees. And for Yankel the action abruptly shifted from happening too fast, to happening so slowly that he could do nothing except examine and reexamine everything he had done leading up to this moment.

A door finally opened, and a girl in a silk kimono glided toward the vanity, taking a seat there without greeting Yankel.

He couldn't see her face, only the bramble of dark brownish-blond hair that flowed over her shoulders and reached midway down her spine. She was small, which appeased Yankel slightly. For some reason he was terrified that this woman—whoever she was—would be some sort of giantess.

She busied herself rubbing a white cosmetic on her hands as Yankel stared at her. She didn't seem in any special hurry.

"You should take your clothes off," the girl said in an eastern accent, which put Yankel more at ease. She, too, was not from around these parts. He had to give Kasia credit; she had found a girl who attracted him.

He peeled off his jacket, T-shirt, sneakers, socks, and jeans and folded them in a neat mound by the side of the bed, lying down in only his white boxer shorts. But the moment his head hit the pillow he remembered Karol's admonition and sat up, tearing through his pants pockets for the condom. After he found it, he lay back down.

While she was still seated at the vanity, the girl loosed her robe. She looked at herself in the mirror for a few seconds, and then stood up, turning toward her customer.

The girl was beautiful—more beautiful than Yankel could have anticipated.

In the car on the way to the cathouse, Karol had warned him to keep his expectations in check. "These girls aren't going to be Victoria's Secret models, if you know what I mean," he had said. "I've been to this place before and the girls are fine. Who knows, maybe they've got one or two beauties. But the key word for this cathouse is 'affordable.' And while the girls are a little older, they keep themselves up and relatively disease-free. For now you just want to get this whole virginity thing behind you."

Moreover, Yankel had been somewhat terrified at what these women must look like when he laid eyes on Kasia, the madam of the house, who bore a striking resemblance to Hindelle Greenstein, a dwarfish spinster in her seventies, whom many of the boys in Kreskol believed was a witch, or a troll.

The woman at the front desk in the massage parlor wasn't much better. She didn't have any of the exotic beauty of the Orient; her face was moon-shaped and her cheek was dusted with specks of acne.

But this girl was unlike the other two—her figure, though small, was bewitching and flawless. Her skin was fair, as if she were a Saxon princess whose lineage could not be disguised even in the louche, rough-hewn locale where Yankel found her. Her eyes were two blue pools of liquid.

Yankel held his breath as he beheld this vision; he couldn't quite believe his luck.

But as quickly as his good fortune revealed itself, it fled. The girl took another step toward the bed, and Yankel suddenly sat up straight.

His disappointment was so great that he almost closed his eyes and said nothing. After all, he reasoned, he had already left his two hundred fifty zlotys on the dresser. Nobody would have blamed him much if he put out of his mind previous commitments and obligations. What would happen next would have been strictly between himself and the girl. It was, indeed, very unfortunate that Yankel was a man who had a conscience. And whose conscience governed his actions so ruthlessly.

"Hello, Pesha," he said in Yiddish. "You're Pesha Lindauer, aren't you?"

Now, I imagine that many of my readers might have laughed in disbelief when they read this last passage. Surely some coincidences are not possible. The author of this book—you thought—is no doubt pulling your leg.

Indeed, when I found this out I thought it sounded suspicious, too. What were the odds that of all the brothels in Poland, Yankel should have wound up at the one where his lost compatriot had landed?

More than that, what were the chances that Pesha Lindauer would have become a prostitute at all? Or settled in Warsaw? Or been the girl that Kasia had paired Yankel up with that night? A million to one, at least.

Plus, I felt bad for Yankel Lewinkopf. He must have felt there could be no possible disruption of this supreme moment of experience. The fact that he would have been actuated into carnal matters with someone as beautiful as Pesha Lindauer must have made the fleeting moment all the more joyous, and its dissolution all the more painful. As someone who has laid eyes on a clothed Pesha Lindauer, I can attest that it would have taken heroic powers of self-control and discipline to have stepped away in that instance of vulnerability. And yet, Yankel accepted the fact that luck was not on his side that evening.

Upon hearing these words in Yiddish, Pesha Lindauer collapsed on the bed and dissolved into helpless tears, which were so loud and alarming that within moments the little elf, Kasia, was pounding on the door, demanding it be opened at once. ("We know each other," Yankel assured Kasia, standing shivering in his gatkes.* "Believe me, I didn't do anything to her at all.")

---

*Yiddish: underpants.

This is not to say that Pesha was sad; if anything, she assured Yankel after she had put her kimono back on and dried her eyes, that hearing his voice had made her happier than anything had in months. They were tears of joy and remembrance.

So they passed the half hour together remembering.

They had not known each other well when they lived in Kreskol. She had been the daughter of a well-off and respected member of the community, and he was a mamzer. Under normal circumstances, they would have nothing to say to each other. When Yankel first greeted her, she did not place him as someone from Kreskol; she was simply shocked to hear the language she hadn't spoken in six months.

Hearing her name spoken was likewise so astonishing that how the speaker had come to know her name almost seemed incidental.

A few days after Pesha had arrived in Warsaw, Kasia had dismissed the name Pesha with a wave of the hand. "That's a terrible name for what you're going to be doing. You don't want anything too exotic. Something simple. You might also want a saint's name. How about Teresa?" And Pesha had been known as Teresa from then onward.

But she never grew accustomed to it; when Kasia, or one of the other tarts, would call her she wouldn't respond. Not out of malice or haughtiness—she just didn't notice it in the din of words that she barely understood. Some called her "Deaf Teresa" behind her back. Others called her "Saint Teresa" because they assumed she was taking on an air that was too good for a low-priced brothel.

"Who are you?" she whispered, under the choke of her tears, after Yankel had shooed away Kasia.

"Don't you recognize me?" Yankel said. "I'm Yankel Lewinkopf, the baker's assistant."

Yankel had never seen someone so happy to see him. She grasped him close to her and sobbed on his bare chest.

Half-clothed, in the semi-darkness, she told him as much of her story as she could in half an hour.

Pesha's story began the night before she left town, as she lay awake in bed reflecting on the rabid anger and rage she had seen on her former husband's face. She decided that the man might be crazy enough to kill her. It was enough to make her want to flee.

Besides, she wondered what kind of fate could be awaiting her once the evil man went through the time-honored ritual of dragging her name through the mud?

She had already gotten a brief glimpse of this. In the weeks before her divorce she had heard the wagging tongues of rivals. The fact that a beautiful girl from a respectable family had stumbled upon a bad marriage delighted the yentas* and busybodies of Kreskol. In the coming weeks these busybodies would no doubt go running to Ishmael to hear what a monster she was. It was supremely unfair.

Once she began thinking of the injustice of it, she was unable to stanch the flow of tears. It was in this moment of helplessness that her father knocked on her door and asked her if he couldn't bring her a glass of tea.

"No, Papa," she said—and they would be the last words she would speak to him. She fell asleep a little while later still fully dressed, with only her shoes at the foot of the bed.

Sometime in the night, she awoke. Her face was no longer damp with tears or sticky with snot. She dragged a handkerchief over her cheeks and smoothed the wrinkles out of her dress as she coldly, soberly began weighing her options.

Frankly, she had never been able to understand why more of her fellow villagers didn't pick up and leave town.

Unlike the rabbis and some of the wealthier members of the community, Pesha didn't have much undue romanticism about Kreskol. (She was hardly the only one, but that's another discussion.) While our town might possess a certain natural beauty, and while we were blessed with fertile fields and abundant enough crops, we were for all other purposes poor.

---

*Yiddish: gossipmongers.

And the beauty of a town—day in and day out—can still grow tiresome when it has been lived in every hour of one's life.

When she was still a child Pesha had even briefly hatched a plan to make an escape to Krakow after she had quarreled with her mother. The catalyst for this argument had been relatively insignificant—a chore the seven-year-old Pesha hadn't felt it necessary to complete—but the subsequent silence and mutual disappointment between parents and child lasted for days. Pesha had bestowed on her parents a curse, and vowed to leave town at first opportunity. She packed a bag, which she left under her bed, and waited for the house to fall asleep. When she was certain that her mother and father would not be woken, she quietly tiptoed through the house and then to the edge of town before she lost her nerve at the loud hooting of an owl. She moodily returned to her room.

Now the idea of abandoning Kreskol without a word to anybody seemed not only possible but her only conceivable salvation.

Naturally, there were a few considerations. Her father, for one. He was old, and old men do not recover from the loss of a daughter so easily, even one who has left home of her own volition. (But, as Pesha asked herself, would a good father wish that his daughter's future should be steeped in unhappiness?)

Second, there were her sisters to think about, the youngest of whom was unmarried. She wondered what this would do to Hadassah's chances of finding a husband if the matchmakers concluded that the Rosenthals were trouble. But she waved this concern away, too. Hadassah would rise or fall on her own.

Finally, she would have been a fool if she hadn't worried at least a little about how she would transport herself to Warsaw, or Paris, or America, or wherever she wound up. And the more she thought about it, the greater the realization that it was *this* obstacle more than any other that kept the emigration rate low—nobody would take a chance going through the woods unless they absolutely had to.

But she discarded this last objection as well. How big could Poland possibly be? How long could she really be expected to wander the woods before she found *something*? Perhaps it was a gamble, but if her only alternative was an unhappy life in Kreskol, she was willing to spin the wheel. She needed to leave that night. Right now. If she slept on the idea, she would talk herself out of it.

She packed very little; a shawl, a scarf, a locket that her mother had given her before she died, a kitchen knife to defend herself in the wilderness, and nothing else. She made the bed before she departed (more out of a sense of habit than anything else), and took what was left of a kugel out of the pantry.

The town was fast asleep and she was in such a hurry to be gone before the fishermen or farmers awoke that she didn't even remember to write a farewell note or give herself one last look as she walked into the woods.

A week later—as she faced starvation and dehydration, and had been chased by wild animals (although whether the bear in question was actually chasing Pesha or caught up in his own affairs is a matter of interpretation)—she still refused to turn around and go back the way she came. "The woods were terrible—terrible," she told Yankel. "But the idea of turning around and going home sounded much worse. I was fool enough to think that death would be preferable."

"I know the feeling," Yankel said, quietly.

"But that first week was the worst of it," Pesha continued. "It was on either the seventh or eighth day out of town that I came upon a farmhouse, and the farmer gave me a lift to Lublin.

"I can tell you. It was a pain-in-the-you-know-what getting him to take me. I didn't speak a word of the language. And he certainly didn't speak any Yiddish. But the fellow liked what he saw when he looked at me. I don't blame him—I got a look at his wife, and she was no beauty queen. Not by a mile. So I started saying 'Bialystok' and 'Warsaw' and 'Lublin,' and he got the idea that I wanted a cart to take me to one of those places. He couldn't resist the idea of being alone with me all the way to Lublin."

This might have been where Pesha, who was always a wily creature, figured out that she might be able to capitalize on her looks.

The farmer's wife put up a fuss. She could see the dangers of letting her husband drive two long hours to Lublin with a woman like Pesha in the passenger's seat, but I suppose she didn't like the idea of keeping the homeless Jewish beauty on the farm, either. Her permission was reluctantly granted, and the two of them took off in a pickup truck. (Which held its own astonishment for Pesha until it gradually melted into the scenery of the world outside Kreskol.)

"He tried some funny business on me," Pesha continued. "I suppose if I had a wife who looked like her, I might have tried something too. But just before we reached Lublin, he put a hand on my knee. And when I didn't say anything right away, he tried to reach a bit farther up—but that was too much. I pushed him away, which, I should add, nearly made him crash the car. And I began crying hysterically. I've never seen a man look so scared. He begged me to quiet down—at least I think that's what he was begging."

She next told Yankel about a hungry day spent meandering around Lublin, rummaging through garbage cans for something edible, when there was a knock at the door.

"Time."

"I'm sorry, Yankel," Pesha said. "But I'm a working girl and she's the boss. You have to go, or I'll have to give her another two hundred zlotys."

Yankel nodded.

"I'd like to see you again," Pesha said, when Yankel was almost fully dressed. "Not as a customer. I'd just like to see you. Talk to you, you know. Are you free tomorrow?"

"I get out of work at one."

"That's perfect," Pesha said, grinning. "Why don't you meet me here at two? I'll leave your name with the girl out front. She'll show you right in."

Even though Pesha was smiling, she looked slightly—ever so slightly—embarrassed. As if the wideness of her grin masked the fact that Yankel had paid for a service she had not provided. At least, this was how Yankel interpreted it. He also decided she wouldn't have mentioned "another two hundred zlotys" if she wasn't feeling at least a little guilty.

Just before he left, Pesha stood up and kissed him on the cheek.

"I guess I didn't have to worry about it being over in thirty seconds," Karol nearly shouted, when Yankel was back in his car, unable to contain his laughter. "I can't believe it—you stud!"

"Yeah," Yankel said with a snort.

"Took to it like a duck to water, didn't you?" Karol said, and he gave Yankel a strong jab in the shoulder. "You son of a bitch, you! You son of a bitch!"

"I suppose so."

"I'll bet the girl wasn't much to look at. Well, as I told you, these places are not the best ones out there."

"No," Yankel said. "She was beautiful."

"Son of a bitch!" Karol howled. "Goes to a cheap little whorehouse for his first time, and he scores a hottie! Tonight's your night, kid!"

As much as he yearned for a little quiet to contemplate all that had happened in the last hour, Yankel had to admit that Karol's enthusiasm was infectious. And Yankel knew that even though he would have to embroider and embellish all sorts of details about the experience, he didn't have the heart to let down his friend, who was so happy for him.

"So, how was it?" Karol asked as he started the car. "Did it match your hopes and dreams, kid?"

Yankel considered this for a moment.

"It was," he answered, "beyond belief."

She was waiting for him outside the cathouse, as she had been warned not to invite the gentleman back unless he was a paying customer. They took a tram to a café that Pesha knew called Trzmiel, which had a wood-paneled sitting room and a nice view of a garden.

They shared a mania for coffee. Karol had given Yankel his first cup a few weeks earlier, which he had sweetened with two overflowing lumps of sugar and lightened with milk. Yankel declared it to be the greatest, most delicious drink he had ever tasted; he also said that it made him feel crisper, more energetic, as if could run clear across Warsaw without losing a beat.

"Don't drink too much," Karol warned. "Too much is not good for you. It'll fuck up your heart and your blood pressure."

But it was an admonition that never stuck. He drank cup after cup and when he found his head swimming, and his heart racing, his immediate cure was more coffee. A few weeks later, Karol noticed that Yankel was never without a mug in hand.

"Christ, Yankel. How much do you drink?"

"Seven cups a day."

"That's way too much," Karol said. "Slow it down. If you can do with three cups a day, you'd probably be fine."

Pesha discovered coffee fairly early during her tenure in Warsaw, and agreed it was some sort of miracle drink. Although Pesha also felt that Coca-Cola and Red Zinger tea were miracle drinks, too. "You're not supposed to put sugar in it," Pesha warned Yankel as he reached for three white cubes. "Put this in—it tastes the same."

Pesha tore two yellow packs of sugar substitute into Yankel's mug.

And after they had sorted their various drink orders, along with Viennese cream cakes and butter cookies (both of them had independently reached the decision that a leveret-like kosher diet was impossible to keep in the big city), they would spend hours talking.

Pesha continued on with her saga, which she mostly got through on their first meeting.

After two days of searching through the rubbish bins of Lublin, she spotted Kasia at the Glowny Dworzec Autobusowy.*

---

*Polish: bus station.

"I had thought of Hindelle Greenstein, too!" Pesha laughed. "In fact, for a moment, I thought it *was* Hindelle. I almost said 'Hello' to her. But the hair was not right. And those glasses."

The middle-aged Hindelle lookalike had her eye on Pesha as well. She had been sitting with another girl when she stood up, whispered something in the girl's ear, and crossed the bus terminal to ask Pesha a question in Polish. Pesha said nothing. The dwarf tried the question in Russian and then German. The German didn't sound right—but it sounded somewhat recognizable. The question ended in the word "*hungrig,*" which sounded close enough to a query she would recognize.

"Yes," Pesha said, and a tear shone in her eye. "I'm very hungry."

"Armste!"* Kasia exclaimed. "Poor dear!"

As if she were her mother and not a complete stranger, Kasia grasped Pesha close to her bosom and patted her on the back, like she was burping an infant.

The other girl—a waifish blond, who looked roughly the same age as Pesha and even more tense and frightened by her surroundings—was summoned with a wave of the arm and the three of them (along with three suitcases and handbags) plopped down at a German restaurant nearby.

"You know how you feel on Yom Kippur, after a day of fasting, when everything tastes better?" Pesha asked Yankel. "When you think you know what butter tastes like, but you taste a little butter on a bagel and you realize that you've never really tasted butter before?"

"I suppose."

"That's what that meal was like. Every morsel was better than anything I had ever tasted before. There was veal schnitzel, potato salad with dill, sauerkraut, and potato rolls. The beer was served in frosty glass mugs—I drank three of them that day. And as we sat there—Kasia, the girl Yulia, and me—Kasia kept on talking. 'Poor girls,' she said. 'Poor, mistreated girls. You'd think the world would treat us better in this day and age. But

---

*German: "Poor dear."

no. Not at all. We've always got to look after each other, because no man is interested in helping us. The men of the world are out for themselves.' After she said that to me in German, she would turn and say the same thing to Yulia in Russian. I'll tell you, Yankel, when an angel swoops down and feeds you when you're hungry, and spends an hour talking to you in a language you somewhat understand—well, you're *straining* to understand—and when she appears to care for you and your well-being and invokes the common bond of sisterhood . . . Maybe I was naïve, but I was desperate."

Yankel nodded.

"'I would like to help you,' she said. 'When I see a young girl off on her own, mistreated, something in me cries out. I want to help.' I suppose it sounds really silly to hear secondhand."

It is an old story, certainly. Even in the backwoods of Kreskol, we had heard stories of white slavery. But I suppose that we all thought that the seduction would be handled by a slick male—none of us would have been on guard against an equally canny woman.

Kasia handed both girls a flier in Polish—which neither woman spoke—showing two happy, laughing girls sitting on bunk beds in what appeared to be an enormous dormitory. One of the girls, smiling and dimpled, had blond hair that had been braided into two golden ropes. She was being embraced in a sisterly way by a redheaded girl, with smoky brown eyes and a slightly more mischievous smile.

"She said, 'I run an organization for girls.' I don't remember what she called it. Something like 'The Warsaw Young Women's Foundation.' But it sounded official. And, I'm a little ashamed to admit this now, but I thought the fliers were impressive. They looked bona fide. Like it required more time, money, and effort than a con artist would dole out. But she told me that it helped young orphans—or, not orphans as such, but women who had no money and no place to go—get on their feet.

"Who would question such good fortune, Yankel? What was I supposed to do? Tell her to mind her own business? How could I do such a thing? She seemed the answer to a prayer. And besides, you saw what she looks like. She's nothing more harmful than a little dwarf! Who could be hurt by a dwarf?"

The three women got up from their lunch and boarded a bus for Warsaw, and all the while, Kasia switched back and forth from German to Russian, telling both girls what they could expect when they came to live in her dormitory. The girls all cooked together, they did chores together, and they also had things like movie nights together (which Pesha didn't understand), and something that Kasia called "Queen for the Day," in which once a week one lucky girl wouldn't have to do any chores, and would have the other girls waiting on her hand and foot.

"'Naturally, the place doesn't pay for itself,' Kasia told us. 'While we never charge any of the girls any money, you are expected to contribute some labor to our endeavor. We are engaged in a number of businesses that we need staffed.' Of course, I said, I would do *anything* to help out. It was only fair. 'That's good, Pesha,' she said. (She still called me Pesha then.) 'That's very good. Well, don't you worry. We'll find something for you.'"

And from the way Pesha told it, she hadn't been so badly treated that first week.

Kasia had the run of several houses and apartments around Warsaw, and for the first few days she left Pesha and Yulia alone in an apartment in a remote section of town. There were twin beds in one of the rooms, and a television in the living room. The refrigerator was stocked with milk, Swiss cheese, eggs, butter, a loaf of rye bread, and a few apples and tomatoes.

"I'll come back tomorrow with some extra groceries, but you can make do with this for today, right?" Kasia had said.

Both girls nodded.

After Kasia left, Yulia turned on the television, which had the effect of entrancing Pesha. "How does it work?" she asked Yulia—but Yulia didn't understand the question and didn't look particularly impressed by the miracle unfolding before her.

Yulia wasn't impressed by much. She never looked at anything in the apartment except the television. Her arms were bruised, scratched, and dried over, and for a moment Pesha wondered if the poor girl had also been lost in a forest. Pesha made an attempt to ask her about these scratches, but the girl showed no interest in engaging her. Pesha could never decide whether the girl was rude or wasn't going to bother trying to communicate in a language she didn't understand. Either way, Pesha stopped trying.

But before it got dark Pesha told Yulia that she wanted to go out for a walk and explore the neighborhood.

She didn't walk more than a handful of blocks from the apartment, but she was away for almost two hours. She passed a flower shop and admired the African daisies. She stopped in an eyeglass store and examined a pair of Louis Vuitton sunglasses. At the perfumer, the girl behind the counter spurted a little Chanel No. 5 on her wrist and told her (in the Polish that she didn't understand) that it smelled of rose and jasmine.

"Oh, I remember what that was like for the first time," Yankel told her.

Pesha's eyes suddenly met his, and she smiled.

"Yes," she said with a light laugh. "You're the only one who knows what that's like."

She and Yulia lived together in the apartment for four days before Kasia arrived and said that she was taking Yulia to a dormitory in Praga Polnoc. When Yulia said goodbye, Pesha wasn't especially sorry to see her go. (Whatever good qualities she might have been hiding, there was no question that Yulia was painfully boring.)

The next morning, Kasia came for Pesha, too.

"Kasia seemed changed," Pesha said of that encounter. "She had been so friendly on that first day—so understanding and generous. Now she was all business. 'This is a special apartment, Pesha,' she said. 'We keep you here for a few days to get your sea legs, but you can't stay here forever. You have to go to another dorm with the other girls. And this is where we'll figure out a work schedule. So get your things and let's go.' But I was a good sport. Of course, Kasia. Anything you say, Kasia."

She was taken to the cathouse where Yankel would later discover her. She was given her new name—Teresa—and introduced to the other girls, none of whom were especially friendly. The rooms were dingier than the ones where she had been staying, and Pesha was frightened by the dirt and grime. But she was also aware that she was living on charity and determined not to kick up a fuss.

"I'll leave it to the other girls to get you up to date on how things work here," Kasia said. "But just settle in for now."

She didn't remember much about the first night. Before business started for the evening, someone suggested a toast to the new girl. Pesha was handed a drink in a red plastic cup, and a few minutes later she felt woozy. She woke up the next morning naked in one of the beds. Whatever imp or foul demon had crept into the bed and defiled her in the night was long gone.

Pesha looked down at her coffee and away from Yankel.

"It isn't so bad, you know. Not really. That first time was terrible, no question. I guess they figured they had to lure me in. Once I was initiated, there would be no turning back. And I have to give Kasia credit—she was cunning about it. I would have run a thousand miles away if she came out and said what it was that she wanted me to do. And I cried and cried the next day. But once the vilest deed had been committed, the rest doesn't seem quite so bad. At least, it didn't for me. One of the things you learn when you've been away from Kreskol for a while is that the world is a far less modest, less moral place. But modesty isn't everything."

"You don't mean that, Pesha," Yankel answered.

She smiled and looked back at him.

"That's where you're wrong," she continued. "No, I don't like what I'm doing. Not at all. And yes, if you said that I traded one nightmare for another that wouldn't be so far off the mark. But if you asked me right now if I would like to return to Kreskol I would say no. A thousand times no. Never."

Yankel looked away, before he returned to her gaze.

"I was sent to Smolskie to look for you, you know," Yankel finally said. "Rabbi Sokolow and the rest of them gave me a note to give to the authorities saying you were missing, and that your husband probably killed you."

Pesha looked surprised.

"They thought Ishmael murdered me?"

"Yes."

She released a one-note staccato laugh.

"And, you know, your family was grieving for you."

Pesha blanched.

"No, I didn't know that," Pesha said. "You're right. I should have left a note." But that appeared to be the extent of her regrets.

Yankel remained downcast as they continued drinking their coffee.

"Let me tell you something, Yankel. The girls at these brothels are idiots. I don't know what you know about drugs, but there are a lot of them at the brothel. Kasia gives the girls their allowance and their tips, and they turn around and spend it on all sorts of terrible stuff. But not me. I'm figuring out how to get out of there. And I've got my money stashed away. Someday I'll go to Paris or New York or Jaffa and I'll open up a café or a flower shop, or I'll wait tables. *Something* better. Don't you feel sorry for me—not for a second. I've made my choices, and I'm happy enough with them."

Her voice dropped, slightly, with this last pronouncement; as if she had imprudently invited Yankel into a private reverie she had never intended for his—or anyone's—ears.

Perhaps she already learned that indiscretion was dangerous in her line of work; that it was wiser to keep any fantasies to herself. However, this moment of incaution was also a gesture of trust. An involuntary vote of confidence in him. Yankel couldn't help but be moved.

They continued chatting for another hour before they both decided it was late and they should go.

"I have a question for you, Yankel," Pesha said just as they went their separate ways. "So when you said that everyone thinks that Ishmael murdered me, does that mean he's locked up in chains?"

"No—he fled town, too. Just before I was sent off to alert the authorities."

A shadow fell on Pesha's lovely, doll-like face, and her mouth curled downward in a frown.

"He's on the loose?"

"Yes."

"Do you know where he went?"

"Nobody knows."

Pesha looked more angry than fearful.

"I wish you hadn't told me that," she said, looking at him for the first time with eyes bespeaking something other than affection.

Yankel fell in love with Pesha as only the very young can love: instantaneously; unquestioningly; implacably.

Truly, Yankel felt a certain astonishment that emotions could overwhelm him so completely for a woman he didn't know very well. And for a woman whose moral history, under normal circumstances, he would have been appalled by.

On the tram back to Karol's, he had to stuff his hands into his mouth and bite into his fingers to keep himself from howling with rage that this woman—whom he suddenly felt so tenderly toward—should have endured the degradations and abuses she described. When he got off the tram a few stops early, he stomped his feet on the pavement, like an angry ogre, eager for the world to take notice of his displeasure. As he passed an unattended car, he kicked one of the headlights with all his might, leaving shards of yellow glass on the asphalt. Dismayed at this gratuitous act of wrath, he sprinted the rest of the way home.

Back in Karol's apartment, he had no interest in eating dinner or dis-

cussing the events of the day. He merely asked to be left alone, and meditated solely on Pesha and her misfortunes.

When he realized that the next time they would see each other, Pesha
would have been with a dozen different men—or more—none of whom
loved her or cared for her, his anger became unbearable. He wished he
hadn't just kicked out a headlight—he felt a savage urge to heave a rock
through the windshield; slash open the rubber tires with a knife; burn the
remains to the ground. If he had access to enough gasoline, he might have
ignited the entire block.

In the abyss of his rage, Yankel went out later that night and lost his
virginity.

"What are some of the other cathouses around town, Karol?" Yankel
asked his friend. "Do you know any others?"

"Whoa, tiger. You just went to one. I know you had a good time, but
you're trying to save money—remember?"

"I know."

"We'll go again in a few weeks. Believe me, I understand why you want
to go back."

Yankel stared at his friend for a few moments before he spoke.

"Tonight," Yankel said. "I want to go tonight."

Karol was taken aback. His roommate was such a passive chap that it
was almost unthinkable that one of Karol's edicts should be challenged.

"Why do you have to go tonight?" Karol asked—but Yankel didn't
answer.

Karol considered this for a few moments. He was not Yankel's father,
after all. If the kid wanted to throw away another couple hundred zlotys,
it wasn't really his business. Plus, the kid spent almost nothing. He never
went to the movies, or out to clubs, or bought himself Italian leather
shoes, or even a pack of cigarettes.

"All right," Karol said. "I'll take you back."

"Not the place we went," Yankel said. "Somewhere else."

This was peculiar, given that Karol had been under the impression that his friend had done very well at the last cathouse. But he decided not to say anything. He drove Yankel to an address in Srodmiescie, and pointed to an apartment building. "It's number twenty-one. Do you want me to come up with you?"

Yankel shook his head.

As he got out of the car, Karol said, "Do you want me to wait for you?"

"No," Yankel said firmly. "Thank you. I'll find my way home."

I have long found Yankel's behavior here difficult to fathom. The only explanation I have been able to come up with is that there's a demon of pride in every man, and Yankel was determined that if he should be cuckolded by the woman he loved, he would cuckold her in return. It was, perhaps, faulty reasoning, but the heart is tethered to a different set of rules than any other part of the anatomy. His fingers trembled as he rang the bell, but the only behavior that seemed to make any sense to Yankel was to do with another woman what Pesha was undoubtedly doing at that very moment with another man.

The door to this brothel was answered by a stocky, bald, and somewhat frightening man.

"What do you want?" the gatekeeper asked.

Yankel was unprepared for questions—but he knew that the request needed to be cloaked innocuously.

"I want to meet one of the girls."

The gatekeeper eyed him up and down, and led him into the living room of what seemed an otherwise normal three-bedroom apartment. Seated on the couch were three bored-looking girls: a blond and two brunettes. Two of the girls were in bathrobes, one was in her underwear. All three were smoking cigarettes.

"Okay," said the gatekeeper, dispensing with unnecessary protocol. "Take your pick."

They were all ordinary-looking. Yankel settled on the blond, who was short, with puppyish brown eyes and rounded lips, simply because she looked less like the other two.

The girl stubbed out her cigarette and got to her feet.

"Let's go," she said with an affected cheeriness, and led Yankel down the hall.

Before they entered the bedroom, Yankel found the gatekeeper standing behind him. "Hey," the gatekeeper said. "It's gonna be three hundred zlotys."

Yankel took a moment before nodding.

"You leave it on the dresser *before* she does anything."

Yankel nodded again, deciding he didn't like this fellow very much.

"One other thing," the gatekeeper said, giving Yankel a final look in the eye, and apparently deciding he didn't like Yankel much, either. "No rough stuff. You hurt one hair on her head, and I'll break your arm."

"I understand."

The room was more dimly lit than the one in the other cathouse. A lamp with a red lightbulb was the only illumination, which made the girl's flesh look as if it were glowing.

She was quicker about her business than Pesha had been. There were no unnecessary creams or makeups to add or subtract. Once the door was closed, she discarded her robe and lay down naked on the bed.

As ordinary as her face looked, the robe had done a good job concealing how exceptional the girl's form was. Her breasts were enormous, even as the rest of her frame was small. Her skin, more honey-colored than Pesha's, was unblemished. And even though he was fully dressed—and a muddle of different emotions—Yankel was aroused. He began unbuttoning his shirt.

"Three hundred on the dresser," the girl said, not moving.

Yankel wordlessly counted the money and left it where she told him.

"Do you have a rubber?" the girl asked as he proceeded to undress.

She needn't have asked; the prophylactic remained unopened and untouched in his pocket, slyly taunting him for failing to consummate his first encounter.

"How does this work?" he asked, showing her the condom.

The surprise passed from the girl's face as quickly as it appeared, and she removed it from Yankel's hand, tore off the wrapper, and unrolled the device into place. But Yankel's question softened the girl. She moved slower, raised his chin with her fingers, and kissed him. Whether it was simulated or authentic, there was warmth in the kisses, thrusts, and moans that followed. As Yankel groped blindly through his first sexual act, he felt something greater than the clumsy dread most males feel during their inaugural moment.

When he finished, she slid off him and, rather than get dressed right away, lit a cigarette.

"That was your first time, wasn't it?" the girl asked him.

Yankel nodded.

"I didn't think that when you came in," the girl said. "You can usually tell."

Yankel didn't say anything.

"The virgins are always so timid. Afraid of their own shadow. You looked determined. Like nothing was going to stop you. But then you asked me about the rubber and I knew . . ."

Neither of them spoke for a minute, as the girl smoked.

"Well, I'm honored I was the one you picked," the girl said. "I suppose you'll never forget me now."

"I suppose not."

"Did you enjoy that?"

The moment he finished had been filled with regret. He felt like he had betrayed an unspoken promise he had made to Pesha. Of course, no vows had been exchanged, but Yankel was convinced of his indecency nonetheless.

However, the physical sensation had been so much greater than anything he could have been prepared for. The eruption in his loins had felt at once so abnormal and yet so liberating. As if his entire essence had joyfully tumbled into a vast, bottomless ocean.

"Yes," he said. "I enjoyed it."

Yankel and Pesha continued meeting every Monday.

At their second rendezvous, Yankel began telling Pesha his story, and she listened with the same rapt attention he had shown her.

He loved her more and more after every encounter. He thought of her at the bakery and when he went home. As he walked the streets, he looked for Pesha's face on the shoulders of every woman he passed. He went to the Trzmiel café that she had taken him to in the hopes that she would return on a random Tuesday or Thursday and he would have an extra hour or two alone with her. He could no longer sleep on Sunday nights, as he lay on the couch, staring up at the ceiling, and wondering if she would really be waiting for him at Trzmiel.

And yet after each encounter with Pesha, Yankel would find himself in a different cathouse, in a different part of Warsaw, with a different prostitute. (For some reason, he tried not to visit the same brothel twice.) He would come home from these houses of ill repute and wordlessly climb into his makeshift bed, where the tears would silently fall down his cheeks. Karol began to grow concerned that his friend might have mistaken that first dalliance with a harlot for love, in which case he would have to wise up the poor sap. But whenever he asked Yankel if anything was wrong, Yankel insisted everything was fine.

Sometimes Yankel and Pesha would sit and have coffee as they talked, sometimes they would wander through the Galeria Mokotow. They exchanged their impressions of Warsaw; their constant amazement at the pace of things. How quickly affairs were decided. How plentiful food and luxury were. How fast people traveled. How lonely it was to live in a city where you didn't speak the language. How confounding the technology proved.

And they remembered Kreskol with nostalgia; the cobblers and wine-makers and butchers all garnered laughs and smiles. They talked of how secure it felt walking the streets and recognizing every face. They rarely spoke of the things they both despised about Kreskol.

"Next week, do you want to meet me on Sunday morning at the Kolo Bazaar?" Pesha asked one Monday. "It's only open on Saturday and Sunday. It's supposed to be something to see."

Sunday was Yankel's busiest day at the bakery, but given his otherwise punctual and uninterrupted attendance record, the request for a day off was granted.

They walked through the bazaar like two dazed children. It reminded Yankel of his journey to Smolskie all those months back, when he had sat in the back of the gypsy wagon. The bazaar was a strange mixture of old and new; there was a Prussian Pickelhaube on one table, a used DVD player on another. Some of the crazy old gypsies had put out their soiled underwear on the ground, hoping to find the right customer.

Pesha tried on a fur coat, and examined herself in a full-length mirror for several long minutes before she conceded that it was too expensive, even if she haggled it down to its proper price.

"Try this on," Pesha instructed Yankel, handing him a leather jacket.

Yankel obeyed.

"Oh my!" Pesha said when she saw him. "Oh my. You're getting that, Yankel. No questions asked."

Yankel blanched when he saw the cost—four hundred zlotys—and he was about to say so, but before he had a chance Pesha was bargaining the jacket down in price. "One hundred," she told the old woman who was selling jackets, winter coats, and blazers off a rack.

The proprietress laughed at Pesha's brazenness, and counteroffered: "Three hundred."

"One-fifteen."

And after the two went back and forth for a few more rounds, they agreed on a price: 170 zlotys. Before Yankel could reach into his pocket and buy the jacket that he didn't really want, Pesha had already paid the woman.

"That's a gift, Yankel," she said when he tried to reimburse her. "Just wear it. You look handsome in it."

The love he felt for Pesha at that moment was uncontainable. He wanted to buy her something. Anything. He almost went for the fur coat that she had discarded, but another woman had already picked it up and had begun bargaining with the crone.

"Thank you," he said in a hushed voice.

"You're welcome."

As brashly as she had purchased the jacket, she took his hand in hers and walked him to the next stall.

"Your hand is sweaty," she said.

"Sorry."

She laughed sweetly at his embarrassment.

He could have died right then and there with a glow of contentment on his face that no undertaker could have disguised. He laughed, too. And when their eyes met, Yankel was convinced that she shared his affections.

They spent the morning walking through the bazaar, going from table to table, examining antique brooches and bonnets and admiring photographs and old movie posters. "Who's that?" Yankel asked when he saw an over-sized black-and-white poster of a lean, clear-eyed man wearing a sweater, sitting astride a motorcycle. "Steve McQueen," the merchant answered. Accordion players and guitarists ambled slowly through the market serenading the shoppers. When Pesha said she was hungry, they shared a bag of popcorn and had the same ticklish reaction to the dryness, saltiness, softness, and crunchiness of each kernel.

He almost said the words "I love you"—but stopped himself at the last moment, too terrified of what she might say in response.

Pesha went to look at a table of handbags while Yankel meandered around a table filled with pipes, cigarette cases, and Zippo lighters, when he heard a voice say: "Hey!"

He looked up and found the blond prostitute with the puppyish eyes from the Srodmiescie cathouse smiling at him.

"I thought that was you," she said.

Never had such a feeling of dread swept over Yankel. He instinctively turned around to look for Pesha, but did not see her, which filled him with both relief and panic at the same time.

The girl looked a bit older when she was fully dressed. She wore a wooly indigo sweater, a peasant skirt, and long leather boots. Around her neck was a small, barely noticeable gold cross. Her blond hair was tied in a ponytail poised off her shoulder. She didn't try to hide her genuine cheeriness at seeing Yankel.

For an instant, he wondered if he shouldn't take off running and find Pesha later. But the girl spoke again before he could act, and the sound of her voice chilled him.

"Don't tell me you've forgotten me already." The blond laughed. "I thought you said that you'd never forget me."

Actually, she had been the one who predicted that he would never forget her, but there was no point arguing.

"Of course I remember you."

"Good." She smiled. "I would have been pretty lousy at my job otherwise."

At the moment, Yankel turned around and saw Pesha coming closer to him, with her eye on the girl.

To her credit, the girl sensed that there was something between Yankel and Pesha, and her friendliness vanished. "Well, good to see you," she said, "so long." She quickly turned in the opposite direction, wending her way through the crowd.

But the damage had been done. Pesha likewise sniffed the intimacy between Yankel and the girl. And there was a look of surprise in her eyes, as if she had stumbled upon a burglar sizing up her property.

"Who was that?"

"Nobody. Just somebody who comes in the bakery now and then."

Pesha continued staring at the girl as she slowly grew smaller and more difficult to locate in the crowd.

"Who is she?" Pesha repeated. "What's her name?"

"I don't know."

"She seemed awfully chummy for somebody whose name you don't know," Pesha declared.

Before Yankel could say anything else, Pesha marched into the crowd and swiftly began making her way toward her rival. Had he been thinking more clearly, Yankel might have given chase, but he froze.

It was only a matter of seconds before the commotion blazed up, and Yankel began running through the crowd.

When he reached Pesha and the prostitute, they were circling each other like a pair of feral cats. Pesha, losing any thread of Polish she might have held, was screaming in Yiddish. The prostitute looked frightened and not a little angry. She scowled back in a guttural Polish that Yankel didn't understand.

"Just who do you think you've got your eye on?" Pesha scowled. "You keep your tits to yourself, you goddamn korva!"

The crowd surrounding the two of them was incredulous and fascinated. None of the spectators were sure what this fight was about, precisely, yet both women looked angry enough to draw blood, which enticed nearly everyone in the vicinity. The fact that both women were attractive (Pesha exceptionally so) lent an even greater depth of interest.

Even though she was the less angry of the two, the prostitute was more dangerous, and when she spotted a mason jar at one of the nearby stalls, she picked it up, smashed its top, and waved the jagged glass in Pesha's direction. Everybody watching took a leap backwards.

The only person who did not scamper away was Pesha. As swiftly as if she had been a trained dancer, Pesha leaped over to one of the nearby tables and grabbed a golf club.

The fervor in this latest act startled her adversary, who was now the one to involuntarily take a small step back. But this extremely minor victory did nothing to allay Pesha's anger or her heightened state of self-defense. She swung the club at the mason jar, which shattered and left the prostitute's hand a gushing, bloody mess.

It was at that moment Yankel could not bear any more. He jumped forward and enveloped Pesha in his arms.

"Let it go," he said. "Let it go."

The fury slowly trickled away, and Pesha dropped the golf club. All the while, Pesha never took her eyes off the blond harlot, who was now on her knees, cradling her bloody hand. It was as her breathing slowed down that a police officer arrived.

The prostitute's wound was wrapped in gauze that one of the merchants kept under the table, and she was driven to the hospital by one of the Samaritans who had gathered to watch the scene unfold.

Pesha was handcuffed and taken away.

"Can I ride with her?" Yankel asked the arresting police officer.

"Are you kidding?" the officer smirked, slamming the back door of his squad car in Pesha's face. He wouldn't even deign to give Yankel the address of the police station.

11

POCZTA

As with any mighty endeavor, the attempt to drag Kreskol into the modern era required the efforts of a great bureaucrat.

The government functionary we found ourselves paired with—Rajmund Sikorski—possessed many of the good qualities that accompany such a title. He was organized. He had great respect for procedure. And he knew the exhaustive checklist necessary to complete before successfully planting a school or a medical clinic in the middle of nowhere.

He spoke to us respectfully and tamed the many negative traits that usually chaperone a bureaucrat.

And like the systematic, intelligent official that he was, Mr. Sikorski realized that this transition would be expedited much more seamlessly if he didn't have to deal with someone who obviously hated him and was determined to see that his efforts failed—like Rabbi Sokolow.

One afternoon, during his regular bimonthly visit to Kreskol, Mr. Sikorski said through a translator: "I would appreciate it if the next time I came you could bring me a young fellow we could train to become the postmaster of Kreskol."

A few months earlier, we had been told that after the service road from Smolskie was paved, the first government building to appear in our town would be a poczta. "Many things can come later," Sikorski explained. "But keeping open the lines of communication between Kreskol and the rest of the province is the first and most essential step."

"Why do you need one of *us* to run it?" Rabbi Sokolow asked. "Shouldn't you get someone who's done it before?"

"Probably. But an experienced man wouldn't be better at weaving the post office into the fabric of life in Kreskol. We need someone local for that."

Which made a certain amount of sense, I suppose.

"Intelligence and self-reliance should be the two most important character traits," Sikorski continued. "Whomever you pick will need to go to Warsaw for four months of training. So we'll need somebody who can take an accelerated course in Polish without falling behind. Someone who we can entrust with an important task when he comes back here—making sure that the mail comes in and out of town without problems, and without much guidance from the administration in Szyszki. It's more difficult than it sounds."

A moment later, Sikorski added: "I'd pick somebody young over somebody old. Less set in their ways."

When Sikorski returned, Rabbi Sokolow presented him with Berel Rosen, the young nephew of Esther Rosen who had an equal number of admirers as he had detractors throughout the village.

There were some who said that Berel—with his droopy eyes, round face, sandy hair, and small, wiry body—was an incandescently brilliant young man, whose intellectual abilities were unlike those seen in Kreskol in generations. There were others who said that he was an arrogant, unserious lout, who flaunted the gifts that God gave him and was destined to squander away his life. Both descriptions were at least partially accurate.

But Rabbi Sokolow suspected that Berel wouldn't have much trouble mastering Polish, or any other training these Poles intended to throw at him. Berel wouldn't grow homesick and beg the Poles to return on his first shabbos by himself. And he finally concluded that an atheist (which is what Berel Rosen was widely presumed to be) would adjust to the big city better than a more devout candidate.

Berel returned from Warsaw four months after he left, with his beard shaved, his yarmulke nowhere to be found, his trousers and shirts modern, and his knowledge of Polish as quick and breezy as his knowledge of Yiddish. And he had a bit more spring in his step, as if he had done marvelous and mischievous things in the time he had been gone.

A day or two after his return, Berel stopped Itcha Bergstrom on his way home from yeshiva and asked for a moment of his time.

"What about?"

"How'd you like to be my assistant?" Berel asked. "I'll give you five hundred zlotys a week."

It was an astonishing sum for someone whose family normally cleared less than that in a year.

"Five hundred a week?" Itcha said. "To be an *assistant*?"

"It's chicken feed," Berel said. "A street sweeper makes more than that in Warsaw. But if you want the job you can have it."

"All right . . ."

Berel reached into his jacket pocket and pulled out ten five-zloty coins that he handed to Itcha. "Here's an advance on your salary. Meet me at my flat tomorrow morning. Number eight Thieves' Lane. I'm on the second floor. Wear a clean shirt. Buy a new one if you have to."

The next morning, bright and early, Berel was buzzing around his rented room like a hummingbird, and Itcha Bergstrom had to struggle to keep up.

"Take a pen and paper," Berel instructed Itcha, and he presented him with a half dozen blue ballpoint Bic pens (something Itcha had never seen before) and a yellow legal pad. "Write this down."

Itcha removed the cap from his pen.

"First, we need to make a list of everybody in town."

This first task would take weeks. Not that our town's archive didn't keep records. Like every other village, births and deaths were recorded in due course. But I would be lying if I didn't admit that these records were treated by most as an afterthought. Sometimes a birth was recorded after the bris. Sometimes it would take place at the bar mitzvah.

"Second, we're going to need to make a grid of the town. We need to record every address. Everything. From the poorest, shabbiest shack to the grandest mansion, everything must be put on paper."

"Why?" Itcha asked.

"Because when mail comes through our office, everybody needs to be found easily and systematically."

It sounded ridiculous to Itcha. Kreskol had done well enough without a postal system all these years. Who would be sending us mail now? But Itcha figured he wasn't getting paid to argue. So he began canvassing each and every block in the town, mapping every building and writing down its living and dead inhabitants one by one. "You can double-check everything in the town archives after," Berel instructed him.

Some of the people who answered their doors thought the boy was off his rocker. "You've known us all your life, Itcha," said Yetta Cooperman. "What do you mean by asking me who's living here?"

"I'm supposed to ask everybody."

Others, who didn't know Itcha (or knew him as little as one could in a town of our size), were suspicious.

"Did the Rabbi say you could do this?"

"No . . ."

Before he had a chance to finish, they would slam the door in his face. Itcha learned to simply tell them what they wanted to hear. "Sure," he said. "The Rabbi said it was fine."

Itcha had to endure the humiliation of going to the doors of people whose faces he knew, but names he forgot.

"You don't remember me?" asked one of his mother's friends.

"Of course I do. But I have to ask everybody. Just for the record."

And somewhere along the way, Itcha realized that the easiest way to deflect embarrassment on this was to ask everybody the proper spelling of their name.

"Well, of course you should be getting the proper spelling of their

name," Berel told his young charge after Itcha boasted about this ingenious face-saver. "I assumed you were doing that from the beginning. Go
back and get the spelling in the Latin alphabet as well as Yiddish."

Itcha couldn't help hating his boss for that. But he was raking in too
much money to complain.

Besides, Itcha had to admit it was vaguely thrilling to watch Berel at
work when he would come back to his boss's apartment every day at four
o'clock and drop off his notes. Berel had an enormous satellite photo of
the town, which he had hung on the wall, and he made notes on the glossy
paper with markers. Little scraps of square yellow paper were attached to
the photo, without glue or safety pins—a modern miracle so unimportant
that Berel never felt it worthy of commentary. He simply stood over this
map, absorbed in it as if it were a tapestry.

"You have no idea how much better life is outside this backwater," Berel
would tell Itcha when he chose to engage his assistant. "The goyim have
basically invented everything. Believe me, Itcha, I'm no slouch. I don't
intend to abandon this job until I've put in my time. But I'm certainly
envious of Yankel Lewinkopf—he had the right idea."

After the road to Smolskie was complete, trucks loaded up with lum-
ber, metal, glass, and construction crews began moving back and forth to
the designated site of the post office (just outside the walls of town, so as
not to create too large a disturbance). Berel would stop by every morning
to check on the progress as the trees were cleared; as the foundations were
dug up; as the first concrete was poured; as beams were raised and pipes
laid.

"When it is finished," Berel stated, "it will be the greatest structure
erected in Kreskol."

One weekend, a group of eighteen or nineteen American Jews (mostly in
their fifties and sixties) who were touring Poland showed up in our town

square. They sashayed through the streets like they owned them. "Shalom aleichem,"* they said to anybody who they passed.

One member of their assemblage spoke a Russian-accented Yiddish, and some Kreskolites were polite enough to answer his questions.

And when they arrived in the marketplace, cash in hand, and began buying up whatever trinket they could find to memorialize their expedition, nobody could find reason to complain.

The next weekend, four groups arrived in four separate buses and stormed our marketplace with the animation of Norman invaders.

"What a bargain!" one Polish woman nearly screamed at the top of her lungs, brandishing an ear of summer corn. "I'm coming back here every weekend!"

Some of us blanched when we saw the way these gentiles were dressed. A few of the women wore trousers, like a man. And although it was cool out, several others wore low-cut tops, exposing the cleft between their breasts, and shorts that left their knees and thighs naked for the world to see. The more pious looked away. But by the end of that Sunday, many hundreds of zlotys had been dropped into our economy, and the mood amongst Kreskol's merchants was along the lines of ebullience. It had been the greatest sales day in anyone's lifetime— some making as much as six months of their yearly income in a single afternoon.

Shifra Rothstein, who sold out her entire inventory of white summer gloves, went back to her supplier, Motke Weyerhoffer, for two dozen more.

"Two dozen?" Motke said. "When do you need them by?"

"As soon as possible."

"It'll take me at least a week."

Shifra looked disappointed. "Whenever you can. These goyim are spending money like it's going out of fashion. We don't have a minute to lose."

---

*Hebrew greeting meaning "Peace be unto you."

These first fleeting weeks of midsummer were unlike any we had ever experienced before; those who had been skeptical of how our rediscovery would ultimately turn out were suddenly at ease. Rabbi Katznelson's comment that the female tourists were dressed like a bunch of korvas failed to stir any great sense of outrage. Even those who hadn't sold anything that day found that the poor flower girls and bagel hawkers unexpectedly had money in their pockets, and were eager to spend it.

The new postmaster was one of the few who saw the dangers lying ahead.

"Don't get too comfortable," Berel instructed Itcha. "Things are good now, but it will end badly."

"Why?"

Berel rubbed his chin.

"Inflation," he finally said. "These tourists are buying from us because it's cheap. Eventually we won't have anything left to sell them. Try buying a jar of honey when there's only a dozen pots left in the whole town. The price will rise dramatically."

How Berel had come by the word "inflation" during his travels was anybody's guess. Berel was a great talker and a great reader, and the time he had spent in Warsaw was apparently not wasted.

"I thought you were in favor of progress," Itcha said.

"Of course I am," Berel answered. "Perhaps I misspoke when I said it would *end* badly. The ending hasn't been written. I just think it needs to be managed smartly. One solution would be to inflate prices now, before the economy goes too crazy. But anybody who's been saving any money will be wiped out."

Itcha had no idea what his boss was talking about.

The pending economic problems were also foreseen by Rajmund Sikorski, and the rest of the administrators back in Warsaw.

Of course, the contemporary tools for inflating or deflating a currency had little purchase in a place like Kreskol, where few businessmen ever advanced credit and the idea of changing an interest rate, or debt forgiveness, would have no effect.

There were one or two economists who said that no matter what else was said or done, supply would fall, prices would rise, and poor Kreskol was in for years of financial woe. These economists began studying the case of Zimbabwe as a possible model of what our hyperinflated future would look like.

But most blithely dismissed these forecasters as worrywarts. Kreskol's supply of cheap goods might take a temporary beating, but its potential tourism market was a gold mine. If anything, after a period of adjustment, the town would receive a once-in-a-century economic jolt.

One summer morning—a few weeks before the Poczta opened—the beadle went around town knocking on doors, telling everyone that there was an important meeting that evening at the main synagogue that every head of a household should attend.

Rabbis Sokolow, Shlussel, Katznelson, and Gluck were seated at the bima, and their discomfort resembled that of men waiting to be ransomed. Sitting with them was Rajmund Sikorski, a translator, and a bespectacled Pole in his middle years introduced to us as Professor Filip Pruski.

"The currency you had a hundred years ago is worthless in today's economy," Mr. Pruski said after he made his introductory remarks. "This is just a fact of life. Inflation has risen more than three thousand percent since then. Kreskol could never sustain this distortion in the market that is coming. Prices will have to change."

At first this was greeted passively, as the Kreskolites didn't understand what the man was talking about. But as Pruski began outlining what the change would mean—that the price of a loaf of bread should rise from two groschen to roughly two zlotys and forty groschen—a bloodcurdling cry swept through the synagogue, and several of the mothers in attendance burst into tears. The council of holy men (who had been briefed on what would be said several days ago) nervously stroked their beards, and we all understood why they looked so unsettled.

"Please, people," Mr. Sikorski took it upon himself to say. "Please, good people—quiet down. Let Professor Pruski speak. He's worked out solutions to this." But it took the translator many minutes before the clamor died down enough for Pruski to get a word in.

The solution, Pruski said, was that the Sejm* had voted to swap our town's coinage on a grand scale—there would be an exchange. It would be run out of the Poczta, and it would award 37.8 zlotys in modern currency for every prewar zloty recovered.

"Hold on to your money until the Poczta opens," Pruski advised. "We're setting aside two weeks where we'll have money changers in the town for ten hours a day, six days a week. The swap will allow you to make the adjustment. Nobody will go broke. Just turn your old money in, and you'll get new money. Simple as that."

It was at this moment that Shifra Rothstein shyly raised her hand.

"Excuse me," Shifra said. "But you said that we had to turn in old money . . ."

She waited for the first half of her question to be translated.

"But the Poles have been coming into town for weeks now. And they've been giving us new money. We'll be able to swap that, too, right?"

It was perhaps the most prescient question of the evening. A few weeks earlier, when word came back that tourists were already streaming into the town and deep in the throes of a spending spree, the officials in Warsaw decided that the currency swap had to be rushed into place because of that very issue. However, the Sejm had felt it was being generous enough, and that it wouldn't spend a couple of extra million enriching individual merchants who had merely been lucky.

*One of the two houses of parliament.

"No," Mr. Pruski said. "Unfortunately we're not going to be able to swap any money that was issued after 1941."

Another howl (not quite as loud as the first) reached the rafters of the synagogue, and several of the merchants looked as if they were ready to riot.

I suppose nobody could blame them much. It's one thing to live your life poor, with nothing more than a few vague fantasies about striking it rich some day. But it is quite a different matter to hold these oft-dreamed-of treasures in your hand only to receive the cold, unfeeling news that this is not the case. Not at all. In fact, you might be poorer than you were. Some of the newly rich refused to believe this. "He's not talking about *us*," one of the fruiters was overheard saying to his son.

Others believed no greater villainy had ever been visited on our town. "This is rape and murder," proclaimed Moritz Lemkin, who had recently made a fortune selling honey to the tourists, raking in almost two hundred zlotys in a week. "This man—Sikorski—is a modern-day Bogdan Chmielnicki!"*

However, the rabbis in attendance had seemingly made their peace with this plan.

"Good people," said Rabbi Sokolow over the murmuring that had infected the synagogue. "We should all try to keep in mind that riches are for this world, but they will not buy entry to the next." A comment that was largely beside the point. He then added, a little more relevantly: "For better or worse, we cannot get undiscovered. That page has already been written."

And the stark truth of those last two sentences hushed the audience long enough for Filip Pruski to finish his presentation, and for the masses to moodily go home.

Over the course of the next three weeks the town underwent a constant

---

*Bogdan Chmielnicki (1595–1657) was a Ukrainian revolutionary and notorious anti-Semite who led an uprising that resulted in the deaths of tens of thousands of Jews.

feeling of foreboding. There were some who declared, flat out, that they would never turn over their savings to the Poles, no matter what they promised. Never. This was some kind of trick; this goy, Sikorski, had charmed the kahal* into going along with him. When their money was safely in his hands, Sikorski would make a run for the woods and leave us with nothing.

"That's silly," Rabbi Shlussel said to his congregation at the beggars' synagogue. "The government just spent millions of zlotys paving a road to our town. Why would they do that if they just wanted to cheat us out of our money?" But common sense and reason are poor companions next to the much more lively entertainment provided by alarm and dread.

The morning after the meeting, when a lorry of tourists came from Bialystok with their cash for the taking, the merchants refused to sell them anything. Or, as the hat salesman, Fishel Pashman, told a customer: "I'll take your money, but only if the coins are a hundred years old or more."

Transactions slowed to a level not seen since our years of infamy. The newly moneyed, who now had possession of thousands of modern zlotys, couldn't get rid of them. The bagel sellers tried to do business with the fruiterers, but until the currency issue was resolved, nobody would accept anything other than old coins, or trade. For weeks, everything from silver to potatoes to salt was hoarded. Gold was the most valuable commodity of all; a little gold ring or a pair of earrings was now worth six or seven times what they were a week ago. Those who would not accept money were offered massive wooden wardrobes or cushioned sofas for jewels.

At the merchant's shul, each call to prayer ended with the congregants bitterly moaning to one another how unfair the whole thing was, and that the entire beit din should be replaced, as they had so obviously failed to stop the pending calamity.

---

*Local Jewish administrative body.

It was a weird time to live in Kreskol. No two people in our town had the same opinion of developments.

Others who were excited about the arrival of the gentiles the previous year—who listened to the stories of their gleaming cities and endless invention with rapt attention and were relatively untroubled by second thoughts—had to rethink the whole proposition.

Some now believed that Rabbi Sokolow had been right to be skeptical; we hadn't known what we were getting into, and the good Rabbi had been the only one who had sense enough to see this.

Others, who had been doubters from the get-go, thought that Rabbi Sokolow had been too weak-willed in allowing all this to unfold under his very nose. "Maybe he's too old to take on these shmegegges,"* one housewife opined. "If he knew this was such a bad idea, why didn't he try harder to stop it? The man could have put his foot down."

"Besides," another replied, "did you see him there at the meeting the other night—up there with the rest of the beit din and the gentiles? He's no better than the rest." Rather, it was obvious to all that Rabbi Katznelson had exhibited much more contempt for the process from the very beginning. Maybe he should be leading things.

And some now spoke of Rajmund Sikorski with the same spite and hatred as we would normally reserve for a Cossack. "Who is he, exactly?" was the question that came up again and again—as if we might be able to discern his motives slightly better if we knew a little more about his personal life.

Still, for a majority of Kreskolites the voluptuous future still bowed, strutted, and shimmied before us. We had even had our first taste when a young boy—Reuven Kornstein—caught a cold and collapsed a few days later in cheder. After hot soups, ointments, a visit from Dr. Aptner, and a séance didn't do the boy the slightest bit of good, he was airlifted to the nearest clinic, where he proceeded to make a speedy recovery.

---

*Yiddish: bunkum artist.

The powers of Sikorski, and the rest of the gentiles, were temporarily restored.

"Who cares what they want to do with our currency when they can heal a child whose grave is already waiting?" asked Esther Rosen.

It turns out, many disagreed.

The opening of the Poczta (to be followed by the money exchange) was set to take place two days before Tisha B'Av,* and the naysayers pointed to this coincidence as a harbinger of doom.

"It has been an unlucky day for us throughout our history," Rabbi Katznelson would tell whomever he could rope into listening. "Why the goyim decided that this was the time to institute all these changes is beyond my reckoning."

But at least Rabbi Katznelson was walking around town and making his voice heard. Rabbi Sokolow, on the other hand, was nowhere to be found. In the weeks leading up to the opening of the Poczta he barricaded himself in his study, not even showing up to shabbos services.

Some guessed that he was too depressed to show his face around Kreskol. Others hoped he was at least using his solitude to form some collective response; some unmistakable message that could be sent to the gentiles indicating we would not go along with these changes passively. It was not simply a matter of money; something greater was at stake.

Regardless, preparations went on for the opening of the Poczta. Itcha went around to every house in town and explained that in a few days they would get their own red mailbox with a lock and key, which would be affixed to the side of their property. He left each family with a four-page pamphlet in Polish and Yiddish explaining the intricacies of the postal system, from the price of standard mail to warnings against putting hazardous liquids and powders in a parcel.

---

*A fast day commemorating the destruction of the First and Second Temple.

Five teenage boys were recruited to work a mail route in five different parts of the village. They were each outfitted for uniforms, each given a few rudimentary lessons in Polish, each told to study an alphabet book, each taken on a tour of the grid system that Berel had devised, and each paid four hundred zlotys a week for their efforts.

All that summer, power lines were being laid through the forest to link the town to the nearest plant, about forty miles away, and shortly before the Poczta opened, linemen could be seen putting up poles at various discreet points throughout town. Distribution panels were ordered for the more than four hundred houses and buildings in Kreskol.

"You'll also be giving out pamphlets about electrical power when we start the mail routes," Berel told his recruits. "But before you do so, you will all become familiar with electricity and what it will do for Kreskol when it is installed, because you'll be getting many questions about this."

12

HERESY

"Gentlemen," Rabbi Sokolow began. "I have been meditating about developments long and hard. And I think we have to face certain unpleasant facts."

Four days before the Poctza's ribbon-cutting ceremony, Rabbi Anschel Sokolow finally reemerged from his study and called the beit din to order. The holy men of Kreskol rushed to his court to hear what their leader thought after weeks of brooding and meditation.

"I think that if this money exchange goes through, it will be the end of Kreskol as we know it," Rabbi Sokolow pronounced. "I believe that the gentiles are determined to see us sin. The new currency will make us more dependent on them and slowly wipe out the way of life here. I think that Rajmund Sikorski is as much a menace to this community as Tomas de Torquemada was to the Jews of Spain."

These words—shocking as they were from such an esteemed, level-headed figure as the main rabbi of our humble town—were somewhat stale by the time Rabbi Sokolow spoke them. Since the day Moritz Lemkin had compared what was happening to the foul deeds of Bogdan Chmielnicki, the exchange had been likened to every disaster that had befallen our cursed people since the time of King David. Rajmund Sikorski had been equated with Nebuchadnezzar and Titus;* the attempt at

---

*Nebuchadnezzar was a Babylonian king who conquered the kingdom of Judah and destroyed Solomon's Temple in 587 BCE; Titus was the Roman military commander and emperor who captured Jerusalem and destroyed the Second Temple in 70 CE.

changing the currency a second People's Crusade;* the townsmen willing to go along with it were Hellenists or apikorsim.**

With Sokolow's words, Rabbi Katznelson finally looked pleased; his old friend had decisively declared where his loyalties lay and was taking the situation seriously.

"However," the Rabbi continued, "the truth of the matter is there is nothing to be done about this. I'm not Simon Bar Kokhbar, and this is not Betar.*** Kreskol has no good options to preserve itself—our fate is sealed. We must accept all this craziness, and pledge our personal fidelity to God."

Rabbis Shlussel and Gluck were moved by these words and the pain written on the Rabbi's face. Despite the fact that both believed the sentiments were overblown (after all, did exchanging money really equate to the Spanish Inquisition?), to see a man as educated and as esteemed rendered helpless appealed to an ancient sense of respect. A small drop of solidarity rolled down Rabbi Gluck's cheek.

But as he turned away from the beloved Sokolow, Gluck caught the eye of Rabbi Katznelson, who appeared to feel nothing of the sort. He looked disgusted.

"Nothing to be done?" Rabbi Katznelson ejaculated. "*Nothing?*"

Rabbi Sokolow did not look up at his challenger.

"I've thought long and hard about this, Meir," he said, surprising everyone in the room by using Rabbi Katznelson's given name. (Rabbi Sokolow spent years insisting on proper etiquette during beit din meetings.) "There is no way to stop this."

"I disagree."

In the past few weeks, Rabbi Katznelson had moved swiftly away from anyone in town who argued that the gentiles should be given a chance. No one, Katznelson said, appreciated the dangers posed. "The exchange

---

*Populist Crusade in the year 1096 that led to the slaughter of many thousands of Jews living along the Rhine.

**Hellenists are secularized Jews; apikorsim are skeptical or heretical Jews.

***Simon Bar Kokhbar led a revolt against the Romans in 132 CE; Betar was the fortress where he was soundly defeated.

could very well be the first step on the road to something even more sinister," he would say. And merchants like Moritz Lemkin believed that Rabbi Katznelson had things exactly right. Desperate times call for desperate measures.

"I think there are hammers available to us we have not used," Rabbi Katznelson declared. "I think we've been entirely too accommodating. We should tell our people no. Firmly and unambiguously. They are not permitted to participate in the new exchange. Anyone having anything to do with Rajmund Sikorski should be driven out of Kreskol. If we have to issue a herem* against half the town as apikorsim, I believe we should do so."

Now, this was a shock. Nobody—not even the most implacable enemy of Sikorski—had toyed with the idea of excommunicating Kreskolites who did business with the gentiles. It was the kind of radical idea summoned from hundreds of years ago, where whole towns were infected with the heretical ideas of Sabbati Zevi or Jacob Frank.

"Moreover," Rabbi Katznelson continued, "I believe that some of the apologists who have poisoned the atmosphere are in this very room. I think there are members of this very court who have not yet appreciated the seriousness of the changes that these gentiles are proposing."

Well, it didn't take a genius to figure out whom he was talking about; Rabbi Katznelson was no longer interested in shielding Sokolow from his critique.

Rabbi Sokolow's eyes darted around the rest of the council, perhaps hoping that one of them would have the courage to challenge this rogue in their midst. But the hush in the room after these fateful remarks spoke for itself.

Rabbi Shlussel finally broke the silence.

"I'm confused. What do you mean by a herem against anyone having anything to do with the gentiles?"

---

*Hebrew: boycott or excommunication.

"Anybody who changes any money."

"What are the violations of the law?" asked Shlussel. "Are you really saying that doing business with outsiders is such a transgression that we are willing to treat fellow Jews like gentiles? *Worse* than gentiles? What are the relevant passages in the Talmud? I would like to examine them."

Rabbi Katznelson turned to Shlussel and stared at him coldly, without speaking.

"Katznelson," Shlussel finally said, "I'm only asking questions. Since when is that a transgression worthy of being an apikoros?"

"I agree," Rabbi Sokolow said. "If we're going to speak about taking such drastic steps there would need to be a firm basis in law."

"I'm not sure I trust everybody's reading of the Talmud," Rabbi Katznelson said, his eyes fixed on Sokolow.

If there had ever been another beit din meeting like that one, I have not heard about it. The notes from every single session weren't necessarily entered into the town archives, but nobody could recall a member of the court suggesting that the court itself was infested with apostasy.

When the shock wore off, Rabbi Sokolow's instinct was to placate his friend. "There are two questions at stake here," Rabbi Sokolow said. "The first is the legal basis for a herem. There is certainly an argument that inducing others to sin is itself a sin. I don't think it's such a leap of the imagination to say that those who are encouraging the tourists to come here are guilty of something."

Rabbi Katznelson remained still.

"But the other issue—which is at least as important—is the issue of following secular law," Rabbi Sokolow continued. "These laws might be perverse; they might do damage. But nobody says that the Poles don't have the right to do this. If they decide that they want to change our currency, we don't have the right to challenge them. That's the way it's always been."

"There is a third issue," Rabbi Katznelson replied. "And that is one of time. Once we switch our money over to the secular system, we will never be able to go back. We will have to abide by that monetary system forever. In a few days we're not going to have any recourse. Today we do. We should issue stringent warnings tomorrow morning. We can't fritter away the next few days—they're too valuable."

"There is not a Diaspora community in the world that does not use the local currency," Rabbi Shlussel pointed out. "Or abide by the local laws. As long as the parliament or potentate are not asking us to explicitly disobey Jewish law I fail to see how changing money constitutes a violation of any command in the Talmud."

The conversation lingered on until Rabbi Katznelson couldn't stand it anymore.

"I sometimes think I'm the only one who's looking at the situation as it now stands," he said when the rest had said their piece. "This isn't a matter of following the laws of Poland. It is a matter of preserving Jewish law. And I say that any man or woman who feeds or clothes or aids one of these gentiles is aiding and abetting their blasphemy. As far as I'm concerned, any Jew who cooperates is an apikoros. Their meat, bread, and cheese are as unclean as a sausage!"

"What if we issued a warning first?" Rabbi Sokolow proposed. "Why do we have to go straight to the biggest and most destructive arrow in our quiver? A herem against hundreds of men and women? And their children? For just *listening* to the gentile authorities? I'm not saying we should do nothing. We should warn everybody about the dangers and temptations of gentile society. Maybe we can appeal to the gentiles to delay the exchange and give everybody a chance to think about it."

"You just said we should do nothing," Katznelson said flatly.

"No, no," Rabbi Sokolow said, looking more and more alarmed by the implicit provocation coming from his once confederate. "I never said that."

"When we sat down," Katznelson said. "The first thing you said was that there was nothing that could be done. Our fate was sealed."

"I didn't mean we should do *nothing*. I even said that we all had to behave like the best upstanding Jews we could. I meant that whatever we did would have very little effect."

"You said what you said."

"Maybe I misspoke," Sokolow conceded. "Yes, you are right. This is all very troubling, Meir. And, yes, we must act. But I think you're taking it too far. A warning is better than excommunication."

"The Poles aren't going to delay this exchange by so much as an hour," Rabbi Katznelson stated. "We either accept the gentiles and what they do to this town, or this is the time to take our stand."

And as the other members of the beit din countered Katznelson, rather than disabusing him of these ludicrous ideas their opposition only calcified them; he believed that he was the only one with enough courage to stand behind the path of virtue.

"All of this chatter is beside the point," Katznelson finally declared. "Either you think the gentile law is dangerous, or you do not. Either you think it will lead to a violation of the higher law, or you do not. I think it's dangerous, and I don't think we should restrain ourselves in fighting it."

He looked past all his other challengers, and rested his eyes on the figure of Rabbi Sokolow. Their long-standing friendship was not lost on anyone in the room. Sokolow merely turned away and looked down into his beard.

No edicts were issued that night. No warnings would be forthcoming. No directives that pious Kreskolites should resist these monetary changes were given. The beit din did not dissolve into two camps, each accusing the other of apostasy. At least not presently. The meeting ended with future plans more or less unchanged.

But some other form of sorcery took place that evening that would become apparent in the coming days.

13

DISQUIET

Children are far stricter adherents to the lines of seniority than adults, and because Meir Katznelson was six months older, he was the dominant partner in his friendship with Anschel Sokolow in its earliest mold.

Being of lesser status did not diminish Anschel's affection and admiration for the wise Meir. He absorbed every lesson his friend had to teach. And, after they listened to Leonid Spektor speak about World War II, it was Meir who understood that they heard something more consequential than a simple ghost story, and made sure it was an important topic of conversation between the two boys.

"I had a dream last night that I was in the woods hiding from the Germans," Meir told his friend weeks after Leonid Spektor had arrived in Kreskol.

Anschel considered this.

"That's odd."

"You haven't had bad dreams since we heard that?"

"No."

But, as if his friend were stage-managing his unconscious mind, the next evening Anschel had one such vision. He dreamed that Leonid Spektor was directing him to dig a tunnel out of Kreskol—but the hole kept going straight down. As they got closer to the center of the earth everything grew hotter, like he was approaching the fires of hell. Shortly before they reached bottom, a mysterious figure—covered in grime and filth, who had been bloodied within an inch of his life—appeared tucked into a tunnel and begged Anschel to turn around and go back the way he came.

(In the elusive way that dreams follow their own logic, Anschel implicitly understood that this half-dead character was an angel.)

Meir and Anschel were among Spektor's most loyal listeners after he opted to stay in town and began telling his stories of the macabre to the yeshiva boys. But they instinctively kept to themselves what they had heard that night underneath the Sokolow sofa.

"How much of that do you think is true?" Anschel asked one afternoon as they walked home from cheder after hearing about a boy who had the fat of his stomach turned into bars of soap by a sinister wizard with a snappy mustache.

"All of it."

But that couldn't be the case. Spektor spoke of warlocks and witches and other creatures of the supernatural that the boys were old enough to know were likely imaginary.

"They're disguises," Meir surmised. "They're real stories, but he's dressing them up as fairy tales."

Other questions arose; the boys wondered what had happened to the German perpetrators of the crimes he originally spoke of—but they didn't have the nerve to ask Spektor to sort the truth from fiction. (They missed the part Spektor related to Herschel Sokolow after they had been sent to bed where the Russian army liberated the camp.)

While Anschel was the less troubled of the two, he would nevertheless stare out into the woods on Shabbat afternoon and wonder what nightmares lurked in the forest before rushing back home and under the covers.

One evening, Anschel asked his father if the one-eyed man's story was really true.

"I'm not sure," Herschel Sokolow said. "But I think so."

"Should we tell the rest of Kreskol about this?"

Herschel pondered the question.

"No."

"Why?"

Herschel ran a hand through his beard—a habit his son would mimic many years later when he was considering a question he wasn't fully sure how to answer.

"Panic," Herschel finally answered. If war and mass murder had recently scorched the rest of Poland, Herschel continued, telling everybody about it could instigate village-wide hysteria. So far, none of this business had touched them—so why worry everybody?

Maybe there's a reason to worry, Anschel thought. Maybe we should get busy coming up with the escape plan. Maybe involving the town's smartest minds would be the best way to arrive at a solution. Maybe we were wasting valuable time.

But saying something like that felt like a challenge, and Anschel Sokolow respected his father too much to press the matter.

"The war is over," Herschel Sokolow assured his son. "That was how Spektor managed to get away. The Germans fled. The Russians have taken their place. You don't really need to be anxious."

Meir's fears were not allayed when Anschel related this to him.

"So, the Russians came," Meir repeated.

"That's what my father said."

"Are the Russians any better?"

Truly, every piece of history they had been taught about their neighbors to the east indicated that the Russians were drunken, cutthroat maniacs with a particular distaste for Jews.

"And I suppose when all the murderers fled," Meir added, "their helpers melted away with them?" Like, say, the blond witch with the chipped tooth only too willing to abet the slaughter.

The urgency of these questions might have faded over time, but the fixation was kept alive sitting at Leonid Spektor's feet and faithfully taking in all he said—until one day Spektor announced there would be no more stories. Not now, not ever. He gave no explanation for the precipitous reversal.

As Spektor's narratives came to a halt, so did Anschel's attention to the matter. He began to think that the kidnapping, mass murder, and slavery Spektor spoke of was not the immediate peril the first accounts seemed to imply. He even began to wonder if, in fact, Leonid Spektor was utterly meshuggenah* and had invented the whole story.

However, the same stories left footprints in Meir's personality that endured for the rest of his life.

Years later (*decades* later) Meir Katznelson never quite stopped thinking about Leonid Spektor. Even after the absence of any corroborating evidence might have corroded his faith. Even as Spektor grew laconic with age and withdrawn from his pupils and former pupils. Even when the world outside Kreskol remained as unknowable and foreign as the surface of the moon, and Meir—like a lot of the residents of Kreskol—sometimes forgot it even existed. Even after marriage and a child came to supersede the larger, ethereal questions raised by his brief association with Leonid Spektor. Even after the passions of his friendship with Anschel Sokolow cooled, and he began to notice the personal and intellectual flaws in Herschel Sokolow's heir apparent.

Then one day Rajmund Sikorski plopped down in Kreskol, passed around the photos of the war and the concentration camps, and Katznelson felt a rising sense of shock; as if a shameful secret about himself had suddenly been revealed.

There was the photo of the dead sprawled out by the hundreds in a ravine. There were photos of prisoners crammed on top of one another in the concentration camp bunks. One photo showed a terrified little boy with his hands up in the air in surrender—a pair of German soldiers stood casually cradling their rifles in their arms, unimpressed by his fear. Looking at that photograph, Meir Katznelson's emotions so overwhelmed him that he was fearful he would break into tears. He looked up at Sokolow, who appeared sheepish.

Katznelson said little during the next few days to dampen the general good mood in Kreskol. The war and what it all meant wasn't much of a concern for anybody except Meir. An announcement about it was made

---

*Yiddish: crazy.

after services the next Shabbat: There had been a war, Rabbi Sokolow said. It was cataclysmic. Most of the Jews of Europe perished. But he didn't say much more and nobody seemed very interested in it. Rather, there was a much more overwhelming spirit of wonder among the Kreskolites. Flight was what the populace wanted to talk about. Photography was what the people wanted to talk about. The state of Israel was what the people wanted to talk about.

But as the first dizzying days after rediscovery receded, the long-buried dread of Meir Katznelson's youth was exhumed and soon it was the only thought on his mind.

"What's wrong with you, husband?" Temerl Katznelson asked one night months after the helicopter landed, as he tossed and turned in his bed.

"Nothing."

Temerl sat upright and stared at the dark outline of her husband.

After a few moments, Katznelson finally lit a candle, sat up in his dressing gown, and proceeded to tell her he was thinking about what Sokolow had told Kreskol about World War II.

"But he didn't tell it right," Katznelson said. "He glossed over the worst of it."

"What do you mean by that?"

"I heard the real story from a witness."

Katznelson proceeded to recount the foggy, misty memory of the night more than seven decades earlier, which upended his wife's calm.

"Leonid *Spektor* was in the middle of all that?" she said when he finished.

Temerl was several years younger than her husband and not quite old enough to hear Spektor's after-school tales, even secondhand. Spektor was merely the town's one-eyed, childless oddball, confined to Kreskol's outskirts. He was slowly decaying by the time Temerl paid him any attention, limping through the marketplace in search of sustenance. It seemed impossible that this small, insignificant man should have served as witness to such towering evil.

"Are you going to tell the people of Kreskol about this?" Temerl asked.

"I'm not sure," Katznelson answered. "Maybe."

"There is no maybe about it," Temerl declared. "This is important. The rest of the Jews were exterminated! We *must* know about it!"

Katznelson was taken aback by his wife's moral clarity and it made him feel ashamed—almost as if he were helping to cover up the great crime.

"Yes, you're right."

However, the question of how to inform the citizenry of Kreskol about this indisputably critical—but indisputably long ago—calamity was not as simple as one might think.

Kreskol had no printing press and Meir Katznelson had no congregation for his sermon.

He thought of calling together all the schoolteachers and instructing them to include the story of the Holocaust in their lessons. That way, the next generation would at least have it foremost in their minds. But should the youth really know before their parents? What would the parents say when asked the inevitable questions?

He wondered if he should call a town meeting and relate everything he knew. But how much, truly, did he know? While Leonid's descriptions of the gas chambers and the bloodthirsty Huns were seared in Meir's brain, the prologue to this—Versailles and the Anschluss and the September campaign—was much fainter. He had gleaned the terms "Hitler" and "Nazis" from Rajmund Sikorski, who had spent less than twenty minutes of his initial visit outlining the political history of the tragedy.

The first thing to do, Katznelson decided, was to find out what happened.

"I want to know more about the Holocaust," Katznelson told Rabbi Sokolow. (This was many months before their impasse over the currency exchange.)

Rabbi Sokolow wasn't sure how he could even accommodate such a request.

"Ask Sikorski for some books about it," Katznelson volunteered. "And make sure they're in Yiddish."

"All right."

But Katznelson wasn't finished.

"I think the whole town should know about it. Really know about it. I don't know why we didn't tell the town everything."

Rabbi Sokolow ran his fingers through his beard.

"What do you mean by 'everything'?" Sokolow finally asked.

"Everything. What Leonid Spektor told us."

Sokolow hadn't spoken the name Leonid Spektor in nearly two decades. Even when the man had died and Sokolow delivered the hesped* he hadn't breathed a word of Spektor's story. He merely said that this grizzled, intelligent stranger had made his home in Kreskol and Spektor was "greatly concerned with the preservation of Kreskol." It was a peculiar addition—but nobody thought to question it at the time.

"I don't know if it will make sense," Sokolow finally said.

"That's exactly why I want to find out more," Katznelson replied. "We need to tell the whole story."

A few weeks later, Sikorski related the disappointing (but not unexpected) news that there wasn't enough Yiddish readership to support the translation of the large scholarly tomes of Holocaust history such as *The Rise and Fall of the Third Reich* or *The War Against the Jews*. However, there were some memoirs and books written originally in Yiddish. Plus, shorter books that had been translated fifty or sixty years ago, when there was still a secular Yiddish-speaking population. By way of example, Sikorski presented Sokolow with *Dos Togbukh fun Ana Frank*.**

"Sikorski says he's going to bring more as he finds them," Sokolow told Katznelson.

Sikorski was true to his word; he brought lithographs about the

---

*Hebrew: eulogy.
** *The Diary of Anne Frank.*

destruction of Warsaw; small accounts of life in the Lodz Ghetto; memoirs of those who had escaped from Poland to Shanghai; and a 346-page examination of German war crimes by a Lord Edward Frederick Langley Russell of Liverpool, that had been rendered into Yiddish as *Di Baytsh Fun Haknkrayts.*[*]

Katznelson retreated to his house with these histories and slowly grew more consumed with the tragedy. The months passed, but he didn't leave his house. He merely sat and read, wasting away to the point that Temerl could see the outline of his vertebrae as he lay on his side.

The road into Kreskol was finished, and Katznelson didn't care. Tourists started coming into town, and Katznelson merely did his best to avoid meeting their eyes. They were, after all, gentiles. Or so he assumed. He hadn't realized just what gentiles were capable of. It angered him. It frightened him. It depressed him.

And as the good people of Kreskol grew more comfortable with the promise of their future place in Poland, Katznelson grew more resolved to make a stink.

When Rabbi Sokolow called him and the rest of the elders of the beit din to a meeting to discuss what would happen with the new currency exchange, from the deepest depths of his soul, Katznelson felt a helpless, bottomless howl of rage. This would not stand. Never. Never. Never.

His fellow rabbis looked shocked by his invective, but Katznelson was long past caring. His old friend Anschel looked genuinely hurt by the rawness of his anger. He didn't mind one little tick. When the meeting was over, with the conviction of Jeremiah, Katznelson marched home, picked up a sheepskin scroll and a goose-feather quill, and wrote in Yiddish all that he knew about the Holocaust. He began thus:

To the citizens of the lost shtetl of Kreskol, this is the story of Leonid Spektor and all he endured in the conflict known as

---

[*]*The Scourge of the Swastika.*

World War II. His account was known to me and a few others—but out of respect for his wishes not to disseminate his story, we kept it secret. However, I have come to believe everyone who is living in Kreskol should know it. We should know what this man who lived among us endured. We should know how widespread was the tragedy of World War II. We should know exactly what we were spared. We should wonder why we were fortunate and others were not. And all of us—from the righteous to the venal—should feel guilty!

It was a peculiar way to begin such a document—particularly if its purpose was to inform. But it was a good way to draw notice. It certainly captured the attention of those who arrived in synagogue the next morning after Katznelson had hammered the scroll to the door. A small crowd formed around the document—which was some three thousand words long—and patiently read about gas chambers and the burnings of bodies and the figure of six million of their fellow Jews (along with millions more of their fellow human beings) who had been incinerated—none of which had been reported in more than a curtailed, piecemeal way before.

The crowd stood around the synagogue's door for hours. Not everybody could get close enough to read it at once. But all were curious. And over the course of the day, as each man finished the document, they peeled away and morosely went off to their plows or stalls, not bothering to pray. Katznelson's ominous warning ended on the following note:

I ask you—how could anyone possibly believe anything the Poles say? How can any among us put faith in this government, or any other? History has shown us that we were led to slaughter by the very kind of people who are now proposing to lead us again to salvation. Are we really so trusting and foolish? We cannot be

destroyed a second time. We cannot succumb to their charms. Let
us remain the way we were. Boycott the exchange!

I never completely understood the connection between the exchange
and the Holocaust. But, I suppose, Katznelson saw in the story of the
Holocaust a vision of the future that Kreskol narrowly avoided. He saw
all the great advances of technology that had been honed and perfected in
the service of mankind's most primitive and horrific instincts.

Now the future was calling. The exchange was Poland's attempt to re-
route Kreskol into its proper place, whether we liked it or not. Katznelson
shuddered at the prospect.

And while the people of Kreskol might have been avoiding the questions of the Holocaust for the many months since our rediscovery, this
new manifesto meant that no one could ignore it.

It got around town that Katznelson had been studying the Holocaust,
and that he was tutoring townsfolk about it in private. Men, women, and
the elderly sought him out over the next few days and asked him about it.

Many were sickened by what they heard. A dark cloud formed over
the town and everything we had experienced in recent months. Suddenly
vital questions arose such as why we should have been so fortunate to
have been spared when so many good towns were thrown into the chasm.
What did such evil say about the nature of mankind? Why did this happen to the Jews? There were many more.

Plenty of other Kreskolites were indifferent. After all, it had happened
many, many years ago. Life moved on. Similar things had happened
during the Babylonian conquest, the Roman conquest, the crusades . . .

"Not like this," Katznelson jabbed back. "It was nothing like this. This
was a singular moment in history."

"Regardless," said Landz Bronfman, "what does it have to do with the
currency exchange?"

Katznelson could not contain his rage.

"It has *everything* to do with it!"

14

SCHISM

The first inkling of the extent of the damage Katznelson had done to the town and the pending currency exchange came from a young boy with brownish blond sidelocks who passed Rabbi Gluck on the street two days before the ribbon cutting. "Is it true that the money that we're going to get from the Poles is cursed?"

Gluck was, at first, too surprised by the question to take it seriously.

"What a lot of nonsense!" he said. "Run along."

But throughout the ribbon-cutting ceremony a few days later, nervous mothers kept coming up to Rabbi Gluck and asking him if it was really all right to hand their money over to the exchange.

"Why wouldn't it be?" Gluck asked.

"I hear some of the rabbis are saying that anyone who uses the new money will be punished."

"Punished for what?"

The woman shrugged. "Transgression," she finally offered.

"Where did you hear that?"

But the antecedent of a rumor is as elusive as the father of a bastard.

"I can assure you," Rabbi Gluck repeated to all who asked, "it's perfectly safe to turn over your money. Nobody is going to forbid its use."

Even those who wanted to believe him had their doubts.

"The safest thing to do," opined Esther Rosen, as she knitted on her veranda, "is to do nothing. Just wait."

"Wouldn't the safest thing be to listen to the Poles?" asked one of the wives. "So far we haven't heard any of the rabbis say we should do otherwise. Except Katznelson."

"Maybe the *smartest* thing to do is just to listen to the Poles," Esther continued. "I'm not saying that they're actually *going* to outlaw the new money. The *likely* outcome is that the new money works out just fine. But I'm talking about the very safest. It's a risk. What if in six months the rabbis change their minds and say that whoever touched this new money is a sinner?"

One young man, Koppel Nagel, went to the marketplace on the day after Tisha B'Av, stood on a sack of flour, and began sermonizing.

"Hear ye, hear ye, good people of Kreskol," Koppel began. "Everybody knows that tomorrow the exchanges are to open. We've been promised thirty-eight new zlotys for every old zloty. It sounds like a fair trade— but I, for one, am not going to give them a single groschen. They're only doing this to make it easier for *more* gentiles to come into town—not to make life easier on us. I say, things are good enough! I say, boycott the exchange!"

This soliloquy might have been less effective in the mouth of an indifferent speaker, but Koppel Nagel had a previously unrealized genius at oratory. People all around the marketplace stopped what they were doing and spontaneously broke into applause.

Early the morning after the ribbon-cutting ceremony a truck arrived from Smolskie carrying Kreskol's first shipment of mail.

Each family got the same three pieces: a four-page letter (written in Polish and Yiddish) describing the currency exchange; a postcard from the Szyszki administrative and civil affairs bureau (also in both languages) urging all the townspeople to visit the Poczta for the issuance of a photo ID; finally, an ungrammatical letter from an Israeli developer who wanted to erect a hotel next door to the Poczta.

Berel walked his new staff through the forms behind the front desk at the Poczta. "This is for passports," Berel said. "This is for photo ID. This is for voter registration. This is the form for money orders. This is for registered mail . . ." (Being that there was no municipal building in Kreskol yet, all parties agreed that voting and passport matters should be handled out of the Poczta until this was remedied.)

Berel demonstrated how to use the scale; how to print out bar codes using the Poczta equipment; where the stash of stamps would be kept; how to lock up the building every night and input the security code; how to restock the toilet paper in the bathroom; where the fluorescent lights were kept and how to change them; how to operate the generator in the basement that would be used until the electrical grid was functional.

An armored truck, two representatives of the Ministry of Finance, and five armed guards appeared at the Poczta at six o'clock on the appointed morning of the money exchange.

Berel and the rest of the postal employees were there to greet these Poles.

"Be prepared for a very busy day," said one of the men from the Ministry of Finance, shaking Berel's hand. "Now where should we set up?"

Berel led the ensemble into the back room of the Poczta. The guards hauled three oilcloth sacks of cash to a wooden table, where the packs of 10-, 20-, 50-, and 100-zloty notes were stacked on top of one another and counted.

"Verify," one of the treasurers said to Berel. "I have counted one hundred ten-zloty notes, for one thousand zlotys."

Berel nodded. "I verify."

The treasurer went on to the 20-zloty notes, and continued on—counting and verifying—until opening.

One guard stood near all the money in the back room. Another stood behind the counter with the two treasurers. A third one stood in the middle of the waiting area, to maintain order among the crowds that were expected. A fourth was stationed at the door. A fifth waited by the armored truck.

When the doors of the Poczta finally swung open, about half a dozen Kreskolites were waiting. All but one were men.

The highest amount changed was by Zemel Reiss, who brought in 348 zlotys in old coins, leaving with the gargantuan sum of 13,154 zlotys and 40 groschen. A receipt was written up in Polish and Yiddish, which Berel signed.

"I feel like a millionaire." Zemel laughed as he stuffed the stacks of hundreds and fifties into his trouser pockets, his coat, and his socks.

"Be careful with it," Itcha advised.

But the number of people who came into the Poczta over the course of the afternoon was worryingly small.

The unofficial census that had been conducted after Berel had mapped all of Kreskol put the population at 1,793, give or take. It was estimated that each household consisted of six people: an average of three children, two parents, and some other older relative—be it a grandparent or an unmarried aunt. There were just over three hundred residences in town, and another hundred or so commercial properties.

But only thirty people showed up over the course of the day to change money.

"This is not quite as big a disaster as it seems," said one of the treasurers at 5 p.m., when he started packing up for the day. "We can expect only one person per household will change money. What would be the point of husband, wife, nana, and junior coming to the exchange? But this is still not good. We should have hit a much higher target than two percent of the population."

"Do we have a backup plan?" asked Berel.

"If we do, nobody's told me about it."

The next day eighteen Kreskolites showed up—even after Berel sent Itcha out into the marketplace to tell everyone he saw that the currency exchange was open for business and there was no line to get through. Nobody cared. Those who did show up looked pained—as if they weren't entirely sure they were doing the right thing. (One such Kreskolite changed his mind just as the treasurer began filling out the receipt, snatched his coins up, and strode out the door without saying a word to anybody.)

This was alarming enough that Rajmund Sikorski came to town to observe the next day.

"We mustn't panic," Mr. Sikorski said as he stood in the quiet of the Poczta and examined the receipts. "There will probably be a spike of interest as the deadline for closing the exchange approaches."

Which, while not alleviating anybody's worries, sounded like a reasonable prediction.

"However, I'm slightly more worried that some of the wealthier people in town have not come in yet," Mr. Sikorski added. (Berel was impressed that his gentile counterpart remembered the moneyed names of our town, like Yechel Mazer and Abushula Dorfman.) "If they don't go along with this, then it'll be a doomed effort."

Mr. Sikorski continued to study the receipts.

"And why the hell isn't Rabbi Gluck or Rabbi Shlussel on this list?" Sikorski asked Berel, as if he had personally forgotten to rouse them out of bed. "They should have been here on the first day. They're our only allies in this. What are *they* waiting for?"

And so, with little better to do, Berel and Sikorski found Rabbi Gluck in his wood shop and asked him why he hadn't visited the exchange yet.

"What's the rush?" Gluck asked.

"What's the *hold up*?" Berel countered. "There's not a soul there right now. Why wait until the deadline?"

Rabbi Gluck looked discomforted. "Look," Gluck said. "I have every intention of going down to the exchange. I promise you both. But I should really be one of the very last to do it. For complicated reasons that I can't get into."

Sikorski tried to catch Berel's eye without success.

"Well, at any rate, would you at least pester Yechel Mazer to come down and change his money?" Berel asked.

"Maybe."

Rabbi Shlussel was easier to convince—even if he was the rabbi of the downtrodden, and his actions carried less weight.

"Certainly," Shlussel said. "I'll go this afternoon."

As if to punctuate his complicity, Shlussel hung a sign outside the door of his store saying that he would accept only modern currency, and setting the new rates for carpets and repairs. (The new figures he posted were high enough that Reb Shlussel's hands trembled as he nailed the sign to his door.)

But by far the most important citizen to participate in the exchange that day was Abushula Dorfman, who—when Sikorski and Berel visited him—agreed that all the talk about holding on to the old money was a lot of nonsense. He turned over more than 8,600 zlotys to the exchange. He also agreed that he would no longer accept older money in his business dealings. Given that he was one of the two largest distributors of cattle and goats in Kreskol, every merchant who heard this was suddenly a lot less persuaded by the argument that they should sit on their old coins.

The next day, more than two dozen of Kreskol's most prominent merchants followed suit, and hung up signs in their stalls saying they would accept only modern currency.

On the last day of the exchange, a hundred families showed up with their life savings. For the first time since the exchanges started, there were lines out the door.

Reb Mazer changed his many thousands of zlotys. Rabbi Gluck's wife, Raisa, quietly turned over the family's modest savings. (Gluck was nowhere to be seen.) Reb Bernstein made a point of saying that he would only turn over half of his savings. (A practice that a number of families, including ones who claimed they supported the exchange, secretly did.)

Even the Rebbetzin showed up at the Poczta and wordlessly handed over the Sokolow family's life savings.

Many of the old ladies who came with the gold coins that they had owned for as long as three quarters of a century wept as they handed them over. The hundreds—or in many cases thousands—of modern zlotys in compensation couldn't cheer them; it was as if some great era of the past was violently dying before their eyes.

"This has nothing to do with reason," Itcha told his boss that night as they counted up the receipts. "Everybody with any brainpower knows that this is the only sensible thing. It's been explained well. But it doesn't matter. I was also terrified—and I don't even have any old money."

Still, despite this last-minute push, only 486 people participated in the exchange (more than one member came from numerous households). A full third of the town's families had stayed home completely—including some of the wealthy.

The day after the exchange closed for good, one-third of the weavers, cobblers, bakers, glassblowers, and farmers of Kreskol kept prices the way they were a year ago and refused to accept modern currency.

It was akin to a village-wide boycott. As the months wore on, more and more accepted trade in lieu of money; but the trades were conducted grudgingly—as if those of us who participated in the exchange had permanently soiled ourselves and were now unholy. Unholier, even, than the Poles.

Two separate Kreskols emerged. One grew wealthy. The other grew poor. The poor sneered as they walked past their neighbors. They gritted their teeth. They stopped having anything to do with any of the rabbis of the beit din (except Rabbi Katznelson, who never changed his savings) and attended smaller, more fanatical shuls.

Kreskol was never the same.

15

BROTHER WIERNYCH

Shortly before Kreskol's story broke in the press, a farmer named Oskar Kowal realized that a transient was living in his barn.

He had been picking up signs of something amiss for weeks. First, when he would come in to milk the cows in the morning one of their udders would invariably be dry.

Second, going up to the hayloft one afternoon he discovered the bales had been rearranged. The impression of a body had taken form in the hay, with a pronounced lump where the pillow would go.

Finally, he stumbled upon a small hole that had been covered with dirt in the corner of his barn. When he kicked some of the dirt away, he found that it was filled with excrement.

Kowal asked his wife if she had noticed anything funny.

"No," she said. But a few hours later when her husband came in from the fields she revised her answer. "You know something. There have been a few things."

"Like what?"

The wife, Zuzanna, wrinkled her brow as she considered the question.

"Food has been disappearing from the refrigerator," she said. "And the cupboards."

Whoever the thief was, he had been notably restrained. One night, Zuzanna had put away eight leftover pierogis—there were three the next night. Cakes and loaves of bread would be slimmer than when they had initially been put away. She would open a bag of pretzels and a day later there would only be crumbs left.

It was never enough to call attention to itself, but when considered in its entirety the evidence looked unmistakable.

In the Kowals' private little island of civilization—miles and miles from the nearest town and, unbeknownst to these humble farmers, roughly halfway between Smolskie and Kreskol—critters from the forest would occasionally pierce the house's varied protections and help themselves to whatever was in the cupboards. But they did so without stealth. A trail of incriminating scraps followed them out the door, as if to inform the Kowals that they were vulnerable.

This, however, looked very different.

Kowal went for a walk in the surrounding woods just before dusk, looking for signs of a vagrant. His son, Jakub, stayed in the hayloft with the family hunting rifle, just in case.

A few hundred feet into the woods Kowal uncovered a small, makeshift firepit. Near the pit was a bag filled with clothes and a blanket. A few yards away were more signs of an ad hoc commode that had also been covered with dirt, much like the one in the barn. Among the refuse was the paper wrapper for the Bursztyn cheese that the Kowals ate regularly.

"Did you see anything?" Kowal asked his son when he returned to the hayloft.

"I didn't see—I heard," Jakub said. "Somebody prowling around. But the moment they heard *me* they turned around and fled."

For the Kowals, the experience was more thrilling than upsetting. The family convened a meeting in the kitchen and wondered aloud how long this spectral figure had been living among them.

"At least since January," declared twelve-year-old Jakub, who was the most unaware of the phantom before that day. (It was July.)

Zuzanna was more conservative; she believed it could just be one or two months.

Oskar was the sole member of the family who believed it was a recent phenomenon. "I think it's only been a few weeks. If it had been any longer we would have noticed him."

How to shoo the phantom away was of greater immediate concern. "We're going to have to camp out in the barn," Oskar said. "We're going to have to remain watchful. Doors locked. The barn door closed, not just the stalls. And we have to keep it up. If we do it for a few days and then forget about it, this guy will be back."

"How do you know it's a guy?" asked Jakub.

"Don't be stupid," replied Zuzanna.

So they held their vigil; in the early evening Jakub sat in the loft with the hunting rifle, an iPhone, and a battery of comic books. Zuzanna took over at around 11 p.m. Oskar took the 2:30 a.m. shift, going about the rest of his day in a state of exhaustion and crankiness.

However, the vagrant returned only a single time, so far as the Kowals were able to tell. One night in the middle of a rainstorm, Zuzanna heard the barn door rattle. She unlocked the breech of the rifle.

The young intruder was slippery with mud. His hair was unkempt and he had a long beard. He was rail thin, and wore a pair of black trousers and a white button-down shirt.

He walked slowly through the barn. When he passed one of the cows he affectionately ran his hand along the animal's back, as if he knew her.

The Kowals agreed that at the first sign of a stranger a call should be made to the house phone with the single codeword: "Reksio."*

As he got closer to the loft, Zuzanna rang the house, shouted "Reksio!" (without making sure anyone was on the line to hear), and stood up brandishing the rifle.

"Stop where you are!"

The vagrant froze. He stared at Zuzanna for a moment, and neither party knew what would happen next. After another second, the stranger turned around and dashed toward the barn door.

---

*A popular cartoon dog.

Zuzanna was no amateur at handling a rifle; she took aim and fired at the ground near the tramp's feet. He didn't stop or show any fear—even as the previously peaceful animals around him went wild—sprinting headlong into the rain.

A moment later, Jakub and Oskar came running into the barn, and Zuzanna spent the rest of the night reliving the thrilling one-minute encounter and trying to describe the unwashed vagrant. As they sat in the hay, the family agreed that they could no longer allow the stranger to come and go without consequence. Retaliatory action was needed. The next morning, Oskar went out to where the transient had set up camp and seized his meager belongings.

Nobody compared stories until years later, but what was probably the same transient appeared in Saint Stanislaus Abbey's pantry the next evening, his fingers sticky with honey and a vinegar stain on his shirt.

The monk who had stumbled upon the 2 a.m. theft had taken a vow of silence, which he proceeded to break with a cry loud enough to wake up a dozen or so nearby monks.

Unlike in the barn the previous evening, the transient had no obvious path of escape. He merely put up his hands in a gesture of surrender. And what was Brother Konstanty going to do, exactly, other than to clutch his chest to make absolutely certain he hadn't just suffered cardiac arrest as he waited for reinforcements?

Several of the monks came running into the pantry still in their nightclothes and stared wordlessly at the intruder.

"Who are you?" one of the older monks asked.

The intruder said nothing.

"Are you hungry, brother?" the monk asked. "Have you come here looking for food and shelter? All are welcome at Saint Stanislaus. There is no need to steal. We will take care of anyone who needs it."

Still, the intruder said nothing. He resembled an animal from the wild, trying to assess the trap he had stepped in. He looked up and down at the men who had surrounded him but said nothing.

"What's your name?" the monk asked.

Silence.

"Come, sit down," the monk said. "Let us give you something proper to eat."

They gently took the intruder's arm and led him to the kitchen table, and Brother Bogomil went into the larder to produce a loaf of bread, butter, an apple, a wedge of cheese, dried sausage, and a cold helping of stewed lentils.

The intruder ate without speaking or taking his eyes away from the monks who had cornered him.

"You needn't fear," the older monk said. "You can tell us your name. No one is going to harm you."

The intruder stopped chewing for a few moments but didn't speak.

"Do you speak Polish?" the monk said.

The intruder was silent.

When he had finished his meal, the vagrant was led to a spare bed and told that he shouldn't feel any rush to leave. He looked distrustful, but accepted a nightshirt, a bar of soap, and the cot.

It was not an uncommon phenomenon; the hungry, leery wanderer who one day appears on the abbey doorstep. After being conjured, such a vagabond would invariably disappear again when he had a full belly, as if he had never been there at all. But the monks at Saint Stanislaus didn't mind. Providing for the meek was part of their mission. Nobody expected praise or gratitude.

The vagrant's inability to speak was also not so uncommon. The blind, the demented, and the deaf were all entrusted to the abbey over the years. It usually happened when the invalid was still a child whose parents hadn't already invested too many years of their lives in its upbringing. But it was well-known that the monks would endure worldly burdens that weaker souls could not.

This vagrant, however, didn't look slow-witted; just uncertain. And, perhaps, nasty. Like he had a poor opinion of the earth and those who inhabited it.

A few hours later, the vagrant was still on his cot when the wake-up bell sounded and Brother Bogomil came into his room to escort him to morning mass with the rest of the abbey. He looked embarrassed to still be in his nightclothes. He accepted a mug of black coffee (which he stared at curiously before tasting), and a few minutes later followed Brother Bogomil into the chapel.

The monks later noted that he was clearly not an observant Catholic; as the Abbot said the Latin prayers, the transient leaned forward, like he was trying to grasp the words.

The transient stayed silent through mass, and after it was over followed Brother Janusz to the kitchen, where he was told he could help him make breakfast.

The transient became known as Brother Wiernych.

This is not to say that he ever claimed the name as his own. He remained scrupulously silent, despite persistent efforts to get him to speak. But the monks needed something to call him. "Wiernych" means of the faithful, which sounded as good a name as any for a man who seemingly wanted to live the life of an ascetic. (None of the monks could detect any symptom of faith in him, but they weren't about to call him "Brother Moody," which probably suited him better.) So it was decided, and the silent man acceded to it.

Of course, any historian has a duty to be equitable to the players of his epoch; to see them as they see themselves. And, I concede, it is very possible that I am being unfair to Brother Wiernych. He was entirely veiled in his outlook, so there remains much that is unknown. He ventured no opinions. No eccentricities. No expressions of taste or favoritism. He remained a cipher, and only the creator of the universe knew the multitudes he might contain. But to the monks of Saint Stanislaus his mysteries were secondary to the discomfort he lent every room he entered.

This, and worse, was reported to the Abbot shortly after his adoption.

Brother Bogomil, who had taken it upon himself to look after the vagrant, made an appointment with the Abbot and told him that Brother Wiernych didn't understand manners, which was making everyone stay away from him.

"What do you mean?" the Abbot asked. "What does he do?"

"Basic table manners. They're nonexistent."

"I see . . ."

"He looks at everybody—*stares* at everybody—like he hates them. It's unnerving."

So the man stared. There were worse things, certainly, the Abbot pointed out. The good lord was the only one who knew the travails this man of the forest had endured before coming to Saint Stanislaus. Patience should be observed. Or, if Brother Bogomil preferred, he could talk to Brother Wiernych one-on-one about his behavior.

"I already spoke to him about this," Brother Bogomil said. "He didn't appear to understand or be interested."

"Oh."

"But that's not entirely it. There's more."

"Oh?"

"He steals."

That, of course, was a far larger accusation with a greater standard of proof than Brother Bogomil could offer.

"How do you know?"

Things had gone missing since Brother Wiernych had taken up residence in the abbey. While the monks of Saint Stanislaus owned relatively little, what they did possess was of great sentimental importance. A gold cross that Brother Gawel's sister had given to him when he was a child had vanished from his night table. A picture frame disappeared from another monk's bedroom, and the photograph it contained—of the monk's mother—reappeared in the rubbish bin a day later without the frame. Sausages and jugs of beer went missing from the larder. A silver chalice couldn't be found in the storage closet.

"Still," the Abbot said, "as the Good Book says, judge not lest ye be judged."

"There's more."

One of the monks, Brother Kacper, was an accomplished professional artist, whose oils and watercolors not only hung on the walls of the abbey but traded for hundreds—sometimes thousands—of zlotys in Warsaw and Budapest. The previous day (in an incident that would push Brother Bogomil to call for this meeting with the Abbot), as Brother Kacper had dabbed one of his paintbrushes into his box of watercolors he had discovered that someone had replaced the brown paint with human dung.

The Abbot was so taken aback that he knocked over a lamp on his desk.

"He took out the brown and put in excrement?" the Abbot repeated, astonished.

"Yes."

"But how do you know it was Brother Wiernych?"

It was a childish question, even if it was a legally critical one. This mischief had not visited the abbey a few months earlier, and now it had. The only change had been in the presence of the new, disliked monk. The services of Hercule Poirot were unnecessary in decrypting the riddle.

However, beyond these inescapably damning—but inescapably circumstantial—facts of the case there was nothing else to connect Brother Wiernych to the desecrations. He refused to speak and thereby could not be induced to offer evidence against himself. There were no witnesses to any of these crimes. None of the pilfered items were ever found in Brother Wiernych's possession. He was never observed in the toilet stalls handling fecal matter in anything other than the prescribed way.

But little thereafter could convince the rest of the monks that he wasn't responsible. Even the Abbot conceded that he was likely the culprit, as he tried to fathom what could push a man to such a revolting, arbitrary act.

"Assuming he's guilty," the Abbot concluded, "there's very little that can be done. We're not going to turn an obviously unstable man out into the forest to be devoured by wild animals."

Many of the monks believed that was precisely what should be done. Or, if not turned over to nature, at least turned over to the police. It was not a violation of Christian ethos or brotherly love to protect oneself from a predator. But the monks of Saint Stanislaus also believed in obedience, and they were not about to contradict the Abbot.

Precautions, however, were necessary. Doors were bolted. A new lock was installed on the kitchen door that was fastened at night. Brother Wiernych was no longer allowed to work in the kitchen or around the chapel, but was given a mop and a toilet brush and asked to clean the bathrooms as his prime labor in exchange for room and board. He performed this with the indifference the other monks had come to find so enraging.

It was also understood that the other monks should monitor him. As he mopped the floors, another monk scrubbed the sinks. When Brother Wiernych cleaned the toilets, another replaced the towels and soap. When he went to the dayroom to watch TV (the greatest repository of Brother Wiernych's free time), another monk watched with him—even though television was something generally frowned upon.

Still, it is remarkable what men can become accustomed to, and gradually Brother Wiernych became nothing more than a single chipped crystal in the great chandelier of Saint Stanislaus.

His status was low. He would never be trusted alone among the valuables of the abbey, or where he might have opportunity to micturate in the holy water. But his monitoring became less rigorous over time.

He still didn't speak to any of his fellow monks, but that was to be expected. (He was not the only one at the monastery who brooded in silence.) Instead, he wandered the abbey grounds and sat alone in the garden. He walked in the woods. He removed his shoes and stalked barefoot along the banks of the lake.

A year after he arrived at Saint Stanislaus, a bolt of gray suddenly struck down the center of his black beard one night, which caused a certain amount of chatter among the monks in the morning. But, as always,

Brother Wiernych left this unremarked on. He grew from lean and undernourished to heavy and deliberate.

On a purely physical level, he remained repulsive. He crammed food into his mouth like a starving animal and chewed with his mouth open. He expelled gas out of both ends of his body whenever the mood struck him, even if it was in the middle of a meal. He often slept through sermons and his snoring even annoyed the Abbot.

But while he was obviously strange, he also lived among strange men. The monks of Saint Stanislaus had removed themselves from the company of other men for an abundance of reasons, some of which were noble, and others suggested a certain immaturity in matters of the heart and body. Brother Wiernych was probably more normal than his peers, in that sense.

One of the reasons he watched as much television as he did was because he yearned for the form and company of women. When a beautiful actress appeared on the screen, he was transfixed. In the library he discovered a book of Renaissance art and gazed in awe at *The Birth of Venus*, which, fanciful as it was, stirred his desire.

Not long after Brother Bogomil first appeared at the Abbot's office he came a second time, to request that Brother Wiernych be given a room to himself.

"How come?"

"He sins against himself every night."

"Oh."

Brother Wiernych sinned without even the artifice of shame. He left stiff Kleenexes on the floor next to his bed, not bothering to drop them in the wastebasket.

The flesh is weak, the Abbot believed. If Brother Wiernych could understand the language it might have been worth warning him that he was imperiling his mortal soul—but in the end it was a matter solely between him and God.

He moved Brother Wiernych to his own room.

16

FLESHPOTS

I would never recommend a life of poverty—but I will also say that once lived, it makes an appreciation for the finer things all the greater.

Yes, most of us were extremely pleased with our newfound fortune. And like any other carnivorous animal allowed its first taste of flesh, our appetites grew with every passing week. After a while, the treasures of modernity were no longer novel and filled with wonder; they came to be expected as a fair and just addendum to our lives.

Visitors kept streaming into our marketplace and leaving their money behind, and the merchants and innkeepers and craftsmen of our town had no intention of sitting on this good fortune as the Katznelson Jews did. (Which is what we wound up calling those who refused to participate in the exchange; they eventually opened their own market on the other side of town.)

Sora Goldman, who knitted and sold sweaters and gloves that wound up commanding a fortune from the tourists—some going for as much as eight hundred zlotys—was the first to decide that her little cottage was an eyesore, and she was entitled to something more substantial.

She spent the next month nagging, wheedling, cajoling, and threatening her husband, Eidel, to build a grand, two-story house on the side of Kreskol opposite the Poczta and the new hotel.

"I just don't know," Eidel said. "What if what everybody says is true, and the currency collapses?"

"Then we will look very smart," Sora replied. "Instead of keeping a lot of worthless paper lying around our little mouse hole, we at least bought a nice big house to worry about our finances in."

A point that Eidel had to concede made more sense than he would have initially thought.

The Goldman house was finished at the beginning of autumn; almost immediately—after the furniture was moved in, rugs laid down on the floors, and the new chandeliers connected to electricity—Sora invited nearly everybody she knew (friends and enemies alike) to come through and inspect it.

A tradesman was summoned from Smolskie who installed a porcelain sink and commode for the second structure in town (after the Poczta) to have indoor plumbing, and one by one, the women of Kreskol put their fingers under the hot and cold running water to test it for themselves.

And the esurience for new real estate only increased. Chatzkel Ackerman, the woodsman who had constructed the Goldman house with six other men he picked, was suddenly besieged with requests. When he quoted seemingly outrageous sums for construction, plenty of comers told him that they wanted the winter to save, but would like to reserve his time next spring.

Construction proved such a financial boon—with more than two dozen planned by the time it became too cold to work—that men who had been previously employed in perfectly respectable professions such as tanning and engraving decided that they couldn't afford to miss out and began calling themselves roofers or housepainters.

It was an open question what would become of the empty hovels in the center of town when Brina Pressman had the brilliant idea of putting her son and daughter-in-law in her old house. She thereafter began matching deserted abodes with budding young families, becoming Kreskol's first real estate broker, and a wealthy woman in the process.

But in those days there was still little by way of luxuries readily available—so, I suppose, there was really no place to park our riches except real estate.

One of the tourists from Smolskie who came through our town could sense the rising opportunity. The fellow—a tall, scrawny chap named Cyril Mierzejak, who spoke no Yiddish and had no previous profession that we've ever been able to discern—appeared on Brina Pressman's doorstep one afternoon with Berel Rosen, who said: "Cyril here wants to live in Kreskol. Do you think you could find a home for him?"

Mierzejak seemed pleasant enough, even though he made no effort whatsoever to learn the local language or customs. He had chestnut-brown hair and brown eyes, and wore a sizable gold cross that he kept visible at all times, as if he were worried we might forget he was not one of us.

Mierzejak turned the outer parlor of the small house he rented into Kreskol's first appliance store, filling it with blenders, toasters, lightbulbs, fans, dust busters, compact refrigerators, and dozens of other doodads that we had never heard of before.

He hired a teenager who was reasonably fluent in Polish—Bunem Nudelman—to act as his translator and sat back and waited for us to throw our money at him.

"What's this?" asked Basha Richter when she came into his store and opened up the compact refrigerator.

"A teeny-tiny ice house," Bunem answered. "It'll keep fruit, meat, milk—or whatever you want—ice cold. There's a bigger one that stands roughly six feet high, but he'd have to order it from Warsaw."

The refrigerator proved to be Mierzejak's biggest moneymaker; he sold more than a hundred of them (some big, some small) over the course of his first six months, turning him into a rich man with minimal effort. Toaster ovens became his second-biggest seller, even though one of them nearly burned down the Applebaum house and sales briefly plummeted before recovering.

Several other gentiles from nearby towns and villages also appeared before Brina Pressman soon thereafter. A hardware store opened, followed by a pharmacy. Another goy had the idea of selling televisions and DVD players, which must have sounded like a proposition that couldn't lose given that TV was another wellspring of fascination, but the idea was overripe. Few of the townspeople were willing to plunk down 1,500 zlotys on such an extravagance. There was nothing on TV in Yiddish if they had. And while the moving images might have been riveting, they were also unnerving; they operated outside the known laws of the day-to-day, and few townspeople intended to bring black magic into their house.

One of the gentile wives opened a beauty parlor and nail salon out of the front room of her house. At first, it looked like another idea ahead of its time, but the proprietress, Jadwiga Wozniak, refused to accept what seemed preordained. She snatched three teenage girls off the street and offered the full makeover, free of charge.

When they claimed they were uninterested—and had no idea what a "makeover" was—Jadwiga raised her hands, the fingernails of which were manicured and painted red.

"How'd you like me to do your nails for free, too?" Jadwiga said in Yiddish. (She learned this sentence and six or seven others before embarking on this mission.)

The girls' eyes stayed fixed on the nails and then crept over to Jadwiga's violet eye shadow and scarlet blush.

"What do you have to lose?" Jadwiga said. "You might enjoy it."

And with that final inducement, Jadwiga had her first customers. A pack of a dozen or so young men spontaneously formed outside the Wozniaks' house (Jadwiga left the door conspicuously open) and watched silently as the metamorphosis was undertaken. When the girls left the salon two hours later—their eyebrows plucked, the lids blue, their faces white with powder, their lips crimson and fingernails pink—they were a vision.

Thereafter, there was a line outside Jadwiga's salon six days per week, starting when the sun went down on Saturday evening.

The gentiles mostly kept to themselves. The attempts they made to speak to us in anything other than Polish were modest. They could be seen smoking cigarettes behind Mierzejak's house, laughing at jokes. They put satellite dishes on their roofs and merrily whooped and hollered as they watched football games moistened with beer and vodka. One of their houses served as Kreskol's makeshift Catholic church, where they assembled every Sunday morning to consume the blood and body of Jesus Christ.

Far stranger additions came in the form of several black-clad, bearded Israeli pioneers.

"Israel," their twenty-five-year-old leader, named Uzi Yagoda, told Rabbi Sokolow in a Hebrew-flecked Yiddish, "was a historical mistake. It should have never been settled before the Messiah had arisen. Jews should not be living there. The ones who do live like the goyim."

It sounded peculiar, but Rabbi Sokolow was not prepared to challenge a stranger. A dozen single Israeli men, and five families, took up residence in the town's empty houses and bestrode the town like they were our long-lost brethren, greeting every weaver and glassblower with a hearty "Shalom!" However, after they heard of the rift that had taken place within our town, they instantly took the Katznelson side, and stopped speaking to the rest of us.

In the midst of our buying and spending sprees, the greatest hunger was for daily (or at least weekly) reports from the outside world.

A year after our rediscovery, some American tourists came through Kreskol carrying a faded tabloid newspaper that—much to our surprise—was printed in Yiddish. It caused a sensation.

The newspaper was passed from hand to hand until the newsprint became smudged and faded and the stories readable only if your eyesight was sharp. Still, we pored over every article—from bombings in Syria, to an actress named Gwyneth Paltrow, who, despite her gargantuan height and straw-colored hair, was Jewish. Or partly. (Gwyneth Paltrow became the first real celebrity of Kreskol; when the matchmakers were trying to sell a girl to a boy's family they began saying: "She's a regular Gwyneth Paltrow.")

When it got out that Kreskol might be a big news consumer, a distributor for *Fakt* and *Gazeta Wyborcza** came on a fact-finding mission to our town—only to be disappointed when told how few of us spoke Polish.

Bunem Nudelman—who still had his job at the appliance store—came up with the idea of ordering a half dozen of the Polish journals every day, and charging the men and women of town five zlotys each for translations, which he would administer orally to groups of twelve at a time. After a while he realized it would be simpler to wake up early, handwrite summaries of everything, take them to the Poczta (the only institution in town to possess a copy machine), and pay some kid to hand them out on a street corner for two zlotys apiece. He called it *The Kreskol Crier*.

It became something of a badge of honor to be able to discuss current events. "What do you think of Mateusz Morawiecki?" one of the housewives would ask at the teashop.

"He sounds like a decent man," came the considered answer. (Given that we considered Morawiecki's rank roughly akin to that of a tsar, few felt entitled to offer more muscular criticism.)

We talked about Radoslaw Majecki, the goalkeeper for the Legia Warsaw football team, and Robert Lewandowski, the captain of the national team—even though few of us really understood the rules of football. But the sports sections appeared in our news summaries every day, and most of our citizens felt duty-bound to take an interest.

Even the Katznelson Jews, who claimed that they had no use for tabloid rags ("Gossip," Rabbi Katznelson pronounced, "is just like murder in that it does irrevocable damage to its victims"), could usually be seen leafing through discarded, day-old copies of the *Crier*.

And then, one day, we started reading about ourselves in the *Crier*.

No one in our town had ever heard of Zbigniew Berlinsky, the scholar.

After the scandal broke, Rajmund Sikorski went around town with a

---

*Two Polish newspapers: *Fakt* is a tabloid; *Gazeta Wyborcza* covers national and international news.

photo of Berlinsky, and asked every shopkeeper if he had come into their establishment asking questions. "No," came the reply, "but many have come through town in the last few years."

Dr. Berlinsky, a professor of modern history and Judaic studies at the University of Krakow with degrees from Cambridge and Hebrew Universities, was (we found out later) one of the world's foremost experts on contemporary Jewish history.

Like many others in our town, I have since looked over the translation of the paper he submitted about Kreskol at a conference of Holocaust scholars at Bar-Ilan University. And I will concede that he is a persuasive and engaging writer. His credentials and erudition are beyond dispute, and one could see the evidence of this in the throwaways and asides throughout the document. Still, this doesn't change the fact that what he wrote about our town was filled with the worst flights of fancy and irresponsible speculation.

I feel slightly uneasy quoting such a false source at any length. But in telling the story of Kreskol, it would be a dishonesty all its own to leave it out of the record.

"I speak to you as a mere onlooker in this latest discovery," Dr. Berlinsky began his paper, which he read before an audience of about two hundred. He was an old man—well past seventy—and he had a hunched back, wrinkles, and gray hair. "I have observed from the sidelines the breathless reports about this latest—and, possibly, last—major addition to the scholarship on pre–World War II European Jewry. Naturally, the idea of an untouched, undisturbed specimen of Jewish life that escaped the Nazi invasion of Poland would have been intoxicating to any of my fellow scholars.

"Let me revise that; it would have been intoxicating to *anyone* who had the least amount of interest in World War II and the Holocaust—be it the scholar or the lay reader—which is checkered with so many ghastly, horrific stories that it is a palpable relief to delve into an unambiguously happy one.

"A subject as elaborate as Kreskol would require an extraordinary amount of time and energy devoted to it—time and energy I do not possess at this advanced age and stage of my career. Still, make no mistake, the time would be spent debunking an obvious fraud.

"I do not believe that the Nazis skipped Kreskol during their migration east, because I do not believe that Kreskol existed then. Kreskol is a sham. It is not a Jewish village. It is not a Polish village. Honestly, I have no idea what it is. My suspicion is that it is the well-financed prank of some demented person or group of persons who have either brainwashed weaker-minded compatriots into believing their obvious nonsense or bribed them into being accessories to this hoax.

"But it is simply not possible for Kreskol to have existed as a Jewish village in the location it stands today and escaped notice of the German army.

"It is not possible that a village of several hundred Jewish souls should have lived, breathed, and died for hundreds of years and failed to pay taxes to the Jewish councils and tribute to the local nobility. The lists of towns used by the Einsatzgruppen during the liquidation of Jews from Poland came directly from the Jewish councils, and it is not just doubtful—it is unthinkable—that an entire village should have escaped their notice. Kosher inspection alone was an elaborate bureaucracy employing many hundreds of Jews throughout the Pale of Settlement, and the inspectors would never have allowed a purported Jewish village to fail to adhere to its regulations. Kreskol is the greatest lie ever perpetuated on academia in the forty years since I handed in my dissertation. And, frankly, I'm surprised that I'm the first to say so out loud."

The paper caused a great commotion in the hall. Within moments, the spectators collectively unsheathed their blackberries and iPhones, and began frantically typing. Hushed exclamations of disbelief rolled through the auditorium, and of the five other scholars seated on the stage with Berlinsky, three turned red with outrage.

Berlinsky was oblivious to the chaos he had fermented. He continued reading his paper as dryly as only an academic septuagenarian knows how, pausing to refresh himself from the paper cup of water on the podium and wink at the fluorescent light. And after the thunderous, prosecutorial manner in which he began the paper, he reverted to a very mundane rec-itation of facts: Tax structures existed in Poland from the late eighteenth through the early twentieth centuries—including the Protection and Tolerance Tax, the Property and Occupation Tax, and the Kosher Meat Tax—which, he argued, no local government, no matter how corrupt or badly organized, would forgo. And once this village was on the books, there was no way the Germans could have missed it.

He then pointed out that for a small village to have spent a century in isolation, there had to have been significant inbreeding and our gene pool would no doubt have been polluted. "If Kreskol had been really left alone all those years, problems such as Down syndrome and mental retardation would not be a rare occurrence but one of the dominant characteristics in the town. That has never been reported."

It appeared that Professor Berlinsky had been unaware of Kreskol's name change, even though this point of information appeared in the offi-cial government report about Kreskol. Or, if Berlinsky did know, he chose to ignore it. And this business about our mongolism was sheer fantasy. As was pointed out later, our population was not in the low hundreds, but well over a thousand (closer to two thousand), implying there was plenty of room for diversity in our breeding. (He would be corrected on this point on the dais a few minutes later, but it remained a major element of the story.) However, Berlinsky took pains to say, he had never really researched Kreskol—this was just his reaction as a scholar of more than four decades.

"This paper," he ended, "is meant to introduce necessary skepticism into the conversation. I do not pretend to know the solution to the mystery of Kreskol. That should be left to younger, sprier historians. I only hope that this raises the right questions that academics—and the greater public—should demand and that a thorough debunking follows. Thank you."

Dr. Berlinsky then took his seat amid the uproar, with his audience frantically waving their hands to get his attention.

The moment the report hit our newsletter, most of us were full of an even greater sense of outrage and disbelief than Dr. Berlinsky's intended audience. Who was this altercocker* to say that we were a sham? What did that even mean, anyway? How could this guy know every village, hamlet, and city in Poland? How could anybody?

"So we're a *sham* village," joked Zanek Boscowitz. "If Berlinsky should pay us a visit, I'll be sure to punch him in the nose with my sham fist, and he'll no doubt be happy that he's only in sham agony."

But Dr. Berlinsky's accusations were taken seriously by other academics and important people.

Berel Rosen (one of the few in our town at the time to possess a mobile telephone) was bombarded over the course of the next few weeks with requests for an interview. Calls came from as far off as Tokyo and Cape Town, with reporters who wanted to know how we, the good people of Kreskol (or, *once* good people of Kreskol), wished to respond to these allegations.

"They're insane," said Berel.

A few of the reporters chose to argue with him. "But surely some of the allegations *aren't* insane," countered the reporter from *Le Monde*. "You read Berlinsky's paper, didn't you? He raises serious questions. What do you say about this tax issue—how did Kreskol slip through the cracks?"

"It's insane because it's not true," Berel replied. "Either something happened or it didn't. Either Kreskol is a real place or it isn't. I assure you, Kreskol is real."

"And how do we know you're not in on this hoax, Mr. Rosen?" the reporter asked.

He would be the only such journalist to offer so direct a challenge, but that insinuation was lurking in the shadow of each pointed question.

---

*Yiddish: "old fart."

The reporters, at least, would ask their questions and go on their way. A few of the politicians got it into their heads that this scandal was a monstrous case of duplicity and they made impassioned pleas in the Sejm to "get to the bottom of the fraud of Kreskol."

Indeed, an auditor and a panel of three government experts were chosen to come to our archive and reexamine all our records. When their report was deemed inconclusive ("Everything that's in the records supports the history of Kreskol as the Kreskolites have told it," the report said, "which can mean that this narrative is correct—or the hoax has yet to reveal any flaws"), a geologist was sent to Kreskol to examine the soil and the buildings in an attempt to find any chemicals or materials that could have been used after World War II.

"Aside from the houses that were recently built, the Poczta, and the hotels, there looks to be no discordant xenobiotic chemicals—such as solvents, pesticides, lead, heavy metal, or hydrocarbons—in the village or the surrounding areas," the report stated. "This would support Kreskol's claim as to its limited interaction with other towns and villages."

But a member of the Sejm got another scientist (who had never been to Kreskol) to say that the evidence could have been tampered with, which was enough to keep the seeds of doubt alive.

Even the tourists—who had been so kind and generous—turned against us.

What had been several hundred tourists per day was suddenly cut in half. And the tourists who did come usually had some wiseguy in their ranks, eager to trip us up. He would toss a phrase in English or Russian at us, expecting our masks to slip. Or he would interrupt the tour guides as they expounded on the history of Kreskol's synagogue, calling it all a lot of baloney. And in many cases this troublemaker would convince his fellow tourists not to buy anything in any of Kreskol's shops as it was obviously fake and what was the point in buying leather gloves or a wool coat from a fake town?

Some of the Poles from Smolskie were outraged enough by this hoax that they drove into Kreskol and began telling us to our faces how dishonest and treacherous they thought we were.

"You Jews never change, do you?" one wobbly, middle-aged man who had been deep in his cups slurred to Reb Zelig Minkin. "Always figuring out some new way to pick a pocket. It's pure horseshit."

And with that, this sinewy, mustached fellow proceeded to spit on the elderly Reb Minkin's coat, and kick dirt at him—much to the shock of everybody who witnessed it.

The next morning, a swastika was discovered painted in red on one of the houses next to the words "Jews out!"

A few days after the swastika appeared, and its meaning fully explained (nobody appreciated just how deep an insult it was, at first), another swastika appeared, this time on Sokolow's shul. And it was also accompanied by the words "Go back to Israel"—but this time, the words were written in Yiddish.

While we might have guessed where this second missile came from, the Poles did not. At least not initially. And the one good thing that came from this whole sordid episode was that the Poles were suddenly filled with a bit more trepidation as they hurtled their accusations of fraud against us.

Our prime tormentor in the Sejm was a fellow named Henryk Szymanski, who constantly stood before his colleagues demanding more audits and investigations into our history, and demanding that the state be paid back every grosz of taxpayer money if we could not prove our origins. But now he prefaced each attack with these words: "We all condemn the defilement of the synagogue in Kreskol on July twenty-second."

The heads of several international Jewish organizations rose to our defense, and even planned trips to Kreskol to meet with Rabbi Sokolow; the prime minister's office sent a letter expressing his regret on behalf of fellow Poles everywhere.

Only the instigator of all our problems, Dr. Berlinsky, remained unmoved.

"It wouldn't surprise me if they did it to themselves," Dr. Berlinsky pronounced when a reporter asked him about it. "After all, the second message was, if I read correctly, in Yiddish. That leads me to believe it was some joker in the town."

After he made this prognostication, the fiendish Henryk Szymanski revised his previous condemnation of the attacks on us, now demanding that the culprits be uncovered and their ringleaders carted off to jail for fraud, vandalism, violations of article 13 of the Polish constitution, and articles 196, 256, and 257 of the criminal code. (Those who knew the honorable Mr. Szymanski's political history found this *j'accuse* laughable, given that the last four violations concerned hate speech and membership in a fascist party, and Mr. Szymanski had been a member of the Polska Partia Narodowa* a few years earlier.)

We read reports in the *Crier* that the Sejm and the senate had launched official investigations, wherein all those who had played a role in our re-discovery were hauled before investigators and asked what they had seen and when.

Rajmund Sikorski was the first witness to be called, and as precise and composed as he seemed in every interaction he had with us, he seemed different when the klieg lights were shone on him.

"I should say from the start that my only interest in Kreskol was as the liaison between Szyszki and the village—nothing more," Sikorski said. "I never sought this assignment. It came to me from my boss, Mika Pawlowska, and I merely followed her instructions in trying to integrate the town into the region."

When asked flatly if he believed that Kreskol's story was genuine, he refused to take a stand. "That's not my place," he replied. "I am not a his-

_____

*Literally, Polish National Party; a far-right, ultra-nationalist political party.

torian, a sociologist, a geologist, or anyone else that could form an expert opinion. I am a bureaucrat."

Even in the final moments of his testimony, when Sikorski was asked if he had anything left to add, he used the opportunity to make his own little dig against our town. "From the very beginning, they've been extremely difficult to work with."

Rabbi Sokolow was summoned to Warsaw and, through a translator, answered the committee's many questions—reiterating that we had simply had no dealings with any other town over the past decades. He was versed enough in the history of our village to explain the origins of the rift that had taken place more than a century ago and why our fellow Jews took pains to avoid us.

The more preening members of the investigative committee tried to trip him up. "Kreskol no doubt has a Bible in its synagogue, no?" asked one fellow. "Where would you have gotten such a book if you hadn't seen any other town in a hundred years? Did Kreskol have its own printing press?"

"The Torah isn't written on paper," the Rabbi replied. "It's written on sheepskin."

The committee members looked skeptical.

"You're trying to tell me there was never one single slip of paper in Kreskol before three years ago—not one? Everything was written on sheepskin?"

"No, no," Sokolow continued in Yiddish. "I didn't say that. But you asked about the Torah. There are books in the library. They've been passed down for many years. Nobody buys new books. There are no booksellers in Kreskol. I'm no expert, but from what I understand, merchants once drove through Kreskol with their wagons and they'd sell books, but this stopped after the rift between Kreskol and the other villages." (Sokolow failed to mention that Leonid Spektor bought books from the gypsies, but he was probably unacquainted with this fact.)

This prompted the investigators to drive out to Kreskol that afternoon and impound three books from the library at random, which were taken to a laboratory to verify their age. All three were judged to be more than 130—and less than 180—years old.

Next, several psychiatrists from Our Lady of Mercy were questioned as to how they could possibly have gone from seeing an obvious fraud before their eyes into believing in it.

Doctors Antoni Polus and Ignacy Meslowski said the kindest words they could about the mental patient who had appeared in their hospital claiming to be from this legendary shtetl in the forest.

"There is no question that the young man who reached out from Kreskol was sincere in his beliefs," said Dr. Meslowski.

"Is it possible that he was manipulated by others into believing all this business about Kreskol's history?" asked one of the committee members.

"I suppose it's possible," said Dr. Meslowski. "But there are a few things to consider. First, he didn't know much about the history of Kreskol. He only knew it as the place where he had grown up. He knew its customs and ways, but he didn't know its story. Second, whatever manipulation might have been going on would have been going on throughout Mr. Lewinkopf's whole life. If Kreskol is a fake, whoever engineered this fraud did it twenty years ago or more."

Until the final day of scheduled testimony, it looked very much like the investigation would have found little to challenge in Kreskol's purported authenticity. Not that the investigators didn't still have their suspicions, but the evidence pointed to a village that had at the very minimum collected quite a number of artifacts to tell its tale convincingly. No ringleader could be unmasked with a motive for perpetuating the hoax. And as Rajmund Sikorski and Rabbi Sokolow pointed out in their testimony, there were many hundreds of Kreskolites who shunned the trappings of modernity and yearned for their past anonymity—which seemed to undermine the idea that this had all been a ruse to generate tourism.

After Dr. Polus had testified, the lead investigator remarked to a reporter: "There will likely be no consequences for Kreskol."

Not even Yankel Lewinkopf was expected to appear. "What's the point of going out and finding this young man?" asked Dr. Meslowski when the committee asked about Yankel's possible whereabouts. "He's not going to tell you anything different than you're hearing from me. Or anyone else." The committee was inclined to agree.

On the final scheduled day of hearings, there were only two witnesses. The abbot of the monastery a few miles from Kreskol, whose testimony (that the abbey had been entirely unaware of Kreskol's presence for hundreds of years) confirmed very little, and Dr. Bartek Krol.

Dr. Krol showed up at the hearing with his hair neatly combed and his goatee groomed, wearing a black Ermenegildo Zegna suit and silver Rolex, looking the very portrait of sleekness and professionalism.

By that point in the hearings, the only press in the room were the Polish newspapers and two from Israel; after an initial burst of interest in Dr. Berlinsky's accusations, the rest of the international press had grown weary of the story.

"I do not know whether Mr. Lewinkopf was truthful or deceptive," Dr. Krol said before the committee, reading from three typed pieces of paper prepared for the morning. "But I do know that he had a vested interest in feeding his doctors more and more of these stories about Kreskol—because they kept spending more and more money on him every time he did."

The moment Dr. Krol uttered these words the hearing was interesting again.

17

REPARATION

It is with some regret that I must conjure, again, the unfortunate Yankel Lewinkopf.

I did not see him myself, but those who did a few days later say that he walked slowly into the committee chamber, not like a spry twenty-four-year-old, but a man whose body has been flayed by the punishments of time.

It was not just the heaviness of his movements or the circles under his eyes that made him appear different. His shoulders were still muscular, but he looked thicker than the lithe, slender teenager who had been originally sent out of Kreskol. His beard was gone, and his hairline had ever so slightly receded. He was dressed in a pair of tan corduroy trousers and a button-down black-and-white checkered shirt.

He didn't speak at first, but when he did, his accent was discernable only to those who were listening for it. If you had asked Poles, they might have guessed that he was from the boondocks, or possibly one of Poland's eastern neighbors, but few would have supposed that his first language was Yiddish. He resembled—as everyone agreed—a gentile.

An officer huddled next to Yankel's side, suggesting he might make a dash for freedom if not actively patrolled. But the guard was the only one who would get close to him. The rest of the Poles looked fearful; like he carried a contagion that would cause all manner of bodily harm. Yes, it would seem that one and all had decided before he sat down that Yankel Lewinkopf was guilty of something. (I suppose they believed he had, at the very least, committed some form of dishonesty. But I cannot speak for them.)

However, I am getting slightly ahead of the story here. Dr. Krol's testimony had not ended with that first set of fateful words. He had more.

"Again, I must state for the record, I say this only as someone who worked in the hospital and looked at the audit for the various departments the summer that Mr. Lewinkopf was being treated," Dr. Krol pointed out. "But I will also say—and I don't know where these rumors got started— that there was other talk about Mr. Lewinkopf and specific demands he had made of the psych ward."

"Like what?" asked Szymanski, who was so surprised by his good fortune that he couldn't even summon the wit and heavy-handed sarcasm that won him his political career.

"For one thing, I had heard that he had made a reparations request."

The room turned into pandemonium. When another questioner asked Dr. Krol where he had heard such a wild story, Dr. Krol answered with a shrug. "It was a long time ago—I don't remember where I first heard the rumor, but it was all over the hospital. Ask anybody who was working at the hospital at the time and they'll back me up."

Since the beginning of Kreskol's rediscovery, the word "reparations" had largely been unspoken in public—but many Poles spoke it to their most trusted friends and family when no one else was listening. These conversations were always muted; as if the speakers knew there was something slightly obscene in making an accusation against so abused a people before any proof of a crime had been presented. But it was nonetheless something on many a Pole's mind.

Enough of this worry had seeped into the collective mood that on the anniversary of our rediscovery two years earlier *Gazeta Polska* published an editorial under the headline "What Does Kreskol Want from Us?"

Ever since World War II ended nearly every Pole expected to one day hear a knock on the door with an ancient Jew on the doorstep brandishing a deed to the property. Or, if not a deed, the tormented memory of what had happened to them and their home—and whether this came with or without documentation was beside the point. It drove millions of Poles to apoplexy.

However, the idea that the Jews would come into their windfall not by coming right out and demanding a specific plot of land or specific sum of money, but would take advantage of the Polish government's guilt to cheat the country out of millions in tax benefits by forming a fake village . . . Well, that was too unlikely to be believed, until it appeared to be happening before their eyes!

At least this was the theory that a member of Szymanski's staff leaked to *Fakt*. "Yes," the unnamed source told the newspaper. "The Jews got their reparations. And we were fool enough to give it to them without a fight."

The day after Dr. Krol's testimony, other members of the hospital staff were summoned to the committee and they, too, admitted that they had heard the rumor that Yankel Lewinkopf had asked about reparations.

This was countered by Wojciech Kowalski, the head of the hospital, who appeared before the committee and said that Yankel Lewinkopf had never asked for any reparations of any kind whatsoever—but by that point it hardly mattered.

"Do you mean to say that you heard *none* of the rumors that the rest of the staff heard?" asked Szymanski—with the suggestion in his tone that Kowalski would be an imbecile for having missed such important news.

"Yes, I heard some things," Kowalski admitted.

"Ah!"

"But these were just rumors. It had no basis in reality."

"How do you really know this?" Szymanski asked. "Have you read all of Mr. Lewinkopf's psychiatric evaluations?"

"No."

"Then how do you know?"

Kowalski was no stranger to official proceedings; in his professional career he had advised local and national political panels all the time. And he was not easily confounded by having a spotlight thrown on him. "Because, sir," he replied evenly, "when such an outlandish accusation arises any responsible administrator would look into it. As I did. I questioned the psychiatric staff about this matter and they denied that Mr. Lewinkopf had ever made such a request. Why would my staff lie to me?"

Szymanski was equally unrattled.

"I've heard that certain members of the staff developed some affection for Mr. Lewinkopf," Szymanski said. "Perhaps they were seeking to protect him from himself?"

"Preposterous."

But even Dr. Kowalski's authoritative dismissals could not spare poor Yankel Lewinkopf. His future was written on the witness chair.

And in describing the somewhat shabby figure Yankel cut when he appeared before the committee, I must go back a bit farther and tell you a little of how he had spent the last two years.

The afternoon at the bazaar had, as I already said, ended with Pesha Rosenthal being carted away in shackles—and Yankel making a desperate attempt to find her.

He begged anyone he passed in the street to point him to the nearest police station. It was a similar task to the one he had performed the previous year in Smolskie, with much worse results—he now frightened people away, not with his appearance, but with the tears streaming down his cheeks and the look of desperation in his eye. (One woman he approached threatened to call the cops if he didn't steer clear, and when Yankel said, "That's exactly who I'm looking for!" she failed to make good on her threat and merely strode away.)

It was hours before he came upon a police station, but when he asked the booking officer if Pesha had come through, his curt response was: "We don't have any Pesha Rosenthals—or any Peshas at all."

Yankel considered this for a moment.

"What about a Teresa? Have there been any Teresas booked today?"

There was, in fact, a Teresa in the holding cell, but it was not Pesha.

Still, the booking officer took enough pity on Yankel that he called over to a nearby police house and asked if they had booked a Pesha Rosenthal over the course of the afternoon.

"There's a woman who won't give her name," the officer said, writing down the address for Yankel. "And she doesn't speak Polish. That might be your girlfriend."

An hour or so later, Pesha and Yankel were reunited, but the affection Yankel had seen in Pesha's eyes earlier that morning had been supplanted by rage. He had expected they would speak of what kind of trouble she was in; what their next steps should be to secure her freedom; what the ultimate consequences of her actions would be (depending on whether her victim had been seriously hurt or not)—but none of those things were on Pesha's mind. The one and only thing she wanted to discuss was the apparent rivalry between her and her victim.

"We're both adults, Yankel," Pesha said after the guard had moved beyond earshot. "I know there was something between the two of you. Who is she?"

Of course, many millions of men throughout human history have had to decide on a few seconds' notice between providing their lover with an unbearable truth or a merciful falsehood. A few will stumble between the choice and offer a slightly less-damning half-truth. Perhaps if Yankel had more time to properly consider his options he would have come down firmly on one extreme or the other. However, this did not happen.

"Yes, I knew her," Yankel admitted. "But it was well before I knew you were in Warsaw."

"How did you know her?"

"She's a prostitute."

The moment the words had left his mouth Yankel realized that he had chosen poorly. Pesha had sensed intimacy, but she hadn't fully realized the extent of it. From the astounded expression on her face, she had clearly hoped that Yankel would answer her falsely.

Yankel watched the rage in her face dissolve quickly into the shock of betrayal. As her cheeks colored, Yankel ran his hands over his own face, as if he were too ashamed to show himself without some covering.

Neither of them spoke. And Pesha's eyes moved from Yankel to the table before she finally broke the silence.

"Oh."

The word hung malevolently in the air for a long time. In its understatement, it summoned both Pesha's surprise and agony effectively. And after the word completed its devastation, Yankel could merely put his head down on the hard wooden table between the two of them and whimper, "I'm sorry, Pesha. It was before I knew you were here."

The rest of their interview proceeded along its preordained path. There was recrimination, disbelief, and anger—none of which was spoken out loud—that was only broken by Pesha with one-word answers to his questions, until Yankel told her, "They say they're going to set bail tomorrow. I'll be back."

Pesha didn't answer him.

"The bail will be expensive—more money than I have," Yankel continued. "Thousands of zlotys."

"I don't want your money."

These words carried more devastation. Yankel's face turned white with sickness, but Pesha refused to look him in the eye.

"Well, I'll be back tomorrow," Yankel said.

But it would be the last words Pesha would exchange with her suitor for a very long time.

When he arrived at the police station the next morning, with Karol by his side (having made a long and tortured confession of everything that had happened since he met Pesha that night in the cathouse), the bailiff told them that the assailant had no desire to see him, and would not accept his money for bail.

"What happens now?" Yankel asked.

"I haven't the slightest idea," replied Karol.

Yankel felt obligated to sit around the police station for the rest of the day, in the hope that he might pry out some nugget of information. "I think you're wasting your time," Karol replied after they had sat for an hour in the waiting area. "If she doesn't want to see you, she doesn't have to. You'll just be waiting around here for nothing when you could be working."

Yankel looked crushed to be handed such a sober assessment.

"And I'm afraid I can't wait around here all day with you," Karol said, a little too cheerfully. "I've got to get to work. Got a job to keep and an ex-wife to support. You know what I mean, right, sport?"

Still, Yankel could not bring himself to exit until lunchtime, when the female officer who had been eyeing him carefully all morning ordered him to pack it in and leave. "Why are you still hanging around here?" she barked. "Get lost."

Yankel stood and backed away, spending another hour standing outside staring at the station before giving up and returning to the bakery. Nonetheless, Yankel appeared again the next day and was told that Pesha had been summoned to the court the afternoon before, with bail set at 10,000 zlotys, and a trial set for two months hence.

"She was bailed out," the male officer on duty told Yankel. "She's not here anymore."

Yankel was surprised to hear that.

"Bailed out—by who?"

The officer looked Yankel up and down, and apparently decided that there was no harm in telling him.

"A lady dwarf."

Yankel went to the cathouse straight from the station.

The same moon-faced Oriental—whose pimples had only gotten worse in the months since Yankel had last seen her—waited for him in the massage parlor with a foreboding curl on her lips.

And while Yankel certainly stumbled through the past few days, not sure what words or actions would best secure entrée to the object of his desires, he had enough foresight to have emptied the shoebox under his bed of all the money he had been saving for a future apartment before he left Karol's apartment.

"I'd like to see Teresa," he told the Chinese woman.

She said nothing.

"Please."

Even though this gatekeeper was breathing heavily, she tried to maintain a casual affectlessness about her—as if she found this interloper more boring than worrisome.

"I don't know Teresa."

Yankel didn't argue with her. Instead he pulled roughly half of the money he had brought with him out of his pocket and presented the girl with it. "Please," Yankel said.

She stared quizzically at the crumpled, clammy notes before her, not daring to touch them.

"Your money no good."

Instantly, he put the other half of his savings before her.

Raising the ante caught the girl's attention. And, for a moment, she stared at the bills and wordlessly looked as if she was counting them to herself.

"*You* don't have enough" was all she responded—and the way she jabbed the word "you" made Yankel wonder whether she meant that he was the kind of poor, scruffy tramp who would never be able to bribe her enough to reverse previously purchased loyalties, or he had simply failed to produce the requisite ransom.

"How much do you want?" Yankel asked.

But the girl had lost interest in the conversation. She picked up the glossy magazine on the desk in front of her and began leafing through its pages, stopping at a list of skincare tips. Her next words were spoken with none of the tripping hesitation or Asiatic inflections of her previous speech:

"Fuck off."

Oh, how Yankel suffered. He had no intention whatsoever of allowing the woman whom he loved so passionately to slip away. He returned the next day with all the cash he could borrow from his boss—telling him, through a stream of hot, humiliating tears, that his girlfriend had been arrested and that he would pay him back as soon as he could—and presented the Chinese girl with 7,000 zlotys. But she was having none of it.

"Don't you come back here" was all she said, not bothering to look at the money for nearly as long as she had the previous day. "You come back, you regret it."

When Yankel returned the next day (this time with an extra 3,000 zlotys he had wheedled out of Karol), a muscular fellow in a white T-shirt and jeans, with a blond crew cut, stood outside the massage parlor, arms folded across his chest, as if daring Yankel—or any other troublesome character—to proceed across the threshold.

Yankel stood for a very long time across the street, observing his adversary. And while Yankel possessed the valiant impulse to charge head-first into the fray—come what may of the consequences—he was also no clod. He could see that this figure had been planted there because he was twice his size. Each arm swelled out of the sleeve of the sentinel's shirt as immense and solid as a tree trunk. It was one thing to sacrifice oneself when the chance of success was slim; certain death was another matter altogether.

After a few moments the sentinel caught sight of Yankel, and turned his bulk toward him.

The two stared at each other for several long minutes, the minotaur taking the full measure of Theseus, before deciding that he did not have anything to fear. Any struggle between the two would end with Yankel's defeat. But the menacing look in the sentinel's eyes did not abate. After a few minutes, Yankel decided he'd better leave and come back when he had some kind of plan.

Passion makes a point of muddying the thoughts of those it seeks to infect, and Yankel spent many fruitless weeks trying to come up with a scheme to see Pesha, without any success.

His first thought was simply that he must be persistent; every afternoon, when work was finished for the day, he should visit the cathouse and wait for an opportunity to reenter, or see the cherished object of his affections take in the afternoon air—but every day he saw the blond sentry standing guard.

Sometimes a different sentry would be posted outside—another big Pole, who looked similar to the first one, except he had longer hair and a wider nose.

The second sentry in fact looked so like the first that Yankel wondered if the two men weren't brothers. Yankel got a bit closer to this one, but when the brute said, "What do you want?" he shook his head and said, "Nothing," before striding off.

After more than a month, Yankel accepted that these two guards might be permanent fixtures, and that if he expected to see Pesha again he needed an alternate strategy.

"Why don't you send her a letter?" Karol asked, quite sensibly.

Yankel spent the next week composing and recomposing a letter in Yiddish for his beloved.

The letter was, I am told, not the words of a natural writer. (The original has been lost, so I can't quote it precisely.) It totaled almost fifteen pages, and was used to wallow in its own titanic misery; Yankel detailed how unhappy he was without Pesha, and how sorry he was to have done anything to hurt her. The prostitute—whose name, he honestly attested, he did not even know—meant nothing to him. He begged Pesha to send word of herself, even if it was just to let him know that she was all right, and how her legal case was proceeding. He unthinkingly addressed it to "Pesha Rosenthal Lindauer"—but a week later it was returned to him unopened.

The next day, he sent another, leaner letter, which he addressed to "S. Teresa" asking only that she meet him for coffee at their appointed spot, at the usual time. This letter was not returned, but when he showed up at Trzmiel on Monday the café was empty.

He showed up the next day—and every day after, for the next two weeks—but Pesha never revealed herself or sent word.

Again, the only solution he could come up with was persistence, and he wrote more letters, day after day, to S. Teresa, in which he detailed (somewhat numbingly) his misery and his longing.

Karol disliked seeing his friend in such a state. He begged Yankel to come out with him during the normal Saturday-night crawls around the neighborhood pubs, but Yankel refused all offers. "Listen, old man," Karol began one of his talks over the dinner table, where they both sat before a microwaved turkey and mashed potato dinner, "I feel it's only right to wise you up a little bit . . ."

"Yes?"

"The worst person in the world you could fall in love with—and I mean the very *worst*—is a whore."

Yankel looked up, insulted more by his friend's choice of the word "whore" than the suggestion that he had been played for a fool.

"I wouldn't say anything if she were an undertaker, or worked in the sewers. But, let's be honest here, Yankel, don't you think you're kidding yourself? Do you really think that a woman who sells her body by the hour is someone to pour your affections on?"

"Don't call her a whore," Yankel replied. "She was kidnapped."

Karol considered this a moment before he advised his friend: "You shouldn't believe everything everybody tells you."

Words to live by, certainly, but not words that Yankel could take to heart at that moment. If anything, they set Yankel's fevered state of mind ablaze with anger; and in an instant, his friend became an adversary. Karol was a man looking to poke holes in his deepest desire. A man who clearly thought his avowed enemies owned the better part of the argument. "You know what, Karol," Yankel said, dropping his fork loudly on the tin tray in front of him, "I can find Pesha on my own. I don't need help from you."

And with his pride suddenly swollen, ready to burst, Yankel added:

"I don't need any help from you at all anymore. In any matters. I'll be on my way. Tonight."

Karol tried to talk his friend out of any rash action, but Yankel was having none of it.

"I have money now," Yankel said simply when asked where he would go. "I'll find my way. You needn't worry yourself."

Karol pleaded with Yankel to be sensible, following him as he went to the drawer he had been allocated, and began stuffing socks, T-shirts, and underwear into the white plastic garbage bags Karol kept stocked in the kitchen. "Where will you go?" Karol asked. "Where will you sleep?"

"It's not your concern," Yankel replied simply.

The packing was done quickly. As he was leaving, Yankel offered his host his hand—which Karol grasped urgently and used as a last occasion to talk his friend out of leaving.

"I'm sorry," Karol said. "I didn't mean anything about your girlfriend. I'm sure that what she went through was hell. Really, Yankel. My deepest apology. Please don't go."

Yankel nodded, but his pride was stronger than his feelings of fellowship.

"Thank you," Yankel said. He opened the door and looked back at his erstwhile friend one last time. "No hard feelings."

And without another sound, Yankel was gone.

18

ERUPTION

It was difficult to ascertain what exactly happened to Pesha in those dusky weeks, but a faint sketch emerged.

First there was a court date, although little came of it. Pesha arrived in a dark blue cotton dress that a more sophisticated woman probably wouldn't have worn to a formal hearing. Her lawyer was an older Pole who told the court that his client had no criminal record, was a respectable seamstress living with a friend, and had gotten into the fight when she believed her victim had run off with a gold bracelet her mother had given her.

"Your honor," Pesha's attorney said, "my client doesn't defend her behavior. She throws herself at the mercy of the court. And, while the fact that my client mistook Ms. Bilas for a thief is certainly no excuse, she simply thought she was recovering her property. Obviously this was a mistake. She's an immigrant who could not speak Polish well enough to address Ms. Bilas properly."

The court had listed Pesha's name as Teresa Mularz. The prostitute she had assaulted was named Ada Bilas.

And while Ms. Bilas had told the arresting officers that she expected the full weight of the law to fall on her assailant, the luster came off her rage over the course of several weeks.

The bailiffs (some of them, anyway) knew Ada Bilas. And when the court clerk scheduled the trial for five weeks hence, one of the bailiffs merely scoffed: "Two hundred zlotys says Ada backs out at the last minute."

There was wisdom in this prediction. The week before the initial hearing, Pesha's lawyer visited Ada Bilas at her Srodmiescie address, and after he departed Ms. Bilas called the prosecutor's office and said that she was no longer certain that she wished to lodge a complaint.

"From what I understand," Pesha's lawyer continued, "the complainant doesn't even hold a grudge anymore and accepts that this was all a misunderstanding."

The judge looked up from his papers at both Pesha and Ada Bilas, sitting two rows behind her, as if he were trying to piece together the real story behind their brawl.

"Where is your client from?" the judge finally asked Pesha's lawyer.

"Kazakhstan."

"They don't teach people to get a cop when they think someone's been pilfering their jewelry in Kazakhstan?"

"I'm sure they do, your honor," Pesha's attorney replied. "From what I understand she's from a very rural town. But, of course, you're right. Even someone from there knows you don't take the law into your own hands. There are no excuses. She's very sorry."

Again, the judge shuffled through his papers. Documentation (forged documentation, but realistic enough to deceive a careful bureaucrat) was provided stating Pesha's alias and the village in Kazakhstan from where she supposedly hailed. A note from the bailiff's office attested to the fact that she had no previous criminal record in Poland.

The prosecutor was asked if, indeed, the complainant had withdrawn the charges. "Yes," the prosecutor replied.

"Do you wish to proceed with the case?"

"No, your honor."

The judge took another moment to look over the documents in front of him and then—sensing something amiss—asked a question that caught Pesha's otherwise steely defender off guard.

"Why does the defendant have a Polish name if she's from Kazakhstan?"

The defense lawyer turned to Pesha for a long moment, hoping, perhaps, for some assistance from his heretofore mute client before deciding to consult a folder on the table in front of him instead.

"I believe her father was from Poland," the attorney finally replied, without looking up at the judge. "Which is why she came back here."

It certainly sounded suspicious, but there were other cases to get to that day. And while this judge (himself a former prosecutor) could no doubt strip away more inventions and unplanned contradictions, curiosity has its limits.

So that was that. Pesha was returned to her freedom, at least in the eyes of the law. She arrived back at the cathouse with no further impediments from the court other than a promise to check in with a kurator* once a month for the next six months.

Back at the cathouse the other girls eagerly anticipated her return—but then, they had sought out news of Pesha and her travails ever since the incident at the market took place.

Not that they had changed their opinion of her; they all thought that Pesha was haughty, and haughtiness was one of the higher sins in their line of work. But there is no question that they each shared a certain shameful pleasure in seeing a snobbish woman get her comeuppance. The idea that Pesha—who never drank, who never took drugs (not even a puff of pot), who never complained and never even spoke to any of them—was brought low by a savage outburst of violence was too rich not to be thoroughly enjoyed.

"How's your case going?" they would ask malevolently, even though Pesha never knew enough Polish to answer. (Besides, she didn't need to. The expression on her face said it all.)

The girls had also more or less figured out the original source of Pesha's misery. Pesha had spent the past few weeks in the run-up to her court date trailed by the nimbus of grief that every woman can recognize. She would break into tears at unemotional moments of the day. She would stare at

*Polish: parole officer.

a coffeehouse menu that she kept in her bedside table, as if it were a sacred totem of her past. ("Probably something she saved from one of their
dates," one of the girls correctly surmised.) She looked more revolted than
usual by the cadre of johns who shared her bed.

They had even guessed which man was causing all this desolation. It
was the slight, lean fellow who had arrived at the cathouse a few months
earlier. And in that brief period after Pesha was arrested but before her
court date, he had been spotted slowly ambling past the house, peering
into the windows, hoping to catch a glimpse of something or someone
inside.

These theories were cemented when Kasia went around the house and
asked each of the girls if Teresa had had any visitors. Or any boyfriends
they knew about.

"Why?" one of the girls asked.

"That's for me to know," Kasia responded. "I just need to know who
she's been seeing on the sly."

One of the older girls—a woman named Roza—reported that she had
seen Teresa at a coffeehouse with a young man.

"What did he look like?"

Roza pondered this for a moment.

"I'm not sure."

"Young guy?" Kasia asked. "Very thin? Dark hair? Not too tall? Seemed
a bit shy?"

"Perhaps."

A day later, Kasia took the unusual step of posting a guard outside the
cathouse. Not that security details were unheard of in their profession,
but when the girls found the muscular Dobrogost and his cousin Andrzej
standing outside their house in shifts, they naturally asked Kasia what the
rumpus was about.

"Don't worry."

"Some psycho that should concern us?"

"*You* should not be worried," Kasia said—which suggested that somebody else in the house had reason to be concerned. The only person suspicion fell upon was Teresa, which only delighted the girls more. Not only was Saint Teresa heartbroken, but the man she was mooning over was apparently a psychopath.

Granted, this didn't quite make sense. If a maniac was lusting for Teresa's blood, why should she lust over the maniac's body in return? But none of the girls stopped to fully think it through. The more heartbreaking implication never occurred to them: namely, that this was an instance of two lovers being kept apart by the mistress of their house.

Still, life went on. The guards stayed put in front of the cathouse for the time being. The girls went about their business. And after a while, they remembered why they hated being in Teresa's company: She was so damned dull. Beautiful, certainly, but dull. And stupid—couldn't speak a word of Polish. Moreover, they resented her popularity. If a john was shown four or five girls to pick from, he invariably chose Teresa. Some johns began asking for her by name before they had even time to take off their coats.

And while one can delight in an enemy's misery in short volleys, over time misery has a way of seeping into one's own mood and altering it. Soon, nobody wanted anything to do with Pesha again.

Pesha stopped eating with the girls at breakfast. In fact, she stopped eating all the food prepared by Luba, the old whore who was Kasia's second in command. She ate only fruits and vegetables—refusing to even touch a slice of toast.

"You're going to get too skinny," Luba told her after a week. "That's almost as bad as getting fat. The johns don't trust skinny—especially not these days. They think you got the AIDS."

After weeks of brooding, agonized silence, a trembling Pesha approached Kasia and told her (in Yiddish, which the crone only half comprehended) that she didn't intend to work anymore from Friday night to Saturday night, ever again. "The Jews of ancient times said that they'd rather be slaughtered than work on shabbos, and I don't intend to, either.

"If you don't like it," Pesha added with a flourish, "you can kiss my you-know-what."

Strong words. Strong enough that Kasia realized that she was being challenged. But while Kasia was a wicked woman, she had mastered the finer details of a successful enslavement. She knew how to squelch a rebellion before it got out of hand and when it was not worth the trouble.

Pesha was largely unrebellious. She had gone along with everything forced on her, and—save for this recent episode involving Yankel—wasn't nearly as problematic as a few other girls Kasia could name. Kasia didn't see how leaving the girl alone for twenty-four hours per week would be a great strain on her bottom line.

"Fine."

"And I want to go to synagogue," Pesha added. "You take me to the nearest one on Friday."

The second request was more problematic. Kasia recognized just how great an advantage it was that her hostage spoke no Polish. (It took her a week or two before she realized that Pesha's guttural German was Yiddish, and Kasia didn't believe it at first. She was under the impression nobody spoke Yiddish anymore.) She had girls who spoke Bulgarian and Ukrainian and Romanian over the years—they were likewise kept in line by the fact that they couldn't get around if they managed to escape.

The idea of putting Pesha in a synagogue with other Jews seemed like the only way Pesha could possibly break free from Kasia's grip. That, and this boyfriend that she was suddenly in love with. Neither one could be tolerated.

"I'm sorry dear," Kasia said—she always spoke to Pesha in endearments, even when she was being cruel. "There will be no trips to synagogue."

Some observers might have guessed that Pesha was testing the limits imposed on her; seeing how far she could push her mistress before she was pushed back. They would also note that a revival of piety was somewhat ludicrous given her recent history of unwedded carnal activity.

But if Pesha was insincere she certainly acted with newfound religious devotion. When Luba harangued her to eat more she finally barked: "Kosher!" And when a kosher steak was finally produced, she said to Kasia, "It must be cooked separate. Served on separate plates." She stayed in her room for days on end, merely sat on her bed, murmuring softly the Aramaic prayers she still remembered, and weeping as if she were one of the ancient Israelites banished to the banks of Babylon.

Some of the Friday-night johns felt compelled to say something when they heard her sobbing through the wall. "What's all that wailing and moaning about?" one of them asked. "You got some creep in there flogging the girls?"

It drove Pesha crazy that she picked up so little Polish.

When anybody asked her a question, she stared. She squinted. She pursed her lips and furrowed her brow. It didn't do a lick of good. She had no ear for languages, and for a long time this depressed her almost as much as the other harrowing facts of her life.

She could only follow Kasia's German if she was very careful; Kasia was a spirited cat trotting along a thin, spindly beam—but Pesha eventually caught up. Not so with Polish. Wading through the babel of voices that came out of the mouths of the johns, her fellow whores, and the people on the street was impossible. When she discerned one of the handful of words that she knew—"*lazienka*,"* for instance—her ears would perk up, but the term would rapidly be lost with all the others. Somebody had mentioned the lazienka . . . but what? Did they need to use the lazienka? Was there a wait for the lazienka? Had the *toaleta*** in the lazienka overflowed?

She felt very much like a baby. There was so little she could say. So little she controlled. So much discomfort and frustration. Nothing she under-

---

*Polish: bathroom.
**Polish: toilet.

stood about what the people around her were doing. Everything depended on the whims and kindness of others, and none of the girls ever seemed in the mood to dole out kindness. As such, she constantly felt a desire to throw a wailing, tear-streaked tantrum. But she resisted because the last thing she was willing to do was let the other girls see her upset.

Just as Pesha was sized up and despised by the other girls for her reticence and perceived haughtiness (and the laughable contention that she was boring), she made her own estimation and decided that her fellow prostitutes were rowdy, frivolous, and ugly.

There was a girl who bleached her raven-black hair the color of ripe corn, and had to redye it every week as the roots grew in. She looked ridiculous. She perfumed herself in a revolting floral fragrance. And she kept the music she played in her room at head-splitting volume.

There was another girl whose chest had been surgically enlarged to such proportions that she looked like a hunchback whose head was screwed on backwards. But the girl believed that she was a great beauty, and traipsed around the cathouse with the countenance of nobility. She treated the other girls with modest upper endowments—Pesha especially—as serfs. (Pesha couldn't fathom who would find this woman's enormous mounds of flesh attractive—but after her many months in Warsaw she learned that there wasn't much in the world that didn't appeal to one male hunger or another.)

There was a girl who was only four and a half feet tall, whose smallness distorted her soft blond hair, green eyes, and healthy bust to make her eerily childlike. Her squat stature couldn't help but remind Pesha of Kasia. Her high, infantile voice drove Pesha apoplectic.

There was the gaunt girl named Zofia who kept herself locked in the bathroom for hours doing god-knows-what and who continued to waste away in the preceding months until she looked as bony as a skeleton. Early in her tenure at the cathouse, Pesha accidentally opened a bathroom door and witnessed Zofia injecting a needle into her left arm—a display that shocked Pesha, even if she didn't truly understand what the girl was up to. But Zofia never forgave Pesha for the judgment implicit in her surprise. Thereafter, when the girl saw Pesha she would give her the evil eye. One time, as they were crossing each other in the hallway, Zofia violently slammed Pesha against the wall, looked her straight in the eye, and hissed: "Zyd!"

It was the first time anyone in the cathouse mentioned that Pesha was Jewish—at least to her. And, up until that very moment, it was not something that Pesha was sure the other girls knew. At least not all of them. The other girls wore crosses, and would disappear for a few hours on Sunday mornings, presumably to attend mass. Perhaps it had been noted that Pesha did not join them. Or maybe someone heard Pesha's weeping prayers from behind her closed door and deduced that what she was saying was Aramaic. Or, for all Pesha knew, they looked at the architecture of her face and recognized something distinct—from an ancient and despised people. Regardless, this nasty, pallid girl decided this fact could be used in the indictment against her. "Who knows," it occurred to Pesha, "maybe that's the reason they all hate me."

But there was little comfort in reaching this diagnosis, only a greater feeling of solitude.

Her treatment began to remind her of the days when she was still married, and she and Ishmael would sit together in their little hovel in abject silence and mutual disgust. Neither had anything to say to the other. The only thing they could do was pretend that they were alone.

Not that she was very surprised that it had come to that with Ishmael. Shortly before the wedding she told her father and her sisters that Ishmael was all wrong for her. She tried to be as matter-of-fact as possible. "Listen, Papa," she began, "I know I've been fussy. Apparently, a lot of people said this—and they were right. But aside from the first date, there's been nothing I liked about Ishmael Lindauer. He might be handsome and he might not be *too* annoying. Fine. But what else is there? If he's just a big, dumb chair who sits in the corner all day, I'm going to go crazy."

Her father and sisters told her this was just a case of cold feet and that it was too late to cancel all the plans.

"Men and women are all essentially the same," said Hadassah. "One is as good as another. Dig a little into this man and you'll find every quality that you desire. You might just have to coax it out."

As if Hadassah knew squat about it—or about anything. She wasn't even married. It was, perhaps, the single dumbest piece of wisdom Pesha received.

Still, she tried her best to make believe her younger sister was right. She remembered that first meeting when Ishmael made her laugh—and none of her other suitors had been able to do that. That was *something*.

But she laughed only once. Just once. And not since. Was that the reed on which she was to hang the rest of her future? Had she really chosen to overlook the fact that the man was downright gloomy? (As a number of funny people are.) When the marriage contract was signed and the two spent several months in pained, uncomfortable silence, she wondered if this was simply the way young husbands treated their wives.

"How often does Yoshke talk to you?" Pesha decided to ask her older sister, Ruth.

Ruth looked at Pesha quizzically.

"What do you mean?"

Pesha didn't really need to elaborate; the puzzlement on her sister's face said enough. No, it was not normal for two married people to sit in their home with nothing to say. You couldn't shut her sainted mother up for all the borscht in Russia. (God rest her soul.) And for a moment Pesha was embarrassed that it took her a few months to figure this out. She felt the first churning, nauseating sensation that she was trapped.

Still, she tried to make the best of it. She asked her husband about his day. She asked about his brothers. She asked about his father. She asked about the customers at the store. She asked how he liked his gefilte fish. She asked his opinion of the tablecloth she had purchased. She asked about the latest gossip concerning Widow Tischler. She asked about the weather.

"It was fine."

"They're fine."

"He's fine."

"They were fine."

"This way is fine."

"It's fine."

"I haven't heard anything."

"It's fine."

It was as if this lousy shmendrick* wasn't even trying! After each curt, stiff answer, he didn't think to ask anything in return. Not about the house. Not about her father. Not about her sisters. Not about her earrings. Not about the fact that the gefilte fish was particularly free of bones that evening. "What is wrong with the man?" Pesha asked herself. She wondered if her husband had noodles in his head in lieu of brains.

It went on like this for weeks with Pesha trying to tease something interesting out of Ishmael, and Ishmael refusing to play along:

"I heard Freidel Schwartz was sweet on your brother . . ."; "Kalmen Jacobs just raised the price of meat—it's a fortune!"; "They're never going to fix the roof of the women's bathhouse . . ."; "Have you seen Zlata Feldman—she's grown as fat as a horse!"

One night this culminated in a reprimand from her husband that was sharper and more wounding than Pesha had been prepared for.

"Don't you *ever* shut up?"

A slap across her face wouldn't have jolted her as much.

It is possible that these brusque, unfriendly words could have been spoken in jest. (They were not.) It is also possible that they slipped out in an unguarded moment of honesty and were at least a tactical error. Cruel thoughts can tramp through even the most saintly mind—but the good husbands are the ones who don't let them linger. However, the look in Ishmael's eyes bespoke honest-to-goodness opprobrium and annoyance. He meant precisely what he said, and he didn't care if he damaged Pesha's feelings.

---

*Yiddish: fool.

Pesha's face turned bright red and she nervously ran her hands over her shoulders, as if to shield herself from further missiles. However, now that he had made this rebuke, Pesha's laconic husband had nothing more to add. He merely stood up and began undressing for bed.

Instantaneously, humiliation mutated into loathing. Pesha sat quietly in her chair, staring off into an empty corner, as her husband finished his nightly ablutions, turned away from her, and fell into untroubled sleep. And she continued to sit, as hour after hour ticked by, filled with too much rage to undress in front of him, even if he was asleep. She certainly was not about to lie down next to *him*.

How dare he, she angrily mused to herself. *How* dare *he?!* Who did he think he was? What kind of man says bubkes* to his wife for the first three months of marriage and then when he decides to open his mouth he does so with an insult? What was she interrupting that was so damn important that he needed to deliberately go out of his way to bully and chasten her?

Of course, millions of husbands have accused their wives of blabbermouthism without permanently severing the marital bond. But this was early enough into their life together that Pesha felt certain underlying assumptions needed to be redrawn—and going to the trouble of amending a first impression makes the adjuster doubly resentful, as one of the sages noted. (I forget which one.) It wasn't that she didn't like her husband after that evening. She despised him. It wasn't that some of her other suitors were cast in a more sympathetic light—all of them were. She thought she was crazy to reject *any* of them in favor of the mean, boorish creature she wound up with. How did such a thing happen?

She didn't sleep next to Ishmael the next night. Or the night after. She decided on that first smoldering evening never to touch him again without meaningful concessions and contrition. (However, Pesha was an astute enough reader of character to know that would never happen.)

And while one couldn't begin to fathom Ishmael Lindauer's peculiar

---

*Yiddish: nothing.

mind, he, too, sensed that something had changed between him and his wife.

Dinner would be set out for him when he got home, but Pesha had already eaten and refused to share her company with him. She sat in the rocking chair and fiddled with her knitting. The meals she served were much less inviting than previous ones. The carrots were undercooked and hard; the fish was mealy; the chicken was dry and flavorless.

Her duties as a seamstress were likewise treated in a perfunctory, uncaring way.

"Could you patch my trousers?" he asked.

"Leave it on my sewing pile."

That was the end of the interaction. He would find the trousers in his wardrobe a week or so later, without comment. The effort that she put into them was pathetic.

She busied herself with housework over the course of the evening and usually fell asleep in her rocking chair. She curled up in bed only after he had left for the day.

And even though mutual hatred between man and woman does not always preclude physical intimacy (it is, I've heard, sometimes inflamed by it), Pesha was having none of it. She would accept not so much as a handshake from her husband. After a few weeks Ishmael's patience ran out.

"Why won't you sleep next to me?" he asked her one night after he undressed for bed and sat watching her at her sewing table.

She didn't look up from her work.

"What do you care?"

Ishmael considered this for a moment.

"A man has needs."

She did not respond. Let him be angry. Let him simmer and stew, as she had these past weeks. Let him feel aggrieved. Why should it bother her?

"And a wife has duties," he added.

The conversation died there, but Ishmael began to look at her with the same fury as she looked at him.

"This is not how a woman treats her husband," he said the next evening when she again refused to come to bed. "Don't forget who's lord and master."

Pesha did stop her sewing and looked him squarely in the eye.

"Lord and master?" she repeated. "Lord and master?"

Ishmael was unbowed by what he assumed was a taunt.

"Every man is lord and master of his own house."

Pesha could no longer control herself.

"Lord and master?" she screamed. "You're thinking of the wrong words. The one you want is 'tyrant'! You're a tyrant!"

If it was an insult, it didn't bother Ishmael as much as the woman's insubordination. Without a word he marched to the wardrobe and removed the trousers that she had patched a few days earlier. He spun around and marched them back to her.

Ishmael had split the right knee of the black trousers and Pesha had sewn it in white thread. The threading was loose, and rather than joining the two pieces together at the seam, she had merely tacked the upmost piece on top of the bottom. It was unwearable by anybody except a pauper.

"You see this?"

Pesha didn't answer.

"You think you've been a decent wife when you give me *this*?"

In case she wasn't getting the message, Ishmael grabbed her by the nape of her neck and pushed her eyes toward the trousers.

She let out a yelp, but it was more out of surprise than anything else.

"This," Ishmael said, "is dreck.*"

He let go of her neck and, before she could figure out what he was up to, ripped the pants in two.

She didn't say anything.

He took the severed fabric and tore it again, before looking at her and issuing his command:

"Fix them."

---

*Yiddish: filth, trash.

Pesha didn't move, but Ishmael had apparently decided that nothing would happen in the house until his trousers were mended. He stood above her and waited.

I imagine that many women in Pesha's position would have succumbed to whatever he wanted. Ishmael was not a physically meek man. Quite the opposite. And laying hands on one's neck can reduce anyone—man or woman—to tears. Moreover, the shredding of the garment had its own implied brutality; as if he were saying that what had been done to the trousers could be done to the wife.

"You . . ." Pesha began softly. "You disgusting pustule!"

A look of surprise appeared on Ishmael's face. And when Pesha spoke next it was even louder and more thunderous.

"You revolting, slimy, stinking pig!"

If Ishmael was preparing to physically force his wife to repair his clothing, or whatever else he had in mind, her courage caused him to lose his nerve.

"You cunt!" he screamed back.

"You call yourself a man!"

The two of them went at each other for the next hour. They screamed and belittled and cursed. But Ishmael did not lay his hands on his wife—instead, the battle reached its zenith when he picked up the wooden rocking chair (which had served as Pesha's bed for the last few weeks) and bashed it against the wall, wrecking it beyond repair.

The chair had been in the Rosenthal family for generations and had been entrusted to Pesha's safekeeping. Seeing it destroyed brought tears to Pesha's eyes. Ishmael was so surprised to see the effect on his wife (after he had called her a "cunt" and manhandled her he didn't think there was any making her weep) that he wondered if he had indeed gone too far. He went to bed, but he didn't sleep. She stretched out on the sofa and didn't bother hiding her sobs.

They returned to silence for the next week. But it was only a matter of time before Ishmael's virile urges reappeared.

"This has gone on long enough," Ishmael said a little more than a week later. "It's shabbos. It's a mitzvah and a commandment to make a child."

"Get away from me."

He didn't argue with her. Instead, he went to her side of the bed, picked up her jewelry box, dropped it on the ground, and stomped on it as if he were a groom cracking the glass goblet at a wedding. He crushed the box and ruined much of her jewelry.

She looked at the broken box sadly, but as if it were a disaster she had been waiting for.

"I want a divorce."

For the first time in weeks, Ishmael laughed.

"Over my dead body."

After that, they split their time screaming at each other or brooding in silence, and Pesha couldn't tell which she hated more. The only thing she knew was that he was a monster. The sole interruption of their misery came when Rabbi and Rebbetzin Sokolow attempted to mediate their marital woes—something that didn't do anything good. The Rebbetzin asked her what she objected to in her husband, but Pesha didn't know where to begin. It was not just Ishmael's meanness (although that would certainly be enough), or even the fact that he wrecked things when provoked (with the implicit suggestion he might do the same to her), but the fact that he was silent. Pesha had never heard of a woman getting a divorce for boredom before, but it was surely as potent a complaint as a husband who's an adulterer or refuses to lay off dice games.

But the Rabbi had instructed them to treat each other well, and Pesha felt she couldn't argue with him. So she was reasonably nice to Ishmael. She roasted the chicken he liked, and sat at the table with him while he ate. But she was not about to return to the bed.

One night, as Pesha lay asleep on the sofa, she woke up when she sensed Ishmael near. She turned, and even in the dark she could see that he was standing next to her naked, his loins engorged. Before she could say anything, his hands were on her nightgown, searching for an opening.

She shrieked, and with every ounce of strength she possessed, she kicked—landing a blow to the groin.

He slumped over on the ground, in agony.

Pesha was so terrified that she jumped up and ran for the front door. But, as wounded and miserable as Ishmael was, he stood up and grabbed her.

In a moment of rage, he threw her to the floor, blackening her arm. For a moment, she was convinced that he would kill her. The look in his eyes was unlike anything that Pesha had ever seen. But, apparently, he was in too much pain for anything more exertive than the initial attack.

He hobbled to bed, where he dressed himself and went to sleep. She huddled in a corner with her back turned to the monster. But she did not close her eyes. A few days later Pesha moved to her father's house.

The only thing that she preferred about being with Ishmael as opposed to her current predicament was that she knew how to properly curse him out. There was great pleasure in that.

Pesha resolved to learn Polish if only to properly tell all the prostitutes off.

She asked Kasia for a spelling book, or a phrasebook—*anything* to teach the basics—but was summarily denied.

"And why would you want to learn the lingo, my dear?" Kasia asked. "I'm here to translate for you."

"But you can't be around all the time."

The little dwarf shrugged. "I'm around enough. And you know plenty, Teresa. More than you realize. Besides, learning a language is an undertaking. You wouldn't want to be distracted from work, would you?"

Pesha didn't need to be told twice that she would receive no further assistance.

But when Kasia wasn't around, Pesha would hold up a teacup at the breakfast table and ask Luba (the friendliest one in the brothel) what the word was in Polish.

"Huh?"

Pesha smilingly shook the teacup.

"Filizanka?" Luba asked.

"Filizanka," Pesha repeated. She wrote it down and muttered "fili-zanka" to herself all day. The other prostitutes shook their heads at this latest incarnation of bizarre behavior.

However, Luba didn't have the patience or the inclination to teach. After a week of Pesha pointing to the butter on the table ("maslo"); the napkin ("serwetka"); the saltshaker ("solniczka") and watching her scribble the words down in Hebrew lettering, Luba stopped answering.

"My translation services are over," Luba finally declared—not that the idiot would understand.

Pesha wondered if she might learn something from television. She sat next to Ling, the house gatekeeper, and watched soap operas with her—but Pesha could make little sense of the moist eyes and pinched, worried faces of the actors on the screen. It seemed like a waste of time.

She learned "Co to jest?"—*what is this?*—and she took it with her on her outings, which weren't monitored. (Even though Pesha wasn't trusted, per se, so long as she was back by dark nobody fussed much with where she spent her daylight hours.)

Pesha largely wandered the streets. "Co to jest?" she asked, holding up a lemon at the grocer. Sometimes they would answer. More often they would look at her bizarrely.

But then one day she struck gold. She found a little bookshop along Poznanska Street called Pan. The bookshop was intended for children, and the walls were decorated with fresco scenes of rainbows and elves, a peasant girl being fitted with a pair of crystal shoes, two children leaving a trail of breadcrumbs in a dark wood, and a tiny girl in a red cloak staring intently at a lascivious wolf dressed in bedclothes. Pesha wandered in to look at the walls when she saw a blond woman seated on the carpet holding up a picture book before a three-year-old.

"Kot," the woman said. "Kot. K-O-T. Kot."

The woman showed the child—a little girl, blonder and plumper than her mother—a picture of a white-and-orange cat.

"Czy mozesz powiedziec 'kot'?"* the mother asked.

"Kot," the child answered.

"Dobrze."**

Pesha sat in a nearby corner and watched in fascination, careful not to give away that she was eavesdropping.

"Pociag," the mother said.

She showed her daughter an image of a train.

"Pociag," the mother repeated again. "P-O-C-I-A-G."

"Pociag," the little girl repeated.

"Dobrze."

And Pesha continued watching for the next hour as the mother taught her child these words. When the mother gathered her belongings and left, Pesha settled into her spot on the floor and began rummaging through the picture books on the shelf.

She stayed at Pan until it closed, and returned the next day, right after breakfast, staying through lunch until closing time. Pesha tentatively began sounding out words for herself.

On the third day, the mother and her chubby daughter returned. Pesha silently listened as the mother taught her daughter about the barnyard: kurczak (chicken), krowa (cow), rolnik (farmer).

When Pesha got home that night, she happened upon Zofia in the hallway. As if overtaken by impulses that she could not fully control, she pushed Zofia up against a wall. The girl was too surprised to react.

With a little sparkle in her eye, Pesha spat:

"Swinia!"***

---

*Polish: "Can you say 'cat'?"
**Polish: "Good."
***Polish: "Pig!"

19

BOLT

One night, several months after the charges against Pesha were dismissed, an older, stooped fellow with a cane and a gray mustache shuffled into the cathouse.

Kasia was tending to the front (Ling, the normal greeter, was at the drugstore picking up paper towels and disinfectant) and greeted the old man warmly; more warmly than normal, given that the elderly were entitled to respect.

"Good evening, my dear man," she said with a grin. "I don't know if I've ever had the pleasure."

The old man shook his head vigorously. "No, no," he said. "First time here."

He was dressed formally with white gloves on his hands and polished shoes on his feet. His jacket and trousers were houndstooth and faded, as if they were purchased several generations ago. He wore a burgundy bow tie and a gray fedora. A pair of thick, brown-framed glasses enveloped and distorted the caller's eyes.

"What can we do for you tonight?"

"A friend," he started—but then corrected himself, "an acquaintance, actually, told me that there was a girl here who was the most beautiful in all of Warsaw. I wanted to meet her."

Of course, Kasia had accommodated plenty of dirty old men before. They usually looked more spritely than the creature hunched before her. The story she generally heard was that their wives had decided that they were no longer interested in carnal matters, and—they pleaded, self-pityingly—there was no convincing them.

However, they rarely waited until they were as aged and delicate as this man to scratch that particular itch. Even men who looked a decade or so younger and in good physical condition had to swallow a couple of Viagra pills if they expected to perform. What, Kasia wondered, would a codger propped up on a gigantic wood cane do with a young girl?

But business was business, and Kasia was not about to send him on his way. "Which girl did you mean, my good man? All the girls here are exceptional."

The old man looked momentarily vexed, as if he hadn't expected additional inquiries.

"I don't know her name. I just know she doesn't speak much."

Kasia nodded.

"I think I know who you want."

The old man was led into a small bedroom where Kasia told him he could wait. "The girl you want is indisposed at the moment," Kasia said. "But she will be with you in a few minutes."

And with that, Pesha was summoned to Room 4. "Be careful," Kasia warned in German. "This one is old. You don't want to break him."

Pesha dutifully entered the room without looking at the dandified, elegant gentleman. She went straight to the bed and under the covers. Without looking up, she blindly tossed a black brassiere and a pair of underwear on the floor.

She was a sad sight, truly. And the elderly gentleman who had rented her time and affections for the hour was moved by her unhappiness. He slowly inched toward the bed and sat on top of the covers, still fully dressed.

He removed one of his white gloves and touched Pesha's shoulder.

She turned her chin, slightly, and looked at his bare hand. It was surprisingly unwrinkled for a man so old.

"I don't want to do anything to you," the caller said. "I just want to look at you."

Pesha didn't understand this so she said nothing, just waiting for the moment of consummation. But when it didn't come, she turned and looked in the eyes of the man who was sitting on her bed.

He was at once familiar and unfamiliar. He merely stared at her. And even though his eyes were hidden behind a pair of thick spectacles, she could have sworn he was weeping.

"Pesha," he said, in a fully recognizable voice. "Forgive me."

He ran a hand up to the top of his head and removed his hat. He then pulled off the glasses, a false nose and mustache, and revealed himself. It was Yankel.

They both shed tears as they held each other. She, still underneath the blanket, only her arms visible as they grasped him closer; he, still in his costume, clutching the cane—not wanting it to fall to the floor and possibly rouse the old crone.

"Please, my darling," Yankel sobbed. "Forgive me. I'm so sorry."

"I'm the one who's sorry."

And this went on for many minutes—their rush of passion and emotion at seeing each other after so long an absence; their mutual regret (his for betraying her; hers for making him think that she didn't love him); their uncertainty for the future. They apologized profusely to each other. They kissed each other. They whispered, "I love you," to each other for the very first time.

"I'm going to take you out of here," Yankel said. "Tonight. Right now."

She shook her head.

"There's no going anywhere," she replied. "I'll die here."

Yankel laughed. "Don't be so dramatic. You'll leave here tonight."

"How? I'm a prisoner."

"You'll come out with me."

You had to give Yankel credit for bravery. It's not just that he was slender and short that made this promise unlikely; it was the fact that he was dressed up like a child at Purim. He had been able to deceive the guardians of the cathouse because he so clearly inhabited the role he was playing—he

was frail, gentle, unthreatening. The thought of him standing up to a physical menace was simply absurd.

Pesha loved this devil-may-care daring, but she still allowed a little
laugh to escape before covering her mouth with her hand.

"Don't laugh," Yankel said. "I've been plotting this out. They all think
I'm an old man. So I'll limp my way out the doorway. And just as I get to
the door—whack! I'll hit the guard with my cane. Feel this thing."

He handed Pesha the weapon in question. It was heavier than it
appeared.

"Then we make a run for it. I've got a taxi waiting around the corner.
You just have to make sure you follow me close. As soon as I get to the
front door, you should hurry after me—even before I whack the guard
with the cane."

I have often wondered what made Yankel and Pesha fall so deeply in
love with each other so quickly. The first answer I have been able to come
up with was proximity and familiarity—Pesha and Yankel shared a past,
even if they hadn't shared it together. They knew each other's sufferings
and loneliness. They knew where the other one came from and they shared
the same sense of befuddlement at where they wound up. And I'm sure
Pesha's bewitching beauty was all the encouragement Yankel needed to
fall in love.

But Pesha was a different story. She was more particular. She would
never accept a match of convenience and mere familiarity. Whatever
else could be said about her, she was starkly unwilling to compromise
her affections—if she had, she never would have divorced her husband
or left Kreskol. I have come to the conclusion that there was another
element that explained her passion for Yankel. I think she loved his
courage.

The two of them shared a pioneering willingness to fling themselves
into the unknown. Yankel—the bastard, the scorned, the orphaned, the
crazy—had marched uncomplainingly to Smolskie when the wise men
of Kreskol asked him to, and talked his way into journeying to Warsaw

when he saw the opportunity appear before him. His willingness to take risks could have overwhelmed many women with a romantic sensibility. Pesha apparently possessed such a sensibility.

Without another word, Pesha threw her arms around Yankel's neck and kissed him. She quickly scrambled out of the bed and began putting her clothes on. Pesha wiped away her tears and was smiling now.

If only I could report that they made their escape as planned . . .

It would have been a happy ending to this otherwise odd tale. But long ago, the creator of the universe—blessed be his sacred name—declined to write a happy fate for Pesha and Yankel in the book of life. As Yankel was putting his false nose back on, the door burst open. The monstrous Dobrogost—the same guard whom Yankel had planned on doing battle with on more favorable terms—was standing in the doorway, snarling with rage. Curled up along his left hand was a metal chain. In his right hand was a crowbar.

Standing behind Dobrogost was Kasia, arms folded over her breast, a look of seething contempt on her face.

Lord only knows what made Kasia stop by Room 4 and listen a few minutes earlier. She did this, now and then, with troublesome johns. Or troublesome girls. And when she heard the low murmuring of Yankel and Pesha's conspiracy—and none of the thumps or grunts she expected—she looked through the keyhole and was stunned to find the troublesome boyfriend beneath the hat and mustache she had greeted a few minutes earlier. She didn't even need to hear the details of their plans to fetch Dobrogost immediately.

The chain came swinging at Yankel's face first, and a couple of back teeth were knocked out of his jaw.

It took Yankel so much by surprise that he didn't have the wherewithal to defend himself when the crowbar landed on his chest, breaking three ribs. These blows landed with the same surprise that Yankel had planned for Dobrogost; the winner of this contest was chosen the moment the fight started. But the punishment continued, unabated.

Yankel, splayed out on the floor, was kicked in the gut. He was kicked in the groin. He was kicked in the face and his fake nose flopped over onto his cheek. (His actual nose behaved similarly.) And with a kind of murderous frenzy, Yankel's adversary brought the crowbar down on his arm and his chest, again and again, until Yankel passed out. When Pesha tried to put herself between Yankel and Dobrogost she was shoved aside, so that Dobrogost could finish his evil work.

As Yankel lay on the floor, the girls of the house—in various states of undress—and three men (one of whom was fully naked) assembled outside the room, and tried to get a glimpse of the carnage. It was so dramatic that one girl who got close shuddered in disgust and strode back to her own room.

When Dobrogost finished the bulk of his torture, he dropped the crowbar and the chain to his side and got on his phone.

"Ling," Kasia called, and the Chinese woman appeared. "Take Teresa upstairs and don't take your eyes off her until I get back."

Forcefully, Ling grabbed Pesha, who was in such a state of shock and disbelief that she couldn't even scream.

"Nothing to see here," Kasia said to the other girls. "Go back to business."

Slowly, as if they were unsure of what they should do, the crowd disassembled.

"Let's get him to the back door," Kasia told her henchman.

Yankel's half-dead body was rolled onto a sheet that slowly turned red with blood as he was dragged through the halls of the cathouse until arriving at the back door. There, Dobrogost and Kasia waited.

After a few minutes, Dobrogost's cousin Andrzej pulled up behind the building with his van.

Kasia played lookout. When she was certain that the streets were empty, she gave Dobrogost a signal and he hoisted Yankel into the back.

They drove for less than an hour until they were outside the city and away from the highway. When they reached an empty spot along an untrafficked country road, Andrzej pulled over to the side. Yankel was hauled out of the back.

Calmly, Kasia told Dobrogost to retrieve their captive's wallet. The wallet had a couple of hundred zlotys in cash, no credit cards, and no driver's license. "Wake him up," Kasia demanded. Dobrogost did it with two slaps across the face.

"What's your name?" Kasia asked.

But Yankel was too battered to speak.

"Tell her your name, or else," Dobrogost growled.

"Yankel Lewinkopf."

The whispered name meant nothing, as Kasia stared at her victim, wordlessly.

"This is not your first warning," Kasia finally pronounced. "This is your last. There are no more warnings after today. There is only punishment in the future."

Yankel said nothing.

"And if you think you're tough, let me tell you something else: the punishments won't be yours. They'll be hers."

Yankel stirred, slightly.

"Do you understand what I'm saying, young man?" Kasia asked in a voice that was so temperate and untroubled that it sent a quiver down Yankel's spine. "If I see you again, I won't hurt you. I'll hurt her. Believe me, I can make her suffer in ways that you wouldn't want to picture. Do you understand?"

Yankel nodded.

"I'm not too worried about you," Kasia continued. "Teresa isn't going to stay at that house anymore. That's another thing I'll make sure of. I have many connections, young man. She will go somewhere far away. And I will make damn sure she never sees you ever again."

Yankel closed his eyes.

"Do you understand that?" Kasia asked again. "Do you realize that you will never see her again? Not ever?"

Yankel didn't answer. And for a moment, Kasia considered demanding the final humiliation of making him acknowledge this sad truth, but she continued to stare at him, intently. As if she were trying to place him. And after a moment, her eyes widened.

"I remember you," Kasia said with a smile. "Karol Bugaj brought you around."

Kasia's two henchmen shared a somewhat confused look, as if they weren't quite sure what their boss was driving at.

"Oh, I know Karol. I know what he does, and I know where he lives," Kasia said. "That's something else to think about. We'll be sure to check in from time to time. We won't forget about you anytime soon—Yankel Lewinkopf. That much I promise. Now, my advice to you would be to get yourself to a hospital."

And with that, she slammed the van doors closed, and the vehicle drove away, leaving Yankel to bleed on the side of the road.

Some of this came out during the hearings about Kreskol. Yankel told the Sejm that he had been assaulted two years earlier, and went through a long and painful recovery, which was why he had limped into the hearing room, and why he couldn't fully raise his right arm anymore. He also said that this had made his career as a baker a daily exercise in pain and suffering. (After the incident described, he took a job in a Krakow bakery. He cobbled together his meager savings for a bus ticket and rented a room in the Kazimierz, the old Jewish quarter, which was now largely empty of Jews.) But, by and large, the investigators had little interest in Yankel's health or well-being. They seemed a lot more interested in the fact that he was getting freebies and preferential treatment when he was a patient at Our Lady of Mercy and that he had seemingly mastered the particulars of the Polish language so quickly.

"You don't speak in much of an accent," said Henryk Szymanski, who framed his questions with the sharpest suggestions.

"Thank you."

"I don't mean that as a compliment," Szymanski spat. "What I mean is that's very suspicious. How did you learn to speak Polish so well if you'd spent your whole life speaking Yiddish?"

Yankel shrugged, not appearing to take his interrogator very seriously.

"What else could I do? Nobody speaks Yiddish in Krakow or Warsaw."

A reasonable-enough response, one would suppose. But it caused Szymanski to go down yet another path.

"How did you get to Warsaw, anyway? I mean the second time you left Kreskol?"

Yankel looked slightly embarrassed by the truth.

"I stowed away in the press helicopter."

"Excuse me," said another member of the Sejm, "but how did that happen? Didn't anybody notice you?"

"I suppose not."

"How convenient," Szymanski spluttered.

Szymanski's modus operandi throughout the hearing was to poke and jab at the rocky, uneven realities of Yankel's story. He pointed out Yankel's many instances of luck: from getting a ride with the gypsies, to winding up in the hospital where the doctors were ready to believe his crazy story. And the words "How convenient" were the way Szymanski gave voice to his skepticism.

Next, Yankel was asked how a stranger to Warsaw—someone who had never been to the town before, never paid taxes, and never had any work experience—could have gotten a job and roof over his head so quickly.

Yankel winced, slightly, at this question.

"I got help from a friend."

One of Szymanski's eyebrows shot up.

"A friend?" Szymanski repeated. "How could you have friends if you had never left Kreskol before?"

"Somebody I had just met."

"You *just* met them?" Szymanski repeated incredulously. "When?"

"That day. The same day I left Kreskol."

Szymanski stared at Yankel.

"Was this someone you met at the hospital?"

"No."

"Who was it? What was this person's name?"

Yankel remembered the promise he had made to Karol years earlier: if anyone asked, he would not mention Karol's name. It was a promise made on the fly, and it was made before they had become good friends. (And, just to dispel any doubts, no, they had still not spoken since the day Yankel stormed out of Karol's apartment.)

Moreover, who could say if Karol still remembered having elicited the pledge in the first place? Even in his unsophisticated, rube-like state, Yankel realized that the promise had been extracted to keep Karol's colleague, Mariusz Burak, at bay—but could Karol really care now? Was there anything Burak could do to damage Karol?

Still, Yankel was not one to abandon a vow lightly. "Just a friend," Yankel replied. "I'd rather not say his name."

Szymanski looked as pleased a kitten who had just spotted a mouse.

"I'm afraid that's not up to you, Mr. Lewinkopf," Szymanski responded. "You're obliged to answer our questions."

"Yes, but I promised him I wouldn't tell anyone his name."

Szymanski was pleased.

"How convenient."

I do not wish to mislead anyone as to the importance of these hearings; they were a relatively low-grade affair—at least as far as national consequences were concerned. Some members of the Sejm (notably Szymanski) wanted to remove the subsidies that had been promised to Kreskol. Others did not. Life would undoubtedly go on whether this effort was successful or not.

It was the media attention that these hearings garnered—which reached previously unrealized heights after Dr. Krol's testimony—that was the truly remarkable thing.

Even in Kreskol we became aware that we were again an obsession for our fellow countrymen—more so than ever before, even if we weren't getting the same number of tourists. The only visitors now were reporters, eager to learn our take on how things were unfolding.

"Are you worried?" they asked.

The answer varied depending on whom they ran into.

The disparate members of the Sejm had apparently not assigned much importance to the details as Yankel was reciting his testimony, but the reporters in attendance knew a racy story when they heard one. With smutty delight, the Lindauer divorce, the unknown catalyst in Kreskol's reemergence, was splashed across the pages of the news. "LUST, BETRAYAL, DIVORCE IN 'PIOUS' KRESKOL LED TO REDISCOVERY," read one of the headlines. There were many others of a similar disposition. (Yankel tactfully left out the parts about Pesha's current profession in his testimony.)

There were no photographs of either member of the divorce party; they were merely described by Yankel. She, the most beautiful woman that had ever bestrode the earth: dark brown hair, eyes of china blue (as one reporter put it); a form and figure that Helen of Troy would find enviable (another reporter's embroidery).

He was a bulky, muscular, putrid-smelling, fire-breathing brute. (I had never found Ishmael Lindauer to be either bulky or muscular, but this was what appeared in the papers.)

And in the wake of these headlines and the interest in the story, every reporter assigned did their best to find some way of tracking down the mysterious Pesha and the wild Ishmael—even though Yankel claimed (truthfully) not to have the slightest idea where either of them was. One of the reporters on the beat was Mariusz Burak, who had been with Karol on the day they had both helped Yankel escape from Kreskol.

It didn't take much for Burak (who was watching the proceedings from the press gallery) to figure out which "friend" Yankel had been talking about, and where he had stayed.

As Burak and Yankel had left things several years earlier, Yankel would check in with Burak when he got settled. After a month, having heard nothing from Yankel, Burak came to the conclusion that he had been played for a sucker. He even asked Karol whether he had heard from Yankel or knew anything about where the young Jew had wound up.

Karol merely shrugged at the time.

But by then the idea of doing a report on how Yankel had adjusted to life in the big city seemed a little stale. Mariusz Burak always had a number of irons in the fire at any one time—he proceeded to forget about Yankel. That is, until Yankel resurfaced in this hearing.

"You were less than truthful with me," Burak said to Karol with a chiding lilt in his voice the next day in the office.

Of course, Karol knew what his colleague was getting at. But given the circumstances, he also felt obligated to make things as difficult as possible for Burak.

"I don't know what you're talking about."

"Cut the shit," Burak said. "You know I'm talking about Yankel Lewinkopf. Look, before you start playing all innocent, let me tell you right off the bat: I'm not mad. Well, I'm not *too* mad. I don't give a fuck about Lewinkopf. Everybody in the media has his story, so I guess that ship has sailed. What I care about is finding Pesha Lindauer. If you help me out there I wouldn't see any reason to tell the higher-ups that you were holding out on us. Do you know anything about her?"

Karol didn't owe Pesha Lindauer anything. He had never met her. And if he thought about her at all, he believed that she was trouble. She had turned his otherwise sensible, innocent friend into a crazy person. Whatever spell she cast over Yankel had—in Karol's eyes—been done malevolently; she was a predator who discovered vulnerable prey.

I should probably add that after Yankel walked out of Karol's apartment, Karol was for the first few weeks enraged at the mention of Yankel's name. He made a clean breast of the whole situation to his girlfriend, Tanya, one night after taking her out to dinner and sounded like a man who had been scorned by a lover rather than a friend.

"Such stupid pride these young guys have," Karol sighed, looking gloomily into a glass of Merlot. "And such a lack of gratitude. He moved out of my apartment as coldly as if he were saying goodbye to a motel room."

"Maybe because he's Jewish he thinks he's got to prove that he's got honor."

"That's not it," Karol said. "All young people have pride. Doesn't matter if they're Jewish or not."

Karol didn't take his eyes off his wine and remained silent for a while.

"This is stupid," he finally said. "What do I care about that little punk, right? Here one minute, gone the next. I've got more important shit to worry about."

Tanya nodded, and that was the last Karol would speak of Yankel for a few months. But weird things started happening in Karol's mind.

He had a dream in which he was being circumcised on a hospital bed by a rabbi in a long black beard. "I'll do it for Yankel," he uttered in the bizarre hallucination. He had several other dreams in which Yankel would fleetingly make an appearance and then vanish behind a corner or in a cloud of vapor. When the latest flare-up between the Israelis and the Palestinians appeared in the news, Karol instinctively took the Israeli side, despite the fact that he had never thought seriously about the conflict before, and Yankel certainly had never expressed an opinion.

After a few weeks, he went by the bakery where he had gotten his friend a job and asked if Yankel was in the back. But the owner had no news of Yankel other than that one day he just stopped coming in—not even to pick up his last week's salary. "That was pretty annoying," the owner said to Karol. "I thought you said he was a good kid."

"He is."

"Well, he could have given me some notice. I had to call Lech in on his day off."

And then early one Sunday morning while getting into his car to go to the grocery store he instead took a turn onto the highway and drove four hours out of town in the direction of Kreskol.

This was shortly after the road into Kreskol had opened, and the villagers were still excited to see outsiders like him.

Karol bought a basket of raspberries and a scarf in the marketplace, and asked any passerby if they knew Yankel. Only one person understood him.

"Yankel Lewinkopf? Sure, everyone knows Yankel."

"Have you seen him?" Karol asked, hopefully. "Is he in town?"

"No," the villager replied. "He left a long time ago."

Karol (much to his own surprise) could scarcely contain his disappointment; he found himself unable to speak lest he begin sobbing.

Karol went to the cathouse where he had taken Yankel, just on the off chance that Yankel had returned. Besides, maybe he had gotten the object of his affections out of there. There might be some scrap of information to go on. But Kasia wasn't there when Karol stopped by—only Ling, keeping an eye on the merchandise like a vigilant shopkeeper. When Karol asked if there was a girl working there named Pesha, Ling seemed genuinely confused. "Who?"

And that was the last Karol spoke of Yankel until the hearing. On occasion, he would spend a few miserable hours thinking about his friend, but he would do his best to turn to other matters. And, with time, he barely thought of Yankel at all.

That is, until one day his baker said to him when he went in to get his morning rolls: "Hey, Karol, isn't that Yankee in the news? Isn't he the boy from Kreskol?"

Karol turned ashen, but the baker didn't seem to notice.

"Wasn't he from Azerbaijan?" the baker asked.

"Yeah," Karol stammered. "That's where he said he was from."

The baker looked at Karol somewhat perplexed. He didn't recall their conversation a few years ago word-for-word, but he remembered something about Yankee being a relative of Karol's. Or something along those lines. But Karol looked so stunned that the baker didn't feel much like dwelling on the modest deception.

"You haven't been following?" the baker asked.

"No, I hadn't noticed."

Karol's interest in news was almost exclusively what his assignment editor and the reporters told him to shoot. But that evening he watched the coverage of Kreskol and the hearing, and even read some of the newspaper stories about it.

It was a day later that Burak cornered him in the breakroom.

"What do you say?" Burak asked. "Did Lewinkopf tell you anything that can help us find this Pesha everybody's been looking for?"

"Yes, he found her," Karol said.

Burak's eyes widened.

"He found her?" Burak repeated. And with that reaction, Karol almost instantly regretted what he had just said. It was as if he had sold out his friend. He fervently wished he could take it back.

"Where?" Burak said. "Where is she now?"

"All I know," said Karol, "is that she was a working girl, if you know what I mean. I don't know where."

"A prostitute!" Burak exclaimed. "This gets better and better! What did he say, exactly? He didn't mention where he found her? A neighborhood? Anything?"

Karol decided that was as helpful as he would be. "No, he didn't say anything else." But the damage had been done. Say what you will about Mariusz Burak, he was a dogged reporter and within minutes he was on the line with his sources on the police force. He was looking for a Yiddish-speaking prostitute who had gotten into the racket about three and a half or four years earlier. Brown hair, blue eyes, not too tall. (As per the testimony Yankel had given.) Answers to the name Pesha. Anybody like that fit any descriptions?

"Does she go by any aliases?" one of the bailiffs asked.

"Possibly," Burak replied. "Come to think of it, almost certainly. They all use aliases, don't they? But I don't know for sure."

"I'll see what I can do."

Burak skipped the hearing that day; he called all his friends in the police department, and when that didn't come up with anything fruitful, he tried a few women's health clinics. Then he tried a friend in the prosecutor's office. Then a couple of kurators he knew. Finally, Burak called a friend who was a bit of a freak, and visited those houses all the time, collecting stories of debauchery and depravity. This friend had the added benefit of being half-Israeli, who spoke a reasonable amount of Yiddish.

"Daniel," Burak said to his friend, "have you ever met a prostitute who spoke Yiddish? Goes by the name of Pesha?"

"Yiddish-speaking prostitute?" Burak's friend chortled. "I've met two!"

"Oh?"

"One was in Amsterdam. And she wore a big Jewish star—but that was a long time ago. Not the first Jewish star I ever encountered, but the first Yiddish-speaker. Before we started she said, '*Du bist a Yid?*'"*

Burak laughed.

"She was nice enough, that Amsterdam girl. The other was in Lodz last year—the girl said something to me in Yiddish. And that was all she said; she couldn't speak Polish. But her name wasn't Pesha—at least I don't think it was. It was something Catholic. I think it was something like Maria. Or Teresa."

---

*Yiddish: "Are you Jewish?"

20

UNREST

Brother Wiernych was mopping the floors of the day room at Saint Stanislaus, a few miles from Kreskol, when he heard her name coming from the television. "Pesha Lindauer." He dropped the mop and turned.

One can only guess how much he understood of the reporter, Mariusz Burak, who spoke over the footage of Pesha, or if he understood the crawl that appeared at the bottom of the screen which read, "Devout Kreskol Divorcee Made Career as a Prostitute."

"The latest twist that TVP Kultura has uncovered today in the saga of Kreskol was that the woman whose disappearance prompted the town's rediscovery is living today in Lodz as a sex worker . . ."

While the anchor spoke, a helpless, frightened Pesha scurried away from a camera crew that appeared out of thin air and began hurling questions at her. She implicitly understood that the ruckus she had somehow been ensnared in was dangerous and fled into a nondescript house for which she apparently had the key, as the camera crew followed closely on her heels. (Subsequent footage of the house showed a first-floor curtain peeking open for a moment, but whoever was looking out was shrouded in shadow.)

The reporter recounted what was known about the investigations of Kreskol to that point; how questions about Kreskol's authenticity had been raised and were currently being debated by the Sejm; the slim outline of Pesha's role in the rediscovery, and how Yankel Lewinkopf had given testimony last week about his cushy life at Our Lady of Mercy

Hospital; and, finally, he insinuated a connection between Yankel and Pesha.

There was not much more to the story. It appeared and a few seconds later it was gone. The results of the football match between Poland and Northern Ireland were the next story. But Brother Wiernych looked as dazed as if he had just been hit on the head with a hammer.

He remained perfectly still until one of the monks, Brother Konstanty, asked him if he was all right, and he picked up his mop and immediately went back to work.

But Brother Konstanty later said that he had never seen such a look of intensity on the face of the man previously. Or, come to think of it, on any monk before.

The next morning, Brother Wiernych was gone. A lock had been forced on one of the cabinets and some of the bejeweled artifacts were missing, prompting even a man as trusting and passive as the Abbot of Saint Stanislaus to agree it was time to call the police. But there was little that could be done at that point, except to take down a careful description of the gold plate and scale, the silver medals, the laptop computer, and the Seiko watch that had been filched. As for finding the culprit, the police sounded skeptical.

There were no photographs of the man. No previous addresses or known associates. Nobody even knew his real name.

"It won't be hard to find a man who's dumb," the Abbot said, as the interview wound down.

"I don't think he's dumb," injected Brother Bogomil.

"How do you know that?" the Abbot asked, not waiting for the interviewing officer to speak.

"When we shared a room together he would talk in his sleep."

"What did he say?" the officer asked.

Brother Bogomil considered this for a moment. "Well, it was a couple of years ago," he finally said. "I was never sure what he was saying. It sounded like gibberish."

The Abbot turned red, feeling foolish for not asking enough questions of the monks to know this critical fact.

"There was one word he kept saying over and over again, though," Brother Bogomil added. "It didn't sound like a real word to me but he kept saying it. And one night he woke up nearly screaming it."

"What was it?" asked the officer.

"'Pesha.'"

When the story of Pesha appeared in the pages of the *Crier*, it was as though a great dam burst and every pent-up complaint about the loud construction noise early in the morning, to the rudeness of tourists, to larger questions of economic uncertainty, flooded Kreskol.

A group of mothers spontaneously took to the streets and picketed in front of Rabbi Sokolow's court. Feiga Lutnick, to whom Rabbi Sokolow had not spoken since she became an avowed Katznelsoner, led the protest.

"We will not stand by and let hussies like Pesha Rosenthal destroy Kreskol's good name!" she cried to the crowd who had answered her call to arms.

The other mothers cheered.

"No Sodom, no Gomorrah!" Feiga cried.

The other women repeated: "No Sodom, no Gomorrah!"

"Purity for Kreskol!"

"Purity for Kreskol!" came the echo.

"Gentiles out!"

Where Feiga got the idea that gentiles should be banished from our town, nobody could say—or, honestly, what the gentiles had to do with the matter at all. Still, this denoted a level of confidence that Jews had not possessed since Roman times—and the historically educated would note how poorly that ended for the Jews. The other ladies unquestionably repeated the chant without stopping to consider the rowdy, radical sentiments within it.

Rabbi Sokolow watched the demonstration with bemusement. He, too, had read the account of Pesha in the *Crier* and was suitably scandalized— but also immensely sorry for the girl. A member of his flock had strayed; the fact that she had succumbed to a dishonorable fate was something to be pitied rather than scorned. Desperate people do desperate things, Rabbi Sokolow thought. The girl had almost no choice.

The rest of the town, however, was in no mood to be nearly as sanguine.

This piece of news came when everyone's livelihood was poised on the knife's edge and signs of disorder were enough to make anyone lash out. The tourism crisis was in full flower and consumed every waking hour of the day since Zbigniew Berlinsky read his outlandish paper. It made many mild-mannered, forgiving Kreskolites snarl at the smallest digression.

Four houses had been under construction when Berlinsky's accusations against us appeared in the paper. Within weeks, the four families building these domiciles were seriously overleveraged and at a loss what to do.

The first family to stop work on their house—the Coopermans—tried to sell their half-finished mansion in the Hotel District. (The Hotel District consisted at that moment solely of the Kreskol Grand, but the name was extremely catchy.)

"We're offering an extremely good deal," Yetta Cooperman would tell anyone whose attention she could commandeer for several consecutive minutes. "We've poured more than forty thousand zlotys into it already; we're willing to let it go for just twenty-five thousand. There's nothing wrong with it—when it's finished it will be beautiful. We just need the cash right now."

But the chill in Kreskol's financial future was unmistakable, and spending 25,000 zlotys on top of the tens of thousands more to finish construction was a burden no one wanted to endure. "Sorry, Yetta," she heard again and again.

She adjusted the price down to 20,000 zlotys and then to 15,000 zlotys. Finally she settled on 12,000 zlotys—a figure so meager her voice would catch every time she said it out loud—but even that was considered too steep for a property still under construction.

Finally, the Coopermans spent the last of their savings ordering heavy-duty tarps from Warsaw and covered the site up to protect it from the elements while they waited out the economic storms.

Yetta Cooperman came to Rabbi Sokolow's house almost every week to bemoan her fate: "How could I have been so foolish to lay out all our savings like that . . . ?" "How could Berlinsky have concocted such obvious lies . . . ?" "When will the tourists be back—they can't stay away forever, can they . . . ?" There were many similar laments.

The Rabbi tried to be as sympathetic as possible, and even promised her that if anybody came to him asking about finding a new house he would tell them to go to her immediately. But, he warned, she mustn't expect a surge of visitors anytime soon. The public buses that came into and went out of town were like ghost ships; the drivers would park the massive, empty vehicles at the appointed bus stop, wait the allotted fifteen minutes, throw away their cigarettes, and drive out of town with nary a soul making the passage either way.

"You're not interested in buying a new house, are you?" Yetta asked, wiping away a tear.

Sokolow turned red. "It's not for me."

"I'd even give you the site for ten thousand zlotys," Yetta said, and began whimpering again when she realized just how pathetic and desperate she had become. "But just for you. Please don't tell anybody else I'd go that low."

"I'm afraid I don't have that kind of money even if I wanted a new house," Rabbi Sokolow replied, truthfully.

The Coopermans had engaged several draftsmen and carpenters that they had paid handsomely. They, too, were suddenly out of work and unsure of their financial future. As were the draftsmen who were working on the other three houses around town that were mid-construction. They offered to do fix-ups around town for a song. Suddenly, some of the strongest and most capable men in Kreskol were just sitting around their houses, or helping their wives sell goods in the town square.

The unfortunates all came to Sokolow, begging him for advice. "Maybe you should try to learn a different profession," the Rabbi suggested a little helplessly, but he didn't know what else he could say.

Reb Zlotowitz, the head of the alms society, reported that there was very little money in the treasury and a sudden spike in charity cases. Sokolow couldn't believe his ears.

"But how could the treasury be empty?" Sokolow asked. "You said that we had been getting tons of tzedakah!"*

It was certainly true that when times were good the people of Kreskol had been generous. When times were great, however, some of the wealthier families had cut back, opting to save for a big new house rather than give to the needy. In the wake of this financial calamity the wells of charity ran completely dry.

"I'm not going to lie, Rabbi, we spent a lot of money fixing up the mikvah," Reb Zlotowitz said of a project embarked on the previous spring to retile the bathhouse. "A *lot* of money. But so much had been coming in lately I didn't even think about it at the time. I figured we'd replenish the funds soon enough. The timing really couldn't have been worse."

This frightened Rabbi Sokolow more than anything.

"How long will we be able to feed the hungry?" he asked.

Reb Zlotowitz shrugged.

Rabbi Sokolow called an emergency meeting with Rajmund Sikorski, who hadn't visited the town since his testimony before the Sejm and seemed reluctant to come now. "Can't we do this over the phone?" Sikorski's translator asked. (A year ago, the first phone tower was erected in Kreskol and a flip phone was generously provided to Rabbi Sokolow.) Rabbi Sokolow was stunned; Sikorski had never turned down an in-person meeting before.

---

*Hebrew: charity (literally, "justice").

"I suppose so," Rabbi Sokolow said.

Sikorski listened patiently as Sokolow sketched out Kreskol's many new problems and his translator rendered the dilemmas back into Polish.

"Under normal circumstances I'd tell you not to worry," Sikorski said calmly. "But all the funds—and I mean *all* the funds, social services as well as the special ones earmarked just for you—have been frozen pending the outcome of the investigation."

The Rabbi was struck dumb as he listened to the translation.

"I'd say you should ask some of your rich friends in Israel or America, but I fear your reputation has suffered there, too. If they're not visiting because they think you're a fraud, they're certainly not about to cut you any checks."

Sokolow didn't say anything as he considered the implications.

"Why do you sound so devastated?" Sikorski broke in before Rabbi Sokolow had the chance to ask anything else. "You always said you wanted us to leave you alone."

Even before the question was converted into Yiddish, Rabbi Sokolow could discern the glib pleasure in Sikorski's voice.

And yes, he had to admit that Sikorski had been right. The Rabbi had seen the town grow prosperous without any of the catastrophes he had feared. There were no conversions. There was no sudden laxness in religious observance. (Aside from a few oddballs who were never truly devout or interested in spiritual matters.) There were no outbreaks of antisemitism, at least until the Berlinsky paper. The only real problem was the schism between the Katznelson and the Sokolow Jews. But even that was no great hardship; the sensible Jews of Kreskol were well rid of those insane Katznelsoners.

As visitors from the Orient and South America had come through Kreskol, even a man as restrained in his habits as Anschel Sokolow had begun to fantasize about someday traveling to China or praying at the Western Wall in Jerusalem. Like anything else in life, he came to realize the changes had both advantages and disadvantages. But the longer he lived the new life, the fewer the disadvantages he saw. Until now.

"Goodbye, Rabbi Sokolow," the translator said abruptly.

The phone had gone dead before Sokolow said, "Wait!"

The protest was neither the beginning nor the end of the public scorn heaped on Pesha. Pesha was spoken about incessantly. The Lindauers were, as one might expect, in an uproar since the news broke and Batsheva Lindauer (wife of Ishmael's youngest brother, Shmuel) began openly saying to the other women at the marketplace that it was a scandal that a prostitute like Pesha should have run off to the big city, and that her dear departed brother-in-law (to whom she had never been introduced owing to the fact that she had married Shmuel less than two years ago) was left to the wolves.

"Think of the poor man," she said. "Think about what we know of her character now, versus his. Think of what he must have endured during their marriage."

Many agreed with her. They allowed themselves to blame Pesha for all sorts of misdeeds she could not possibly have committed—and freed Ishmael of crimes in which his guilt was never in question.

Whatever bouts of fury Ishmael displayed had to have come from somewhere—she had probably driven him to it.

"If I were married to a prostitute I would probably be cranky, too," Inna Solomon remarked. And a handful questioned the very premise that Ishmael exhibited any signs of wrath in the first place.

"How many people were really there to witness that incident?" asked Feiga about the public display that had occurred just before Pesha ran off. "I wasn't there. And if I didn't see it with my own eyes, I can't say for sure that it happened."

Even among the witnesses to the incident, some of the weaker minds began questioning what they had seen.

And while most were certain that Ishmael had died in the forest, there was a surge of speculation that he possibly survived. After all, nobody knew Pesha was alive until a few weeks ago. "How could a simp like Yankel Lewinkopf and a girl like Pesha Rosenthal have made it, and not a strong fellow like Ishmael?" Inna asked. "He must have reached Warsaw or Krakow."

The forest was less forbidding than once believed. He could very well still be living there, at this very moment, even though we would never see him again. "He probably doesn't want to have anything more to do with us," Inna continued. "Poor fellow. He's hiding for something he didn't do."

And some saw a larger problem in Pesha; she presaged the greater, fundamental change that had taken place in Kreskol. The shift from morality to immorality.

Many more people began showing up at Katznelson's shul. And even though the official posture from Rabbi Katznelson was that anybody who used modern currency was a Sokolowite, and Sokolowites were no different than apikorsim, these new arrivals received a warm reception. It was as if they were ba'al teshuva* returning to the fold. After Rabbi Katznelson's service ended on Saturday morning, the newbies approached their old friends they hadn't spoken to in ages.

"Looks like Katznelson was righter than Sokolow about a thing or two," said Leibish Applebaum.

The Katznelsoners were dizzy with excitement. Yes, they said, Katznelson was right.

Right to be concerned about spiritual decline, as evidenced by Pesha.

Right about the currency, too. Nobody knew how to haggle or bargain with these crazy, inflated prices. And the fact that the tourists had abandoned us—well, what had been the point of the whole exercise? What had we endured the heartburn and anxiety for?

And right about the interlopers who moved to Kreskol. True, Katznelson's break came before the gentiles set up shop and began living among

---

*Hebrew: a transgressor who has had a change of heart and begins religious observance again.

us, but the gentiles were another sign of encroachment that was accepted by the Sokolowites, and despised by the Katznelsoners. Now it appeared that the Katznelsoners had the better part of the argument. The transplants served as a permanent reminder that we were chained to all these things that we never wanted. It was outrageous that they treated Kreskol—which we had lived in, loved, and cared for for generations—as their home. Like they were entitled to what we rightly earned.

What made it all the more galling was the fact that they were so transparent about their mercenary motives. They were there for a quick buck—they had no interest in the town beyond that.

Nobody cared much when we were rich, but now that we were poor it felt unbearable. These mamzers wouldn't even lower prices or offer trade in lieu of cash—even though we were in the middle of a financial crisis. And, perhaps, this was where Feiga Lutnick's call came from.

One fall morning, Cyril Mierzejak arrived home from a Saturday-night jaunt to the city to find that someone had broken into his store and looted it. The appliances that had not been carted off were trashed. Springs, knobs, screws, coils, nails, glass, metal, and plastic were sprinkled liberally on the floor.

Aside from the store, the villains had gone into the back room that had served as Mierzejak's residence and taken a knife to his bed and pillows, smashed the framed photographs on his wall, and, most revoltingly, left something foul on the floor that I'll leave to the imaginations of my readers to figure out.

A livid Mierzejak summoned the police and a squad car was dispatched from Smolskie. The investigating officers dutifully scratched out notes and inspected the scene of the crime, but Mierzejak felt they were simply going through the motions and he could feel his indignation rising.

"Those assholes," Mierzejak scowled to Szymon Wozniak after the cops had gotten into their car and driven home. "Those fucking assholes. They're too lazy to come back out here and investigate it right."

"Amen to that."

"I don't know what I'm going to do," Mierzejak said.

Wozniak considered this.

"You're insured, right?"

"Yeah," Mierzejak said. "But, I have to wonder, is it really worth sticking around this dump?"

Financially, the gentiles had been among the groups most affected by Kreskol's diminished reputation. While some of the gentile transplants quietly thought that the question of Kreskol's authenticity was worth examining (and confirmed some of their worst opinions about their neighbors), it didn't change the fact that it was decidedly bad for business. After the tourists stopped coming, their normal customers didn't have money to spend. They were offering ludicrous exchanges: a dozen eggs and a quart of milk for coffee filters and a toothbrush.

The only reason people like Mierzejak and the Wozniaks had settled in Kreskol in the first place was that these Jews suddenly had money to spend, and didn't know diddly-squat about what anything was worth. Kreskol was easy money. But it was a decidedly unpleasant place to live. The town pub was filled with smelly bearded Jews who didn't speak a lick of Polish. Internet reception was appalling. One had to drive forty minutes through the backwoods to get to a decent restaurant. And if an unmarried man wanted to get laid, he wasn't about to do so in the village he now called home. (Mierzejak hadn't been curious enough to explore Thieves' Lane and its debauched offerings.)

"I might just take the insurance and leave," Mierzejak said. "If business has dried up, why should anyone stay in Kreskol?"

Mierzejak was not the only one thinking this. Other gentiles had the same idea. The fact that Mierzejak would be getting a significant check from his insurance company made his fellow gentiles wonder if he wasn't, actually, very fortunate to be the victim of wanton vandalism. More fortunate than themselves. (Some wondered if he wasn't fortunate at all—if there had been something shaping his luck. And a lot of them started making calls to their carriers and asking what their coverage was like for theft, vandalism, and arson.)

A few days later, as one of the public buses drove through the town, an errant rock came careening through the driver's windshield.

The driver lost control of the bus and skidded along Market Square, crashing into a stall. A young woman named Glika Bamberger was run over.

What followed was chaos. Throngs of onlookers came to the scene to help and investigate. When the bus driver saw the anger in the faces of the crowd he fled. He turned up a day later hitchhiking along the road to Szyszki.

Tears and howls went up in the air and an ambulance helicopter was eventually summoned, but it couldn't save poor Glika, who died on impact.

The next day, when the public bus came through town on its normal route, a mob was there to meet it. More rocks came through the driver's window, along with soiled cloth diapers and garbage. Fists came pounding on the door and the windows. The driver didn't wait around for yet another disaster, so he turned around and sped back to Szyszki.

Later that evening, the bus company suspended service to and from Kreskol for the foreseeable future.

21

MISDIRECTION

Yankel Lewinkopf held his breath.

Sitting on a bus, more than a week after his public testimony before the Sejm, he saw Pesha's face. It wasn't her actual animated face—rather, it was a photograph. A chunky, blond woman seated next to him had the most recent edition of *Fakt* in her hands and had stopped on a spread about the Jewish seductress of Kreskol. Pesha was captured gazing absently at the camera as she entered a sandstone house in Lodz.

Yankel hadn't heard the TV report a few nights ago. Until that moment, the whereabouts of his beloved was a mystery whose trail had long gone cold.

After Kasia taunted him that Pesha would be sent away, Yankel didn't see any purpose in staying in Warsaw. He didn't know where Pesha would be exiled to, but it wouldn't be there. Besides, he had grown to despise the city. Everything reminded him of Pesha. So after he was released from the hospital he used the last of his savings to purchase a bus ticket to Krakow, and began wandering from shop to shop in the tourist section of the city, asking if anyone was in need of a good baker.

Yankel's inherent cheerfulness—which unsettled many people on the streets of Smolskie the previous year—faded as his Polish became refined. He no longer inspired quite the same cautiousness, even if there might have been other reasons to distrust him. (A careful observer would note that some of his teeth had been knocked out, and that he walked with a limp. The doctors had given him a cane, but he decided it was better not to use it when asking for a job.)

On the fifth bakery he tried the owner asked him: "Where have you worked before?"

"Warsaw."

After Yankel told him the name of the bakery and correctly answered a few more questions—average punching time for a sourdough and amount of yeast typically used in babka—the owner decided to try him out.

Yankel rose at dawn, worked until 3 p.m., and slept in the Jewish cemetery in Kazimierz for the first week. He furtively washed himself in the bathroom at the bakery and hid the sleeping bag he'd acquired before leaving Warsaw behind the oven. "Yes," the owner said, "you'll do." The day he received his first paycheck he moved into a spare room in an apartment occupied by two other young men.

Yankel worked with an older baker—a Turk named Orhan whose Polish was worse than his—and after he felt he was more or less settled, he began nosing around Krakow's brothels, asking if they had a Pesha or a Teresa working there.

Most of the pimps and madams found him suspicious. No, they told him, they didn't know anyone with that name. But eventually one of the madams produced a woman named Teresa.

Yankel shook his head.

"No, this is not who I mean."

The madam didn't mask her annoyance.

"What do you think this is, Facebook?" she asked. "You came by to look someone up? Well, sonny, you're not going to waste my time or my girl's time. Whether she's the right Teresa or not, you owe us fifty zlotys for a peek. If you want to take her in the back room it'll cost you another two hundred."

Yankel gave the madam fifty zlotys—a somewhat modest sum, but one he could scarcely afford to spare—without arguing. But it occurred to him that he was going about this all wrong. If Kasia had taken precautions against him, walking into a cathouse and simply asking for "Teresa" or "Pesha" was surely a doomed effort.

"You should hire detective," suggested Orhan, to whom Yankel confided a heavily edited selection of his troubles. "Private detective. He figure out where she is."

It was worth a shot. Yankel went for a consultation with the first name Orhan found for him on Google.

"I charge one hundred fifty zlotys an hour plus expenses," the private eye, who operated in an office on the southern bank of the Vistula River, said after Yankel had laid out his case. "For an investigation like this, I think it would be a minimum of forty hours."

Yankel didn't have anything close to 6,000 zlotys. It would take him a year to save up such a wild sum. And the private eye was careful to remind him that the forty-hour number was a probable minimum. It could be a lot longer and more expensive.

"I don't have that kind of money."

The private eye nodded sympathetically.

"Best of luck to you."

Yankel's disappointment was unmistakable and, for a moment, the investigator felt bad for him.

"Do you have any advice?" Yankel asked.

If he wasn't going to entice Yankel to become a paying customer, the private eye decided there was no harm in giving away a few scraps of trade know-how.

"Some of these escort services have websites," he said. "Look through them for a photo of your sweetheart."

Yankel seemed perplexed.

The investigator smiled. It was obvious that this weird fellow was socially warped and technologically maladroit; when Yankel had filled out the agency application he had left the space for a telephone number and email address blank. When the detective pointed this out, Yankel innocently replied that he possessed neither.

"Look, pal," the private eye said, "if you really want to search, your first purchase has to be a smartphone. Trust me, it will help you in every other area of your life, too."

Yankel took the advice to heart, and saved up for months. On the day of the purchase he consumed the entire afternoon of the sales clerk, asking question after tedious question on how to work the device. When he got home, he spent weeks scrolling through the pages of Krakow's escort services, looking for any photo that resembled Pesha. He never found anything close.

So he kept returning to the phone store with new queries. He asked how to use the phone to find a criminal complaint; how to use the phone to find out if there was some kind of bureau of missing persons; how to use the phone to find out if there was a sex workers' guild and who was a member; how to use the phone to find venereal disease clinics where—god forbid—Pesha might have been treated. (All of which were dead ends.)

The staff at the phone store rapidly grew sick of Yankel and his endless stream of inquiries that were grossly fixated on sex and prostitution. It was as if he had no sense and no shame. Only his affect of dumbness kept him from being banned outright from the store.

"Mr. Lewinkopf," a salesgirl named Alicja finally said after Yankel's tenth visit in two weeks, "if I gave you a lesson on how to use your phone—I mean, a real lesson, took all day to go over it with you—would you promise to stop coming in here?"

"All right," Yankel said, "unless it's an emergency."

That was probably the best Alicja could expect, so she pawned her customers off on the other clerks and carefully explained to Yankel how to properly google; how to use the app store; how to text and save phone numbers; and so on.

Google, she explained, is the great Delphic oracle of our times. "You ask Google a question and it spits out an answer. Every question you ever pose should go through Google first."

Over the course of the afternoon it dawned on Alicja that most of

Yankel's requests seemed to focus on finding a long-lost person from his past, whom he believed had become a sex worker.

"Have you tried Facebook?" Alicja asked.

Yankel had heard of it, but didn't understand what it was.

The two of them spent the next hour creating an account for Yankel—and for a giddy second Yankel thought he had struck gold.

"Yes—there's a Pesha Rosenthal on Facebook," Alicja said.

However, the user in question lived in Tel Aviv and was a good two decades older than the Pesha Rosenthal he was looking for.

I suppose the daylong lesson served a purpose in that Yankel became more or less conversant in how to use his phone, and he abided by his promise not to return to the store. (Opting, instead, to try a different store one neighborhood over when he needed help.) But it was largely a false lead. Pesha certainly wasn't about to leave a trail of digital breadcrumbs for Yankel.

After months of fruitless online searching, he took to wandering the streets, looking into the faces of the women he passed. And Yankel grew morose. He would think about Pesha until he dissolved into tears. He fantasized about a rescue. He likewise fantasized about a confrontation with Kasia and her goons. But in his more realistic moments, he recognized how unlikely it seemed. He would go to the nearest pub and quietly deaden his feelings with vodka. And unlike in the days when he first found out about Pesha and her dishonorable profession, he felt no desire to one-up her with another woman. Attractive young ladies would spot the handsome Yankel and catch his eye. He merely looked away.

And then, as if hit by a bolt from the blue, there was Pesha. On the pages of *Fakt*. For a moment, Yankel thought he would faint. He brushed his hair back with trembling hands and felt the perspiration on his forehead.

He didn't dare ask the woman next to him if he could look at the paper. He simply got off at the next stop, went into a sundries shop, and purchased his own.

He rushed back to his apartment, went into his bedroom, and opened the paper to Pesha's story, which he read and reread with a strange mixture of giddiness and sorrow.

Yes, Yankel resolved, he would go to Lodz immediately. He counted out his savings, told his roommates that he would be gone for a little while, and told his boss that he would need a few days off.

Within two hours he was on a bus headed for Lodz. As he stared out the window he realized that he didn't have the faintest idea what he would do when he arrived in the city.

It occurred to Yankel that *Fakt* might not have been the only publication to report on Pesha and her rediscovery. He began googling and found a story that mentioned the neighborhood the house was in, even if the publication declined to provide the exact address.

Yankel was a different man in other ways than the wayfarer who ambled through Smolskie more than three years earlier. He was more organized and he wasn't as easily impressed with the new city. Certainly, he was eager to get to the industrial part of town and look for houses matching the one in the photograph. But once the sun set he realized how pointless it would be to wander the streets in the dark. He found a youth hostel for fifty zlotys a night that advertised free Wi-Fi. He bought himself two bubliks,* lay on the thin mattress, and spent the night searching Google Street View for possible avenues.

It took Yankel a day of walking around the appointed neighborhood before he found what he believed was the house.

At least, it looked very, very similar.

There was a café situated across the street, and Yankel took a seat and watched men go in and out, with a greater gush coming after dark. Yankel felt that had to be a pretty strong sign.

There wasn't much else to go by. The curtains of the house were drawn.

---

*A dense, ring-shaped bread.

The only display of character the house exhibited was a garden in the back that was overrun with chrysanthemums, corn poppies, and crocuses.

Yankel kept his eye on the red front door. He continued to consume coffee after coffee—to the point where his heart began to race and his head began to swim—but there was no sign of Pesha.

He came back the next day and the day after, sitting at the café from opening until closing. She didn't appear. And Yankel began to wonder if he had been too quick to settle on this as the right house.

One thing he was very wary of doing, however, was entering the house without a plan. For all he knew, Kasia had put up a giant poster of him warning anyone manning the door that he was not to be allowed entry. And while (to his great relief) there were no praetorians keeping watch over the entrance, one misstep and there likely would be. He couldn't try the same tricks he had before. There could be no shoddy disguises or half-baked escape schemes.

He thought of paying someone off to check it out for him; offer them a couple of hundred zlotys to go in and ask for Teresa and report back. But the idea of sending yet another suitor to Pesha—even if he made it a condition of their taking the assignment that they *not* do anything carnally with her—sickened him. Where would he find such a character? And what would stop such an agent from bedding Pesha anyway? It didn't matter to Yankel in the slightest that she slept with new men every day; he would not be a party to any more.

He tried to think of a credible excuse for sending a woman to check in on her. Maybe she could pose as a long-lost relative coming for a visit? Maybe she could come bearing a parcel for special delivery? But every excuse felt contrived and inadequate. There was only ever one reason to visit a house of ill repute. They would never accept a female caller.

And it occurred to Yankel that the media glare on Pesha might have thrown a fright into Pesha's jailers. Anybody asking about her would probably be turned away. Who knows. She might have been moved already. Or, if she hadn't been moved, perhaps they would do so in a few days.

The more that Yankel thought about it, the more concerned he grew. His chance to find Pesha might have already vanished. If she was still there, he had to act quickly. "How?" he wondered. "How? How . . . ?"

And as he thought this, he turned his head to the other side of the café and saw Ishmael Lindauer sitting quietly at a table, staring at the very same sandstone house and red door.

It had been only a few years, but time had thickened Ishmael's physique and grayed his hair and beard. He was dressed in a black tunic that looked unwashed. He had a cloth satchel by his legs. Most surprising of all, however, was a metal cross on black beads that was hanging against his chest, which made him look like a priest. While Yankel hadn't known him particularly well back in the old days, he recognized the sneer on Ishmael's face. Except for the clothing and the grayness, he was unmistakable.

Yankel wondered if Ishmael had recognized him, too, but figured the chances were slimmer. Yankel's beard and sidelocks were gone. As were whatever pimples dotted his adolescent face, which was the last time Ishmael would have laid eyes on him. And while the gigantic cross around his neck didn't make Ishmael look Jewish, it did make him look like someone who had been excluded from the fashions of the day—something you could not say about Yankel, who was dressed in jeans, T-shirt, and Nike Air VaporMaxes.

Nevertheless, Yankel was nervous enough that he asked his waitress to move him to a table out of Ishmael's line of sight.

So Yankel spent the day seated in the back of the café, watching Ishmael watching the cathouse.

With increasing alarm, he tried to conceive what this swine was up to. It was obvious that Ishmael intended to do Pesha some kind of harm. Perhaps he had a ridiculous plan to carry her off once again to be his bride, in the demented way that love clouds good judgment and inspires great folly.

It even occurred to Yankel that Ishmael was very possibly acting out the scenario that he himself had written three years earlier when he had gone to the cathouse in Warsaw in disguise, and attempted to snatch Pesha—a thought that shocked Yankel to his very core. After all, Ishmael's disguise was merely that of an Orthodox priest instead of an old man. Yankel felt himself go limp, imagining that there was any similarity between himself and this monster.

These and a thousand other tangled thoughts appeared in Yankel's brain.

When evening finally came and the café cleared out the last of its customers, Ishmael paid his bill and stood out on the street, continuing to gaze at the house. Yankel stood a block away.

Ishmael inconspicuously leaned against the unlit side of a lamppost and waited for the street to be completely empty.

After he was comfortable that he was alone, Ishmael moved slightly nearer to the three-story, freestanding house, and when a customer left, Ishmael watched closely who opened the door and what he could see of the interior from the street.

But he did not approach the front door; when the customer was out of sight, Ishmael wandered into the garden in the back. Yankel cautiously followed and watched from the shadows.

Ishmael opened his satchel and pulled out a can of black spray paint. On the back of the house he wrote, "Whore." When he was pleased with how it looked he next wrote, "Cunt." He looked up at the house to make sure none of its inhabitants had heard anything.

Yankel grinned. He assumed that Ishmael Lindauer's intentions were more nefarious than petty.

But Ishmael wasn't finished. He went into a spot in the bushes where he had apparently hidden something away—and that alone served to make the hair on the back of Yankel's neck stand up. Ishmael had been to the house before; he had more carefully laid plans than Yankel.

Ishmael returned from the bushes brandishing a sledgehammer and two canisters of petroleum.

With utter conviction Ishmael smacked the sledgehammer against the cellar door. The lock broke instantly.

Ishmael dropped the hammer, opened the cellar, picked up the petroleum and disappeared into the house so swiftly that Yankel could scarcely believe what he was seeing. He called emergency services.

"There's a crazy man who just broke into a house," Yankel cried. "He might be trying to burn it down. It looks that way." He gave the address but hung up before he could give any information about himself.

Yankel ran into the cellar as fast as his legs could carry him and found Ishmael scattering the petroleum on the cellar floor. Ishmael froze when he saw Yankel.

"Just what do you think you're doing?"

Ishmael was taken aback to hear the question in Yiddish. And he stared at Yankel for a brief moment before dispelling whatever surprise or puzzlement he might have harbored. Ishmael didn't have time for distractions. He tossed the petroleum canister against the wall, reached into his pocket, and pulled out a book of matches.

The look on Ishmael's face was not wrathful or frightened. Rather, it was pleased. More than pleased—it was ecstatic. He had discovered his greater purpose, and felt joy. Having a witness to the destruction made it even better.

Yankel charged toward Ishmael, but he was too late. Ishmael ignited the pool of oil on the floor, and in moments half the cellar was engulfed in flames.

Yankel took off toward the staircase to the house, where he could at least sound the warning for everybody to get out—but Ishmael wasn't about to allow that. He grabbed Yankel and savagely threw him to the floor as Yankel yelled.

I suppose if he could kill a houseful of people with fire, Ishmael didn't mind killing one more with his hands. He locked his fingers around Yankel's throat and began choking him with all of his might.

Yankel clawed back and reached hopelessly for Ishmael's throat.

The smoke filling the cellar caused Ishmael to lose his grip for a moment and go into a paroxysm of coughing. As he did so, Yankel called out. But Ishmael soon recovered and fixed his hands again on Yankel's neck.

"You want to know what I'm doing?" Ishmael snarled at his victim. "This is what I'm doing. This is what I'm doing!"

Just at that moment Yankel heard a loud smack.

Ishmael's grasp slackened, and he slumped over on top of Yankel. Yankel looked over his shoulder and saw a young woman dressed solely in scarlet bra and underwear with a lamp in her hand.

Yankel had never seen the girl before. She was tall and slim with dirty blond hair, and she looked terrified. She had opened the cellar door a minute earlier to investigate the smoke and the cries for help and had been shocked by the roaring flames. She turned around and screamed for everybody to get out of the house, and—almost as an afterthought—grabbed the nearest instrument she could find to prevent Yankel's strangulation. She applied one quick swing to the assailant's head, and fled the scene.

Alongside the other girls who were pouring out of the house engorged in flames, Yankel staggered onto the sidewalk, where he collapsed.

He didn't come to until the emergency workers were strapping him to a gurney. "Pesha," Yankel murmured. "Where's Pesha?"

He looked into the sea of girls, all fixed on the disaster. Next to them were a fluttering of johns, all of whom had the good sense to grab their trousers before bolting out of the house.

As he was wheeled along the street to the ambulance he saw the woman who had saved his life, who was now wrapped up in a fireman's coat.

"Please tell me—where's Pesha?"

The girl looked surprised for a moment.

"You mean Teresa?" she said.

Yankel nodded.

She wasn't entirely sure whether she should be talking about Teresa. She looked over her shoulder at the pyre raging once more before she answered.

"Teresa ran off a few days ago."

22

DENOUEMENT

From the beginning, Yankel's account was distrusted. When the authorities asked what had happened the night of the fire, Yankel said he was simply walking past the house when he saw what appeared to be a prowler entering the cellar. That was when he phoned emergency services.

"Had you ever seen the man before?" Dawid Zielinski, the chief investigator, asked about the still-unnamed arsonist whose charred remains were lying on a metal slab in the morgue.

Yankel shook his head.

"Never."

The investigator felt the itch common among law enforcement officers when they discern a fabrication.

"Were you spying on him?"

It hadn't occurred to Yankel to come up with a proper cover story, and he was taken aback by the question. It suggested something sneaky and nefarious about him.

"No, not at all. I was just taking in the night air."

There were multiple flaws in that version of events, as truncated as it was. The cellar, in the back garden of the freestanding house, was not visible from the street. To reach it, one had to walk down a small grassy lane separating the house from its neighbors.

Plus, Zielinski had listened to the recording of the call that came in on the night of the crime. Yankel hadn't used the word "prowler." He said "crazy man" who looked like he was about to burn down the house. This might have confirmed that Yankel wasn't the perpetrator of the crime but it also proved that he was changing his story.

"What are you doing in Lodz?" the detective asked. "I thought you said you live in Krakow."

Yankel nodded.

"Just visiting for a few days," Yankel said. "I had never been to Lodz before."

"Who were you visiting?"

"Nobody," Yankel said. "I was here by myself. Just a holiday."

A good lawman will keep his most damning critique to himself until it becomes necessary or useful. But this was veering into absurdity. Zielinski practically felt that his intelligence was being insulted.

"Mr. Lewinkopf," the detective began, "you're telling me that you just *happened* to pick Lodz to visit. And you *happened* to go by the house that had been inhabited by Teresa Mularz—the woman who came from the same town as you did. And you *happened* to be there when this nut decides to burn the place down."

Until that moment, the detectives hadn't uttered Pesha's name or pseudonym in Yankel's presence. Nor had they suggested (even obliquely) that they knew who Yankel was and where he came from. But their skills with Google, apparently, outshone his. Yankel reddened, embarrassed by his obvious prevarications.

"Do you think we're *stupid*?" Zielinski finally thundered. "You expect us to believe that bullshit?"

Yankel's chin merely sank into his chest and his eyes darted away. "Yes," Yankel finally croaked. "I agree—it sounds fishy." But he refused to alter the details of his story.

I suppose Yankel clung to the notion that he could still find Pesha once he was released from the hospital. Letting the authorities in on his designs would only insert an obstacle in his path. Therefore, he could only offer new information parsimoniously.

This had the unintended effect of making the detectives wonder if

Yankel's call to emergency services hadn't been contrived. Maybe *he* was the arsonist and the dead man was *his victim*. Maybe all his seeming idiocy had been an act.

But that didn't make sense either. If the call was intended as an alibi it was made prematurely. Receiving the call when they did prevented the worst from happening. Plus, none of Yankel's fingerprints had been on the canisters of petroleum or any of the other pieces of evidence that survived the fire. The dead man's fingerprints were everywhere.

Finally, Marta, the girl in the red underwear who had saved Yankel's life (and everybody else's in the house that night), confirmed the most important parts of Yankel's story: The dead man had been trying to strangle Yankel. Yankel had been the one calling out, trying to alert everybody to the immediate jeopardy. He was as much a hero as she was. Almost.

Marta was much more lucid and helpful than Yankel. While she couldn't say who this demented arsonist was (thanks to his all-black getup and a metal cross recovered around his neck, it was believed the perpetrator might be a priest), she wasn't at all shy about offering up her opinion.

"It's pretty obvious that this psycho saw Teresa on the news," Marta stated, sensibly.

That was more or less the working theory among the detectives. The case had all the hallmarks of a perpetrator seething with hostility to women and ambivalence about sex. The brothel's notoriety would have made it a prime target for someone with mental and sexual afflictions. The priest part was a somewhat beguiling element—but then, you saw something new every day in their line of work.

The other serious alternative was that the crime was the handiwork of a Jew hater. Or a Kreskol hater. (The terms had largely become conflated in recent weeks.) Either way, the connection with Teresa Mularz was unmistakable.

"Why did Ms. Mularz flee?" Zielinski asked Marta.

"I don't know if she liked the life," Marta said, sipping from a paper cup of coffee she had been offered. "And she didn't get along with anybody in the house. Maybe with the spotlight on all of us she figured nobody could try too hard to stop her from leaving."

This interested the detective.

"Was she living in the house involuntarily?"

Marta shrugged.

"A girl's gotta eat."

Marta proceeded to tell the detective how the house had braced itself for disaster when the news report came out and a media scrum formed on their doorstep. The housemother called all the girls together and said that nobody should text or email or call about the topic of Teresa until the storm had passed. Nobody. There would be consequences for anyone who didn't listen. She sent out for food and toiletries and refused permission for anybody to leave the house or receive customers.

The girl whom the fuss was all about remained as silent as she had been throughout her tenure. Nervous-seeming, yes, but she kept her thoughts to herself.

The morning after the cameras left, Teresa's room was empty. She hadn't escaped through the front door—rather, it looked like she managed to lower herself from a second-floor window in the wee hours of the morning. Whether she had taken money or provisions to look after herself was anyone's guess.

"Oh, she's prepared," Marta postured. "I never saw her spend a penny on herself in the three years she lived here. I think she was saving up for the right moment."

"Saving for what?" the detective asked. "Where do you think she went?"

"I haven't the foggiest idea."

The detective jotted down a note.

"Did she have any troublesome customers?"

True, Teresa was extremely popular among the clientele, and that always carried with it the possibility of danger. Some men couldn't get enough and would ask for her again and again. But you had to give Teresa credit for refusing to dole out false hope. There were no counterfeit whimpers, or kisses, or winks—everything was strictly business. She usually didn't even look the men in the eye. It got to the point where the housemother took Teresa aside and told her that if she was a little warmer she could make much better tips. But this coldness proved extremely useful at preventing fixations from taking hold.

While some of her steadies betrayed a look of disappointment upon exiting Teresa's boudoir, none of them looked capable of violence. Marta had seen the other types before; she even batted off a few. The only men Teresa had bewitched (to her good fortune) were losers.

"This guy wasn't a john," Marta answered.

"Yeah, I know," the detective said. "But was there anybody else who might have been obsessed with her?"

The one area where Marta was less than fully candid with the police was on the inner workings of the cathouse, for obvious reasons. Marta didn't even reveal the correct name of the housemother, who conveniently disappeared the night of the fire and had not yet resurfaced. Troublesome johns seemed like they might fall under the category of house business. Marta decided that the detective didn't need this extraneous detail.

"Not to my knowledge."

The detective moved on.

Within a week his report was more or less finished. The only remaining facet of the case that still perplexed him was the Hebrew lettering sprayed on the back of the brothel.

The exterior wall had been blackened by the smoke and soot that had belched out of the cellar, so nobody noticed this peculiar defacement for more than a week. But when Zielinski went to make a final examination of the crime scene he stared at the wall—realizing something was slightly askew, but unable to pinpoint what—until he distinguished the faint discoloration between the black of the fire and the black of the paint.

More than any single element it served to make Zielinski think that Yankel shouldn't be written off as a possible suspect. Aside from Teresa,

Yankel would have been the only actor in this drama who would have known these letters.

"Did you spray anything on the back of the house?" the detective asked Yankel the day after discovering the graffiti.

"No," Yankel said, and then, remembering something important, added: "But, come to think of it, I did see *him*—the crazy man—writing something on the back of the house when I came along!"

Zielinski opened his notebook.

"You previously said you saw him casing the house—like he was a prowler," Zielinski said, carefully. "He was doing this *after* he vandalized it?"

Yankel immediately saw that this addition did not help his credibility.

"Well," Yankel said. "I saw him *finishing* it up. I didn't actually see him spray painting. He was putting away the cans. And then he went to the cellar. It all happened pretty quickly."

"How come you didn't mention anything until now?"

"I suppose I forgot."

Zielinski recognized the value of finality in these investigations. There was always something that didn't quite make sense. The evidence here was too overwhelmingly stacked against the dead man to justify delving into a slippery secondary character. It was possible that the decedent had, indeed, spray-painted the back wall just as Yankel claimed. Maybe the crime was more motivated by religious animus than the investigators originally believed. (Or perhaps it was some toxic combination of antisemitic and sexual rage.) And while Hebrew graffiti was certainly an unusual thing for an anti-Semite to indulge in, Zielinski was well aware that people who are tormented by a topic study its intricacies. Maybe the dead man was leaving a message for an audience of one (Teresa) in the language she knew best.

But the prime reason not to look into Yankel's suspiciousness was that the police department received all sorts of clumsy hints from the prosecutor's office that it would be best for all concerned if they wound down the investigation. Everybody was sick of Kreskol. A case related to Kreskol (even tangentially) shouldn't receive undue attention.

And so while there could remain an ongoing effort to identify the dead man, he was adjudged the most likely culprit. The case was closed.

Two days after that quiet decision was reached, a few of the nationalist members of the Sejm introduced a bill rescinding official recognition of Kreskol.

All revenue for improvements would be discontinued—not just frozen, which was Kreskol's current legal state. Its name would be struck from history books—except where it would be identified as a sham. Not even the funds to keep Poctza services running would be approved. A few of the more strident voices in the Sejm tried to insert provisions in which Kreskol would be responsible for returning the investments the government had made in the town—but that was considered going too far. At least for now. (Several kingmakers in Prawo i Sprawiedliwosc* assured the grumpy backbenchers that they would look into a separate bill next year, but they should pass this one now.)

"The obvious result from our investigation is that the town is a con," Henryk Szymanski declared before the assembled Sejm. "Plain and simple. And we must distance ourselves. Whoever's involved should be treated as a criminal. We must not be taken in."

Yankel watched the reports from his hospital bed with escalating incredulity. It almost made him feel some sympathy for his former townsmen.

Granted, when Yankel was summoned before the Sejm to face Szymanski a few weeks earlier he grasped the politician's odiousness. He wasn't sure whether Szymanski really believed what he was saying, or had figured out a pat way to stick it to the Jews without having to be too explicit about it. Whatever way you looked at it, the man was a snake.

However, when the topic of derecognizing Kreskol came up, Yankel didn't believe anyone in their right mind would fall for such a risible fantasy.

---

*Polish: Law and Order, an ultra-nationalist and populist political party.

Numerous brainy, well-groomed figures appeared on television to declare that the populists in the Sejm were trying to make political hay out of a nonissue. Just as Zbigniew Berlinsky had elucidated all the reasons Kreskol was a hoax, they explained as convincingly why it couldn't possibly be a hoax: Land would have to be procured in the forest. The town would have to be built without anyone noticing cement mixers or bulldozers going back and forth. The fact that there had been no working road before made this doubly difficult. A road would have to be forged and then dismantled before anybody noticed. Thousands of people would have to be induced to lie. Plus, there had been records of Kyrshkow before the war. Not a ton of records, to be sure, but this seemed fairly definitive proof of the larger narrative.

And yet there was Szymanski and his allies reading the audit of what had been already sunk into Kreskol: Millions and millions for construction and land improvements. Millions for electric panels. Millions for a post office. Millions more promised for future endeavors.

"The motive is there," Szymanski declared to the Sejm. "The con has paid handsomely. And the sinister minds who contrived this know that this is only the first payment. Do we really want to invest many millions more in something that we're not even sure is real?"

The recent news from Kreskol about unrest and hostility toward official vehicles going in and out could well have had the ironic effect of boosting the arguments of those claiming the town was authentic. After all, if the town was only in business to scam Poland out of tax revenue, why should they suddenly be antagonistic and eager to distance themselves? But it didn't work out that way. The populists were the ones invigorated by the recent news, and took umbrage at the fact that Kreskol's gentile residents were singled out for abuse.

"This town is filled with violent people," Szymanski chided. "Dangerous people. And dangerous people do dangerous things. This is yet another argument for keeping our distance."

When time came for the opponents of the bill to speak, they summoned none of the zeal of the populists. "Szymanski and his party have not introduced a single piece of evidence in all of these proceedings to prove their case," said the head of the opposition. "Their case is not *partly* speculative—it's *totally* rooted in sheer conjecture. It's a lie."

But, for prudent politicians, doubt is a more persuasive argument than certainty. The populists said that there was reasonable doubt about Kreskol's origins—whereas the opposition contended that there was no doubt whatsoever. The wobbly members of the body convinced themselves that the judicious thing to do was to pass the bill. Recognition could always be reinstated later. And what a lot of the prognosticators assumed would be an easy defeat turned into a narrow victory for the bill. Funds were cut off forthwith.

A victory cry went up among the assembled legislators when the tally was announced. Even the marshal of the Sejm grinned with satisfaction.

As the news came in (the day before he was to be let out of the hospital) Yankel felt a shock for which he was unprepared. He told himself that in the unlikely event the bill passed . . . well, what did he care? Kreskol wasn't his town anymore. He knew what was true and what was a lie. The gentiles had been passing ordinances and laws to put his fellow Jews at a disadvantage since time immemorial. Was this very different? Besides, his singular goal was finding Pesha.

And yet, as the female broadcaster spoke, he found himself so stunned that he was unable to speak. A nurse came into his hospital room with his dinner tray; he couldn't look at her. He merely looked away as she set it down.

Almost nobody in the hospital brought up the vote with Yankel. The only one who dared was his doctor.

"How's the news sitting with you, my boy?" he said, without bothering to say what news he was referring to.

Yankel didn't answer for a few moments.

"I don't really understand it."

That was to be expected, the doctor replied. (He courteously didn't offer any of his own suspicions about Kreskol.) He handed Yankel a purple pamphlet with white lettering. If he was feeling blue he shouldn't hesitate to call the number at the bottom. There were all sorts of resources for people with depression. He shouldn't be afraid to try one out.

Yankel didn't thank him, as was his custom. He didn't say anything. When the doctor left, he stared for a moment at the pamphlet and then dropped it in the wastebasket.

That night, lying in his hospital bed for the last time, Yankel plotted his next step. In his reckoning, Pesha could have gone to one of three places: Israel, America, or back to Kreskol.

He remembered the way that she spoke of their shared home with nostalgia. (For the moment, he ignored her equal impatience and exasperation with Kreskol.) He remembered how her eyes had watered when he mentioned the fact that her father had been worried sick since she left. He remembered how vexing and overwhelming she said the modern world was. If Ishmael was gone, the first place she would probably go would be Kreskol.

Yankel's reasoning was hardly watertight, but it made sense to begin a long search with the closest and easiest-to-survey location. The next morning after the administrators checked him out of the hospital he strapped his rucksack on his back, went to the bus station, and asked for a ticket to Kreskol.

The young woman behind the ticket counter—with black-framed glasses and straight black hair tied in a bun—smirked.

"There is no such place."

In the old days Yankel would have taken her posture with self-effacement and good grace. But those days were over.

"Give me a ticket to Smolskie then," he replied impatiently.

Her smirk never quite went away. With a slowness designed to incite him, she accepted Yankel's cash, counted it carefully (holding one bill up to the light), gave him his change, printed out a ticket, and gave him a receipt. Yankel just glared at her. When he left he rebuked her with a vulgarity that shocked not only the ticket agent but everyone waiting behind Yankel.

Upon arriving in the Smolskie bus station late that afternoon, Yankel felt a shiver. He hadn't been to Smolskie in more than three years and he hadn't walked past the town's modest bus terminal more than once or twice; but even this vague totem of his past threatened to summon the overwhelming, crushing sentiments he had been fending off. He simply stood in front of the bus station, not moving a muscle until these emotions passed. And standing frozen and devastated on the sidewalk—with an expression veering dangerously close to tears—he looked crazy.

When he finally thought he could move without sobbing, he spotted a pool of drivers sitting on the hoods of their taxis, smoking cigarettes.

"I'm going to Kreskol," he said.

At first, none of the drivers responded. Finally one of them said he would take him for four hundred zlotys. There were stories about cars being hit with rocks when they approached Kreskol, after all. It was a huge drive. And he had practically zero chance of getting a fare back.

"Fine," Yankel said, even though it was about a third of the money he had to his name.

And so Yankel got in the back and watched as they drove out of town and the road suddenly gave way to farmland and become dotted with linden trees.

"I used to get a lot of fares out to Kreskol," the driver said. "Not so much anymore."

Yankel grunted.

"You heard what happened this week?"

Yankel didn't say anything for a moment. But the man was just trying to be friendly.

"Yes."

The driver took the hint that Yankel didn't feel much like talking; he kept his eyes on the road as the lush fields gave way to the denser, more primeval forest. Yankel quietly took in the explosive greens and browns, and he looked through the thicket for the animal inhabitants of the wilderness—but they kept themselves too well hidden to be seen from the road.

"Fuck."

The driver stopped the car.

"What?" Yankel asked.

"I missed the turn."

The driver cautiously turned the taxi around and headed back the way they came.

The driver took his mistake as a good excuse to resume chattering—about how he hadn't even *seen* the turn. How bad these country roads were. How now that they'd passed the new law the roads would get worse. And on and on.

After they had gone back the way they came for half an hour, the driver stopped again.

"Something's off."

Yankel didn't respond.

"How the fuck did I miss the side road twice?"

The driver was a young fellow with dark skin and a bushy beard. He looked genuinely flummoxed by the circumstance.

He turned the taxi around again and drove the car in a slow crawl up the road.

"Sir," the driver said. "This is very, very strange."

"What?"

The driver didn't speak for a moment.

"I have done this drive plenty of times," he finally said. "Dozens. The turn is right around here. We've gone past it three times now—and I've been looking for it. But it's not there. Something's fucked up here."

The driver got out and began looking helplessly through the trees before he turned to address his passenger.

"The turn is right around here," the driver said, almost pleadingly. "Maybe not here exactly, but within a few hundred feet."

Yankel didn't say anything.

"Could the government have ripped up the road?" the driver asked. "They just passed that law, no? Maybe they wanted to close it up?"

That was ridiculous. Yankel reached into his pocket and pulled out his phone, but there was no signal all the way out in the forest. He opened the back door.

"I'll get out here."

The driver looked worried.

"Are you sure?"

Yankel nodded. He reached into his wallet and paid him.

"Look," the driver said, "why don't you keep two hundred. I didn't take you all the way. It's only fair."

But Yankel was no longer paying attention.

"It's this way?" Yankel asked, pointing east.

The driver nodded. "More or less."

So Yankel stepped into the forest. "Are you sure about this, sir?" he heard the driver call after him. "Maybe I should just take you back to Smolskie. No charge." But Yankel didn't respond, and after a few yards, he heard the taxi start up and head back the way it came.

He walked over the jagged rocks and uneven dirt until night fell, with a rising revelation: Kreskol had once again vanished.

Yankel hadn't ever heard of Leonid Spektor (he died when Yankel was too small to know him) or his solitary campaign to protect Kreskol from the wider world and its savage, ruinous ways, but he intuited that the hidden road was the handiwork of his fellow villagers. They had probably gotten it into their heads to do something similar to what Spektor dreamed up. Now that the pomp and attention that had been shone on Kreskol was gone there was a rare opportunity never to have its solitude disturbed again.

Yankel speculated about what must have happened in these last weeks;

an army of bearded men and sidelocked boys, marching in step, were led to the known edge of existence. The place from which all the town's recent woes emanated. He could see Rabbi Sokolow (or, maybe, Rabbi Katznelson) commanding his troops: "Go—destroy the road!"

And with the ardor and inspiration that God inspires, this horde would have let themselves run amok. The road would have been annihilated. The signs would have been pulled up. The gravel smashed. Trees felled. Others would have been replanted to mask the turn into the forest. The havoc could have been complete in only a couple of days.

It might not have happened exactly that way; for all Yankel knew, it could have been the gentiles. Not in any official capacity, mind you. The government was too conscious of the world's good opinion to take quite so dramatic a step. But the same could not be said of the peasants of the nearby settlements. Their sensibilities didn't rock back and forth with the latest fashions; whatever crowns or governments came and went, they remained steadfast and true to the enemies of their fathers and grandfathers. Perhaps they did the heavy lifting of casting Kreskol back into oblivion.

Who knows; maybe the two peoples reached an understanding and worked together in temporary alliance.

When it got so dark he could no longer see his feet beneath him, Yankel stopped.

He stretched out on a flat strip of dirt and closed his eyes, but he didn't sleep. Rather, he was visited by the haunting thoughts that torment a man in moments of loneliness. He remembered the dead and the long lost. He thought of his mother. If she'd lived, she would be elderly by now. She died before he was old enough to fathom what she was truly like; most of what he could remember about her was reduced to her bewitching smile. But he wondered what she would make of all the curious circumstances in which tiny Kreskol had found itself the last few years.

And after a few minutes, he thought of his father—who was still in Kreskol. Either above the ground or below it.

The fictions repeated throughout his youth—that his father was a citizen-in-good-standing who had disappeared some years before his birth—gave way to a dishonorable truth some years ago. Back when he lived with Karol, his friend had asked him about his parents and he repeated the sorrowful end of his mother and the preposterous mythology of his father.

"So who do you think your father really was?" Karol asked.

The revelation was so stark that it assumed no force whatsoever—yes, *of course* his father was one of Kreskol's other men. He had no doubt met him hundreds of times. Still, he had never said this obvious truth out loud, not even to himself. It took Yankel a long time before he answered prudently: "I'll never know."

Karol shook his head.

"That's not the case, buddy. You can figure it out. If you get a blood sample you can get a paternity test. It'll tell you if someone is your father or not."

As in many instances during that first year in Warsaw, Yankel was momentarily humbled by the powers of technology.

"Really?"

Karol nodded.

Naturally, he couldn't simply enlist any man over forty to take an unwanted paternity test. Even if he could, he blanched from the idea. It was one of the facts of the modern world that he both admired and loathed; its insistence on obliterating life's most poetic fables and closely guarded secrets.

There was some comfort in knowing that his father still lived and slept and ate and prayed in Kreskol, whoever he was. The town might have vanished, but his father remained.

And as the dawn broke, Yankel came to the realization that wherever Pesha was, she was not in Kreskol. Pesha would not go backwards.

He remembered the secret she had shared years earlier in the little tea shop in Warsaw. One day, she had told him, she would escape to Paris. Or Israel. Or the New World. She would open a flower shop, she had said. Or a café. She had been scrimping and saving for it.

As Yankel stood and dusted himself off, he looked east. Kreskol lay somewhere through the untamed, uninhabited forest; a lonely beachhead of the past. Pesha belonged to the infinite west.

Wearily, Yankel decided to go back the way he came.

Before he started on the march, he reached into his rucksack for the canteen of water he had the foresight to bring with him before starting on this journey, as well as a few other items to sustain him.

Among them were his phylacteries, prayer shawl, and yarmulke. He hadn't used them in prayer for several years, but he'd been unable to discard them.

There was a time, not too long ago, when he wrapped his arms and said the morning prayer every day at first light. And now, alone in the wilderness with his fate uncertain, he felt an uncontrollable urge to repeat the ancient words that had been chanted through the generations when his kind was confronted with the evil of man or nature.

They were all Yankel had.

Yankel might not have ever known his father, but his father no doubt spoke these words. As had his father's father. And on.

They were, he realized, his inheritance. This profound truth brought Yankel to his knees. He bowed his head and his voice rang out:

"Hear, O Israel—the Lord is God, the Lord is One!"

Finis.

GLOSSARY

agunah (Hebrew): a "chained woman"—a woman who has not received a divorce from her husband and is thereby forbidden from remarrying.

amidah (Hebrew): the "standing prayer"; the central part of the Jewish prayer service.

altercocker (Yiddish): old fart.

apikoros (pl. apikorsim) (Hebrew): a skeptical or heretical Jew.

Armste (German): poor wretch; unfortunate.

ba'al teshuva (Hebrew): a transgressor who has had a change of heart and begins religious observance again.

babka: Eastern European yeast cake.

Bar Kokhbar, Simon: ancient Jewish leader of a revolt against the Romans in 132 CE.

beit din (Hebrew): a rabbinical court.

ben Maimon, Moses (1138-1204): Better known as Maimonides, was the twelfth-century Jewish philosopher considered one of the greatest sages of the medieval era.

Betar: a fort in Ancient Israel where Simon Bar Kokhbar took his last stand against the Romans, which was subsequently crushed.

bubbe (Yiddish): grandmother.

bubkes (Yiddish): nothing.

bubliks: A dense, ring-shaped bread.

Casimir the Great (1310–1370): Polish sovereign who introduced a legal code to the nascent kingdom, founded the University of Krakow, and offered protections to Jews.

Chabad: the largest ultra-Orthodox Jewish movement in the world and the only Hasidic movement that missionizes.

Chabad House: one of the Chabad movement's houses of study and outreach.

challah (Hebrew)*:* a braided bread.

cheder (Hebrew)*:* elementary school.

Chmielnicki, Bogdan (1595–1657): Ukrainian revolutionary and notorious anti-Semite who led an uprising that resulted in the deaths of tens of thousands of Jews.

cholent (Yiddish)*:* a long-simmering Sabbath stew made of beans and beef.

Chumash (Hebrew)*:* The Bible, or Torah.

dayyan (pl. dayyanim) (Hebrew)*:* judge in a rabbinical court.

Di Baytsh Fun Haknkrayts (Yiddish): The Scourge of the Swastika.

dobrze (Polish)*:* good.

Dos Togbukh fun Ana Frank (Yiddish): The Diary of Anne Frank.

dreck (Yiddish)*:* filth, trash.

Du Bist a Yid? (Yiddish)*:* Are you Jewish?

dybbuk (Yiddish)*:* an evil spirit.

dzielnica (Polish)*:* administrative.

Fakt: a Polish tabloid newspaper.

Frank, Jacob: eighteenth-century Polish Jewish religious leader, ultimately excommunicated from Judaism, who preached a new mixture of Christianity and Judaism called Frankism, which also advocated "purification through transgression"—i.e., sexual swinging.

gatkes (Yiddish)*:* undergarments.

Gazeta Wyborcza: a Polish newspaper.

get (Hebrew)*:* a bill of divorce.

Glowny Dworzec Autobusowy (Polish)*:* bus station.

Gomulka, Wladyslaw (1905–1982): First secretary of the Polish United Workers' Party.

hamentashen (Yiddish)*:* a triangular cookie filled with preserved fruit, typically served on Purim.

herem (Hebrew)*:* excommunication.

hesped (Hebrew)*:* eulogy.

horah (Hebrew): a Jewish dance.

Judenrat (German): a council of Jewish elders established during World War II tasked with enforcing Nazi law.

kaddish (Hebrew): Prayer for the dead.

kahal (Hebrew): assembly of elders.

Kapo: An internal concentration camp police force, populated by prisoners.

Karaites: a sect of Judaism that rejects the Talmud.

Karo, Joseph (1488–1575): Rabbi who authored the Shulchan Arush, one of the largest compilations of Jewish law in history.

Katz, Naphtali ha-Kohen (1649–1718): Rabbi, Kabbalist and commentator.

klemzer (Yiddish): Traditional Ashkenazic Jewish music.

Koidanover, Tsevi Hirsh (1648–1712): Kabbalist and author of *The Just Measure.*

korva (Yiddish): whore.

kurator (Polish): parole officer.

lashon hara (Hebrew): literally, "evil tongue"; malevolent gossip.

lazienka (Polish): bathroom.

Maimonides: Rabbi Moses Ben Maimon (aka, the Ramban), a twelfth-century Sephardic doctor who became one of the most important Jewish philosophers of the Medieval era.

mamzer (Hebrew and Yiddish): a child born of a forbidden relationship; i.e., conceived in adultery or incest. They are forbidden from being counted in a quorum or from serving as a judge.

Matura (Polish): state secondary school exam.

meshuggenah (Yiddish): crazy.

mezuzah (Hebrew): A small case affixed to the doorposts of Jewish houses that has a prayer written on parchment inside.

mikvah (Hebrew): the ritual bath.

Mój Boze (Polish): exclamation, "My goodness!"

Moshiach (Hebrew): the Messiah.

Nebuchadnezzar II (605–562 BCE): Babylonian king who conquered the kingdom of Judah and destroyed Solomon's Temple in 587 BCE.

Nu (Yiddish): "Well?" or "So?"

Orthodox Union: Contemporary Jewish organization that certifies kosher status of food.

People's Crusade: Populist Crusade in the year 1096 that led to the slaughter of many thousands of Jews living along the Rhine.

Pilecki, Witold (1901–1948): Co-founder of the Secret Polish Army during World War II who was arrested and executed after the war by the communist government.

poczta (Polish): post office.

Polska Partia Narodowa: Polish National Party, a far-right fringe political party.

Prawo i Sprawiedliwosc: (Polish): Law and Order, an ultra-nationalist and populist political party.

Purim: Spring holiday that celebrates the defeat of Haman and openly encourages inebriation.

Rabbinic Council: Eastern European Jewish organization that collected taxes and served as a go-between with local communities and governments.

Reb (Yiddish): honorific, corresponding to "sir" for a non-rabbi.

Rebbe (Hebrew): the religious leader of the community.

Rebbetzin (Yiddish): The wife of the rabbi.

Reksio: a cartoon dog.

rugelach (Yiddish): a small rolled-up Jewish pastry.

Sigismund II Augustus (1520–1572): the last male of the Jagellonian dynasty of rulers of the Grand Duchy of Lithuania.

schmaltz (Yiddish): rendered chicken fat.

schnorrer (Yiddish): beggar; moocher.

Sejm (Polish): one of the two houses of parliament.

Shalom aleichem (Hebrew): greeting meaning "Peace be unto you."

shechita (Hebrew): slaughterhouse.

shmegegges (Yiddish): bunkum artist.

shmendrick (Yiddish): fool.

shtreimel (Yiddish): a large fur hat.

siddur (Hebrew): prayer book.

sofer (Hebrew): a scribe who handwrites official documents.

swinia (Polish): pig.

Talmud: the central text of Rabbinic Judaism, comprising the "mishna" and the "gemarah," originating as the oral law of ancient Israel.

tefillin (Hebrew): phylacteries; a set of black leather boxes that are wrapped around the arms and forehead during morning prayers.

Tibbon, Moses: thirteenth-century French Jewish doctor and author.

Tisha B'Av: a fast day that commemorates the destruction of the First and Second Temple.

Titus (39–89 CE): Roman military commander and emperor who captured Jerusalem and destroyed the Second Temple in 70 CE.

toaleta (Polish): toilet.

Torah (Hebrew): the first five books of the Old Testament.

tzedakah (Hebrew): charity (literally, "justice").

tzitzit (Hebrew): Tassels affixed to the garments of religious Jews.

voivodeship: a Polish province and area of local government.

Warszawa: A post-World War II Polish-manufactured automobile.

yenta (Yiddish): a gossip or busybody.

Yeshiva bachur (Yiddish): Yeshiva boy.

Zevi, Shabbetai: seventeenth-century Turkish rabbi believed by many to be the Messiah until he converted to Islam.

Zlote Tarasy: An office-and-retail complex in Warsaw.

Zoroastrianism: one of the world's oldest Middle Eastern religions.

DEBTS

Those who go diving for mistakes in *The Lost Shtetl* will no doubt surface with a few pearls—I'm no scholar, I'm not religious and I've only been to Poland once. But despite its fantastical nature, I tried to give this book the sheen of as much credibility as I could. For that reason, I leaned on a number of sources, most heavily Yaffa Eliach's epic, commanding chronicle of the Lithuanian shtetl of Eishyshok *There Once Was a World*. There were many other books along the way that informed me, but the ones about World War II that were particularly important to me were Lucy Dawidowicz's *The War Against the Jews 1933–1945* and the works of Primo Levi—specifically, *The Drowned and the Saved*, *Survival in Auschwitz* and *The Reawakening*. My (rudimentary) knowledge of Polish history largely came from Adam Zamoyski's *Poland: A History*.

Several people helped me along the way in my factual pursuits; I would like to thank my friend Steven I. Weiss for introducing me to Professor Glenn Dynner—author of the excellent histories *Yankel's Tavern* and *Men of Silk*—who read the manuscript of *The Lost Shtetl* and offered his notes. Likewise, Rukhl Schaechter, editor of the Yiddish *Forverts*, introduced me to Esther Goodman who went through the manuscript line-by-line with extremely valuable insights and comments. (I didn't take Esther's advice that no Jew would ever be named Ishmael—but that was done for aesthetic reasons rather than factual ones. However, Esther was right about my original ending.)

Finally, my old pal Ignacy Zulawski was kind enough to field a confounding number of queries coming from me via email about contemporary Poland—and, when Iggy didn't know the answer, he contacted friends and relatives in Poland to ask on my behalf.

Naturally, the misimpressions and mistakes are entirely mine, not theirs, but they definitely saved me from a few embarrassments. (Although embarrassments go with the territory. I should note that you could transliterate Yiddish in a dozen different ways—each way with its zealous defender—and I did the best with what I could. Still, I imagine there will be plenty of Yiddishists who will conclude I'm a rank amateur.)

Michelle Brower read an early draft of this book and gave me very astute and intelligent changes—as well as sincerely appreciated encouragement at a time I was very low on the fortunes of this book. My friend Noah Phillips was likewise a fiery booster of the book in its nascent form. My thanks to them both.

I am forever indebted to my agent David Vigliano, as well as numerous people at AGI Vigliano Literary, particularly Tom Flannery, Nikki Maniscalco and Ruth Ondarza. I don't believe this book would have been sold without the indefatigable efforts of Nick Ciani (now of Simon & Schuster) who believed in the book, who kept pitching it, and who kept answering my endless, anxiety-spewing calls with calm and optimism.

Likewise, my gratitude overflows to my friends at HarperVia, including Judith Curr, Paul Olsewski, Alice Min, Maya Lewis, Emily Strode and Stephen Brayda, whose cover for *The Lost Shtetl* left me dazed in admiration. But special thanks must be reserved for Tara Parsons, a brilliant editor, whose enthusiasm was intoxicating and whose edits were incisive and unassailably correct.

My in-laws, Dr. Patricia and Dr. Eugene Wexler, have been a constant source of encouragement and support, which is not something I could ever repay. (I'm also grateful to my mother-in-law for examining the hospital scenes for some semblance of accuracy.)

My parents, Ken and Andy Gross, read every draft of this book (as well as a chapter or two along the way) and offered me the one thing that every writer really needs: complete honesty. Their reading of this book was always considered, intelligent, critical and passionate. When things weren't working, they let me know. (They were almost always right.)

And then, of course, there is my beloved wife and son, Jane and Harry Gross, for whom the debts are too high to be addressed here. Take this volume as a down payment; I shall spend the rest of my life working off the balance.

Here ends Max Gross's
The Lost Shtetl.

The first edition of this book was printed and
bound at LSC Communications in
Harrisonburg, Virginia, September 2020.

A NOTE ON THE TYPE

The text of this novel was set in Adobe Garamond Pro, a typeface
designed in 1989 by Robert Slimbach. It's based on two distinctive examples of the French Renaissance style, a Roman type
by Claude Garamond (1499–1561) and an Italic type by Robert
Granjon (1513–1590), and was developed after Slimbach studied
the fifteenth-century equipment at the Plantin-Moretus Museum
in Antwerp, Belgium. Adobe Garamond Pro is considered to
faithfully capture the original Garamond's grace and clarity, and
is used extensively in books for its elegance and readability.

HarperVia

An imprint dedicated to publishing international voices,
offering readers a chance to encounter other lives and other
points of view via the language of the imagination.